# THE UNSTEADY OBJECT OF HOPE

# THE UNSTEADY OBJECT OF HOPE

*A Unique Crime Novel*

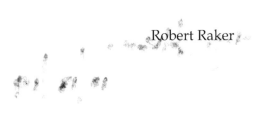

Robert Raker

# ACKNOWLEDGEMENTS:

This novel could not have been written without the support of Randolph Simmons, Gabriel Santos, Christine Shroy, Adrienne McGill, Brian Eckenrod, Carrie Eckenrod, my mother and my late father whose deep love of film and literature has led me here…

# TABLE OF CONTENTS

THE DIVER
1

THE MUSICIAN
72

THE AGENT
115

THE MODEL
175

THE BALLERINA
226

THE DOCUMENTARIAN
267

THE PAINTER
301

THE TEACHER
334

# THE DIVER

The bloated, distended corpses of the people whose shortened lives I retrieved from the water were visible in the immature patterns of condensation that evaporated on the mirror the longer I stood there and waited to hear her tap against the bathroom door. She had done that so many times in the last three years. I often didn't notice it, her seeking acknowledgment before coming into the most vulnerable of places. But I wasn't quite sure if I wanted her to anymore, express that level of intimacy because of everything that happened.

When I didn't hear her rise after I left our bedroom, I slid back the glass door to the shower, twisted the end of the brass faucet and let the water run for a few minutes. I watched the quick, sudden burst cover the floor, the droplets clinging to the white and salmon bath sponge she used. It looked like a wilted flower trapped inside of its own failure to adapt to its environment during a snowstorm. Some water trickled over the edge of the shower and onto the floor. The level rose to almost more than three quarters of an inch. It wasn't draining quickly. I crouched down and tapped on the metal screen on the floor. The water moved left, then right. I thought of the rhythm of her body when she crossed a room and how ethereal she looked when she broke the surface of the water when we first swam together. I also remembered that everything we endured began in less than twelve feet of water.

*The water could teach you how to move if you let it.*

I pulled my first body out of less than twelve feet of water over two years ago in the frigid waters off the coast of Rhode Island. I was a certified swimming and scuba instructor who taught corporations the proper use of equipment and the requirements needed in recreational and military diving. But most of the details concentrated on commercial diving. I lived under the disruptive surface of the water, waded in indoor training pools, in rivers, in oceans, submersed in its reckless and intemperate tenderness. A civil engineering firm contracted me to provide training to its employees to repair and construct oil pipeline fittings off the coast of Nova Scotia, some 100 to 150 feet deep. I was there in the bitter cold of the North Atlantic for seven months, isolated from the blighted industrial landscapes that corrupted the rural and urban banks of the small town in Pennsylvania I lived in. Things were unadulterated beneath its distorted colors, the water. Quieter. For me, there should have never been anything dangerous about the water.

As I arrived early in the morning at a port in Providence on an oil barge, I loaded my equipment onto the docks to catch a ride back home when a petroleum worker on another boat cupped his hands over his mouth, outstretched his arms and signaled there was something in the water. With most of my gear left behind, I walked with another worker to the end of the dock and discovered what appeared to be a body stuck in a drift a few feet below the surface. The torso tapped against the wooden posts secured to the inlet floor some 10 to 15 feet from where I stood. We waited for almost an hour for the police to arrive and I was eventually asked to go into the water because a police diver on call in the vicinity could not be located. The weather was also brutal as a cold front had covered most of the East coast in a dense blanket of sleet and freezing rain. Travel restrictions were initiated.

It wasn't something I wanted to do. But I had the most detailed training, more inclusive than any of the others on scene, even though some of them were 20 years older than I. It was a mere matter of circumstance or if you believed in it, fate. I geared up and through a stinging rain listened to the officer on scene communicate over the radio with a dispatcher on how to operate once I had penetrated the water, what to initially look for surrounding the body that might determine an accidental death or a homicide and how not to compromise the integrity of the forensic scene. The coroner would later determine an exact cause of death after the body was removed and photographs of the scene and surrounding areas were taken. Police were requesting we all remain on scene after I came out of the water, as we were listed as material witnesses. I wasn't going in deep so I decided to use a snorkel on the surface and hold my breath when I had to. I was still wearing a diving suit. I couldn't force any spittle from my mouth to clean the inside of the mask. My chest tightened.

*The water could teach you how to breathe if you let it.*

The ladder against the dock was cracked and missing a few rungs so I dropped off of the edge of the dock and felt the cold water collide with the material of the dry suit. Bright lights from an incoming vessel came up over the horizon and provided an aspect of light I hardly needed because the body wasn't submerged that deep. But it looked beautiful nonetheless, all things considered. I swam and positioned myself a few feet away from the body then gathered my breath, the serrated sharpness of the air cutting the inside of my throat. I couldn't speak even if I had wanted to. I trapped as much air as I could inside my lungs and maneuvered down.

The man's body was suspended about three to four feet underneath the surface, entangled in a tattered fisherman's net secured to the dock. The area was well known for its exquisite seafood, especially the production of crabmeat. Fishing was where, for the first time, I went into the water. My back was so burnt from the scalding sun that I dropped over the edge of the boat with my father to ease the constant sting. I remembered the salt water burned my eyes and I kept rubbing at them until my father told me to stop, that I would only make it worse. It looked like I was crying I had irritated them so much. I wanted to pass the clear water over my lips and through my throat, not understanding about the salinity. It tasted so bitter I kept spitting. Being so unfamiliar with it all, it's current and pull, I stayed very close to the boat. The life jacket rubbed at my skin. It felt worse than the sunburn. My father positioned me into his arms so I could see opposite the shore, gaze at the openness and loneliness of the ocean beyond our boat. I had never seen anything so beautiful, so picturesque. The pureness of it all arrested me.

In the burgeoning light there appeared to be nothing the police would consider out of the ordinary. There was nothing binding his hands or his ankles. No one else was in the water. I moved past him on my back and took notice to the small hole off center against his forehead. It looked to me as if he had been shot to death. Leaving the body unmolested, I ascended out of the water as high up on the ladder as I could until someone reached over and pulled me up. The voices above the water were constant and indecisive. It took a few minutes for the fear to subside and I couldn't hold onto the mask I pulled away from my eyes without dropping it. I had seen a dead body before, but nothing like that and not close enough I could notice the fact he hadn't shaven for weeks and his fingernails weren't manicured. But at the time I couldn't tell how long his body had been in the water. I crawled on my hands and knees further away from the water and ripped the snorkel out from between my lips when I tasted the warm bile in the back of my throat begin to rush forward.

After I helped them with the body, I sat inside of a small restaurant at the top of a hill at the opposite end of the dock. It was in dire need of repair. The screen door almost fell off when I went inside. The sound of it closing behind me reverberated throughout and what few people were there regarded me with uncertainty, then ambiguity. Almost all were standing in front of the glass, staring at the scene happening outside. I watched a group of dock workers, police and emergency responders walk up the hill towards the restaurant. I felt weak in the knees so I sat down at a booth. A few from the group broke off from the police and motioned their way towards the parking lot. A waitress came over, exchanged pleasantries and then placed a steaming cup of coffee in front of me. By the time I poured sugar into my cup, the officer who gave me directions outside sat down holding onto an unlit cigarette and a look of sympathy. I clutched the ceramic mug so tightly I thought I would crack it with my fingertips.

Between cups of coffee, he talked to me about the basic forensic procedures I utilized, the importance of gathering details in an investigation. He said something, as I watched his lips move, but I was subdued, struck by his characteristics. I thought he was trying to apologize about my having to go into the water and deal with the situation at hand when it wasn't my responsibility. But he kept asking questions about what I saw in the water. Were there any other signs of trauma? What were the condition of his hands and fingers? Did he appear restrained in any way? At times he wrote longer notations on a small pad. I wasn't sure what else to say to him, so I let him continue. I kept staring at his fingers, his wrists as he often motioned them in the blank area of the table around my coffee. I wasn't sure why, but even though the man in front of me was much younger, I saw salient points of my father in his demeanor, in the displacement of his fingers, the way he curled them closer to his palm to hide them when he wasn't quite assured in what he was explaining.

I placed the cup of coffee to my lips and let the steam soak into my eyes. It reminded me of how it felt when I opened my eyes underwater.

Somehow I thought the action would distract me from the endless questions. It reminded me too much of sitting in isolation with my father, listening to him instruct me in agricultural specifics at farm shows and fairs, as if I was going to mirror his industry as my brother had. Not long after I motioned to leave, the officer asked to me to sign a witness statement, then acknowledged he had to interview the rest of the staff at the restaurant. Yet at the end he added he may have to contact me further at some point during his investigation. I wasn't sure what else he wanted me to say or what use I could be to him later. All I wanted to do was make the rest of my trip home and move passed what had happened here. It started to rain lightly outside, a more relaxing drizzle.

*The water could teach you how to feel if you let it.*

I moved out of the bathroom and stood in the shadows of the hallway outside of our bedroom. She was still naked, asleep in the bed on her stomach next to where I had been, her unclothed thighs exposed from underneath of the dark sheets. I pulled a blanket up over her body, covered it completely and kissed her on the shoulder, caressing with care the small birthmark set against her plunging neckline. It looked like a figure eight. When I kissed her, I allowed the side of my face to linger across her collarbone. She smelled so good but not cloying, not boastful. There was a little more insecurity to it.

I scratched at my chest and wanted to slide underneath of those quilt sheets and enter her from behind, flex my hands across the sides of her hips and secure my body inside hers. I wanted to lick her nipples. But I couldn't. In the moment I could have found the courage to approach her, the phone rang. The dense, vacant tone shattered the emptiness and my indecision. It was the local police department. There were unsubstantiated reports of a body in an abandoned quarry about 11 miles from here. For a few moments I said nothing, cupped the receiver against the side of my face and stared out into the waking morning. They stressed over and over they wanted someone familiar to the area and knowledgeable about the case, as if I had become necessary. It had all been going on so long. No one appeared to care about or taken into account what I had said after the last time it happened. I couldn't do it anymore. Yet they needed me to go into the water again. Looking back on it all, I should have never gone into the water.

Someone had raped and murdered several young children and left behind a vacant trail of motive and tangible evidence. It started in late December of last year right after the holidays and had continued every calendar month since. It was early August now and as another semester of engineering and instructional classes began for me, there had yet to be another reported abduction or sighting of a body. Everyone hoped it had all ended. And so did I.

I didn't want to help the department do it any more, help the unending dead tread water. I didn't give a damn about integrity or forensic procedures. There had to be someone else who could do it now that the federal authorities had become involved as well. I was surprised they hadn't taken over the investigation and relieved me earlier. I scratched at the condensation on the bathroom mirror. The shaving cream remains on the brass handle of the faucet resembled a snowdrift on a model train set. It reminded me of the holidays at my grandfather's. The faint odor of cherry from a pipe seemed to drip along the porcelain, hide itself in the steam. I had gotten the first call to go into the water at the initial outset of what turned out to be a contemptible winter.

*Body Number One: (January) Jennifer McLaughlin, 12 years old. Was discovered floating in a backyard pool on a residential street. No one was present at the address when the body was discovered. Initially, it appeared to be a tragic accident and then declared a wrongful death. After a few weeks of questioning, both parents were ruled out as suspects. They would look into the families' history, searching for claims of abuse, both physical and sexual. It was standard operating procedure for detectives to look at the parents when something like that happened, especially the father. He was an artist, the mother, not surprisingly, a model. After the autopsy the medical examiner determined the body had been violated, traumatized elsewhere and then dumped in the tainted, cold water of the pool no more than a few hours later. The last time anyone had seen her alive was earlier in the afternoon. That left a window, pending an exact time of death, of about five hours. The victim was raped multiple times. They found trace amounts of flower petals in her lungs and common fertilizer underneath of her fingernails.*

My training classes for the winter semester wouldn't start for almost another week. The child was found face down in a backyard pool the morning after the first snowfall of the season, hours before the New Year. There were no footprints on the ground anywhere around the pool. The snow that fell consistently for the last 10 to 11 hours could have covered any useable tracks. It was brutally cold outside. I looked out the passenger side window into the backyard. Something repulsive existed in the complicated stillness that fought its way through the dense air, the smudged windshield before I stepped out of the car parked at the end of a long, crumbled asphalt strip. The crime scene itself was about 70 to 80 feet wide and encompassed a good third of the rear of the property. At the farthest point sat an old stone fireplace filled with dead branches and loose rock. Something had been burned recently. A technician was placing samples from that area into a clear jar. The remains of a rusted swing set resting on an angle opposed it. The fittings that once secured it were snapped and embedded into the ground with cement. With the low light it looked like a tin giraffe broken off at the ankles. I raised my shoulders and inhaled in hopes I could asphyxiate the dread.

I made my way up the driveway towards the faded yellow house where bright, seasonal lights hung from the gutters. They were high up on the building and looked like they were kept up year round. There were shutters missing next to several windows, the once golden shingles a pale ochre underneath. Icicles in the naked branches of trees appeared like helpless prey in winter's silken web. There was a dead bird lying underneath overturned patio furniture. Nothing appeared to move, even the men and women who carried equipment onto the property, one journalist courageous enough to face the weather trying to finally wrap his arms around a story with some substance. Not much happened here. Only one other time had this area ever been involved in something like this. But it wasn't something anyone wanted to think about. The figures that stood there resembled a morbid display from a grade school student's diorama, prolonged hardship in a shoebox. Winter had temporarily stopped the process of decay.

I blew warm air onto my hands, started to stretch out a pair of latex gloves and sat down on a series of stone steps that led up to the front door of the house. The blank stone embraced the frigidity. Curved lines of smoke trailed over the peak of my right shoulder and disappeared into the bitter cusp of twilight. The solitude I governed became swallowed up in the heavy footsteps of a homicide detective in a large overcoat.

"Remember, try to keep your hands behind you and not to touch anything until the scene has been documented, sketched and photographed. Once they mark the precise spot where the body is, they'll call on you to pull her out," the lead detective instructed, snapping a pair of rubber lined gloves over his large hands. The shape of his wedding band bulged against the constituents of the rubber.

It had been some time since Detective Daniel Mull and I stood close enough I could reach out and remove snowflakes from the shoulder of his dark jacket. They sat there introspectively for a few seconds and then disappeared into the shallow grave of the material. There were several cigarette butts on the ground around his feet. He dropped the one in his fingertips and buried it into the dirt and ice with his heel. It sounded like human bones in the hand breaking. I wondered how long he had been standing there in the doorway, watching me.

"Are you sure that you can do this?" he asked as he folded his arms across his broad chest. "It isn't easy, and to be honest, it's something that sticks with you," he added.

"Yes," I said half-heartedly. I could see the disdain he had for me in the way he held his body rigid, the condescending tone of his voice. Maybe I was wrong and it was merely indifference. But he could have just been trying to stay warm. It was hard for me to tell. "I've done it before," I said.

"I know. It was in your file. There aren't more than a few certified divers here in this area of the state and our department here is so small we don't have the budget for one. We called requesting help, but no one else could get here because of the weather. The main roads from the upper portion of the state leading here are closed. There was one other diver we were able to get a hold of in Southern New Jersey, but he isn't familiar with police procedure. In some ways, you are. You took a few courses last year in forensics. It would take days, maybe weeks to train someone else on what to look for. That's why the decision was made to call you," he said and looked at me over the top rim of his glasses. "But if it's all the same, I'd rather have called on someone else," he said.

"I wasn't in the water that long in Providence," I noted. "I don't know how much help I can be. There isn't anybody else that could swim in parts of these waters anyway if something else ever happened so it may be just as well. I've been in them enough to know how they function. Sometimes it moves too quickly," I said.

"Then let's just be glad it's contained here and the body wasn't discovered in the river. If it was summer, no one may ever have found her until she washed up along the coastline." He withdrew a pack of cigarettes and offered one to me. When I declined, he shrugged his shoulders and placed one between his chapped lips. He scratched at them when he spoke as if his mouth were dry. Although he arrived less than an hour before I did, he appeared spent, his eyes lidless and random. He pulled at the flesh below his Adam's apple. The muscles in his throat twitched and it looked as if he swallowed sand a few minutes ago from a cup instead of coffee. He gestured to a group of men huddled around each other, listening to the instructions of another, the coroner. "This may not be the last victim," he said. "There's a strong chance I might have to call you again to go into the water so don't fuck anything up for the forensic guys. It'll just make things harder," he said, his confidence in my resolve and abilities remaining undefined.

There was hope hidden behind his movements, hope in calling on me again, an obsessive arousal that another person would fall victim and he could give credence to the education he felt he was wasting here, in the middle of nowhere. Like many of us, he was isolated here, all because of a girl, a boy and the uncertainty of what happened when you went into the water

"What? You think this could be a serial thing or something?" I asked.

"Not necessarily. Not here. This place is so isolated. In so far, there's nothing to suggest that yet. Most of it will depend on what the coroner's report reads. They can match it up with any previous unsolved crimes, but we've only ever had one here resembling this," he said. I waited for him to say her name. When he didn't, he began again. "The description matches the girl who lives several houses down. We're trying to find the parents now. We found an invitation to an art show inside on their kitchen table. No one knows as of yet if she was supposed to be home alone or with a babysitter, friends. She might have just fallen in, been an accident. But God only knows what people think nowadays when something like this happens, what they're probably thinking." He shot his head to the right and motioned at the other members of the department. "If it's pedophilia or a non-random sex crime, there is a tendency to repeat the behavior though. It could turn out this is just the beginning." He paused and genuflected. "Things like this, that girl, rarely stay simple," he said.

Simple. There was a haunted tone in his voice expressed in that word, his intended connotation, and the way it fell from his lips as if his saliva was weighted by a small stone. Simple. The cigarette that burned slowly in his hands trembled. He looked now like he did when I taught his daughter how to swim, like an anxious father who stood in the shower of the fluorescent lights cascaded on the water from the ceiling, the chlorine smell saturated deep into the towel he wrenched with his bare hands. I wondered if he still did that when he became unsettled. I tried hard to remember the color of his daughter's hair that afternoon, cast in the firelight from a bonfire.

"What's so simple about the murder of a child?" I asked.

"Don't misunderstand me. I'm not trying to be insensitive. I mean it's never as definable as black and white, right and wrong. People try to justify things and it often gets in the way of what is actually the truth underneath," he said, stepping across a patch of ice and down a series of broken, concrete steps into the backyard towards the pool.

"What are you saying?" I asked. I slipped on the ice and reached out to brace my fall on a deck chair. The arm of the chair splintered. The words I expected him to say never came.

"I'm not an expert on sex crimes, especially those involving adolescents, but from what I have read they don't rape or assault someone and then stop. It's often not as isolated as it sometimes appears. It's not a part of their functionality, the perpetrator" he answered. He reached out his hand to prevent me from moving further into the crime scene and continued. "I'm trying to make you understand the consequences of what I am asking you to do. It might not stop," he said.

"Then it'll give you some time to find a replacement for me. What about murdering a victim? If that's what happened," I said, stamping my feet on the ground to keep warm and generate blood flow in my extremities.

"It's too early to tell how brutal the assault was. We don't even know if she was violated sexually. Whatever happened though, it is a bleak scene," he added. "Like I said it may turn out to be a tragic accident. Then no one will need either one of us," he added. A woman in a turtleneck sweater was on her knees sifting through a loose pile of soil around the edges of the in ground pool. He whispered something in her ear. I watched him move from one area of the marked crime scene to another, lithely like a dancer pacing through his marks choreographed from a textbook.

Detective Mull and I had much in common with one another, despite our distant upbringings, although he would never admit it. That, among other things, is probably why he didn't want me here. It was like I was his foil, an altered mirror image, the villain unobstructed who thwarted his attempts at prestige, at destiny, at movement. It wasn't my fault. He looked past me when his attention brought his eyes towards the barren edge of the pool. It made me feel rejected, a novice understudy to the immorality play laid out before us on a stage of fallen snow, concrete and darkness. But there was no audience, no applause, no one to comment on the job you were doing or offer praise. I wanted to be sick. We were men whose truncated lives hadn't turned out as we expected they would. In a blunt matter of speaking, we were impermanent failures.

*The water could teach you how to hate if you let it.*

The oval spectrum of another officer's flashlight penetrated the complex milieu that advanced on my sense of decency, the proprietary standards about society I thought I understood. There was a protective lining that covered the recessed pool. It laid unfastened, pulled back at one corner and folded over from right to left, like the way a person unmakes their bed or removes a blanket from their sleeping body. It appeared commonplace and innocuous. Someone leaned over with a small instrument and removed some of the strands of rope that had been untied and deposited them into a plastic bag with the word "evidence" stenciled across the side. My face must have expressed uncertainty because a woman assigned to the case whispered into my ear that it would be checked for fibers. I welcomed her warm breath against my skin.

"The perpetrator could have used his or her bare hands and left samples of skin behind or hairs, any fragments of DNA, even material from a glove," Mull said. I stepped closer to the pool and looked at her body almost compulsively, as if I were retrieving a moment from my childhood, trying to gain access to something I had no longer in adulthood had the right to see. When she was discovered, the officers suspected the girl drowned, even though some of the water underneath was drained. But a person could drown in less than two feet of water.

I could see the top of the water line where it once had been. Only about two feet had been drained. I wondered why they hadn't winterized. Small bits of ice formed crystals in the girl's hair and along her ears. They looked like earrings she might have taken from the facing of her mother's dresser when she wasn't looking. A fragile touch of frost rested upon the surface. You could still see the darkened color of the once chlorinated and soiled water underneath. Depending upon the angle I stood from, it looked like the ocean along the Canadian coastline at dusk, a majestic body of water uncorrupted by the tragic and pitiful stench of the dead. I wanted desperately to be there, hundreds of feet below the surface alone, warmed by the mists and strands of acetylene from a welding torch floating in the current. When they broke apart they looked like the tentacles of an emaciated jellyfish, tired and skinny.

The photographer arrived in a squad car about 45 minutes after I was called. I felt uncomfortable as I stood there and watched the photographer appear to take pleasure in his odd esotericism. When he signaled he was finished, I zipped up my suit and watched the detective and forensic team stare at me at the edge of the pool. I stepped down the ladder in the shallow end, paused where the ground sloped downwards, and closed my eyes. I should have turned back.

The pool seemed deeper than it actually was with the absence of proper light. Without consistent care and maintenance, the walls looked like faded copper because of the lime stains. I followed the concrete slope into the deep end. The girl wore an indigo dress. Tiny, dark shoes covered her feet. A dark, purple tie struggled to break free from her hair. She looked like she had fallen out of the frame of a country painting. All of it should have been beautiful. The unkempt water swirled around the crown of my head when I moved under to see if anything obstructed her. There was little room underneath of where she rested. I swirled my hand around in the water after being told to look for any kind of instrument that might have been disposed of. I wanted her to have drowned. I flexed my knees and secured the body inside my arms. I was surprised at how heavy she was. After ascending the incline back towards the ladder, I handed her body over and went back down into the remains, although I wasn't sure why. Moving a flashlight back and forth I checked the edges of the pool. The only things displaced in the water besides me were the shells of some cicadas, two mason jars, a few paintbrushes and several petals of a flower.

*Body Number Two: (February) Timothy Reisbaugh, 9 years old. Was discovered in a shallow, manmade fishing pond at the edge of the only playground area for miles, Conemaugh Park. Some children who were going ice fishing discovered the body. Most of the time kids played ice hockey there when the pond froze over and was thick enough for anyone not to fall through. It wasn't any different from other creeks or ponds, consumed by rain and run off from the surrounding hills. The preliminary autopsy showed discernable patterns to the trauma inflicted on the first child I pulled from the water last month. Yet no one was willing to state the cases were connected without any concrete physical evidence. Unfortunately, there wasn't much progress. There were still no suspects in the previous case, not even a person of interest, once the parents had been ruled out. No one who lived in the area around the park remembered seeing anything out of the ordinary.*

I used to fish like them, almost all the kids in the neighborhood when I was growing up did. My father used to call it "poor fishing." Our families were lower to middle class so our parents couldn't afford to buy us actual rods and reels, so we made due with what surrounded us. I remembered raiding my best friend's garage, looking for broken garden rakes or shovels that we could cut off at the handles. Even if they could have had the money, they were smart enough to understand that in a few months' time, or when the pond froze all the way through, the poles would rest like rotted trees in the back of the garage anyway. Our attention was always diverted from one ideal or product to the next. The patience wasn't there. What a waste it would have been to spend decent money on boots, hooks and bait anyway, none of us ever caught anything in the pond fishing our way. At least not what those kids had caught that Sunday.

When I drove up to the edge of the creek basin that drained into the pond, my car tire broke some of the makeshift fishing poles that were left on a dirt path. The few kids who had alerted the police to the body were wrapped in blankets and one of them was taken to the emergency room when he went into shock. It's a frightening experience, seeing the corpse of a human being, especially that of a child. It's not something that could be forgotten or dismissed, especially one that has been in the water for a period of time. It's never how authors describe it in the pages of a book and can never be as singular as a sketch artist makes it out to be.

Three of the children were still being interviewed by the detective. Two were boys and one was a girl. I passed by them at the moment their respective parents arrived, embraced their children, placed their hands on the sides of their faces and looked into their eyes. That was what genuine fear looked like if you had to describe it as a concrete image, the colorless uncertainty in the few moments between a parent and a child when something like that happened. I opened the trunk of my car and started to put on a standard issued dry suit I removed from a long canvas bag. I wore the dry ones when the water was dangerously cold, like it was that afternoon. A large sheet of ice covered the surface of the water. The nose clip I used to wear when I swam competitively still sat in a small plastic bag at the bottom underneath the clothing. It still smelled like chlorine.

"Christ some kids who were fishing with long sticks and twine spotted the heel of a black sneaker propped up against the side of the drainage pipe over there on the other side. One of the kids reached in and tried to pull it out. That's when he saw the tips of fingers. All I can think is when the ice cracked or shifted as the temperatures changed the body must have started creeping towards the surface," Mull remarked as he tapped his pen against the broken facing of a wristwatch then used it to point towards the horizon. "It wasn't completely frozen over until roughly a week ago so we're assuming the body was placed there then. One of the kids we interviewed said he was out here with some friends last weekend and the pond didn't have any ice on it." He offered me a cigarette and again I declined. "The department wanted someone who knew the forensic procedures," he said as he flipped to a blank page in his notebook. I guess they wanted someone who knew the routine of swimming alone with the dead. Most oftentimes in the beginning, I hated being needed like that. But I had no way to tell at the time though it was just that, when I shivered at the edge of a backyard pool trying to remember what the forensics experts coached me on. I never expected that situation again, never expected so many, not here.

The area of the creek and fishing pond the body was found in was generally midlevel year round. We usually didn't get a substantial amount of rainfall during the spring and summer. During the winter, it remained isolated and the only people that went up there were kids, occupying their time with ice skating or hockey, the occasional snowball battle. It was hard to get to when the only road was so often buried by snow. The body would be covered in dense soil and ice and be difficult to move. But depending upon how long the victim had been in the water, the decomposition rate could be advanced. I learned cold inhibited the acceleration unless the victim had been killed and dumped long before the pond had frozen over. I thought somebody might have seen it. There was no way I could tell though until I got into the frigid waters. The body might then be gaunt and insubstantial, spread out across the breadth of my forearms like a costume or a dress. I glanced around at all the people pushed behind the caution tape as I rummaged around the trunk of the car. People who lived nearby were giving statements.

Everything was changing.

I could see it in the distraught and desperate faces of the people in the community, the empty playground behind them and the swings that rocked back and forth in the minimal push of the wind with no one present to enjoy their innocent rapture. I looked out at the crime scene, which was much more detailed than that of the first victim. Someone had cut a large access hole into the ice about 50 feet away from the body. That was where I would go under the water. In all, the pond floor was about 11 to 14 feet down beneath the surface, with some areas dipping to 16 feet or so. A fellow officer helped me secure an air tank over my shoulders and check the regulator to make sure the unit functioned; the routine of precautions, an air of invulnerability suppressed behind what was in essence, a compulsion. There was something comfortable in that though, the routine, warm, like a familiar embrace. I never knew how long I might have to be under the water.

I tightened a mask over my face and walked down to the area the police had cordoned off. I placed a sharp knife under the compensator strapped across my chest and replaced the second regulator into my mouth. Sometimes the body would be stuck or submerged in debris and you had to go underneath to cut it loose in order for the victim to float to the top.

People often called them "floaters," the bodies, but I never did. To me, it showed a complete lack of respect for another human being. It wasn't garbage or hospital waste discovered wading in the drift and tides of the ocean. But the person who disposed of the bodies I was sent in to retrieve, their perspective was different. And that was something you could never allow yourself to forget or you started to drown, even outside of the water where everything was supposed to be intimate and dry. I watched Mull break his attention away from one of the several reporters and look back over his shoulder into the woods, the trees weeping under the heavy ice. I wasn't sure, but I thought I detected a vague sense of pity in the surrounding light reflected from his glasses. All I knew for sure was it wasn't for me.

I stepped onto the ice and moved my way towards the point of entry and stayed close to the taught safety line that an officer secured to the base of a nearby oak tree. I used to play in that creek before the pond was constructed, before time had widened its banks and when the waters ran more rapidly than they did now. We used to grab for crayfish and box turtles. What time does to places, people. Diving classes started for what was considered the spring semester in four weeks. There was talk of postponement. I signaled with a thumb raised high I was ready and dropped through, underneath the ice. It took a few moments for my field of vision to clear when I went underneath water like that, even though it was isolated and trapped. It was kind of like being in a mudslide, the confusion, the anxiety, and the initial shortness of breath. I couldn't panic.

To do something like that, it took persistent training and nerve. But the certification I achieved was a formality, an inconsequential sheet of paper that, in the end, gave you nothing. What people who chose to do that forgot was you still have to look into the puffed faces of dead bodies after the waters cleared aside. And it's immeasurably worse if the enlarged face was a child's. There's nothing in the procedures and equipment manuals that could prepare a person for that. I almost had to think of everyone and everything as indecent, distance myself from the tears that would inevitably cloud up on the inside of the mask if I let them. I still struggled with that, to discover the separation and the detachment from the dead and the inability that I had to readjust to things outside the stability of the water.

The body I was sent to get was someone's child, someone's baby. No matter how old a person got, he was always referred to as somebody's baby. I had it easier than most in the department though. I didn't have to deal with what happened afterwards, the repercussions brought on by the series of abductions, the subsequent murders, the attempted suicides, the lives left behind to rot in the water until there was nothing left recognizable anymore. I felt sorry for the therapists and the caseworkers because there was no interaction between the dead and myself.

It was late midday, nearing 6:00 p.m. and I had to turn on a flashlight to see. Power crews were summoned to bring in portable emergency lights so things could be examined closer. No one on the forensic team wanted to make a mistake. Plain-clothed officers with dogs and several volunteers checked the surrounding woods nearby, searching for possible evidence. Everyone within a 20-mile radius was questioned. I got my bearings after a few minutes and tugged on the safety line in order to let them know I headed towards the body and away from the entrance. Small chunks of ice circled around me like frozen coral broken away from a reef. I turned on my back and tried to figure out how thick the ice was above me. I would have had to break through if I lost sight of where I was or became disoriented.

Water that cold was like steel beams pressed against the arms and legs. My chest hurt. Again I reminded myself I would have to check to see if the body had been tampered with, rigged or weighted to remain submerged and unnoticed so they might be able to connect this victim to the other and establish a pattern. I listened to my breath collide with the apparatus. As I neared a bright marker attached to a piece of rebar they had forced through a small hole drilled in the ice I saw the boy. His carcass was stationary next to the drain inlet and remained several inches beneath the surface. His one shoe was missing and there was a belt tied around his ankles, which strapped his legs together. The coroner would determine if it was placed around his ankles post mortem. I pulled down on the marker flag to let them know I was in place.

Nothing in the pond appeared alive. It looked like a blurred, underdeveloped photograph, images captured in the dark. I took a deep breath, grabbed his hand and tried to move his body. The water and the surrounding environment tugged back. Part of his right hand and the crown of his head must have been frozen into the ice, but not far up enough it could be seen from above the surface. Perhaps it was covered with leaves or blocked by some debris. I and others would have to cut him out. I screamed and bit down on the breathing apparatus. After turning away from his body for several minutes, I removed an underwater measuring tool I used on pipeline repairs and started calculating a spot where we could begin chipping away at the ice from above without damaging the body.

*The water could teach you how to forgive if you let it.*

After I came back up onto some flatland near where I parked my car, I watched everyone's reaction to the body being placed onto a collapsible gurney and loaded into a coroner's van. I assisted Mull in cutting a diameter around the body using a gasoline powered chainsaw. The block of ice was removed from the pond and placed onto a tarp and dragged to the edge of the pond. From where I stood I could see the boy's knuckles. All the fingers on his left hand were blackened from frostbite. It didn't look real. Without knowing it was a child I removed from the water, I would have sworn the ice contained an elderly man or woman, from the worn look of nothing more than a few fingers. Officers started to take the names of the people at the scene again, an attempt by them to be thorough. Mull told me that sometimes perpetrators returned to the scene of the crime to gain some sort of sexual satisfaction.

Someone patted me on the back while I removed my dry suit like I had done something noteworthy or commendable, saved someone somehow. I didn't save anybody. It was the opposite. I ruined lives at times when I provided indisputable answers. I pulled down on the undershirt that had ridden up on my chest. Wisps of gray smoke emanated from the exhaust of the coroner's van as it started back towards town. A woman reached out and touched the side of the van as it drove away from the scene. Until the body was removed from the ice no one would be able to identify him with any certainty. Mull assigned someone to research local missing person's cases in our county and surrounding ones. People always say they wanted closure, like in missing person's cases or disappearances, child abductions. When I looked at the way that woman reacted I wished she would have never known what had happened to that boy. At first she moved through the other people in the crowd, touching the shoulders of a few witnesses, as if she were looking for someone. But as I climbed the hill higher towards my car, she changed.

18

There were no details in uncertainty and that had to be a comfort in some abstract way. It depended on what way you looked at it I supposed. I wasn't sure if she was a relative or a concerned neighbor whose daughter would have someday dated him, took him to pick out his tuxedo for the prom, and slipped him a kiss on his way out of the back seat of the limousine. There was always someone relieved it wasn't his or her son or daughter. That had to be a hard thing to live with, being glad that a different child than your own was dead. No one understood how powerful and destructive the truth could be.

No one stopped the woman as she stood at the edge of the pond. She removed her shoes and stepped out onto the ice. Despite people cupping their mouths and shouting, the woman remained determined and moved further out. Another woman coerced her closer and went out to help her. With her arms around her shoulders, they both sat down at the edge of the pond while a paramedic wrapped a wool blanket around their bodies. I slammed the door on the trunk of my car and tossed the goggles into the back seat.

*Body Number Three: (March) Penelope Marcipio, 15-years-old. Was discovered in partially collapsed silo filled with water, waste product and other residual debris on an abandoned farm. She was the first child who wasn't local. Penelope was reported missing over four months ago from a small town about 40 miles west. No one at the time the body was discovered claimed legal ownership of the property. It was determined later she was most likely the second victim, but the third corpse found. The foreclosed farm where her body was retrieved was on a modest property at the Northern edge of town covering about 18 acres. Forensics teams continued desperately to relate each murder victim to the one previous through proximity, relationships, shopping habits, physicality, schooling, any kind of similarities at all. It was getting harder. Boxes of tagged evidence were shipped to a specialized crime unit within the Federal Bureau of Investigation. The pressure from those multiple federal agencies to provide support had been mounting for weeks. The entire collapse and possible rebuilding of the case from the very first victim created budgetary limitations as well. Tax payers were stretched to their limit. Officials within the remaining hierarchy of the department spoke of reassigning Detective Mull to another case if a lack of progress continued, in order to provide a different perspective on the crimes and establish what the newspapers termed a sense of hope. It would end up being the worst of the crime scenes which had lasting effects on everyone.*

19

Something Mull had said about water caught my attention as I tapped against the window with the back of my hand, waiting. The outside of my knuckles turned rose, the color of a frightened raspberry.

"What did you say?" I asked.

"I said it's extremely remote, more than 17 or 18 miles away from any interchange entrance or exit, making it an isolated place to dump the body. We checked with the county records department. No one has attempted to purchase the land since the original holders were forced into foreclosure. By all accounts it's considered abandoned, but there's still a lot of belongings, records and broken furniture and personal effects still inside," he said. "Whoever lived here last must have left everything behind," he added.

"Is the bank that foreclosed still in operation?" I asked.

"No. It's going to take a few weeks to get the records," Mull added. "We had to track them down, but they're in another state. Apparently they merged two or three times since then, so it's going to take some time to find what we need.   It's a logistical nightmare. But I don't think there's a connection with the people that used to live here and what we found. Yet we still have to do our due diligence so we can rule it out completely," he added.

Foreclosures on dairy and cattle farms were common in this part of the commonwealth, especially over the last decade or so when larger operations opened up in surrounding states. The winters on the East coast were as hard on the agriculture as the dry plains or Midlands and there were very few people who survived domestically or economically anymore. Most farms were only able to produce enough crops to sell off for about two months during the entire year. People who grew up here with farming in their blood had immigrated to larger, more developed cities.

The job market here had been depleted over the last several years and the technological infrastructure required in advancing most large companies didn't exist. Last year a pharmaceutical company backed out of its plans to open up a research center. Attempts to further develop a medical center also deteriorated. Last month, construction was stopped on a scrap metal storage facility. The detective signaled the driver to shut off the flashing lights and the engine of the car grinded to a halt. I sat in the back seat for a while then let the door close, but not latch behind me and stepped around to the trunk and lifted it open. I looked over the roof of the car towards the crime scene.

Cracks and impressions ruined a once quaint concrete path that led up to the front porch. I took a few steps backwards away from the car after shutting the trunk. Near the rear of the vehicle in a ditch was a partial wooden sign that read "fresh vegetables." Several of the letters were missing. I wondered where the cart or stand had been and if anyone had ever driven by this desolate area and bought stalked corn, strawberries or fresh peaches. When my father wasn't around, I used to grab one brilliant peach off of the front porch and run around to the back of our house and sit by the pond, watching the dragonflies skim across the top of the murky water. They moved so fast, like a miniature model plane. I used to let the juice run down my chin. It was always great when no one ever saw me. Sadly, it was the one thing I missed the most when I left home. There should have been more.

A woman wretched in tears was being led away from the barn by an emergency technician towards an awaiting ambulance. As soon as she sat down a paramedic slipped an oxygen mask over her face. Her breathing was quick and shallow. I saw the word "forensics" stenciled across the breast of her black coat. I took a deep breath, fighting against the tightness that developed in my chest, brought upon by the pensive atmosphere and the disruptive familiarity of the farm that, unfortunately for me, came with it. I looked down at my feet when I stumbled because of a large tree root. The ground was littered with them, ridden. It was as if someone had murdered history and buried its body here a long time ago. Only it was beginning to break through the earth, like a bulb, grow and spread. Everything I had tried so desperately to forget about childhood and the past was rushing across my body, like the cold waters off of the coast of Canada, where I again would have given anything to have been.

*Water could teach you how to break if you let it.*

"Let forensics do their thing and then you can go in and pull the body out," Mull said, beginning to take notes on a small tablet. "But be careful. The initial reports say that it isn't pretty in there," he warned.

"Is it a boy or a girl?" I asked.

"It appears to be a girl, but we don't absolutely know yet. There isn't enough light going into the opening for us to make an educated guess. The body also appears to be face down. Anyway, what does it matter?" he asked as he showed his identification to another officer that questioned his permission on the scene. He must not have recognized him. Unfortunately, familiarity here bred uncertainty.

"I guess it doesn't," I said. I stepped into another suit and rubbed my hands together. My breath mixed with the remnants of a cigarette he stepped on. He smelled like he had been up for days. More than likely the lack of progress on any one of the cases started to get to him. But I knew it was more than that. I would have been more concerned if it hadn't. I looked over at him again when he questioned me. His eyes were colorless, empty.

"Are you alright?" he asked.

"Fine. Why?" I couldn't tell if I was shaking because of the cold or what was happening.

"Nothing. Forget it. I'm going to talk to one of the photographers. I want to make sure he gets pictures of the other structures as well and not just the silo, a wider scope of the acreage. I don't want to miss anything," he said. His determination was intense, but sometimes caution led to the corruptibility of certainty.

I moved in front of the car and looked at the decaying silo and attached barn for the first time. It was situated to the direct left of what appeared to be a dairy cattle housing, with metal bars separating the stalls. The paint and the materials underneath the exterior had started to wither away. It was hard to tell what color it had once been. Less than eight feet away from the body stood the barn, one that was being searched and sealed by the department. There were rotted hay bales all around the sides of the structure as well as the dilapidated farmhouse opposite the property. It was odd, but the smell reminded me of old books. Some fall decorations were toppled against an immobile tractor. The tires were missing. The intense flash of a camera flickered in the distance. A photographer came out of the barn and moved along the side of the house towards the rear of the property. Someone said something about getting pictures of the water well outback.

"It'll be a couple of minutes," one of the forensic experts said to me, reaching out for my shoulder as I started to move nearer the scene. When I looked closer I noticed that it was the coroner, Walter Fasman. I had seen him at the other crime scenes, but had never been this close to him until now. I tried, when I wasn't in the water, to keep my distance. "You can wait in one of the squad cars if you want to. Put on gloves if you're going to move around inside any of the buildings, especially the house, in case you touch anything. They haven't checked some of the areas yet. Besides, they'll keep you warm," he added.

I ducked underneath more caution tape and pulled the collar of my coat higher up on my neck. The screen door to the farmhouse, filled with holes, hung off of the rusted hinges. I opened it slowly and hoped what was left of the supports would remain intact. The smell from outside had penetrated the oppressive darkness inside. I felt for a light switch, but there wasn't any power. More portable lights from the fire department were supposedly on their way, but it would take them some time to get here, a direct result of the weather and what it left behind. There was so much mud around the property. The living room windows were broken in and what was left of the glass swayed back and forth like paper moving in the auspicious breeze. Outside the photographer snapped another picture. In the quick light from the flash I could see inside the farmhouse, trying to gather as many details as possible in the limited visibility. There were faded squares on the walls where paintings or portraits had been.

*Another picture flash.*

I could see an old-fashioned steel radiator running underneath of the window ledge. I hesitated slightly then touched the surface. It was terribly cold. I burned my hand on one when I was younger. I pulled off one of the gloves. The scar was still there on the flesh of my palm, but most of the original color of the wound was gone. There was a small, terracotta flowerpot, cracked, the dried soil scattered across the chipped paint. There was a barely legible named imprinted across the rim. Lily. I wondered how old she was when she made it or put her name on it as I leaned against the windowpane. I scrutinized the inundated dusk, the vacancy and the isolation in what was happening here. I tried to remember what color the leaves had been that day, that last day for me when the adolescent sun was burgeoning atop the blighted stalks of corn and oat plants, brightening the peaches, a bleached russet shade that changed from beautiful to dangerous, like a rotting apple to the inside of a woman's mouth. The photographer brushed aside the branches of some dead foliage then concentrated on the empty field behind the house.

*Another picture flash.*

*And another.*

*And another.*

I stepped through the door to the farmhouse and back out into the dark hours of the morning. There was a rusted porch swing on my right that overlooked the woods next to the house. Several men and women were moving through as I noticed the small moons of flashlights scattering across the barren trees. Mull had asked that volunteer firemen and municipal workers be brought in to search the surroundings woods through the morning. The tragedies of a truncated childhood were beginning to scream when I heard Mull call to me from where the body was found. The dirt and soil around the base of the silo were saturated, moist and there were various patterns of footprints indented into the ground even before the scene became compromised with all of the department's people. It appeared to be a bottom loaded storage compartment which made it the oldest style of farm silo. Most modern farms used top loaders because repair to them was made much easier. In all, the stave silo measured some 250 feet in the air. Even though there was no sun, I shielded my eyes with my hand when I looked up towards the top.

"How did it get filled with water?" I asked.

The detective turned around and scribbled something onto his notepad and gave low toned verbal directions to another officer, then pointed in the opposite direction. "Most likely the heavy rains we had the other night raised the level up some. There's a large section of the cone that covers the top that's missing or broken away over time. Snow inside that came in through the opening could have melted. There's been a lot of it this year. The inside of the cylinder appears to be intact, but you could get us a better answer once you're inside. What's in there could have been building up over time. Might be a coincidence. Could be he filled it with water to decompose the body, but I don't see how he could have done it. The well out back of the property was searched and according to the level, it's as dry as a bone and there were no depressed tire tracks leading towards or away from the silo according to the first officers on the scene. Then again, we don't know for certain how long the body has been here. After you pull the body out, go down as far as you can and see what else is in there," he instructed.

I grabbed an industrial flashlight I used in commercial diving and crossed underneath the caution tape. A second photographer stepped down from a steel ladder I would use. He stumbled through a few puddles when he reached the ground, tumbled onto his chest and remained on his hands and knees for a few minutes. His stomach and back muscles contracted violently. I closed my eyes and turned around when he began to vomit. I wondered if it was the first body he had photographed.

"Get in and get out," Mull said when he folded his arms across his chest and began to worry about the integrity of the crime scene. I felt like telling him he was right that things would get worse, but decided to allow his uncertainty and misgiving to remain uninterrupted. Looking into his eyes I knew he was thinking about his daughter. They were watery and doleful. I wished it all would have been as simple as he once said it would be.

I climbed the ladder and leaned in some 60 feet in the air and maneuvered the flashlight's beam around in a clockwise direction, surveying the scene, and came across the body of a girl who floated on her stomach. There appeared to be nothing above the surface that secured her body in place, no wires or cords. There was no movement of any kind inside the silo. I dropped cautiously into the water and was struck instantly with the horrid stench of rotting flesh and animal feces. Some of the fluid splashed across the upper surface of my lips. It was apparent the body had been here for some time, left to waste away in a pool of muck and shit. With my back facing the cylinder I moved along the outside wall and hoped to get as far away from the girl as I could.

Honestly you couldn't tell if it was a boy or a girl. The body rested perfectly in the middle, rising and falling with the displacement of the water. I placed a mask over my eyes, grabbed a quick breath and plunged underneath of the remains towards the bottom of the structure and confirmed what Mull had suggested. The silo was layered on the inside with a dense concrete and steel wall about eight feet thick, which had helped to retain the water and debris inside. Someone would have to check and see what the previous owners had stored there. Not that it would have told us anything. If it indeed had been a dairy farm, it was probably filled with feed or corn. I broke the surface, ripped the mask from my face and gasped for air. There was a body bag already draped over the edge of the crumbled silo where I came in, as ineffectually as a bath towel over the thin construction of a shower rod. I wasn't going to be able to get her down the ladder with me.

A large crane was brought to the sight to aid the removal of the body. I secured the mask back over my face and pulled down on a line attached to what was a submergible gurney, similar to the ones in rescue used by the United States Coast Guard. Giving direction, I told the operator to lower the line. Pulling it towards me, I manipulated the equipment and secured the girl inside. Raising my arm above my head I signaled he could pull the harness up. Her body ascended from the water. Motioning for him to stop, I adjusted one of the straps. For the first time I could see her face. The flesh around the construction of her nose had begun to peel away, the bones of her nasal cavity protruding out from underneath. I covered my mouth. What was left of the hair on her scalp resembled algae or kelp floating on the surface of the Dead Sea.

It was a majestic and historical body of water, the Dead Sea, which was rumored to cover the ancient cities of Sodom and Gomorrah. Because of the overwhelming salinity, life could not exist in its waters. I visited Jordan once during my Olympic career. We were in Europe for time trials near the end of my attempts to represent the United States. I never got a chance to experience the myths and legends of that body of water. I wasn't sure why I thought about it now. The girl's body was almost free of the silo. I searched around again before reaching for the safety line. Voices and sounds echoed in here. I wondered if there was any chance she was alive when she was dumped here. It would be up to the coroner to determine that. Imagine the horror alone, the smell, the isolation and the sick density of the water. If I never saw Jordan again during my lifetime, I realized I had already touched the waters of the dead.

I stepped out of the dry suit and held a moist towel over my mouth and nose. My stomach was turning itself over and over. A truck headed up the farm's gravel driveway pulling the portable lighting. Mull instructed them to set up around the perimeter of the barn. He was going to search the rear fields again. I shut the door to my car after removing a jacket and started towards the battered farmhouse again. When I reached the front steps I hesitated for a moment. The rotted floorboards underneath my feet split and I dropped through the porch. It wasn't that far down and it felt like I was standing in mud. One of the portable lights switched on and the intensity was as high as a sunrise. I shaded my eyes from the glare and crouched down. I searched around for a flashlight and after retrieving one, repositioned myself to see clearer. Beams of light shot underneath of the wood and I could see several cardboard boxes. I asked one of the officers on the scene for another pair of gloves. I crawled through the opening and pulled on the box closest to me. The outside flaps were sodden and pieces tore away. I lifted the box into my arms and went through the front door into the house.

I could hear footsteps from some of the forensic detail upstairs searching the rooms. I heard the coroner ask them to see if there was any physical evidence that the girl might have been violated here then dumped into the silo. It would be impossible to even lift a latent print off of anything in the house. Sitting on the floor with little visibility I removed the contents from the cardboard box, hoping to find and address or something that would lead us to the previous tenants and quicken the process. There were several photographs long faded into a sepia tint, a blank, leather journal and a couple of greeting cards. I wondered what the date was today.

I wasn't even sure what I was looking for anymore, but I kept rummaging through someone's clandestine mementos. Why were they hidden underneath of the house? I felt like a thief. There was a roughed up pocket watch resting on the bottom of the box. There seemed to be nothing special about it. I replaced it and tossed through some letters. Several of them were unopened. The postmarks were gone. Underneath of those letters were several photographs of a stunning woman. No dates appeared anywhere on the photo paper. Each looked recent. Secured by a rubber band was a large bundle of invoices and receipts. I thumbed through them and was familiar with what many of them listed. Some were for goods purchased, but all were for items sold. When I was growing up, our garage was stacked floor to ceiling with identical receipts. Trying to get around them was like moving a mountain aside with a feather.

Dissatisfied and defeated I pushed the box aside and stood. I went through the living room and into the kitchen, stopping when I reached the back door. Outside the window, men and women were still searching the grounds. I stepped out onto the small porch and looked around. A rusted grill sought refuge in the shadows cast by a huge tree overlooked a large patch of dead grass. There was nothing else around besides blackness. All the farming equipment must have been in or behind the barn. Maybe stolen and salvaged for scrap. I noticed a pronounced slope in the ground as I walked. There might have been a pool there once, or a pond. I kneeled and moved my hands across the area and pushed aside a piece of rotted fruit. I dropped it back onto the ground and inhaled to the point where I could no longer compress air within my lungs. I couldn't swim on land as much as I wanted to.

Leaning forward I noticed an insect cocoon. It was still unbroken after all this time. I stood up and looked at the circles from the flashlights pass through the landscape. The corner's van pulled away from the house. When I moved closer to the neglected corn field, I kicked several pieces of petrified cobs. Circles of light still danced in the darkness. There was no noise, the passive moments of the hush of the early dawn. Hundreds of rotted cobs were spread, brave and fallen infantry soldiers of an unrecorded campaign. When someone found my father's body in our pond, he was surrounded by peaches, burning spheres of boldness and authenticity resting on the surface. His lungs were satiated with water. No one had reported him missing for three days. I should have been there. When the chrysalis broke apart between my fingers, there was still the remains of an insect inside.

*Body Number Four: (April) Molly Janikowski, 14-years-old. Her body was found inside a scrap metal storage facility under construction, which had been suspended because of an improper permit. Molly was discovered floating in the basement foundation. The 5,000 square foot area was filled with a little more than 42 inches of water and mud washed from the surrounding rear hillside. The land on the building site used to be a small golf course. A curfew was instituted for anyone under the age of sixteen that started at 8:00 p.m. The Governor of the state was beginning to apply pressure because of the complete absence of any real physical evidence, nothing that could guarantee a conviction in a court of law. It would all be circumstantial anyway without conclusive DNA evidence. The District Attorney wouldn't prosecute without the confidence he would secure a conviction. So many months into the investigation and there were still no suspects reported or named publically, just a few "persons of interest," and no substantial evidence that could be used to determine a clear motive or link an individual to the crimes. All registered sex offenders were accounted for and had been cleared by the department with help from officials in surrounding counties. But there weren't many around here. The radius of the search now covered almost 100 miles. Mull, the coroner and the lead forensic investigator had been called into several meetings over the last couple of days to provide updates to local politicians and news stations.*

There were several leads phoned into local and national tip lines that were set up by volunteers, but nothing materialized from any of them. Pressure mounted from state and Federal agencies to come up with a fresh lead and a suspect. Some parents and local community leaders had scheduled a town meeting to address the situation and possible upcoming changes in the investigation. They felt they weren't being kept apprised of what was happening. An undercover agent, who specialized in cases involving the sexual assault of children, was rumored to have been assigned to the case, but no one in the department knew for sure. That might have been part of the point. All anyone wanted was help.

The soil around the foundation of the structure looked like spilled paint, a bright, rusted color spread out across the ground, a unique hue reserved for antique light fixtures and Southern-styled patio furniture. It came from the color of the clay unearthed during the construction. Detective Mull paced the edge of the scene, wearing a pair of latex gloves and a tortured artist's countenance and perplexity, detailing specific measurements and observations in his notebook. It was overcast and dreary. The power had been shut off to the project site, but a quick call to the utility office had them turned on. Some of the portable floodlights highlighted the haphazard stubble forming along the detective's sharp jaw line. There was dried mud on his coat and blood on the underside of his chin. It looked as if he had started to shave his neck and became lost in thought in front of the mirror, fogged by the inability to solve what was happening.

Mull tried, his body rigid, to light a cigarette but gave up after three matches refused to ignite under the delicate mist. He threw it to the ground in front of him. The wind blew it across the area and into the basement. It went into the water. I glanced down at the body. The petite 14-year-old was resting face up, clothed, her hair swirling in the breeze. The construction site had been sealed off completely and a barrier was set up around the perimeter that extended close to a mile and a half. Instead of getting narrower, the crime scenes were become more expansive yet still remained suffocating nonetheless.

"Did you get any prints?" Mull asked.

"No usable prints yet, unless you want us to identify all the footprints around the body," a forensics team member answered. "Besides, it's been raining for over 24 hour's detective. We're not going to find anything here."

"That would be a waste of time I know. Almost 60 people came through here on a daily basis according to the project foreman we tracked down. It's a fucking mess out here. I'd be surprised if you even got a clear partial heel print. All in all it's a damn smart place to dump the body. Have all the workers been questioned?" Mull asked.

"Not yet. There were in actuality over 70 people employed on this project and that doesn't include anyone from the financing company or the architect. Anyone who entered the site during operating hours was required to log in. The company is sending it to us. We'll have to wait for the coroner to determine an approximate time of death though," he began, "since no one has been on site for a little over two weeks. That's when the permit fell through and the construction shut down."

"That would eliminate some things, but I'd be surprised if she hadn't been murdered in the last couple of days," he began. "It would have given him more privacy, less exposure to wait to dump the body. Has the photographer finished yet?" Mull questioned.

"Almost," he said.

Mull looked over the man's right shoulder into the horizon near the entrance to the worksite. "Are any of the security systems up and running?"

"No. The cameras you saw on the way in by the main gate aren't functional. They were still being installed when the project was halted."

"How did he get in?" Mull asked.

"When we arrived the gate was closed, but we looked closer. It appears he had large bolt cutters and severed the lock and chain. We have it in a bag. It's not a very sturdy lock, not more than a half of an inch thick. He would have cut through it in a matter of seconds," he said.

"You won't find them, but look around and see if you can find what he used. Check the equipment that's here as well. Pull her out," Mull said. I kneeled along the side of the construction, a set of goggles hanging around my neck.

It appeared as some misogynistic, failed session of Macro Polo, a simple children's game where one participant is blind, depending on his or her ears and sense of touch to lead them. I remembered playing it at the local YMCA on the other side of town. I thought of the uncertainty and overwhelming panic I felt treading water in the center of the pool. I remembered that because Molly's ears were badly bruised, almost caved into her skull. She most likely couldn't hear her attacker if the wounds were not inflicted post-mortem. I remembered all of that because Molly's fingers were swelled, partially because of the water. Some of the ones on her right hand were displaced, the joints broken at the knuckles. When it happened, it sounded like a branch breaking in half. I wondered how alone she would have felt in that moment.

"Would he have bothered to even try to rig the body to remain underwater?" I asked, as I readjusted the goggles into place around my eyes. The impact caused me to blink a couple of times.

"At this point, probably not. Either he's wanted the victims to come to the surface or he's gotten uncharacteristically sloppy, but I don't put much credence to that. Whoever it is hasn't made a single forensic mistake. It's more than likely a deliberate act," he added. "You probably won't find her body rigged and possibly not on any of the one's going further."

"Could he have used any of the equipment here to fill this foundation?" I asked the detective as I motioned behind him.

"The equipment he would have needed was brought here on a daily basis and then returned to the construction depot adjacent to another site. Could be some of the equipment was rented from another site. I'll have someone contact them and see if any of their equipment was unaccounted for in the last week or so or what was rented out. He would have needed something large enough to hold at last 2000 gallons of water. Even if he had used it, there wouldn't be any complete latent prints on it. Diadan construction is one of the largest firms on the Eastern seaboard. That equipment could have been on hundreds of different sights over the last several months," Mull added. "That's a lot of elimination prints. We won't know until the foundation is drained, but according to the project foreman we talked to, the water lines were operating to their full capacity when construction stopped. So it's possible he could have broken a line down there in the foundation deliberately. The more apt question may be why would he want to fill it with water? He knows the body wouldn't go undiscovered long enough to decompose. Our man could have killed her in private then placed her body in a bathtub or something similar to allow her to decompose. If he did that in close proximity to other people or buildings, he would have to somehow mask the smell. Unless the water itself is the message," he said.

After pausing, Mull continued. "I understand it because of how destructive water is to a corpse involving DNA, trace elements and the like. He could dump the bodies anywhere though, dismember them, immolate them, make them almost impossible to identify. But he doesn't," Mull said, turning his back and looking out at the surrounding scene, the access roads the perpetrator may have used in the background, the onslaught of journalists and television reporters shouting questions over top of questions so that not one was distinguishable from the other. "He puts them in places where he has to know that they're going to be found. It may be a misjudgment on my part, but I believe whoever he is, is taunting us," he added.

Water seeped into the basement foundation from the runoff and trickled down the imperfect boundaries of the incomplete masonry. Through the clear synthetic material of the goggles I stared at her and slid into the area. The surface was cloudy and dense, littered with twigs and small insects moving from place to place. The alabaster color of the walls was dulled by the red clay around the construction. I turned my back to her body and lowered myself into the basement area. I switched on a flashlight. There were no ropes or bindings that broke the surface of the water. I didn't go under because there was no way that I would be able to see.

It hadn't occurred to me until I neared her body how much she resembled Mull's youngest daughter, Adley. A small echo tripped across the skin of the water. The displacement caused air to move over the opening of sections of incomplete plumbing comprised of industrial plastic. It sounded like someone gasping for air. The images that accompanied it were no doubt excruciating and unforgiving. "You don't have to do this anymore. I'm sure that Detective Mull could find a suitable replacement if pressured enough," a voice began. Standing in a rain poncho at the edge of the basement housing was the coroner, Walter Fasman. He wore glasses but because of the mist, I noticed that he had taken them off and stuffed them into the inside of his coat. "If the perpetrator is using water to try and decompose the body, there aren't that many large areas he hasn't already used, except for the river unless he repeats himself," he concluded. "Besides, without any real progress it's a matter of time until the federal authorities take over the investigation. It'll happen soon and then we'll all be removed from the case. We're not trained enough nor have the experience to handle this kind of thing," he said.

"Something like this shouldn't be happening here," I said, adjusting the dry suit around my neck.

"There's no latitude or longitude to immorality," he said.

"I'm sorry, but this goes beyond immorality alone." The water appeared to move closer to me. I adjusted to the isolation and the desperateness in being in the water at times. At first I was never going to stop, all that space, that feeling of quiet autonomy, the water embracing and patient. I watched him look over his shoulder and motion his attendants to roll out a gurney. Several minutes later I placed my hands underneath her stomach and guided her along the water, as if I were teaching her to swim, as if I were teaching her the history of something more. He kneeled over the girl's body and helped to secure her inside a bag. He was close enough to her I thought he was going to whisper into her ear so I couldn't hear and I would never understand the point of all things.

*Body number 5: (May) Michael Dyer, age 29, civil engineer, father of one girl, divorced. Was pulled from the submerged wreckage of an automobile when the car he was driving veered off of a road to avoid an accident and careened into the river. According to the autopsy results he appeared to have died on impact when the front of his skull was crushed against the steering column. He also suffered a subdural hematoma. Dyer was not wearing his seatbelt at the time of impact. There was another passenger in the car when it went into the water. His was the first body I pulled from the water that wasn't related to the case and wasn't the body of a child.*

There should have been nothing different about it, the body, although under the water, it weighed more than almost all the others. It was hard to tell though, the current pulling, moving the appendages and structure through the fluid with blunt, reckless force. In truth, it was impressively different. It wasn't underdeveloped and guileless with an immature sense of subjection and purpose. It came with an absolute certainty of identity and circumstance. None of the children had. I got the call from the department around 4 a.m. on a Thursday morning. I wasn't asleep at the time so the early hour didn't matter to me. And I was alone. I almost wanted an emergency call to happen so I could escape from the claustrophobia of uncertainty and evasion that saturated our house at its surface. It was hardly noticeable, but I understood it was there.

Mold. No, a spore.

That was its genesis, a small microbial organism cleaving the kinetic balance of our marriage. I had inhaled it into my lungs from the stagnant water I pulled children from, saturated them with confusion and indifference. I carried its characteristics and biology into the molecules of water we drank, the water we bathed in. Hanna was in New York researching for a documentary and I was here monitoring my gear, but hoping I would not have to go into the water again. Yet I knew I would. I could smell her blooming grace overtop of the humidity and the rank in the emptiness of the garage. It was odd I couldn't before.

There was a multi-vehicle accident on one of the back roads adjacent the river and the exact cause wasn't determined, but there were some preliminary reports from eyewitnesses that heavy, dense fog may have played some part in the crash. I wasn't an investigator so I didn't care. It didn't matter to me. As I listened to the scanner on the way over, they called for paramedics and emergency lighting to be brought to the scene. When I arrived some six or seven minutes later, the area around the crash had been sectioned off with one barrier and two plain-clothed officers were setting up to divert traffic into the oncoming lane to give rescuers the room to work. No one else had arrived yet. The only vehicles that usually passed through there that early were school buses or sanitation trucks. It would have to be completely closed.

I shut off the headlights to the car and depressed the button unlocking the trunk. I grabbed a set of road flares. The routine of doing this should have been more of a burden than it was, carrying the swelled honor or dishonor of the dead on my shoulders and placing them into the back of a truck or a van. I didn't know most of them very well, if at all. But the relationships, the false intimacy I had with their lifelessness was simple, unadulterated, uncomplicated by the burden of guilt and apprehension. I couldn't be betrayed because it did not exist in the truncated and limited vocabulary of the dead. I often looked forward to it, putting on the dry suit, swimming under the surface and seeing things through the displaced perspective of the tinted diving goggles. The light cast by things outside and above didn't penetrate the water that deep. Nothing that rested down there could be exposed. Even the truth became suppressed underneath of the rot and the debris.

When I arrived on the scene, I was told two people were pronounced dead and two more would need to be air lifted to the nearest medical center. One of the vehicles had become engulfed in flames when the fuel tank ignited after the collision. Plumes of somber, black smoke suffocated the atmosphere. It looked like the barren streets of a war torn republic. A third car had careened off the side of the road and broken through a barrier. It rested on its passenger side in the thick mud on the edge of the bank though so I probably wouldn't have to go into the water. The water here was resilient, bitter and cut through your suit as if the molecules of its chemistry were serrated. I stepped around some of the damage and set flares down at certain points. It was difficult to see. But it was hard not to notice the charred remains, almost glued into position against the seats, their faces stretched in horror. They looked like plastic dolls, wax paraffin dolls. One of the officers asked me to help him place more flares farther down where the road disappeared around a bend, almost 600 to 800 feet from where the wreckage started. His hands shook when he pointed into the mist. I couldn't tell the difference between the smoke drifting around the bodies and the fog that wrapped them in reticence.

I thought of Hanna's breath moving along the asphalt, searching for me through the ruins, neglecting insignificant places, objects and collapsing on the dark flesh of the water, thinking I was trapped, submerged underneath. I wanted to hear her voice, distant by thousands of miles. I imagined her looking down from the cement rim of a lighthouse, gazing upon an opaque canvas calling me home, her lungs an incredible siren. Her love and her sound so immense and unyielding it could break through ice and stone on the vast desert of oceans, rip through the hull of a ship and unthread the sails of any vessel in an attempt to mute her. I imagined her coming closer, her speech leading me, guiding me to land to sanctuary or a collision upon the irregular debris of desolated cliffs and menace. I begged for sunrise to tear through the dark fabric of ambivalence which tightened against my body.

It sounded like extinction, a series of loud impacts leading to entropy and decay. Mortality. I had no other way to describe what scattered through the density of the atmosphere and the trees. It was something I had never heard before, that sound. If I hadn't been there, I would have never been able to tell what it was. It was piercing, powerful and enduring. In the distance ahead of me a vehicle travelled around a sharp, oncoming curve, the pale, raspberry fog from the flares spinning and trailing off into oblivion. It must not have seen me. Then, not long after, that sound behind me. I turned and ran. In the time it had taken me to arrive, that vehicle had swerved into the shoulder to avoid the wreckage of the accident and crashed hard into the water through the guardrail and past the overturned car that still rested motionless in the mud.

The currents were fast and the chances of the driver and any possible passengers surviving were minimal, especially if the windshield of the automobile had been compromised. No one could say for certain how many people were in the vehicle. There was no movement inside when it first penetrated the surface of the water, although visibility was zero. By the time I had arrived, the car had been submerged for almost four minutes. The most that the electrical systems in an automobile would work underwater was ten.

Luckily I hadn't latched the trunk of my car so I was able to slide into a wetsuit and secure a compressed air tank over my shoulders, struggling to breathe in the thick, morning air, air so sharp it hurt your chest to inhale it, tore through your lungs as if they were tissue paper. I watched the water break around my feet and begin to pull back around my ankles. Soon, I was knee deep in the frigid waters and watched the distant landscape of the high-rises disappear from my line of sight.

Water could teach you how to be patient if you let it

There were construction sites opened up facing the waterfront. The steel frames looked like broken, temporary images of a child's imagination set upon a discolored background. The fog in the atmosphere appeared to sleep along the unstable mattress of water set comfortably into the snapping pockets and concurring ripples. I closed my eyes for a moment and took a large breath, then placed the regulator between my lips again. I clenched my teeth like a boxer before the opening bell of a fight. The steel taste of the apparatus was bitter as always, but still comforting.

I penetrated the infinite colorlessness and descended down, twisting the end of an intense flashlight. I couldn't see anything. I was tired already. The bottom of the river was estimated to be some 300 feet beneath the landline. After three or four minutes I reached the automobile as it rested motionless on the bottom against the passenger side. I maneuvered into a better position and looked through the glass. I pulled on the handle of the driver's side door. The pressure hadn't caused any of the windows to crack, but there was some water trickling into the vehicle through the windshield. There were bubbles that rose to the surface. I didn't have much time. There would be a limited supply of oxygen inside. And I would have to flood the remainder of the compartment to retrieve the bodies. No one moved inside. I thought everyone was dead. I looked around. There was no one else in the water.

I unsnapped a button on a belt around my waist and grabbed the end of a small acetylene torch sometimes used to weld a joint or displace a lock or another piece of metal to untangle a victim. I turned my head away from the welding arc and began to work on the driver's side door along the crushed hinges. It didn't take long for me to violate the car's exterior and the increased force of the free water tore loose the remaining hinge. Water poured into the compartment and the body of the driver shot out of the seat and struck me in the chest. The seatbelt around his waist either dislodged or was never fastened when he entered the car. His belt was undone and his pants were pulled down around his thighs. I clutched his ankle and held his body so I could check for vitals. I touched his throat. It didn't matter. He was dead. There was a large, horizontal laceration across the length of his forehead. The air bag hadn't discharged or inflated. Blood trickled into the water. Most likely he fractured the front of his skull on the steering column. The man must have died instantly. I let his corpse rise to the surface over my shoulder.

There was another body, still strapped into the passenger's side, the water in the river causing her hair to float through the spectrum of dimmed light. I reached deeper into the compartment and cut the line to the lap belt and the one secured around her shoulder. Her head tilted back against the leather seat. I touched her throat. It was tender. She was alive, but unconscious. I gasped for a burst of air from the tank when I recognized the small birthmark on the woman's neckline. It looked like a figure eight.

*Hanna Cohen, age 34, documentarian, married, no children. Was last seen filming a documentary on lighthouses and their keepers in New York.*

I was exhausted ascending out of the temporary lucidity of the water, her body cradled in my arms. I never should have come up. The dead man rested face down some 20 feet from the shore. Another officer had entered the river and helped two others lift his body into a raft. It rested on a tarpaulin against the bank of the river. The other people from the department stood there as I carried her. I looked back over my shoulder. A news photographer stood on the banks of the river and depressed the shutter on the camera over and over again. I handed her body to a medic and walked over and knelt down in front of the male victim and rolled his body over so I could see his face, the sand and deposits from the river staining his mouth and teeth.

Two officers restrained me as I started to remove his wallet. I'm not sure if they understood the woman I surfaced with was Hanna. I lifted the diving goggles over my head and tossed them into the river. I stepped back violently, vomiting hard on the ground several times. Everything looked different again. The bodies, the people I pulled weren't supposed to be alive. They weren't supposed to possess life, breath, characteristics of morality and fear. They weren't supposed to come with direct consequences. I could still smell the salt on my skin and feel the coarseness in my hair the water created. It felt like scattered pieces of dead, fallen leaves, like I had drifted to sleep in the backyard near that pond while my father covered me as a child in that inescapable autumn debris, peaches basking in the sunlight at my feet. The dead had abandoned me in passing.

The morning after I pulled Hanna's body from the water was tense and reflective. While she was admitted to the hospital, I came home to pack a bag of clothes for her and ended up never going back. The telephone rang throughout the deserted places of where we must have faltered as lovers, where we somehow became misguided within one another's arms, within one another's longitudes. Someone left message after message and I could faintly hear their voice on the answering machine with the volume turned to its lowest setting. It was too soft to tell if it was Mull or another member of the department or hospital staff. I remained motionless in our bedroom, nestled in the corner between her dresser full of her intimates and some of her filming equipment. But it all seemed inaccessible to me, the clothes she wore, the photographs she framed, the people she sometimes interviewed at their most vulnerable, their weakest. I felt like a nomad, a wanderer, trapped atop one of her lighthouses with no way to get down.

After being disabled and unresponsive for hours, I dressed and ended up swimming at the local YMCA while Hanna was treated for a severe concussion, lacerations to her shoulders, neck and face, and several cracked ribs. I had lapped the pool for three hours until the muscles underneath of my skin burned, deadening the pain through authority and exhaustion. The muscles in my shoulders and back stretched beyond what was expected from their kinetic construction. I felt like a coward. I never had enough audacity to endure the consequences of what had happened and the layered damage the accident had caused. After five days of round the clock care, she was released. The department offered to send someone in my place to bring her home. In my place. Someone else had already been there.

That morning, all the windows were open in our house, the adolescent sunlight pouring in through the glass in our bedroom. It was early. The light was so beautiful, delicately intense, but gentle enough to be soothing as the landscapes behind remained silent and exhausted. When Hanna found me I was sitting on the tile floor inside the shower. I had been sitting with my back against the door for an hour. The once mildly warm water bit, falling across my neck and chest. There was nowhere else I could go, no water around to hide within.

Hanna dropped her bag from the hospital and opened the door to the shower, the tips of her hair beginning to moisten. She hesitated. There were deep bruises under her eyes. She reached and pulled my body forward, cradled me and secured my head in her lap, moving aside the hair that fell across my eyes. I could hear her labored breathing. I wanted to pull away from her so much, but I adored her, married her years ago because she was intelligent and alluring, but more importantly she understood the emotional complexities and sensitivity I possessed and never admonished me for it, never used it against me. Without saying a word she kissed me on the side of the head and sobbed.

"You never came to the hospital," she stated.

"I'm sorry," I ushered quietly.

"I was there for five days, waiting for you," she said.

"I don't think they knew who I was carrying at first. You seemed so heavy, weighted somehow like all that water from the river had soaked into your skin, what clothes you had on. I wanted to know who he was so much. I should have tried to resuscitate you, but I didn't. Someone else did, one of the paramedics. It was like he was kissing you. After they rushed you away, I sat there on the banks of the river. I couldn't bring myself together enough to be near anyone who knew about what happened, to see the look in their eyes. Pity would have been an endless, arid desert for me. You had the luxury of being isolated. The entire time, sitting here, reflective, the right thing to say to you and everyone else never occurred to me," I added.

"I wasn't sure what you would do. When you didn't come after the second day I thought you might be gone," she added.

"I'm fine. It doesn't matter," I said. I abandoned her embrace and leaned against the glass door opposite her body.

"I'm sorry," she said as moved to turn off the water. "I shouldn't have done this to you."

"Why?" I asked.

"You didn't' deserve this," she admitted.

"No, why did you do it?" I was scared she was no longer in love with me, that I had separated somehow from her, that the intimacy I enjoyed with her was vanishing and I was too naïve to see it.

"I don't' know," she said. "I've been thinking about that since you saved me." Her head rose up and the marks underneath of her eyes resembled smeared mascara. It was hard trying not to desire her then, watching her compassion, her vulnerability, her nipples noticeable through her blouse, the bold, vermillion pattern of the material along the sleeves contrasting with the tenderness of her eyes.

"I didn't save you," I said.

"Yes you did," she admitted.

"Bringing your body out of the water didn't save anything," I said. "I should have never come out of the water." I stood up, my limbs atrophic. She reached her hand and touched the plane of my stomach, paused, then allowed me to continue to pull away.

"What are you going to do? Are you going to leave me?" she asked.

"Can we talk about this later?" I asked. "There's a town meeting scheduled and I'd like to be there after everything that's happened," I said. "The government's going to take over the case soon."

"Are you going to leave me?"

"I don't know." I wrapped a towel around my waist with my back towards her, growing more assailable around the woman I loved.

*Water could teach you history if you let it.*

Moreover the history of a woman, what was an often intricate, beautiful and delicate chronology of passion and sometimes sadness. A woman was a rare thing, a collection of sympathy and power, passion and intellect. A woman was inimitable in the lives of men. The history of a man was constructed on their indelible shoulders. I understood all there was to know about history; the archives of the muted dead, the annals of failed intimacy and privacy, the history of immorality and despair. I understood the sad affliction of circumstance placed upon vibrant young children by the violent unpredictability of man's rash and savage brutality and the complicated nature of water. It was highlighted in the chronology of the investigation, those offensive crimes, bodies and statistics imprisoned in the bronze landscapes, the turned soil, and the cold waters of barren ponds like archaeological relics.

I sat in the back of the school auditorium, watching people enter through the rear door, listening to their concerns and fears as each one poured warm coffee into unrecyclable cups and flicked at their cigarettes, clinging to their individual vices. A candlelight vigil for the victims was starting for those not able to be in attendance because of the smaller size of the auditorium. The local pastor led the ceremony and read each victim's name with somber remembrance. The church bells chimed in the unseen distance. There were about 110 people inside, searching desperately for that promised hope in another person's words and in their actions, expressing their outrage, waiting for reassurances and positivity that couldn't be given to anyone by anyone. The dead wouldn't give up their secrets. I once thought they needed me, the dead. But in that swimming pool on that cold, January night, I should have turned my back on them, let them remain unfounded and never allowed my body to have broken the surface of that water. Mull entered through the door of the auditorium with his wife and his daughter, Adley.

*Water could teach you control of you let it.*

There were so many reasons to leave, resign from the investigation and go home. Nothing was going to change when the murderer was apprehended. All the imposing damage had already been afflicted by selflessness and by the pure tenacity of water. And I was betrayed by it. It had stained the one thing I valued. Some wounds would remain laid bare and the dead would always be gone, archaic and as sunrises turned into long, restless nights, forgotten. It all scared me. I smiled at Mull's daughter. Water had power, pure and simple. It was dangerous to disrespect anything one knew so little about. It had an imposing will, a purpose and could not be enslaved or manipulated by composition or architecture. It could not be instructed or controlled, commanded or tricked. It was then I realized water was as much responsible for death as it was for birth.

*Body Number Six: (May) Jeremy Sundermond, seven years old. The boy was discovered wrapped in a large mesh cloth that was subsequently dumped into the river. The material was commonly used for landscape bedding to prevent the growth of weeds. His face had been nearly unrecognizable because of multiple lacerations and contusions to the face. During the autopsy the coroner would count over 62 separate wounds. There was one witness to the action to dispose of the body, although there appeared to be no attempt at the time to weigh the corpse*

42

*down to inhibit identity. No physical description of a suspect could be provided due to the hour and proximity of the altercation. For the first time, almost six months into the investigation, a piece of physical evidence was recovered from a crime scene; a bullet casing, but not one removed from the body of a victim. It was removed from the side of the riverbed. Ballistics couldn't be matched because none of the children previously murdered had been shot during the ritual.*

*That word, a ceremony or regular procedure, was indiscriminate, violent and referenced several times in that psychological profile created with help from the Sex Crimes Section of the Major Offense Squad of the Pennsylvania Police Department and the Federal Bureau of Investigation. I reread the document several times, trying to understand the difficulties the department had in apprehending a suspect or suspects. Mull instructed members of the department to maintain a watch on the local weather forecasts as well as patrol large areas of water as much as possible within the township limits. There were thoughts the perpetrator would dump his next victim in or near water and may have been noticing the patterns of recent weather forecasts. But no one actually knew what would come from one day to the following. I waited for the next body of water to crash up against the coarseness of my skin.*

I watched the streetlights on the opposite side of the river reflect off of the water and float like diseased fireflies, drowned during the night. I sat on the edge of the bank which was damp and sodden with water. The crushed guardrail at that curve had been temporarily patched. Remnants of police caution tape were still wrapped around the base of a tree, all somber reminders of the accident involving Hanna. I once said everything started on the concrete steps of a small pool occupied by stagnant water and the revelation of truth. But it happened a few months later when the emergency responder pressed his lips over my wife's and broke two of her ribs trying to resuscitate her on the banks of the same river.

I wondered how long she had been seeing him, how often in seclusion they had shared each other's flesh and unrealized dreams. Maybe they never spoke about them, determined not to breach that level of emotional intimacy. Blood was beginning to come through the small cotton gauze on the inside of my elbow the woman at the hospital had taped there less than an hour ago. Some mistakes punish you forever, regardless of the act of contrition, or moreover, the act of forgiveness. In sleeping with him, that swelled, dead man, Hanna had incurred a communicable disease, a virus she subsequently carried and passed. And in a moment of unforgiveable fragility, I broke, forgave and made love to her as I never had or ever will. I grew hard inside her, mere days after being discharged from the hospital after the accident, succeeding her lithe voice wondering aloud if I was going to leave her. When she shut the bedroom door behind me, I paused and yielded to her advances and apology, unable to say all the things I should have.

Was I disposable? Or was I truthfully a representation of permanence, someone she needed when she slept, when she breathed, as if no one else's body could fit so tightly inside hers? Would she touch me in the desolate places of my body, arid plains of uncertainty and fear, where fallen tears of self-pity and regret became grains of sand, burning the boundaries of my existence and feel me or someone else? I once felt safe, needed, and I wanted so much to trust, honor the compassion that existed in the curves of her hips, the tenderness of her fingertips across my thighs, the sensual violence in the crashing of her buttocks against the strength of my pelvis.

Her voice made the muscles in my aching body rigid as her chestnut hair collapsed across her collarbone, her body yearning, her nipples warm against the outer edges of my lips. I wanted her to tell me the truth and caress me, but her touch frightened as well as aroused me, like a child both curious and afraid of the encompassing dark, the terrible secrets that it held within its absence of color, within its bones and skin, secrets I was now discouraged to hear her even whisper as I withdrew and came on the inside of her thighs. In the young twilight I held Hanna, kissed the small of her back as she quietly turned and reached towards me, the light splashing across the plane of her stomach, a smile forming in the corner of her beautiful mouth.

I should have never saved her, merely held her close and drowned and I had a difficult time in dealing with the truth inherent in that. Our marriage, our closeness became poisoned here, not with the rotted bodies of those poor children, gathered in the backyards of Pennsylvania. I thought I could see the depressions left behind, sunken into the eroded soil when I carried her in my arms, laid her unresponsive body across the scattered grass. I buried my hands deep into the muddy bank and removed them, spreading the earth across my face and neck, trying to counterfeit the man underneath. I began sobbing, held hostage by those seven or eight seconds where I wished she would have died. The burgeoning red sunrise bled into the water from the scaffolding and buildings, like oils falling from the stern edges of a mounted canvas.

*Water can grant you knowledge if you let it.*

No one ever told you what to do with it though.

It was calm, but all things placid and still were imbalanced by the inhumanity and the senselessness in everything around me, the dead children, the innocuousness of the ashen landscapes and the marriage I valued. I looked down and tugged carelessly at the band around my finger. While other towns were industrializing and changing, we were suffering at the tense grip of urban decay. Construction lights left on from the previous evening from the development beginning on the opposite side cast shadows under me and across portions of the river. I shielded my eyes with my hand as the sun began to overtake the subtlety of the horizon. A small launch passed slowly on the water, a few thin fishing lines hanging over the side. At the moment it passed, the small floodlight mounted on the front highlighted the silhouette of a figure standing at the far edge of the bridge, arms folded over the railing, hiding in the shadows. The body paused slightly, hunched over as the launch passed, then rose and became rigid in posture.

I stood from the dampness of the bank and unbuttoned my shirt, moving into the water ankle high. I welcomed the momentary cold sting. I closed my eyes and pushed through the bleak water, wishing the hopelessness and the rot would wash across my body and run away in the currents. Pieces of the vehicle Hanna had been travelling in with that man were still lifeless upon the river basin. The department considered it too dangerous to be removed at the time because of the currents and a lack of manpower because of the investigation. It had been a little over a month.

Several other accidents had happened here in the river over the last few years or so. Undoubtedly other objects rested underneath the surface. It was the second time I had been here since it happened. With my guidance, an insurance adjuster used an underwater camera after the accident to capture some of the scene. Some of the photographs were in the preliminary report. It reminded me of a graveyard of ships, pieces of metal and glass, lost architecture rotting at the bottom of the sea. I felt like one of those forgotten structures, trapped fathoms beneath the water where I couldn't breathe, where I slowly deteriorated and rotted in the drink.

An object fell from the darkened bridge and plummeted into the river, near one of the support beams anchored to the bridge and the basin. I held my breath and moved under the water. Nearly 200 feet out I came across a dark mesh covering. Pulling one corner towards me I revealed the mangled body of what appeared to be a boy. His shape was savagely slashed from what was revealed to me. There were layers of skin absent from his cheeks and jaw line. Part of the right side of his skull was crushed and concave. The blood covered my hands and wrists. He looked like a doll cut from construction paper. I replaced the mesh covering over his body. I spun around in all directions, searching the landscape. I could see no one from where I waded underneath of the bridge. Holding on to his left hand I started swimming back towards the landscape. Tightly I held onto his tiny wrist, as if I were his father, trying to lead him from danger. Abruptly a shot crashed into the water beside me.

Over my shoulder, framed by the maturing sunrise and burning fog, was the silhouette of what I thought was a man, standing at the opposite end of the bridge. I let go of the boy's dead hand, closed my eyes and submerged under the surface as deep as I could go without equipment, unwilling to see that small boy's sad, unique lineaments question my quick judgment in going into the water, the probity in dealing with pain or steal the courage I had to find if I wanted to rediscover Hanna, relearn what had been forgotten. As I reached shallower water and resurfaced, a second shot echoed, the slug missing me and pounding into the dense mud and sand. I stumbled onto the river bank and rolled behind a diseased tree.

*Water could punish you if you let it.*

Someone had gotten close. That's what Mull had said. The possible murderer never planned on anyone seeing him dispose of a body, especially so early, nearly 5:00 a.m.

"You didn't see anything?" Mull asked.

"No. I heard the body drop, but I didn't know what it actually was until I got closer," I said. "From where I was under the bridge, I couldn't see anyone."

"What the hell were you doing there at that hour?"

"I couldn't' sleep. I got up to check some of my equipment and then went out to the hospital," I said. Mull softened when he noticed I lowered my eyes to the ground. It must have occurred to him then this was where the accident involving Hanna had happened. But I wasn't sure.

"Where was the body?"

"Near the base of one of the bridge supports about 200 feet out," I said. There was no handgun or evidence discovered near or around the bridge. I was sitting in the passenger seat of my car with a large blanket draped over my shoulders. I rubbed my forearms and my hands, but I couldn't shatter the numbness that overtook my fingertips. I was probably in shock. Four wooden steaks encompassed an area of about 50 feet along the shoreline. Police caution tape bordered the outside as a forensic team member placed handfuls of mud and sand into a small box. Wire mesh was fastened over the bottom.

"It's almost like an archaeological dig," Mull explained. "They're sifting through the debris to find the bullet that missed you. It was fired from such a distance its trajectory and speed would have been affected by the density of the sediment. That's why the area had widened a bit," he said.

"Why would he take such a risk in dumping the body here? Usually at that hour the bridge traffic crossing from here to the other side of the river is considerable," I said.

"Not this morning," Mull acknowledged.

"Why?" I asked.

"The bridge was closed from 10 the previous night until 9 a.m. coming into town because of a burst water main on the other side, according to the permit. Work was stopped about 6 p.m. The road's barricaded about a mile in. That only heightened the challenge of dumping the body here because if he approached in a vehicle, he could have been seen or been boxed in," Mull hypothesized. "Did you see a car, van or a truck, anything at all?"

"No. I ducked under the water when I heard the first gunshot. The sun was coming up right behind him. I wouldn't have been able to see his face at all even if I were standing right in front of him. I couldn't shield my eyes either because I had hold of the boy's body. With the bridge closed, wouldn't that mean he would have to have carried the victim on foot?"

"It's possible. The victim weighed less than 50 pounds. But what he did to the boy would have taken privacy. There's no way he would risk doing that where he could be seen or even leave trace elements behind. So far he's been extremely careful. He had to have parked somewhere close by though." Mull called over another detective and asked him to check to see if anyone was given a parking ticket in the vicinity this morning or late last night. "We'll check for any abandoned vehicles as well, anyone missing plates or tags. The murders are getting worse," he said.

"You mean the violence?"

"Precisely," he said.

"That first night you remarked it was the beginning," I said.

"I know. I was only trying to prepare everyone. I've studied endless case histories on similar crimes, but I never expected anything like this. But it's different than most cases involving children. They're not only sexually abused, but the bodies are mutilated. There's an incredible amount of rage involved in the action. But it does strike me odd that he wanted to dump the body here," he said.

"It matches his apparent water fixation," I said. "Water destroys," I added.

"But all those bodies appeared like he meant them to be found in a quick period of time. All the other victims were isolated or contained. If the body had gone undiscovered it could have ended up down the river hundreds of miles away. What do you think?"

"Well it makes sense if you take into account the currents. It was like trying to swim through wet cement."

"Unless he panicked," Mull suggested.

"Yeah, but why this time? If he's taunting us he'd want the body to be found right? He's been very controlled up to this point as you said, considering the brutality," I stated.

"Maybe he was going somewhere else with the body in the first place, but the construction altered his route somehow. I wish we had something to match the ballistics from that bullet to."

"What about other unsolved cases?"

"We will look, but I don't think we'll find anything. Unfortunately his modus operandi revolves around children. I don't think he'd deviate from that," Mull admitted. "Not after this many victims," he added. "It's possible that could narrow things down some. The only thing he's changed or accelerated in any way is the violence."

"Which simply means our unidentified silhouette is getting angrier," I added.

"He hates, plain and simple. There's no way around it. I'll look into the specifics of the bullet fired at you. Go home," Mull suggested and as he started towards his car, rubbed out a cigarette into the ground near where I had been gradually beginning to fracture because of Hanna. I could see my handprints still traced into the sand. "It could be coming to an end soon, one way or the other." The sound of that gunshot thumping into the water echoed throughout each one of the detective's footsteps. I clamped my hands over my ears and tried desperately to remember the sound of anything, anything else but those shots, the pleasurable moans of Hanna and that man in a passionate embrace and the erratic beating of my own heart.

*Body Number Seven: (June) Mindy Yaris, nine years old. Her body was discovered in an isolated lake that rested on the rear of the McIlheny's farm at around 3 a.m. When she was removed from the water it was evident one of her arms had been lacerated almost completely down to the bone. The coroner revealed the mutilation to be post mortem. No one was able to determine with any certainty how long her body had been there before it was found. After it was discovered and all the examinations had been performed, the coroner resigned. The inherent belief after the first body was discovered that it was meant to be a nonviolent act that the perpetrator was attempting sexual gratification and panicked was unsubstantiated and dismissed, especially after the brutal discovery of the body of Molly Janikowski and the subsequent children. Whereas Mull suggested that the violence would lessen in nature it had matured and increased. I wasn't sure why he didn't tell them what he had said to me in that backyard. That miscalculation was noticed in the course of the investigation and other Federal agencies had gotten themselves involved, especially after I was shot at on the river, even though I was considered by everyone to be a civilian. Some state bureaucrats felt that Mull under reacted and the department wasn't doing enough. Ballistics tests were run on the bullet removed from the riverbed. No matches were found. It was as if immorality itself had materialized out of the soil and vanished, eviscerated under the intense sunlight of what was continuing to be an unfamiliar season. Everyone was starting to break.*

The rains continued to swell, the passing winds pulling the drops horizontally across the once serene aspects of the sweeping farms and houses along Ardmore Avenue. It looked like a thousand sewing needles falling from a basket. The high branches of corn drifted in the failing breath of the wind as it receded and quieted upon the property for a moment. An unsubstantial fog swirled through the beams cast from the car's headlights then rolled over some gaunt, discolored stalks of corn, emaciated remains of fallen agriculture. A few spoiled vegetables were gathered into a pile along with a rusted garden rake along the side of the house. Several rotted cobs had broken from their stems and collapsed onto the dense soil. The dislodged pieces of corn looked like diseased teeth. The landscape, the various kinds of vegetables being manufactured looked exhausted, burdened by veniality and decay.

Some stalks stood rigid, waiting. Others appeared debilitated, surrendered under an arid, barren land of sun. Even though the crime was believed to be contained to the rear of the property, officials had cordoned off the entire farm. The McIlheny's adjoining house appeared deserted. It was set on a small hill about 200 feet from the beginning of the field. No lights were on in any of the windows at the front of the house. I drove a few hundred feet into a cleared and sectioned area beyond the main house near a barn and some disabled equipment and shut off the engine to the car. One of the tractors had no wheels. It rested against the right side of an unused silo that had been filled with cement. I closed my eyes for a second and thought about Penelope, that frightened, distorted gaze almost pasted recklessly across her face. But not all the violence here was physical and it was oftentimes the hardest to determine.

It made me realize I was grieving, but not for that particular girl and not for the victims I pulled from the water anymore. It had started off that way, imagining what they would have felt before they were murdered, the invalidity while listening to the patterns of Hanna's breathing, the rising and falling of her chest and abdomen when I couldn't sleep. Even before what had happened at the river, I wondered what would become of us, the parents of those unfortunate children if and when the cases were ever closed. How would we go on living here after everything we promised each other was ruined by misdeed and mistrust? All the local fairs and craft shows held here would never have the same innocence to them again, the same sense of community and decency.

The rains gathered in a puddle in front of me and I was struck by the color of the water. It was so dark I should have seen nothing, but the complete absence of anything vivid or stunning. At first I thought I saw a bold purple floating on the surface, the burning auburn shade of a sunset. I stepped away from the driveway and noticed a pumpkin underneath of the front porch. It had a face painted on it, but the countenance was worn and faded. I wondered if it had been designed last year and remained unnoticed all this time. But there was no artist here, no one that could represent the fear in anything except in distant grays and carbons. Instead of being assured, I was immersed in a deliberate and ritual occurrence of desperation and self-pity and I wasn't quite sure it would ever stop.

Floodlights shining upon the back of a barn highlighted a group of 40 or so volunteers who were going to attempt to search the surrounding woods. It would be difficult to see anything because of the weather. Reports of winds reaching 60 miles per hour were broadcasted over the airwaves. A member of the department instructed them on how to search properly. Each individual was to stand about 25 feet apart from one another and proceed in a straight line. I hadn't been to church in some time, but it looked like God preaching to his disciples. The shadows cast from their bodies stretched out across the uneven grass like hands folded in prayer. Nevertheless, there was nothing uncorrupted in its existence. Purity had abandoned us all.

There were no tire tracks I could see with limited visibility through the fields of corn except those made by one of the McIlheny's tractors. About 15 of the 560 acres had been tilled over, allowing for some placement of vehicles and equipment. Reaching into the trunk to get my gear, I listened to the coroner's van struggle to gain traction in the mud. Without damaging a substantial portion of the local crop, there was no way to get a vehicle close enough to the edge of lake. It would be difficult to get emergency lighting or generators through the field as well. The news station located across the main river was going to send its helicopter to provide some overhead visibility, but had to ground it because of the dangerous winds. Budgetary constraints as well put a damper on how much money in compensation the McIlheny's would be given if a large

51

portion of their produce was ruined during the investigation. It was difficult for people to understand, but things were becoming economically distressing. It was a sad thought because people were being murdered, but it was an abstract truth not many would see underneath.

I lifted an oxygen tank onto my shoulders and started trudging through a few rows of tilled over corn. The coroner lifted a gurney from the back of his van. All the children had been murdered and suffered an incredible amount of trauma, most of it post mortem. None of them had been injected with any types of illicit drugs. The soil rose around my feet as I walked through the aisles of corn, the blades of the starched stalks slicing across the nape of my neck. We were all a community of victims, only the individual crimes were different. The wheels of the gurney pressed into the soil. The apparatus hitting the ground must have sounded different to him this time, less sedentary. This wasn't the first time he had been here to recover a body. The ground was harder than because of a drought. I slowed my pace and allowed the coroner to catch up.

He was unassuming and appeared inexperienced as if he never examined a human body, struggling to carry his gear through the mud and hide the distraught and solemnity beginning to find its way into the skin of his eyes, face and lips. He appeared sullen, like the vacated sacks of seed that were strewn about, discarded. Lifting the oxygen tank further onto my shoulders, I bent over and took an end of the gurney. The pressure to solve the case, to provide physical conformation of guilt weighed in his demeanor and his hands. The equipment jostled within my grip and it wasn't always because of the terrain. I glanced over my shoulder and observed his grip, watched with interest the muscles in his hand twitch, the veins prominent on the surface of his skin.

"Thank you," he said. The deeper we entered the field, the more intense the smell became. Most of the farmers here used manure as a natural fertilizer. To those from a more industrial landscape it might have seemed altering. It was an odor I would have given anything to forget. But it was more enticing than the smell of the dead. I stopped for a moment in the middle of a gap between rows. The coroner asked me whether or not we were lost. Whenever I didn't know exactly where to go, I always headed for the water.

*Water could nurture if you let it.*

Up behind the house, the volunteers had disbursed into the surrounding woods carrying flashlights. It was going to be a massive amount of ground to cover with some areas over a mile in depth. To me it seemed to be immaterial. After murdering the child the perpetrator could have ran through the woods and either continued on foot or exited via the main road at the far edge, especially if the crime was committed in the middle of the night. But that was a travel of nearly two miles. As we moved deeper into the acreage, I turned when I noticed the angle of the floodlights had changed. There was someone leaning on a ladder, changing the direction of the light to shine upon the field. It wasn't much to navigate by, enough to make the points of the stalks behind us irradiate.

I remembered Hanna and the way her hair looked when the sun fell down across her shoulders, a light honeysuckle shade taking the attention away from her eyes. The incompleteness of the polite color brought back to me the infection on the inside of her elbow. I rolled up my sleeve and ran fingertips along my forearm. I could hear the sobs she muffled in her sleep in the increasing sound of the rain as I tried to put measurable distance between the image of her provocative body and the inundating sadness that made it suddenly difficult to breathe.

It started to rain again. The light that was momentarily behind us had faded into the thickness of the crop and the spray. We quickened our pace in almost utter darkness.

"I can't see anything," he admitted, struggling to maintain his balance on the uneven ground. Loud claps of thunder echoed through the atmosphere and I could feel it through the soles in my shoes. I pulled harder on the gurney in an attempt to keep moving, even though he wanted to stop and find shelter.

"As long as we keep moving in a straight line we should reach it soon," I said.

"We should have gone in through the back end of the property," he added.

"There's no way to get your equipment close enough. We'd end up having to carry it regardless. We need to keep moving, but we might not have a choice," I said.

"Where are we?" the coroner asked.

"I'm not sure how much farther we have to go," I admitted, trying to shield me eyes from the stinging rain. The mud underneath of us was beginning to cling to the wheels of the gurney so pulling it became useless. A line of lightning lit up the horizon for a moment and illuminated the tree line at the rear of the property.

"With all this metal around we're sitting ducks," he said, his lips beginning to tremble. I set down my end of the gurney and held my hands above my eyes, straining to see a few yards in front of where we stood waiting.

"It looks like there's a shed about 100 feet up on the right," I said. We readjusted our grip on the gurney and started through a thick patch of taller stalks. In minutes we were standing on a small, broken concrete slab and the remains of a shed that was in need of repair. There was enough room for the equipment and us. A few bags of feed were stacked in the opposite corner. I sat down onto the heavy burlap bags. The farm had been in the McIlheny's family for nearly 80 years and some renovations and additions were completed, in the last decade or so. The main house was painted neutral beige and one of the old dairy stalls had been torn down. There used to be milking cattle, but expenses grew as the population in the surrounding towns decreased so they switched to vegetables and certain perennial flowers which took up most of the rear of the property. I turned around and set the air tank down against a half empty bag of grass seed. The receipt still attached to the outside of the bag was dated from July of four years ago.

"Haven't seen it like this in a while," the coroner said as he leaned out the broken door and glanced up at the sky. One of the hinges had rusted off.

"These kinds of storms burn out pretty quickly. We'll be able to get to the body in a couple of minutes," I said.

"I'm not sure I can do this anymore." He removed his glasses and was trying to wipe off the spots with his undershirt. The proper words to use drowned in the streams of water that poured in through a small hole in the roof. "I've never seen this level of trauma on a victim before," he said.

"Has a case you worked on ever been drawn out this long without establishing a clear suspect?" I asked.

"Most cases go unsolved after the first 48 hours regardless of anyone establishing a clear cause of death," he said. "That's often followed by years of incomplete evidence chains, false leads, and re-interviewing witnesses' years after the fact. They're called cold cases for a reason. After a while things get pushed aside. No one wants to remember where they were when someone was shot dead on some side street. It's the same for me believe it or not. When cases like this get reopened or assigned to someone new, we get autopsied as well. I don't want to have to recall how much a child weighed when they died, describe in precise and anatomical detail how they were violated. I can't. When I became a pathologist it's like being a doctor in some aspects. We're taught to be distant, desensitized. It's difficult to admit, but if you don't run as fast as you can from it all, well I understand why you're in the water so much," he admitted. He kept looking down at his hands almost the entire time he was conversing with me, obsessively making fists and rubbing the ends of his fingers. I noticed they were very clean, even with the conditions outside. But he scrubbed at them, as if blood and the bodily fluids of victims stained the creases in his palms. "Why have you stayed on the case through all this? A certified diver from another precinct somewhere could have replaced you," he said, without a tone of disrespect for my lack of experience. "Surely they could have found someone else."

"When it first started, I'm not sure, but I felt needed. I know that really wasn't the case. To be honest I became a bit fascinated by what was happening. It allowed me to be somebody else for a while I guess. Until the accident in the river." I raised my eyes and continued. "Now, I don't have anything else," I said. The rains softened a bit, but still pressed down hard. I stood up and gathered my gear.

"I meant to ask you about the river, but I didn't want to pry," he said.

"No I was aware that you knew because you did the autopsy on the man they found with her," I said.

"Yes I did. How is your wife?"

"Distant at times, but apologetic." I stretched my hands across my face and kept them there.

"Did you see the file on him?" he asked.

"Yeah I know about it." I rolled up my sleeve and angled my arm so he could see the mark on the inside of my elbow.

"I'm sorry," he said. I looked behind his shoulder and thought that the weather might be letting up.

*Water could teach you persistence if you let it.*

It took us longer to trudge through the crop than I expected, but we broke through the last few rows of corn and stood at the top of a small hill that led down into the lake. Nothing looked real. There were a few dogs tracking through the woods, but I couldn't see any exact movement. From our vantage point, about 200 hundred feet up on a slope, we could see the lake and some of the acreage surrounding it. There was no mistaking what they found. In the middle of the water, face up was the body of a girl, completely naked from the waist down. She appeared suspended directly in the center. The coroner dropped to his knees and closed his eyes.

If an artist took a pencil sketch of Adley's crime scene and laid it in reverse on the grass overtop what we witnessed here no one would notice the dissimilarities. Not much changed at a place like this. When I saw Mull's daughter at the town meeting, she had struggled to maintain balance in her wheelchair. Adley was spending the night on McIlheny's expansive farm with several of her friends. Local high school football was very popular in Central and Western Pennsylvania and the town was no exception. Players were celebrating a state title, the town's first in over 20 years. The boy she adored at that time in her life was going to be there with several other classmates, as well as most of the team members.

She wanted to kiss him. And in those innocent urges she discovered the burgeoning insecurity of womanhood, the nervousness and frustration in the cycle of emotions and thoughts. Behind a barn she held him, kissed him, her face burning under twinges of firelight that appeared to singe the tips of the corn stalks and the long strands of her golden hair, so delicate it almost dissolved in-between his fingers. She wanted to pull him closer, sleep with his taste on the naïve edges of her mouth while not quite understanding the complexity and intensity behind the apprehension and gratification she experienced. She might not have even been sure why her heart began to beat faster. Adley pulled back from him, tugging on the sleeves of his jacket. She smiled. It was all innocent and harmless. It was the last time she would press her hands against the tightness of his abdomen. No one ever developed a clear picture of what happened that night.

"Jesus Christ," Fasman murmured.

"Oh my God," I said. Fasman removed his glasses. He struggled to hide them in the inside of his jacket.

"It isn't her is it?" he asked.

"No. No, it's not her," I said.

"Thank God."

"Someone should call him," I said. The coroner turned his attention to the open spaces behind me. It was in his eyes, the images, the pain, the numbness in remembering that ambushed muscle and bone. Each one seemed almost hollow, artificial circles of glass unable to absorb the most delicate of color or light.

"He's already here," he said.

Under his trench coat he was wearing a maroon dress shirt and a black tie. I wondered if he was having dinner with his wife, holding her hand across the table like he did years ago, previous to when everything had become so entangled and disjointed. For too brief a moment he would stare at the small, imperfect marks her lips left on the outer edge of a wine glass. And in the smudged color he always thought she looked best in, he remembered what it was like not only to be audaciously in love with her, but the sense of security that he encountered in the passiveness of her voice and the subtle, tender movement of her hands. With his casual shoes possessing no real grip, he slipped on the declining slope of land when he moved closer. His body pushed through the mud and sodden grass. It came to rest a couple of feet from the water. Mull lifted himself up onto his knees and stretched out his arms. Before I started down after him, from where I stood, it looked like he was cradling her in the palms of his hands. When I slowed behind him, I leaned over closer. It wasn't possible to hide regret in a place where it wouldn't be found later.

"You know what to look for when you get in there," Mull said. "Have someone help you bring the body out of the water. It looks like her, doesn't it?"

"Daniel, it's not Adley."

"It could be," Mull said.

"Where is she?"

"With her nurse," he said.

"There are over 40 people here helping. As you said, we know what to look for. Go home."

"We were having dinner when I was called. I haven't spent more than a few hours alone with my wife since this all started. I feel the guilt every time she looks at me when I'm called, so much I can't breathe. She wanted to go to that inn, the one that's always lit up at night past the interstate. We reserved a small table in the corner so we could be alone together. We were going to spend the night. Our food was late, but I didn't care. The McIlheny's gave me flowers to put at the table. Tulips. I drove all the way up there this morning to make sure everything was right. I watched them collapse in an extraordinary glass vase that was hand-blown then painted by that artist, the one whose daughter you pulled from that pool. As it filled with water it swirled around the stems and the level rose higher towards the mouth of the vase. I couldn't stop thinking those tulips were children, drowning, swallowing, necks breaking at the most delicate of places," Mull said.

"Daniel, Where's Molly?"

"We were going to lay there naked in each other's arms, pretend that we were surrounded by, I don't know what to call it, inexperience. I want so much to not know who she is, who I am. What does that say about me, that I wanted to lose sight of her, forget my handicapped daughter?"

"It doesn't say anything."

"I wanted to so much. It had been so long since we talked, but I was afraid that in listening to her, she'd say I've never given her what she wanted," he admitted. "To be protected, cherished, listened to. I have so much respect for my wife that I couldn't make love to her like that, thinking about dead children. After what happened to Adley, there was so much we couldn't do because of the amount of care she needed. She planned so much for her and none of that will happen. It's her child," he said.

"She's your child as well Daniel. You can't let yourself lose sight of that because of what's happened."

"Adley doesn't even recognize me anymore. I've seen it in her eyes, the way she studies me. She communicates so intensely with them," he said. "It's the most remarkable thing I've ever seen."

"She's still a beautiful, vibrant girl," I said.

"I know. I'm so proud of her. She wanted to go to South Africa with Hanna when she began researching for that documentary she always wanted to make. What's she supposed to do now? So much help is needed here, but I don't know what to do." Mull raised his head and I watched streaks of mud scroll down the sides of his face and onto his neck. It was getting so dark. "I let that monster stay untethered and look what the consequences have led to," Mull said.

"You're not responsible for what has happened here Daniel," I said.

"We're all responsible," he said.

I placed the regulator in my mouth and inhaled. There wasn't much I could see. The drops of rain striking the surface of the water were effectual, calming in a way I could never describe, considering what laid near me. The girl was drifting back and forth. There were no preliminary indications her body had been rigged to either stay afloat or submerge. Neither her hands nor feet were bound. I passed underneath of her body and moved the beam of a flashlight over her darkened silhouette. If there was trauma induced, I couldn't tell. I broke the water near her shoulders. Using a flashlight pen, I pulled aside sections of her hair. There was a large contusion on her scalp consistent with what was termed blunt force trauma.

Adley's skull had been fractured in two places as well as several vertebrae in her neck. The wound was estimated to be made by an undetermined blunt instrument, most likely comprised of lead or steel. The indentation from the wound measured almost an inch in diameter.

Moving counter clockwise I positioned myself at her side. The girl's right arm had been almost completely detached below the joint at the elbow. Filleted tendon and bone protruded from the crude incision.

Adley had her pelvic bone crushed. Her left ankle was broken in four places. Adley suffered three broken ribs and a punctured lung. It was determined that she had intercourse prior.

An acrid stench clutched at the fragile breath of night. I inhaled so hard from the tank I thought my ribs would crack. I closed my eyes for a moment and removed the regulator. With as much precision as I could, I searched around her body. The poor girl, later identified as Mindy Yaris, was nude below the waist with severe bruising evident on her thighs, abdomen and feet. Mull still stood at the base of the lake when I started to guide her body ashore. There was a black bag not more than a few feet from him. When I passed around her hips and ankles, I noticed a flower resting on the water, placed between her legs.

It didn't take much. It never did. It could be a sound or a smell. The subtle and tender colors in a painting or a simple photograph. Perhaps it was one of those oftentimes inconsequential things that made Molly come down. The long dress she wore hugged her curves, a black shoulder-less piece which cascaded along her hips and legs. Her guise appeared angelic, inviting while everything around her emerged cumbersome and pestilent. The long wisps of hair she usually pulled up behind her neck were on display across the breadth of her shoulders. There was nothing that could take away the transcending beauty she carried standing there, offset by the savagery and the adversity in her and her husband's lives. When she saw Mindy's pale corpse being held by Daniel she wailed. Mull spun around and regarded her collapsing, her dress ripping along her legs. Regardless of consequence he ran up the incline towards her, Adley's tragedy playing over and over again inside his head. The one chance he and Molly had to be alone was gone, violated by ambulances and divers and memories each one could never escape. Daniel dropped down beside her and pulled her mud ridden body closer, held her in his arms, his lips pressed against the tender flesh of her ear, whispering, hoping to give her everything she wanted but understanding that he never could.

*Water could teach you self-reproach if you let it.*

*Body Number Eight: (August) James Stanachek, six years old. Was discovered in a small abandoned quarry that hadn't been used in a decade. It used to supply limestone, construction aggregate and sand to various portions of the state. It had been shuttered and advertised for sale for the last three years without attracting any buyers. This was the only crime scene during the eight month investigation where Detective Mull was not present. Two weeks after the body of Mindy Yaris was found on the McIlheny's farm, he was reassigned from the case. A departmental hearing found him unfit to make objective decisions because of the similarities between the ongoing case and the unsolved one involving his daughter. The boy was the final victim discovered and it was the last time I went into the water.*

The winds pushed the rescue line from the helicopter across the stretched mouth of the quarry as I held on to the harness that suspended me some 115 feet above the abandoned crevasse. Unused and closed it remained isolated atop a hill set back from the main highway. There was an abandoned car parked behind some brush. That was what led someone to contact the department. That was all it took sometimes. But the sad fact was that most physical crimes went unsolved, regardless of the advancements of forensic medicine and technology.

There were tools that could measure everything. What the computers and the experts could not measure was the human condition, how degraded and violated a sexual assault victim felt and the hatred it bred from within, how contracting a communicable disease from an affair made a woman feel when she tried to put her arms around her husband at night. Those people didn't talk. They suffocated. The bottom of the quarry was filled with loose rock, trash and debris tossed into it throughout the past few months, the waters climbing higher along its side during the flash flooding forecasters had predicted for the beginning of last week. There were various reports of a dense, foul odor. I tugged at the secured line and instructed the pilot to lower me further down.

The stench from the water collided with the consistency of the wind and I thought I was going to vomit into the regulator I had fastened between my lips. Pieces of rickety, broken sawhorses that once blocked off the entrance had made their way into the opening. I looked down upon the soiled waters and felt isolated in the tense situation, alone. I thought I could see portions of a chain-linked fence. The winds picked up and the helicopter had trouble maintaining a steady position above me. In about three minutes I would drop into the water, loosen the cable from my waist and turn on a high-powered flashlight and look for another child. Not long after I established contact with a body they would send down a metal gurney on the same line. I would have to search because there was no telling how deep the quarry was from a first look. The department was trying to contact the city engineer's office to find out. More often than not, I had to go under.

A co-pilot sitting in the opening of the helicopter door motioned his hand across his throat. That was a warning the winds and rain were becoming difficult and they wanted to stop and continue the search when the weather cleared. I raised my hand to wave them off and signaled them to drop a little faster. It was all too important to me. I couldn't stop now. The helicopter passed through a pocket of air at an angle, dropped and the sudden movement of pressure forced the rescue line I was on to bend and shift violently to the right. My frame struck the quarry wall and opened up a tear in my suit. The inertia of my body jerked me back into the center of the opening again and carried me further towards the opposite side. Before I could strike the rock again, I unclasped from the line and dropped the remaining 80 feet into the water, hoping that it was deep enough and I wouldn't strike the bottom. The regulator rolled around inside my mouth on impact and the metal construction rattled against my teeth. I could taste the blood at the back of my throat. The troubled world around me suddenly shuttered into black.

I couldn't see anything for a few moments and the impact of my body crashing onto the rough water confused me somewhat. I wasn't sure where I was initially. I shook my head and through a pair of diving goggles watched the helicopter climb higher and cross the opening of the quarry and disappear. The suction of the water created as I impacted pulled me back under the surface. I could breathe, steadily, but I still panicked for a second as if I were drowning. I bobbed back up out of the water and my arm movements caused some floating debris to be pulled towards me. I regained my composure after a few moments, settled into a rhythm atop the water's flesh and struggled to find the flashlight. The depth of the quarry, the rain and the murkiness of the water from soil run off impaired the poor vision I already had. It was close to dawn.

I pushed away a piece of metal moving towards me and fumbled for the depression on the light. Behind that steel pipe was the body of another victim, a child. It lunged at me as the steel moved, a twisted shape of anger and insensitivity attached to the face. My eyes widened in shock and I screamed although no one could hear because of my deepened solitude and the equipment I began to tear away from my face. There was blood pouring out of my mouth. I gasped for air. I could see other police officers looking down, cupping their hands around their mouths, shouting, their echoes gaining effectiveness against the vastness and stability of the rock. I heard mumblings come from the end of a squawk box. I felt concussed. There was pressure against my ears. I thought I could hear the rotor blades of the helicopter. The tone was dense and barely audible. It sounded like a hummingbird fluttering against an orchid.

The child had been dead for about two weeks. That was what the acting coroner approximated about twenty minutes after the body had been lifted out of the scene, but he would begin the autopsy and establish positive identification right away. The department was still checking to see who might have been the registered owner of the abandoned vehicle. If no one came forward to identify the body, they would run his fingerprints and then match his dental records. His bottom jaw was missing. It looked like it had been blasted off with a shotgun. I leaned against the side of an ambulance as an emergency technician attended to me. There was a large pad of cotton inserted between my gums and the lining of the inside of my cheek. The taste of latex from his gloves lingered against my lips. Another technician stood in front of me and shined a small beam of light into my eyes, checking that my pupils were dilating and that there were no signs of a concussion.

*Water could teach you how to hurt if you let it.*

Blood was still trickling down from the wound that had penetrated my suit. I leaned over and tore the area open below the knee, stretching the hole wider so they could apply some alcohol and gauze. Using a pair of sterilized tweezers, the technician removed some small shards of glass and rock that had seeped into the laceration. After dabbing at the blood and drying up the water from my leg, I said I would dress the wound alone. Watching the man turn around and attend to his emergency kit, I started to wrap gauze around my leg and side and covered up the other scars already embedded underneath my skin. The pilot wanted someone on the ground to notify my wife so she could meet me at the hospital. I said no.

~

I closed the shower door and tossed a navy towel over the top of the pane of glass. I turned on the faucet and let the water run high and uninterrupted along the edges of the sink. It made sense that most of the bodies were discovered in or near outlets of water. Most of the later victims had developed what medical examiner's called adipocere, a fatty discoloration of the skin. The perpetrator took more time to weigh them down, which helped advanced the rate of decomposition. Water did such damage to a body. It washed away the physical evidence and the broken, fragmented sins of the pious. In the distance I could hear my wife stir in the bedroom. I peered out into the hallway. In another hour or so she would wake up. I wondered if she had reached over and traced her fingers along the edges of the impressions my body had left behind on the mattress. Outside the window, a neighbor was loading fishing rods and a tackle box into the flatbed of his truck.

I turned off the water in the sink and dried my hands on the towel spread across the width of the shower door. There were clothes tossed into a pile in the corner behind the door. I bent over and scattered through them and found a shirt I could wear. There was dried mud still stained along the collar and under the arms. I scratched at it. It never came off, the smell from the dampened straw and animal feces saturated deep into the cotton fibers. I stretched the shirt across the breadth of my shoulders, noticing how the muscles in my chest had started to change since I had stopped training over two years ago as I pulled it into place around my waist.

I had been a collegiate swimmer, spending at least eight to nine hours a day immersed in the brine aroma of chorine. It dried out your skin and made your lips insensitive. Your muscles burned when you reached a certain point, when you pushed yourself back and forth obsessively, wanting to become an Olympian, unattainable and forever. But I never reached that accepted pinnacle. And I felt I was a failure. Again everything was changing. The goals and the dreams we held ourselves to were the ones that, in the end, often destroyed us.

*Water could teach you how to relent if you let it.*

I ran my hands across my face in the shower. The hot water steamed up the glass door. I listened to the bathroom door close. My wife leaned against the door of the shower and I watched the pressure from her naked shape darken, then dissolve the steam on the designer texture of the glass.

"Are you all right?" she questioned.

I didn't say anything. I didn't have to. The silhouette turned and her hand touched the side of the shower door. I grabbed the handle and pulled on it so she couldn't open it.

"I'm sorry. I don't know how many times I can keep saying it without breaking," she said. Several minutes later she grew frustrated at my distant emotional position and closed the door behind her. Her beautiful shape stayed on the glass door for a few minutes and then disappeared. I turned off the water and slid the glass panel aside. She had left the room before she could have seen me step from the shower clothed, wearing that shirt I had on underneath the dry suit at the quarry dive and a pair of jeans. My hand slipped away from the brass fixture and I locked the bathroom door, turned the latch and hoped she wouldn't hear it. I removed my undershirt over my head and kicked my dampened jeans onto the floor. I scratched at the stitches from my leg. The incision was still saturated with fluid and puss. I leaned up and stood naked in the center of the room.

The full-length mirror framed in oak wood on the back of the bathroom door was covered in steam and my body appeared red and blistered from the increased temperature of the water. But as the condensation evaporated higher into the paleness of the ceiling and my body began to dry, it became more expository, the degrees of imperfections noticeable across the latitude of my skin. I rotated my body and stared at the lower arch of my back. That was the only part of me that still looked clean, authentic. The door closed behind me, the steam trailing behind me into the hallway.

When I closed the bedroom door behind me she became aware I was inside the room. I watched her move across the surface of the bed, short strands of her hair unseen against the dark sheets. I wondered if I leaned close enough if I could smell the strawberry in her hair, taste it in the fragility of her faint saffron skin. I jostled a lamp she purchased yesterday at the edge of the bed. The shade still had the plastic wrap attached. It made me feel temporary. Her warm breath brushed across the tiny hairs on the edge of my thigh and I felt her body roll closer on the mattress when I sat down.

"Come back to bed," she said as she traced the back of her fingers on my arm. I turned over my shoulder aroused, but frightened by the intensity of her eyes and her lips, pursed together. When she exhaled, they separated ever so slightly. She raised her arms towards the light in the room and her body stretched, opened up and the displacement of the linen exposed her nipples, the structure of the bones in her neck, her collarbone and shoulders.

"I can't do this right now," I said. "I have to go back in. They found another body this morning."

"What about my body?"

"Please don't do this to me," I said.

"It doesn't matter what you do," she began. "All of those poor children are dead. You can't save them."

"I'm trying to save myself."

"What do you mean?"

"Nothing. You wouldn't understand," I said. "I'm not even sure that I do."

"Talk to me," she requested.

"I have to finish this," I said.

Her fingertips caressed the tender spot above my kidney. "Stay with me."

I shut my eyes and tried to summon the courage to stand and leave. She never retreated in her solicitation, grabbing the end of a sheet and lowering it so I could see the enticing darkness of the inside of her smooth thighs. When I didn't move to leave, she put her hands underneath my shirt, moved even nearer and closed her lips on different pockets of my skin. I stood, turned my back to her and stretched a sweater over the width of my shoulders. My body ached from the fall.

"I can't stay here with you," I said.

"You can't or you don't want to?" she asked. "I asked you once before and you never answered me. Are you going to leave me?" I tightened the belt around my waist and stopped when I reached the door of our bedroom. I wanted to leave her, move away from here and what had happened so much, but it would have taken courage I wasn't sure I had anymore.

The lace up slip she wore had fallen down deeper over her shoulders and completely exposed her left breast. In the mirror she looked like a wilted flower suffocating in an intense heat, dehydrated and flaccid. The muscles in her abdomen contracted and she raised her head, her eyes flushed and swollen. She looked vulnerable, the way an injured animal can appear and in the same concurrence, behind the soft frailty, unabashedly licentious.

"Say something," she said, ignoring the soft tears settled into the tenderness of her warm skin, never ashamed or cheapened by the transient exhibition of her breast, her nipple, her small, round aureole that slipped out from underneath the safety of the material. In that artless instant she possessed no regard for her own body's isolation, the partial abandonment of privacy and self. She reached out and clutched for the stability of my hand. I could see the small puncture wound on the inside of her forearm above the elbow and the slight, jaundiced discoloration where the tip of the needle from the injections had penetrated the skin. I fought against the paroxysm of empathy and pity, instead slipping into the comfortable and malicious expanse of hate. I didn't know what else to do and I didn't know where else to go. There wasn't any water for a couple of miles.

"We can't keep doing this," she said.

"Doing what?" I said.

"Walking around listless in this huge space of avoidance and regret."

"What do I have to regret?" I asked.

"You know what I mean," she said, somewhat defeated.

"I'm not sure that I do," I said, with the honest intent to damage her more.

"Is that necessary?" she asked.

"What?"

"Trying to constantly break at me."

She was always beautiful, even here on the bed, fractured and unconsumed, her body disclosed to the small fragments of light that advanced across the unvarnished floor. I withdrew from her and turned away towards the window of our bedroom, pulled the curtains aside without care and watched the rain that continued to fall since I pulled that body out of the quarry a few hours ago, that child, his lower jaw blasted away and detached. I could still taste the artificiality of the apparatus against the enamel of my teeth. With my back towards her, I listened to her struggle to compose herself, to construct a focused thought in between the deep and random gasps for air.

"What do you want me to say that would possibly make a difference?" I asked.

"That you still love me. That you'll touch me," she said.

"I can't. I'm not sure that I know how to do that anymore," I said.

"Yes you do," she whispered. "I need you to touch me," she pleaded.

"You don't get to ask that of me," I began. "Fucking me again and again isn't going to take back what has happened," I said.

"Fuck you, you righteous bastard. You god damn beautiful saint." She slid off of the edge of the bed onto the cold floor and leaned back against the mattress and box spring. Almost all her legs were exposed now, bent insignificantly at the knee, the back of her heels touching the hardwood floor, the tender landscape of her rapturous thighs outspread enough so I could almost see the shadow of her dark pubis. I turned, knelt down beside her and replaced the strap of the slip higher up on her shoulder. In doing so, the back of my hand brushed against the bones that signaled I had reached the lower plane of her cheek. She closed her eyes and craned her neck, stretched, invited, displayed to me the delicate slightness of her features. I spread out the taught uncertainty in my hand and touched the golden flesh of her throat. She opened her mouth and nipped on the edges of my fingertips. I closed my eyes and tried not to externalize the amnesty and the sorrow. I couldn't show it again, even though she desperately wanted me to.

"I hate you," she said.

"No you don't," I responded.

"You don't have to leave," she said.

I touched at the small hole on her arm. "You should put some gauze over that. It looks infected. Have someone else treat you next time. I have to go to the hospital. I'll be back soon," I said. She raised a sleeve of the sweater I had put on and touched the underside of my left arm, studied and admired the rough surface, the tiny scars and the one long scar she once said she understood. She paused at the spot where I had been given an identical injection to the one that troubled her. Her eyes softened at its appearance and became less defensive and her tone transformed into a visceral array of remorse and grief.

"The doctors called yesterday while you were gone. They think that because of your position, what you do and the contact you have with those bodies and the diseased waters, regardless of how careful you are, that they should increase the number of injections because of the high risk of infection. The results just aren't improving rapidly enough," she acknowledged.

"To how many?"

"Two times each month." She reached up and placed her hand seductively around the shape of my neck. Her fingers settled into the

68

grooves of my throat muscles and she pulled me closer down towards her. I could feel her warm breath collide with the anxious instability of my skin. "I'm sorry," she said.

"Jesus Christ," I said. I pulled away from her and retreated back to the overcast sanctuary of the window's edge.

"It might not have to be for that long. Maybe a few months they said, but a lot of it depends on what my next set of results turns out to be."

I watched the increased winds push the water and the decomposed leaves left at the borders of the property out into the edges of the street. At the edge of a driveway across the street an abandoned tricycle entered into the genesis of decay. Recycling bins remained fallen. It disrupted the impassivity of the images that had once been there.

'There's something else as well," she added.

"What is it?"

"There's extensive damage to my reproductive tissue."

"Did they say what that means, in the long run?"

"We talked about this before. They said it was too early to tell. They want to talk to both of us next week sometime. We have to call them back to set up an appointment. They've scheduled me for an instructional class on infertility so we can completely understand what our options are and what those next sets of test results may or may not mean. I need you to go with me," she said.

"When?" I questioned.

"I know this isn't much notice, but the class is tomorrow morning."

"I'll go," I responded.

"Will you stay, here with me? I want you to hold me, just hold me."

"I can't," I said. I closed the bedroom door behind me.

Water could teach you how to grieve if you let it.

Did she really need me? Would she suffer without my love or would she thrive without the intense burden of my hate if I were to leave her? I stood underneath of a light rain at the edge of our driveway and waited. I knew if I turned around I would see her pulling aside the long drapes in our bedroom. She appeared so nubile and sadly intense when I left her, the frail material of a pale yellow slip falling across her breast.

Images of running, forgiving her with violent abandon, pulling her warm body to the distant floor to feast on mine passed in the windows of the bus. There was so much I wanted to ask her, that I wanted her to ask me about love, emotion, children, what I had done to drive her into the arms of another man. The hope Hanna and I had disappeared in the raindrops on the glass as I sat inside the bus wondering, passion aside, if we would ever be as close again, as a man and a woman should be.

On the front lawn of a house across the street on the corner was a FOR SALE sign pressed into the dense mud. The expansive, red brick colonial, recently renovated, had been on the market for a couple of months. That was after the first murder, when the owner's daughter was found murdered, her body dumped in a backyard pool. The photographs and images of that scene lingered along the daily routine I had become immersed in, the deliberate brutality of the crime coercing its way into of all the things I tried to find graceful and beautiful. I didn't realize it at the time, but being in all that water was causing me to drown. The bus idled in front of a rail crossing, the guardrails slowly coming to a stop in their movement. I watched a train slowly travel past as I sat wallowing in retrospect. We idled for at least 10 minutes as an engineer loaded on several pieces of equipment before the gates rose and I continued on towards uncertainty.

The bus had only travelled a miles or so past the crossing when a disabled man stood from his seat, raised his arm and fired one direct shot through the top of the bus. The driver pounded hard upon the brakes and the vehicle fishtailed to the right and spun into the center of the street, intersecting both lanes. The man braced himself on the floor of the bus and the gun scraped across the metal. He reached out his hand and gripped the barrel and pulled it towards him, all the while maintaining his composure and his reticence.

Without breaking even for a second, he looked into my eyes and pointed the gun at the soft spot underneath of my chin. The gun was steady and sure. He changed his position and paused at the edge of the seat I tensed in and the perspiration from his brow dripped onto my forearm. I wanted to taste the salt on the tanned plains of Hanna's skin more than ever. The man turned his attention deliberately to the driver and instructed him to put the bus into park and apply the emergency break. Take the keys out of the ignition. Now toss them out of the window to your right. Using his gun he waved the older gentleman in his uniform to move to the back of the bus where he could see him.

"Any attempt to move towards the front of the bus at all or to try and stop me and I will kill you. Make no mistake in judgment please because I am not here for you," he asserted. A beautiful young woman in the front seat crossed her hands in prayer. He stepped backwards while continuing to watch all the other passengers and leaned over, his breath colliding with the sash around her neck.

"There's no need to pray. Hope and faith are God's lies to us all."

*Water could protect you if you let it.*

# THE MUSICIAN

I sat there and looked at the gun, cocked the trigger back and forth repeatedly like I was an adolescent amused with the physics of a toy and wanted to grasp the technical aspects of it, what made certain parts of it function and react the way it was supposed to. I desperately wanted to study it, concentrated with an abject fear and respect, separate it into its different and unique pieces on the cold tile of the kitchen table, research its history, learn the displacement, the reflex action of the pistol in regards to the human muscle. I wanted to learn specific wind variations affecting trajectory, caliber, repetition, the weight it would carry in the palm of my hand so I wouldn't miss when I had the chance. I knew the single shot chamber was empty at the moment. But I didn't have the luxury of time any longer.

The dimly lit room was empty, the remnants of last night's dinner with my wife ignored in the recesses of the sink. The hot water she ran to wash the dishes in grew cold overnight and the liquid soap was no longer visible to the naked eye. The plug was still fastened over the drain. Even with pieces of food resting throughout the sink, the water was so clear. I didn't remember why she never washed them. Tiny drops of wine clung to the side of a tall glass like dew against the outside of a window the very morning after a rainstorm. My attention from the way she had looked in that long sundress, the top opened up so I could see the sweetness of her exposed neck, a small bead of perspiration disappearing in the shelter of her cleavage broke and I stared back down at the gun.

A gunshot fired at a distance of 10 feet measured 166 decibels. The sound it made when it spoke was deafening. It shattered the atmosphere, the reaction stuttering the world and consequence transversely, like ripples on a pond. I would be much closer than that, within 10 feet. I wanted to be able to feel his spittle scatter across my bottom lip. I looked out the window and listened to the rain splash against the gutters. It reminded me of nails dropping on a concrete driveway. The weather didn't matter anymore. Everything had to happen today.

I turned my right wrist over and rubbed away the discharge that began to form on the end of my nose with the back of my hand and lowered the weapon onto the table. One of the large, colored envelopes in front of me still had the shrink-wrap attached, my brother's name barely visible underneath on a label in the right hand corner. I tore the lining open and removed the contents.

How could he have done this? The man had everything in respect to what I had lost, what I had, in essence, taken from myself during a failed suicide attempt and the repercussions of a subsequent vehicular manslaughter conviction. The packets of information I had uncovered were spread open before me. The receipts from various motel rooms. The surveillance photographs. A blurred photograph of what was believed to be his vehicle passing through an interstate exit seized from a traffic camera. Undercover information from the Federal Bureau of Investigation. The deconstructed, structured alibis. The statements gathered from witnesses who would no doubt be called upon to testify against his person during a trial. Perhaps none of them knew though to what extent. Eleven unmarked recorded conversations from legalized wiretaps were contained in the second envelope I had mistakenly opened earlier. They looked like they were digital copies. According to a small index card inside, in a mere matter of days, authorities hoped all it would be considered admissible in a court of law.

I had turned off one of the recordings after I heard my brother say some of the things he did. Each dialogue constructed to elicit a distinct and precise acknowledgement from the victim, the subtle and seductive nature of his character alluring and unapologetic. It didn't sound like him at all from what I could remember, although it had been some time since he and I had engaged in the familiar constraints of personal conversation. I couldn't think of how long it had been. There was a passiveness to his speech previously, a kind of naïve uncertainty about relationships, environment and intimacy. Almost childlike. The tone of his voice on the digitally enhanced recording was mature, different, evenly controlled and manipulative. Darker I guess. It wasn't the voice of my brother.

That was all included in the preliminary report to the district attorney and the judge who would issue the arrest warrant in less than a few days. Monday to be precise. There was even a section of typed transcript 16 or 17 pages long which detailed a mere three to four minutes during one of the alleged incidents. The rest were still being transcribed. The notations in the report were concise, pointed and descriptive. The child in question on the dictation was an adolescent girl.

I stopped reading it after the seventh page. That was more than enough. The notes included in the small margin to the right of the report by the initial lead detective described the acts themselves, the strength involved, the bruises, the ferocity and the measured depth of the penetration, the vaginal tearing, the lack of DNA evidence because he had more than likely used a condom and the girl's body was discovered by examiners in a decomposed state in a swimming pool. That crime was committed in January. A medical expert determined in an included report that during the violation my brother wore rubber gloves and likely had shaved his entire body, including all his pubic hair to leave as little trace evidence as possible. It was disgusting. The transcript trembled in the tentative tips of my fingers. The muscles in my chest contracted and then released. I held onto the gun, ran into the bathroom and closed the door, locking it behind me.

Were they sure it was him? I had to know for certain it was. But there was no one I could contact in the police department without admitting my guilt in illegally obtaining confidential information. The window above the toilet was cracked open and the rain started to come in through the small holes in the screen. I couldn't breathe. I pressed my face against the window and swallowed the unaccustomed coldness. The thin metal was rough against the plane of my cheek and the grime left streaks across the side of my face. I retreated and wiped away the vomit from the pockets around the folds of skin at the conjunction of my lips. Cold water collided with the dryness of my throat and the complexity of the glass mirror connected to the medicine cabinet. I opened up the door, my fingerprints faded against the small, plastic handle. The simple reflective action caused me to pause. If I left fingerprints at his residence, they could use them to find me. No matter.

I removed a bottle from the second shelf and tried to unfasten the cap. They should have replaced the prescription and filled the bottle two or three weeks ago. I held onto it and retreated into the small sound studio across from our bedroom where I was sure I had others hidden. The thick, glass door closed behind me. I opened several drawers on the desk and retrieved another prescription bottle. I gripped it with my hand.

Hundreds of digital audiotapes were stacked against the wall. Years of research and sound piled up in no specific order.

Scattered shreds of yellow legal paper with physic and logarithmic equations peered out from underneath of a series of insurance required photographs and measurements. Books on music theory and composition rested on a dusty, wooden shelf a few feet above my head. I scanned some of the DAT titles I accumulated during my research and employment: jet engine, chainsaw, shotgun, oil drill, a thunderstorm, sonar, waves on the beach, a radio and a head on collision between two automobiles at 75 miles per hour. It was impossible though to consistently hear the past coming.

As a musician, I held sound in the highest importance. Pitch, tone, and the logarithmic construction of amplitude, frequency, intensity and other characteristics essential to desirable auditory quality. The biology of sound was complicated. It moved in circuitous longitudes, propagated outward from a fixed point. I felt I could see sound move, drip from the strings of violins and cellos in a concerto like water, trickle from the golden mouth of a trumpet like honey. Several musical instruments sat abandoned in the corner, scattered patterns of smudged fingerprints poisoning the luster. Beads of rain escaped in and gathered on the wooden floor in front of them. I pushed myself out of the chair behind the desk and closed the window. I knelt down and reached out my hand to remove the cello from its wooden stand. It wouldn't settle in the cradle of my palm, restless like a newborn baby fighting to get back to the comfort and familiarity of its mother's womb.

I flipped open the door to the DAT recorder, removed the tape of my brother's voice and replaced it with a different one from the pile. Satisfied with the one I chose, I placed the recorder on the floor of the sound room and turned up the volume. I subconsciously wanted to hear more of my brother's conspicuous seduction. Being enraged by his emotional savagery would subdue my conscience, therefore making it easier to pull the trigger. But the honest reality of the notes on the tape spread across the tile floor like sap across the wilted branch of a tree at the onset of winter. My chest tightened. Tears trickled down the sides of my face and gathered all the surrounding light along their way. The chords from a cello, not my brother's voice, echoed against the stone tile. It was a live recording of our quintet from a few years ago. After a few minutes I stopped the tape and the images of previous accomplishment and technique faded.

I hadn't listened to any compositions I authored or played since the accident. I covered my ears, deafened by the pain and loneliness of the circumstances that led me here. The sad composition on the DAT recording abruptly ended during a piano verse and I listened to a long silence, a break I did not remember. Perhaps I had damaged it previously without knowing. Someone's lips parted. It made me think about the taste of my wife's saliva. I could hear isolated sounds in the background I tried to determine, then the fragmented breathing of a woman. She inhaled repeatedly, as if she wanted to break free words lodged against the bones in her chest. The pain, the penetrating disillusionment masked by the compassion in her voice overtook the rain and the discord as it disappeared against the coming morning.

*Can you hear me?*

*You won't answer me will you even if you could? Lately, I could be in a room with you and not even know you were there, watching over your shoulder at the pages of music on the floor of your sound room. It was as if you were trapped alone on the inside of the glass and I couldn't break it to reach you, to communicate with you, even if I tried. But should I?*

*You once said to me after the accident that hope was an illusion, a missing accessory in a child's magic kit. I never agreed with that, although I never admitted it to you. I wasn't sure when or if you would ever listen to any of these tapes again, to hear your once talented and beautiful past played back to you. There are so many sounds that deafen the world around you, drown out all the harmony you used to create and understand. Sometimes in the middle of the night I could see you staring at the instruments in that room, sitting there like imported porcelain dolls, like a glass flower so brittle one touch would shatter the delicate biology of its artificiality. You didn't think I noticed. But I didn't make a sound. That was the only way I could get you to react anymore, was to create some sort of vibration, something audible. A guttural laugh. A broken dish. I was hesitant to wonder watching you if you were afraid. Afraid to succeed again, afraid to touch me in those intimate places where I rediscovered the intensity you possessed, but had only forgotten and how beautiful a man you are. I never thought you were afraid of anything, except for the possibility of losing me. I thought the accident would bring us closer. But the more you try to hold onto something, the farther and farther away it retreats, always slightly out of reach. All things runaway in time, it's a question of when. Things have changed and I am struggling to understand what has polluted the soil of our cultivated life together, what has happened between you and I that complicated what was such a simple joy. No matter how much you might not want to be, you are my husband and my lover. But I wonder, no I hold in doubt, so much of what I once understood to be absolutely certain.*

*It has become impossible to reach you because I cannot touch you, cannot hold your head in the crook of my elbow like I always have. You didn't always have to be the strong one. You carried enough. I could have held that burden for you after the accident. Women have tremendous strength and underneath all the tenderness of our bodies, underneath the sensuality and the compassion lay a grace and an integrity that cannot be argued, cannot be equaled. Your music is all I have and most of that is a distant recollection of scattered sounds. Sadly, they are all hard, industrial sounds. Synthetic sounds. None of what you have catalogued since is ethereal or passionate as it used to be. It has always spoken for you when you were reluctant to. I was intimate with its fragile honesty, with its sometimes savage brutality, an array of rich notes that drip through my fingers and leave my skin cold and broken. I love you, for all your faults, for all your excesses, for all your fears.*

Years after the accident, O.S.H.A., the Occupational Safety and Health Administration employed me to measure the effects of sound pollution on human beings, ecology and other aspects of the environment. In the beginning I surveyed industrial plants, limiting the exposure of employees to higher decibel levels and issuing suggestions to increase long-term safety and the productivity of employees. That role expanded to construction sites.

I removed a few marked DAT tapes from the large stacks and others on the desk randomly. None of them were labeled and I slid them into an empty shoulder bag. I thought most of them were from the police evidence, the ones about my brother. I hadn't listened to all the surveillance tapes yet, but I already knew from details about the wiretap almost all the initial recordings were worthless, routine discussions in his voice about politics, religion, and literature. Nothing incriminating occurred that established or disestablished his guilt, let alone state his coming intentions. After several months the department was about to pull the surveillance until my brother, in dialogue with an undercover agent, via the internet, used the phrase "Each one merely needs cultivated." The innocuousness of the sentence resonated with someone, especially after the discovery of that poor child's body in April.

From a misguided life of desperation, mistakes and tragic consequences, patterns of complete irresponsibility in regards to being an educated musician and a complete husband, it was ironic I was the one who obtained the information before it was released to the press. Before the detectives that comprised the task force made an arrest. I held all within my shaking, misguided hand. Hand. I could still feel the weight of the muscles that had been there before the accident, the structure of the ligaments and tendons against my body, even though the arm had been completely severed. On occasion, when I knew I was alone trying to learn to play again, I would sense the phantom pain project through the blunted stump at the end of my shoulder. I felt myself consistently reaching out with it, but managing to falter.

I couldn't think of any significant reason I should be the one to do it. What about a relative of one of his victims? If I were going to go up there, I would have to leave soon. I didn't want to give him a chance to flee once word got out and the previously unreleased graphic details hit the front pages of the newspapers, because they most assuredly would. Everything would work as long as the police didn't get nervous. In cases like those of abductions and pedophilia, media outlets believed people needed to know, that they had the right to. There were detailed laws for the registration of sex offenders. Amber alerts. But he might even have been tipped off by now though.

I read in the file that sometimes pedophiles communicated through a delicate network, stitched together by ugly threads of abnormal passion and misguided tenacity. A psychological profile included in the package labeled him as an "indiscriminate preferential," an unconscionable offender identified by a broad, unlimited scope of behavior. The police would close in soon enough. I struggled with the duality of wanting to be there when it happened and wanting to escape from everything surrounding the murders, flee from the desperate confines of my own loathing and rejection, the debility I had as a man that was further brought to the surface throughout the months of my brother's alleged crimes.

Deeply though, I needed the acceptance the act would thrust upon me. I would have been smart to leave it alone, to trust the proper authoritative and municipal bodies. Not get caught. Part of me wanted to. Someone told me they were going to place him into custody Monday morning, even though some higher ranks within the department considered him a high flight risk if he should sense he was being watched. They wanted to be absolutely certain about all the evidence before they made an arrest. And the judge in the case the detectives contacted waited to issue the search warrant they would need to seize property from his residence. No one from the department or any federal agency had been inside. It was too risky. But I could get in. My brother lived almost an hour and a half away. By the time the afternoon bus schedule stopped running, hell would descend upon that small town in Northern Pennsylvania, masqueraded as tranquility in the stuttering translucence of the fall raindrops.

I thought to myself over and over I should drive up to see him and confront him first, give him an opportunity, but then someone might recognize my car if things didn't go as I had planned. Someone could have memorized the license plate. It wasn't hard to describe me though looking at me. There were too many variables. Did I have to worry about being identified if someone should see me? After all, he was my brother and I had been there before, although not recently. It would make more sense to take the bus, but trip was an hour and a half longer than by car because of the continual stops. And if someone did see me leave the scene and watched me get onto a form of mass transit, the vehicle and the exiting highways or state routes could be blocked before things ever got started. But I didn't have a choice.

I tried to remember what the area around his house looked like, the trees, the surrounding buildings and the proximity of parking near his front door. There might have been a playground in the backyard, even though he and his wife hadn't any children I remembered. It might have belonged to the previous owner. I wondered if that was how he had seduced them, taken them there in his car perhaps, with the innocent promise of games and adolescent amusement. They had included a photograph of that in the file, the rusted playground, his domicile, the acreage and backyards of the surrounding housing complex that utilized an architect's complete attention to detail. There were even places marked where they could hide their men, leaving them invisible from any point inside the house, from any window. Points of entry into the residence had been highlighted. There was a small circle around an old cellar entrance. Somebody had been extremely thorough.

The fear that manifested itself in something like that was authoritative, carrying with it a sort of passive ambivalence. And that was why they waited and I tried to decide whether to act. That search warrant. They didn't want him getting off on a technicality. That was the most frightening part to me, not the indiscernible acts themselves, but also the fact my brother was so meticulous in not being caught to date, a chronology that encompassed almost eight months, perhaps longer. That he was so systematic in his approach to it, almost scientific. I wondered how many trips he had made here previous to January when that first body was discovered in an in-ground pool. If he drove up and down the side streets, calculated the miles and the speed and the terrain. If he documented every entrance, every corresponding exit or slowed down to a mere idle. Peering into the bay windows of brick houses and the fragile souls of those children while they ran through sprinklers in the front yard or talking about their friends in school.

The small town had been manipulated, the sanctity of people's lives altered by a perpetration of terror, committed by a man I had once understood, but now struggled to recognize. He would have to be placed on suicide watch when incarcerated, the fragile saint. The stigma attached to that word, pedophile, would be written on the cinderblocks and the floors of the small cell, encased in the air pumped in through a small vent in the ceiling some 12 to 15 feet above his head. There were no windows, no sharp edges, only a cot on the floor and a place in the corner where he could piss. There would be death threats, even if the case made it to trial. I would meet you there, brother.

That was small consolation to the people and the families he damaged. I told myself if I hadn't had my accident, I would not be here thinking about doing this. It gave some meaning to things. At least I justified it that way. I couldn't imagine things going to a publicized trial, thousands of reporters and protestors lining the steps of the courthouse, shoving their notebooks and inane questions into the survivors and the misplaced faces of the immediate family members, mothers and fathers, sons and daughters. I anxiously looked out the window again. The couple a few houses down was the first to have their child abducted. It made me sick to know my brother could have killed that child and then been so close, close enough I could have smelled the arid perspiration against his collar.

I looked up at the cheap clock on the wall in the bathroom and knew I would have to leave before my wife Augustina got home. She should have left me after the accident. In fact, I had given her the opportunity more than once and hated to admit to myself I tried to force her out. I was a fucking cripple and indirectly I blamed her. I wouldn't have had to worry about it then, worry about the guilt in the attempt to kill myself. There was no way once she saw the file I uncovered she was going to let me go up there and do it. It wouldn't make things right. I wanted to so much though, abandon her without reproach and kill him without remorse. Then get as far away as I could.

She acted as though I still had choices. Tell that to the doctors who prescribed me all those painkillers after the surgeries I couldn't stop taking. There were four in all, each one a different color. One was an antidepressant, but ingesting the medication made me unresolved and further discontented. I remembered the names in detail: amitriptyline, imipramine, desipramine, doxepin, and nortriptyline, a dizzying vocabulary of synthetic ingredients that led to a vertiginous spiral of emotional and physical dysfunction.

I glanced over at the towel she used to dry her lithe body with last night after dinner, remembering the softness of her touch, the smell of her skin underneath the elbow. Small, light remains of her lipstick were embedded into the corner of the white cotton. Augustina was an amalgam, a sensuous blend of brilliance and carnality, driven in her life by a traditional valued upbringing and a misguided sense of patience. God I loved her, but I couldn't breathe around her anymore, especially after last night. She told me everything with a resonance of disappointment she couldn't hide behind her soothing breath, echoing through the consistent stream of water that was fortunate enough to trickle down the sublime edges of her architecture.

In her soulful eyes though, I was still a clean, accomplished musician, the same determined, beautiful man she had fallen in love with years ago when I was bold, when I was more secure. I could see it every time she touched what was left of my arm, the blurred, rough flesh. When she reached her inquisitive fingertips around my shoulders, her breasts pressed against the crest of my back. I tried playing several times after the accident. It only lasted a couple of days, the inherent determination I had to maintain a foolish semblance of normality. I hated who I was and continuing my existence as I had been would have been immaterial and pointless. I thought about telling her how I felt and having her convince me to try again to be whom I once had been. But recently I had become lost inside a mist of insomnia and nausea, the replaying of past consequences and past mistakes, trying to give a clear definition to the utterly indefinable.

I lowered my head and closed the curtain over the window above the toilet. The gun almost fell off of the top of the porcelain fixture after I had set it there. It made me think I would have trouble holding it steady, the gun, with things being what they were. If I did it from a distance, I would have to lean up against something, prop my back on some building or car so I could steady the gun against my knee in case I hesitated.

I reopened the folder and intently studied the crude topography of the maps, hoping to discover something to satisfy the hesitation building inside. I turned around and sat on the edge of the tub and started to shake. I was supposed to walk up to him as he came out of his front door, or barge in through a kitchen window with his wife having breakfast and place the cold barrel of the steel weapon against his temple. Things about the situation now were objectively hypothesized and estimated.

In the realm of all the conjecture and all the uncertainty, what I couldn't see right then was I had to do it. I was being called upon by the close community of the surviving, the people left with rebuilding hope overtop the broken foundations of the past. Called upon as a savior, a preserver, but not through some religious calling or theological diatribe. People often committed crimes in the Act of God. This wasn't one of them. I knew what I was doing was wrong. But I needed to do this, this one thing. I slid off of the side and down into the tub, some drops of water still clinging to the material underneath me. My shirt was open at the collar. I removed my hand from behind my head, reached up and took the gun from the toilet. The steel was cold against the concavity of my burning chest. There were stains on the tile and the side of the tub. I moved the gun up the ladder of my rib cage, paused at the notch in my throat, stopped when the barrel rested on the underside of my chin. I had only meant to hurt myself.

That was what suicide was, a blatant and undeniable act of pure indulgence. For me, egoistic mutilation brought upon by indifferences of self-worth and the instability of intimacy and emotion. I pushed the gun harder and the folds of skin under my chin collapsed around the opening at the top. Sweat dripped down the length of my spine. I had made the motions, had perfected the technique before, but never went through with it. God, I wanted to so much. But I couldn't. Soon though, if I reached that point, there would be no going back. And I had made mistakes before. No. It couldn't happen. Not this time.

No one would be hurt except for him and I and I would make sure. There could be no doubt, no apprehension in any of my thoughts or movements. I grabbed at my empty shoulder. I once had a prosthetic limb attached to it, a heavy piece of composite plastic secured over my shoulder. It was supposed to augment the healing process, compensate and in turn make me feel more acceptable, provide stability to the surrounding tissue. I hated wearing it. The fucking thing felt so oppressive and heavy. I felt like a department store mannequin, artificial and transitory, dressed and moved around from place to place, window to window.

I struggled trying to open the cap to the painkillers I was now addicted to. I felt out of balance when I was awake, concussed. I hardly slept anymore though. Fucking childproof caps! I slammed the bottle on the edge of the sink and cupped my hand underneath the faucet, guided a cold stream of water into my mouth. The freshness slipped between the cracks of my fingers. The anxiety I felt in my mouth stuck to my teeth like paste. I couldn't breathe. Again I placed my palm over the prescription and couldn't open the bottle. I clenched a fist and slapped at the plastic container, propelling it against the tile wall in the shower. It didn't matter. There were others. The cap rolled off and the pills scattered around the porcelain fixture. Pieces settled onto the drain.

The sunken sound of the small, white disciples became indistinguishable from the pelting rains that punished that horrible afternoon, when everything became as unsteady as a ship at sea, enraged by the winds of my own vulnerability. The pain continued to struggle to tear its way through the fragile seams of my flesh. It was an accident. My hand started to shake. It had the color of a piece of wood bleached by the water. I made a fist and continued to open and close my hand. I had to be able to flex the muscles and utilize the cramped and atrophic joints if I were going to grip the pistol tight enough. In the winds that increased outside I thought I could hear a child screaming.

The shutters on the outside of the bathroom window broke loose and began to collide against the brick on the side of our house. I was supposed to fix them last week. The weather worsened. It was a few minute before noon. I would have to leave soon. I couldn't wait anymore. I reached into the bathtub and wrapped my fingers around one of the colorless circles and placed it on my tongue. I grabbed the empty cylinder and filled it with some of the loose OxyContin and stuffed it into my pants pocket. I opened up the barrel of the gun and double-checked the empty chamber and filled it.

When I turned to open the door and leave, the nausea started again. It was something I had trouble fighting because of the side effects attached to the tricyclic antidepressants. I slumped against a bookcase in the hallway, which led into the living room. The doctors hospitalized me for almost eight months after the accident and I endured four agonizing surgeries, which left me nothing more than hopeless and incomplete. I grabbed the map of his acreage, a group of the cassette tapes and some of the other evidence I had planned to show my brother. He wouldn't be able to deny it then. He would listen to his own hard voice echo around him. I thought about telephoning my brother, warning him for some reason. I wanted him to know I was coming. I wanted him to be afraid of losing everything. I wanted him to be afraid of me.

~

I could feel the gun press against my chest underneath of the coat I had put on right before I boarded the bus. Some of the ink from the lines I drew on the map with a marker ran down the folds because of the rain. It began to stain the ends of my fingertips. No one bothered to look at me, even with my deformity. I couldn't even receive slight blemishes of pity. I wanted to reveal the weapon right there on that ripped, imitation leather bus seat so I could make sure the bullet was loaded into the chamber again. I wanted to sit it next to me, fascinated with the abstract, mechanical beauty surrounding its authority, its finality and its power. I didn't want any miscalculations. The rain came down hard, streaking against the side of the small, glass panels on the bus.

Rain. It made such different tones when it struck other objects like a microphone to record outdoor sounds, other bodies of water, how it hardly made any sound at all when it collided with the human body, the soft palette of flesh underneath a woman's breasts. The window beside me was open and water trickled in. I tried, but couldn't force it shut with one hand. The mist caught up in the wind escaped through and flickered across my glasses. I pulled them off by one side and rubbed my eyes. There were only a couple of stops between here and the entrance to the highway. There was no going back.

I started to shake again. I looked to my right at the people passing on the street below. There was a man removing a black and white photograph of one of the missing children from the facing of a telephone pole. The portraits had been there for months and I passed by them several times. We all did. The man's eyes were flushed, discolored and swollen, abused by tenuous nights of waiting, the horrible anticipation of getting that one call, the hollow, vacant sounds of someone, some stranger on the other end telling you your child was dead. The truth was cold and the truth was definitive. Never was it anything else.

I leaned back against the seat and closed my eyes. Augustina was about ready to walk through the front door and into a quiet and uncertain retrospective of torment. She wanted me to make love to her last night, to reassure me I was still seductive by sliding her body under the black, satin sheets into the pockets of my skin and chest where my muscles tightened when my legs raised as she positioned the shape of my cock into her. Once she went into the bathroom to change her clothes after her morning rehearsal, it wouldn't take her long to understand what I was attempting to do. Spread across the bathroom floor she would find the remainder of the police file on my brother I hadn't shoved into the pocket of my coat and bag. She would brace herself next to the bathtub, the photographs, and the disordered, written words of my brother echoing through her diction against the Aztec inspired patterns of the designer tile. Because she was so honorable, I expected her to tell someone to stop me.

I reached into the outside pocket of the jacket and withdrew a small earpiece plugged into the recorder. The recordings were something I should have forgotten or left behind, tossed into the puddles of water transformed against the side of the bus when it paused at the continuous traffic lights. Things weren't moving fast enough. Each time the bus stopped and opened its doors to exchange passengers I flinched, grabbed the back edge of the seat in front of me and leaned forward as if to stand, to flee. I waited for something to go wrong. The bus came to a complete stop at an intersection, the traffic lights motioning back and forth on the wires suspending the signals above the street. Only one light hung in the exact center of each crossing wire. None of them appeared to be functioning.

There were a few intersections left until the bus would reach the on ramp for the main highway, a long stretch of 80 or so miles. None of the other passengers were close to one other, each of the three men and two women sitting several seats apart. We are sometimes frightened of intimacy, obsessed with the preservation of self, not wanting to open ourselves, not wanting to trust. One of the women stood and changed places closer towards the front of the bus, avoiding contact with the shoulder of a man who sat immersed in his tragedies I supposed. She might have been getting off at the next stop, I wasn't sure. I was exhausted, burdened under the weight of anxiety that constricted the muscles in my abdomen and throat, the complex variables of hate I suppressed. I closed my eyes and wondered what Augustina was doing.

Through a studio window in a building on the corner, a man held a woman around the waist, repositioning his hands along the subtle curves of her hips, reacting to the way that her muscles moved. The man's palms found freedom along the edges of her body, adjusting to the musculature of her thighs. She broke away and arched back, placing her head into the shadow of his collarbone and softened the biology of her throat in response to the tactile brushing of the back of his wrist. Her architecture displaced under his instruction and her body collapsed into a fetal position against his ankles.

For a few introspective moments she remained motionless there, handicapped by the inability to move on her own. The man leaned over her body and lifted her, embracing her frame against the strained muscles of his torso. He raised her submissive body higher and crouched down, lowered his head so their faces touched, flesh upon flesh, previously restrained by years of history and technique. Together they closed their eyes and kissed, their progression devoid of the awkward naiveté of adolescent passion and reverence. I thought about the delicate totality of my wife's body and how I wished I had reacted to what she had whispered to me last night while we dined.

I started to listen to a different tape as the bus passed through another intersection and gathered speed, pulling me closer towards an ending I could see coming, but was too weak to subside. It wasn't my brother's voice I listened to, but a symphony composed by a pianist in the quintet I used to play in. He was killed in a plane crash touring Europe less than a year after my accident. Our bassist moved to London a few months ago and adopted two children, twin girls. The violinist, whom I had played with the longest, moved to California and recorded several classical albums covering Vivaldi, Beethoven and Tchaikovsky. That was the last anyone had heard from him. It was all too apparent I no longer felt like I fit anywhere in anyone's lives. There was no longer a place for me. I turned the volume down on the recorder and closed my eyes. My wife and I had met for the first time underneath the fragile umbrella of those truncated chords in New York during a summer rehearsal. The rain that morning sounded like the one falling against the glass bus windows.

My legs shook when she first appeared and I pressed my knees and thighs tighter against the wooden curves of the cello to steady myself, felt the dulcet tones through the impatience and uncertainty underneath of my skin. It was burning and I wanted to tear through it, rip into it and expose the sturdy alabaster bone beneath. She had bones like a bird. Her name was Augustina. I liked the way it sounded inside my mouth. The outdoor theater was closed for our rehearsal and some minor repairs, the columns and rows of seats unoccupied, a barren field of faded stone and distant applause. Several weeks remained before the theater would reopen for business. A quick morning rain had earlier dampened the boundaries of the stage beneath some of the construction overhead, the water gathering in small puddles, settling into the edges of the concrete in front of the first row of seats. The light shower had given way to an intense heat and humidity, which pulled at me as I leaned forward in my chair, trying to adjust the sheet music in front of me.

The white, uneven light from the overhang attached to her uncomplicated anatomy, dripped down over her exposed collarbone like the loose water falling from the plastic tarpaulin above us. Though her body was petite, she had power, thrusting from different points of the stage as the structure of the music heightened, the emotion in the piece distended. Strands of long, auburn hair were tied up behind her head and when she moved, broke apart and slipped in front of her sage washed eyes, ones that were so assured, so wrought with conviction they appeared to absorb all the colors from the surrounding landscapes, leaving everything a blighted wasteland of ash and salt.

The original composition was written for a quintet, but our bassist was ill and remained sleeping at the hotel downtown. The chords from the piano, once violent and authoritarian, quieted. A violinist behind me lowered his instrument, hushed the remaining strings like comforting a crying newborn. Soon I would be immersed in a long solo, several measures of musical soliloquy branched in by our composer and her choreographer so that his new lead could dance alone at the front of the stage. During an initial pause before the music matured, I loosened the pin at the cello's base and leaned it back deeper into my chest. The bow, under the light pressure of my fingertips, touched the face of the cello, the soft horsehair fibers caressing and collapsing the strings. I wondered how her skin responded, if its tenderness sunk like the feathers of a pillow, if its fragility shaped the way sand upon a beach changed underneath a child's plastic pail. Scattered leaves were carried across the stage and under the base of my feet. In keeping rhythm I stepped down upon them with my right foot, their decomposing biology helpless and withered.

There was a moment during the solo where she stopped and turned around, her body facing mine, the muscles in her abdomen taught. She was a staggeringly beautiful woman, resplendent and alluring, her clothes nestled against her body in response to the heaviness of the air. I felt consistent drops of water strike the back of my neck as we played. A pipe in the overhang that was supposed to be fixed and wrapped in tethered plastic must have ruptured during the rehearsal, but no one could hear it because of the vibrant sounds being projected. Streams of water came rushing down from above our heads and the conductor ushered other dancers to exit the side of the stage. But I never stopped playing. I couldn't. Nothing else existed in that shortened moment, not structure, not balance, not tone, only the repetitive movement of my hands across the cello and her grace. She moved slightly and I raised my head. I could see her darkened nipples show through the light blue and white striped tuxedo shirt she had loosened moments before she went on stage. I watched her exhale and behold me. I was seduced by the candid sensuality in her perspective.

The ambiguity of everything had quieted and became measurably clear. It would be over soon, regardless of the outcome. I thought about pulling out the gun again, tightening my fingers around its body to stop them from trembling. I stopped the DAT tape instead. Sweat dripped along the composition of muscles and bone underneath of my neck, broke apart on the outside of the pile of evidence I spread across the seat. Some of the ink began to bleed across the page. The last thing I had looked at was a crime scene photograph of the girl whose body was discovered abandoned in a crumbling barn silo. In the photograph she didn't look real, more like papier-mâché on display in an art class. There were mud and animal feces all over her body. I wanted to vomit. The scene was violent, moreover sad and overbearing. In less than two hours I would have a chance to be as aggressive as he had been, even more vicious and brutal. I would give him a choice, something my brother had never given to anyone else.

I reached up and tried and close the opened window again. None of the latches moved. Understanding I was solely culpable, I slumped further into the seat and watched the tears dance along the reflection of my face in the glass. I couldn't look into it and see someone else's reflection. I wanted to, to see a better man and husband staring back at me with cold, penetrating, disapproving eyes. But it didn't work that way. There was nothing else I could do. I had reached an end. I squeezed the barrel of the gun inside the pocket of my jacket. I thought about pulling the trigger, dislodging the bullet into my thigh. They would be able to get me to a hospital though. I deserved to die because of what I had done. But it would be easier this time.

The distress, the loss of character and distinction haunted the long steps I had taken to reach this point. I had to become something else entirely. I looked down and closed the folder. My brother ruined what I had wanted to be long before he murdered anyone. I wanted to break some of his teeth as I forced the muzzle of the gun into his mouth, to rediscover the temerity I hid behind my deformity and self-recrimination. I reached into the pocket of my coat and searched for a pill. I didn't care which one.

I removed another DAT tape and placed it into the recorder. It started with a few industrial sounds; a log splitter, the assembly of a car engine in a factory in Michigan, the augmented hummingbird like tone of a military chopper taking off. Nothing was on the tape after that. I changed sides, unsure whether I wanted to hear her voice again. She had every right to be critical, to hate me. But I knew no matter how much my wife convinced me she loved me with her patience and her empathy I would fracture. Another sound began instead. I recognized it immediately. It was a car accident. The automobile gained speed at a steady rate, reaching 30 miles per hour in a matter of seconds. 40. 50. 60. At 75 miles per hour the discordant sound of plastic, rubber and steel collided, where I had once murdered the very strict concept of innocence.

~

The rains started heavier again. It felt like they would never end and the streets and the river would burst and all the people would suffocate and drown, immersed in a landscape of death and barrenness. The clouds above the horizon blackened. I would bring the darkness with me to him everywhere. Not that I believed he would understand the things he had done, possess any form of contrition for the indescribable acts of barbarity and disillusioned hate. The DAT tape continued.

The startling tones of that car accident decreased and were dislodged by further tools of industry. A drill. A motorboat engine. A forklift. A printing press. A heart monitor. A baby wailing. My hand trembled and I stopped the tape. I tightened my hand around the gun. I was so close to pulling it out from underneath of my jacket and tossing it out the open window. I couldn't do it. It would be easier to kill my brother than listen to Augustina's praise and love wither away at the hopelessness I depended upon now. I depressed the DAT tape again. The unending cries of a newborn child abruptly softened and Augustina's voice appeared in her dreams to soothe her. She spoke faintly this time, more deliberate, but calmer.

I watched you try to play once.

It was a couple of months after the accident. Torn bandages still covered the area around your left shoulder. The pale color of them had begun to rust. You wouldn't let me change them. You said they reminded you of who you were. There was no way you could hear me from inside the sound room. You thought I had gone to a rehearsal or out to dinner with my company. You must have tensed standing outside of that door, pressing your fingertips against the glass window, wondering whether to go inside. I watched you cautiously open it as if you were afraid of what might be waiting on the other side. Your body was completely naked. After you left the bedroom you must have never dressed. In our bedroom you appeared vulnerable to me, unassuming and distant afterwards. If you felt assailable now because of your body, it didn't appear that way. Perhaps you were more comfortable alone, without me. I wondered if you would have covered up if you had seen me there watching behind you. But the deformity you attained made you all the more beautiful to me. I was unable to make you understand or believe that though. And that more than anything has led us here.

You walked into the room as if you hadn't been inside its walls for a decade; simply been away and returned, not haunted by the past memories of childhood games and unfamiliarity. At first you paused, reaching out like a sightless man determining what objects laid in front of you. I stepped into the place where you had been outside the room, the shapes of your feet mirrored in the water on the floor. Did you shower after I tried to touch you, feel the need to rinse your ailing flesh from the pestilential touch of my fingertips? It felt that way. It might have seemed trivial and not purposeful, but nothing you had ever done to me before had made me feel that unattractive.

The cello appeared asleep against its cradle. You awoke it hesitantly, wrapped the fingers of your right arm around its neck and sat it between your legs on the floor. It took you a few minutes to find an unfamiliar way to brace yourself with the instrument. The bow was next to you, underneath the chair. It fell weeks ago, but no one had ever picked it up. I watched you pick it up. After a few introspective minutes, it awkwardly laid down against the fibers on the cello. I couldn't hear anything. But it didn't matter what sounds were given birth. And it didn't matter your body just couldn't adjust to its changes. What mattered was you were trying to communicate in some way. But did either one of us understand that, what was being spoken? I wanted to place my head against your shoulders and listen to the notes come through your back, translated for me through your bones, your body a dictionary of words and purpose. The last thing I watched was your body lean in against the cello and surround its frame. Your shoulders rose and then fell. The bow dropped to the floor. It looked as if you were crying. I wanted so much to be in its place, to feel the warmth of your despair crash against the reckless wanton of my body.

The sundress I wore was still spread out across the floor in our bedroom. I loved the color. It reminded me of autumn. I tensed when your fingertips pressed the cold metal of the zipper against my spine and lower back. I left it exactly where it had collapsed along my hips. I could smell your scent in the fibers. When I raised my legs higher and stepped away from it, my toes got caught in the thin shoulder strap. I leaned against your body and removed the material. Your heart pounded through your chest. The wine that accompanied dinner was still present on my lips. The feeling I had to taste you was intense and disturbing. It pulled at me, beckoned. I didn't know what to do. My body glistened with anticipation and sweat. I had never remembered feeling so aggressive towards you.

I watched you take a step back. That surprised me. I wanted so much to assure you I still desired you, wanted you to explore my dark places. Tenderly I took your hand and held it, pressed it against my face and closed my eyes. There were so many things I wanted to tell you. But I didn't want to make a sound. Instead I lowered your hand and started to unbutton your shirt. I ran my fingertips inside the collar and pulled it away from your shoulders, touching your warm skin as much as I could. Slowly you raised your arm and pressed my hand flat against your chest. It still pounded. I tried to continue undressing you, but you stopped me and lowered your head. Using tender reaffirmation, I raised your chin up and kissed your lips, allowed mine to linger along their definition before falling down across your throat. I could taste the salt of your nervousness.

Uncertain, your hands reached up and I allowed you to remove my bra. I guided your fingertips across my shoulders, directing them into the barren places of my skin longing to be discovered again. My breasts became exposed to the light pouring in through the glass. I leaned closer while you caressed my nipples. I shuddered. It had been so long since you and I had been like this, joined, aroused and weakened by one another's imperfections and thirst. I lay down on our bed and guided you inside me, the skin on your back and chest glistening, shimmering almost. It dripped across the plane of my stomach. I said things I never believed I could. They made me another woman and for a minute I understood how you felt, wanting to be someone else. I couldn't recognize the language I spoke. But I know I told you I loved you.

You took me twice, never anxious or impulsive. Several times you asked me if I was okay when my hands quivered against the small of your back. I was only nervous. For a few beautiful hours we were lovers again, unburdened by who we *actually were and the failure of knowing that we could never be anything else. I watched you sleep, your body intertwined with mine. When you moved, your hand ended up resting across my stomach. It was then I knew I had to tell you that I was pregnant.*

I slipped out from underneath her body and stood in the doorway after she told me. God she was so beautiful, her body covered with a light sheet from our bed. Augustina rolled over on her side and I thought of all the things I never did for her I should have as I studied the classical qualities of her face, her high cheek bones and her plush lips. It was clear to me watching her sleep, her hair pulled aside exposing the tender slope of her neck and shoulder and it would be the last time I would feel that calm that composed. I closed the door to the bedroom and stepped out into the empty hallway. Nothing would be the same after this even if I didn't do what I believed I would do, murder him. I couldn't understand how to subsist with the mistakes I had made, to let the guilt and the culpability wash over my chronology of ineptitude and discouragement and raise a child. I couldn't be a father to a son and everything immeasurable to a daughter.

An ambulance rushed passed the bus, the startling sound echoing in the distance of the blacktop. The local hospital was located a couple of blocks up on the left, set atop a hill where an elementary school once was built. Parts of the playground were still intact around the back, remnants of innocence now unfortunately overshadowed by suffering and remorse. The fence that surrounded them was rusted and overgrown grass protruded through the metal. The brakes on the bus grinded to a halt and shifted the contents of the file across to the edge of the seat. I didn't want to look at them anymore. One of the photographs of a murdered child slipped out and I glanced over at it. Half of his face below the nose was gone. It was one of the photographs taken at the scene. Jesus Christ. I gasped for air. But I needed to see what my brother had done. Nothing else mattered. It was penance, plain and simple, retribution for a man scared and afflicted.

It was raining harder. The driver shifted the bus into gear, still putting slight pressure on the clutch and straightened out the wheel. The only people who remained on the bus besides the driver were two men and one woman. All the things I had been running from would be over soon, all the distant recollections of missteps and indecisions left behind. In the glass, I noticed the broken reflection of the woman behind me. Through the grime and the rain clinging to the window, she resembled my brother's wife. I wondered how much she knew about him no one else did, his demons, the weaknesses that made him vulnerable. If there were only some way to get her out of the house before I got there. There were so many things she wouldn't have understood about his death and the crippled things that remained. I couldn't let her get to me. I wanted to tell her there were things a person cannot ever seal, cannot ever destroy.

*It was then I knew I had to tell you I was pregnant. What are we supposed to do now that you know and you understand again our lives are changing? The two of us have been through so much in the continuation of our marriage. In that time, I have trusted you, cherished your emotional sensitivity and respected how rare it is in a man. I never used that against you and although I shouldn't because it's expected of me as your partner, I am proud of that. So many before me have. There are times where I want to blame myself for what has happened and the level of distrust and hate you have for yourself. Did I enable you to feel that way, loathe so much of what you have become as a man and as a husband? Was I not there for you like you wanted me to? I am left to question so much of what once I had been certain. I am still certain though I love you, stronger than ever before. Part of me should be angry at you for shutting me out, but that emotion wavers depending upon how I choose to look at it.*

*It's the same way when I regard your face. At times when the sun is careening in through the front window of our house, uninvited, I see a beautiful man, proud and resolute despite what misguided view you have of yourself. But other times when I watch you trying to still compose music, I see in your desperate eyes a man who is scared to be who he once was, argumentative, but passionate and moreover, brilliant. You never directed any of that contempt towards me though, never once raised your voice or challenged me. But I struck you once and it makes me ashamed. Although you never talked about it, I wanted to. And I have the chance now you were never going to give to me.*

*It wasn't long ago and that is why the details are all still fresh to me, like the aroma of ripe fruit through the open window driving past McIlheny's farm. It's odd, but once you said the spoiled fruits smelled like familiarity. We used to go there for ice cream before the accident. Maybe it was my fault all this happened because I kept pushing you to play your music again. And for some reason that morning I was so irritated because you had the opportunity I expected you would*

94

*take again right in front of you. You had changed after the accident and I'm not talking about the deformity you felt made you look feeble. I thought it gave height to the intensity people always admired in you. The change I guess I failed to notice then was supposed to be emotional. I didn't see it that way, because I never understood how fragile the world had made you previous to what happened. I should have noticed.*

*I should have noticed the times you wanted held and listened to, after those lonely weeks alone when I was travelling with the company, making you feel insecure. Had I given you a reason? Was there someone in your past who caused you to believe in its repetitive history? I always thought your art, the music you created was enough to comfort you when I was gone. Who damaged you in your youth for your self-worth to be questioned so intensely? I can only guess it was another woman who guided you towards the path you have taken us down. Who was she? I wonder if you found her prettier than me.*

*I can still feel the place on my hand where I struck you when I rub my palm. Someone from your old quartet, the pianist, sent you a beautiful new cello that morning with an invitation to play close to the theater where we first met, in New York. It was only a short drive and I would have made it. Inside was a custom designed instrument designed by a specialist in Europe that allowed you to press both areas of the strings, the neck and the breast as one with the unique bow. There was a note attached meant to encourage, not pity you or bring forth an unbearable tide of forgiveness and discourse. He said at the end of the note you always saw the world as a desolate forest of apathy and affliction. I never thought of it as a burden, trying to change your view of us, and the people who passed us by.*

*Not long after you removed the cello from its case, we argued. I wanted to help you become the person you wanted, rid us of the insecurities in our consummation and I was certain music and sound would aid us. You kept telling me I didn't understand music would not tame the beast that existed underneath the surface of your skin. I never saw that in you. Is that how you viewed yourself, as an animal? Never could someone as noble and caring as you be considered anything, but a man. I love you. And I have never stopped, even if you have. Please remember that.*

*I wonder when you listen to this if it will be raining. It was when I followed you into the backyard that morning, but it wasn't very heavy or steady. It was sort of peaceful, like the rain that falls along the beach in the middle of the night. The ground was saturated with water from the night before. You told me to leave you alone. But I never will and you know that. I implored you to take hold of the*

95

*cello. Tears dripped along my cheeks. I wanted to reach you. I was surprised when you sat down on a landscape boulder and started to play. The constructed bow must have been too unfamiliar for you to play long. It only lasted seven seconds. But in those stunning moments I was carried away by the notes you emanated. I wanted to dance again and replay the moments where we kissed for the first time. You were so nervous when I touched the side of your face. Instead, I found myself tearing away at the skin on your chest. You had it all planned out. I should have seen it coming.*

*Minutes after you stopped playing when I turned my back to you, the cello went up in flames on the grass. I watched the strings curl closer together and illuminate under the affects. The stain seemed to drip from the base and pour into the grass. It looked like oil. It was cold outside, but I could feel the intense heat scorched into the atmosphere by the burning body. I started to cry helplessly. I beat my palms against your chest over and over. You never flinched even as I struck my hands hard against your neck and face. The red on your skin combined with the flames reminded me of the red deserts of Arizona where we once spent a weekend. The sunsets were so vivid.*

*Like the night you made me pregnant, I acted differently, kept pummeling you around face and chest, shouting. I called you a selfish cripple. Exhausted by your unwillingness to defend yourself I dropped to my knees and sobbed. I cried harder than I ever had in my life before you, what life I chose to remember. So we both sat there in the sodden grass of our backyard and I cried. And you remained silent. The only time your lips parted were to kiss me slightly below my chin. I was sure you tasted my tears. For a moment I wished they would have poisoned you. The wood from the instrument darkened and after a few minutes the flames died out. I never asked you why you burned the cello.*

The heat was intense enough the inside of the bus windows began to sweat. I tasted bile in the back of my throat. I struggled to clutch the gun, in fear and aggression. The bus idled at a train crossing and the moments we waited were interminable. A man was loading some heavy equipment onto one of the cars. We eventually began again after a 15 minute delay and as the train echoed in the distance behind us, I could see several police cars off in the distance. I pulled the gun out from the inside of my coat, held it between my legs and exhaled. I lowered my head and the barrel of the gun tapped against the construction of the floor of the bus in front of my seat from side to side, mirroring the metronome she used to count out a rhythm to when she danced, moving her body with unparalleled correctness and agility, collapsing with raw purpose at the edge of my feet. I had to succeed here.

Passengers on the bus became alarmed and nervous about what was happening. They could see the police in the distance, horizontal across the road, nowhere for the bus to go. I looked out of the window through the raging rains and wondered if she was out there hoping to be able to talk to me. But someone else, most likely a trained negotiator would talk initially, tell me to give up. Go ahead and try to identify with me, gain my trust. Please. Come on this bus and take my hand. Comfort me and through false words and through the strength of my flesh try to understand the torture involved with a man's determination, every aspect of a man's fragility. And when everything else was stripped away, how uncomplicated we were, how easily we fractured.

Maybe he would speak to me of hope. That birth was full of hope. That religion was full of hope. Come onto this bus and convince me that there was hope somewhere in the darkest corners of my unfortunate miscarriages. Hope had no simple or concise definition. It could be represented by anything. But I had to be willing to see it, understand its possible abstraction, like the misapplied colors of a revisionist painting. The few pieces of furniture left untouched, encircled by blackened cinders scorched and smoldering on top of the ground after a house fire during a holiday. The calming rhythm of a woman's throat while she slept. Hope. It was different things to different people. It was supposed to be what was left after everything else had gone.

I raised the gun above my head and pulled the trigger. People screamed. The driver depressed the brake pedal and I stumbled forward against the seat. The vehicle fishtailed and came to a stop across the center line. I wondered if my brother could hear the gunshot that exited from the chamber and punctured the ceiling of the bus, slicing through the rain and the morning air. I wondered if after everything, someone would finally be able to listen to me and hear me coming.

~

It all happened as quickly as Augustina and I had fallen into the brilliance of one another's love, the abject pain and preference presenting themselves without warning. The sound of the gunshot ripping through steel echoed throughout the arid plain of ambiguity and imbalance. The thick black smoke from the scorched tires scraping across the blacktop faded into the distance. It passed over top of the police cars gathered on a side street and disappeared on the horizon. It wasn't supposed to happen like this. Unfortunately everything else was lost. I had gotten so close.

There was no stillness I wanted to any of it anymore, like the subtle placement of her hands across my stomach when she fumbled around while she slept. Where could a man go when he reached the end of everything he knew to be right, when he stood in the coldness of his own existence, saddened and frightened by the violent truth he had failed? I imagined her coming home and seeing the things I left behind. I wanted to tell her I was sorry. I wanted to tell her why I burned the cello.

I told the other passengers to relocate to the rear of the bus, sitting away from the emergency door. Moving closer to a window I pressed up against the glass and surveyed my surroundings. I squeezed the handle of the gun and pressed it against my chest. It was difficult to get an accurate representation of the situation. With calm instruction I told them all to hand me their cellular phones and any other electronic devices. The driver struggled to move and it was obvious that it was from a disability. Sweat poured along his neck and gathered onto the front of his shirt. His breathing was very erratic and quick. I told him to stop. The man turned, his eyes full of anxiety and aversion. The gun was still pressed against my chest. I leaned closer to him. I let him go. It didn't matter to me what he said when someone would question him. I couldn't cover up any of the windows inside the bus. I didn't want anyone to see me. I wasn't quite sure what else I was going to do.

If I were to surrender, I had a chance to begin again sometime, resurvey the embattled cartography I had crossed. Introspectively I wished I could have, stepped out from the tension and the disbelief and pleaded for help, for someone to understand, not just listen and pretend empathy. Dishonorable amnesty was as menacing as a loaded gun.

I watched the driver move around the right side of the bus. An emergency medical technician ran up to him, wrapped a blanket across his shoulders and ushered him away. The man sat down on the back of an ambulance and was given oxygen. A police officer walked up beside him while he struggled to breathe and started talking to him. No doubt he was asking him questions about what happened. How many people were still on the bus? Was anyone injured? A sniper would be stationed behind a tree, on the roof of a house or underneath of a car, wherever he could ascertain a clear shot. In the eventual dark he would remain there, nameless, faceless, soulless, patient like a noble personification of death itself. It was what I should have been, resolute and assured, waiting for my brother to come, waiting for my brother to see.

The silence I usually loathed and rejected embraced me, gave me a transitory sense of community. I belonged to its quiet spectrum, the small pockets of time where no one spoke. There I wished I could have remained, lost in a blanket of that censorship. I tucked the gun against the small of my back. I reached up and removed the light bulbs on the ceiling from their housing. As I headed towards the front of the bus again, I paused beside the young woman. She was very beautiful. In her trembling hands was an art catalogue.

It had been less than an hour since I pulled the gun. I moved my jacket to the seat in front of me and began tearing through the pockets, desperate for a pill. There had to be some left. I found one and placed it against my tongue. My mouth was so dry. In moving the jacket, I dislodged some of the information on my brother. Some photographs and one of the surveillance tapes dropped to the floor. I struggled to reach over and pick them up. What stared back at me in assailing black and white were images of the different crime scenes. Everything about those places appeared bleak and unresponsive. Things used to be beautiful here.

I adjusted the volume and repositioned the earpiece. The hardened, dispassionate approach of my brother's seduction, his scattered sexuality lingered, weighed upon the auditory senses of my consciousness. I remembered some of the motives and reason approached in the file when a criminal psychologist was brought in to work up a profile. A pedophile was a disordered person with intense urges and fantasies involving sexual activity with a prepubescent child. The person is often distressed by the images of arousal and intercourse. The report hypothesized that he had engaged in the behaviors for at least six months' time, probably longer. But not all child molesters or pedophiles murdered and butchered their victims like he allegedly had. My brother appeared to choose children whose irreproachable fabric he thought was torn and disrupted by fragmented domesticity, the lack of stability or structure in a home environment.

I understood listening to one of the tapes how easy it was to get inside someone through trust, through seduction, through the promise of hope, through moments of intimacy, privacy and in time, hurt them. I learned how easy it was to damage someone. I was beaten down by the barbarity and the tenacity of the human spirit, the individual, the union of man and woman, strewn together by passion and coincidence, hate and consequence. When trust and intimacy were stripped away, when a man was broken, you were doing him a favor by killing him. Everything after became a disparaging choice of externalism. We were murderers responsible for the slaughter of an infinite and incalculable amount of innocuous dreams.

The wiretaps, the inauspicious contents pulled and urged me to listen to its inhumanity, the abducting diction in my brother's voice glossy and precluding. It had to come to an end. The voices were labeled as unidentified except for his. I could hear at least two others and it was difficult to understand specific qualifications about their dialogue. But I knew it was about a little girl. None of the markings on any of the transcripts said which one. I could hear water crashing in the distance. I stopped the tape when I saw one of the men at the rear stand and come towards me. I pulled the gun and pointed it ahead. When he started to speak I cocked the trigger, stood and told him to sit back down. It was my intention not to keep them here any longer than was necessary. And unless someone tried something very brash, no one would be injured. It didn't have anything to do with them. It would all be over soon. I lowered the gun when he turned around.

I pinned the gun against my side and paced the aisle of the bus, waiting for them to call again. It had been almost an hour since the initial verbal contact from a negotiator. There were so many questions he asked me and I never gave him a clear answer on a lot of them. I said no one was injured and no one would be as long I was given some space and some time. The thing I wanted the most was another driver and access to the main highway. But I knew they would never let me leave with anyone else on board. I thought about telling him to bring my brother here.

Unfortunately, that was never a possibility. He asked me to release the rest of the passengers, perhaps the woman. I said no.

I sat down next to the still fallen pile of evidence and took the recording out of the DAT player. I couldn't listen to it any longer. But I had said that before. The things said by the men on that tape were suggestive and galling. Utter depravity. I pulled out another one and depressed a button. The sounds of construction continued throughout until there was a break. It was Augustina again. She had been crying. I could hear the subtle, delicate differences in her breathing, the inequality in her resonance. It was usually so calm, so enduring. I always believed it alone could rid the world of so much famine and violence, that her voice could bring water to the thirsty, comfort to the diseased and dying. I had no idea she had been recording over portions of my sound catalogue, or how long she had been doing it.

*I know you will understand the significance of recording over sections of sound from this construction site. It was the first job you were assigned to when you believed for the first time your past was behind you. It made sense to have you study sound, find better ways to keep people safe, as your music had kept me from harm for so long. Of course I wanted you to play again. But as I said before, I never wanted to push you.*

*I know it was the only time you wore the prosthetic out in public. I watched you from a distance, pulling the resin plastic against your shoulder. It was so hot that day, but you wore long sleeves and I thought you did it to cover your arm. But when I watched you walk out of the house to catch the bus in a thick shirt and jeans, I knew. It was because of what that woman said to you when we went away to the beaches near Long Island for one of my performances. When you said you would go to the party afterwards I was kind of surprised. It was so beautiful out that night and the sun felt so good against my bare skin. You didn't know any of the people there and I thought you might be more comfortable in our hotel room overlooking the pier. You tried to be reclusive, hiding behind groups of people, shielding them from view of your body. I thought that outfit you wore looked so good on you, the light colors bringing out the enticing color of your eyes. And that stupid, ignorant woman set fire to all the grandeur you felt that night.*

*People in my company kept coming up to you, expressing their awe at your courage to be there after what had happened. Some of them couldn't compliment me enough and I kept blushing when you looked at me the way you did when no one else was. None of them would ever see the things in you I did, the way you spoke to me, the sounds you made with your mind and heart when you used to play. The irresistible way you turned into a shy adolescent when I asked you to make love to me. You always tried to hide it, but your hand always started to shake as soon as I lit a candle and came into our bedroom. After all this time you were still nervous around me, like the first time.*

*There was too much alcohol at that event though. But drunkenness could never be an excuse for what she said. You were sitting on a rock watching the tides, sipping from a glass of wine when a few people in the company that I disliked came up to you. The first thing you did was turn your eyes in circles, trying to find me. I would have fought vast deserts of warriors to keep anyone from hurting you. But I wasn't there. Someone started it by making a comment about your arm and your body. Those fiends toppled the strength I was trying to help you rebuild with their recriminations and their jealousy. A man I didn't know asked you if you were sick. And you said no. It got quiet and you stood up to leave. I was proud that you never wavered in your attitude and your demeanor.*

*You had such integrity and pride. It was always there even though you couldn't feel it, like my hand on yours, or my lips across your bones. Then that woman asked you that question. It was the worst thing I had ever heard a human being ask another. We drove home in the middle of the night. I didn't care I missed the performance the next day. I wasn't going to subject you to that kind of abuse again. I kept reaching over to push the hair out of your face while you slept as I drove all those miles home. I could have been with you anywhere and thought out if as home. I can't help but wonder what you're wearing.*

*I am not sure what triggered it, but I thought a lot about the pianist in your quartet last night. Maybe it was the environment I was immersed in at my recital the past few days. It was the first time we could actually get someone to come and play at the studio in over a month. He turned out to be so young I knew none of your compositions would be played. I wasn't sure he had ever heard of you. And I was glad. I didn't want to hear your music played by someone else though. In my eyes, no one had that right.*

*The pianist was the one from your quartet who died, wasn't he? You didn't say anything to me till a few weeks after it happened. I knew you held out hope you would play again together. Is that why you held the truth so close to you? Because his passing was so crippling to you? There was no shame in admitting that. He was so supportive of you after the accident even though you told me not to show you any of the letters that he sent. I am still not sure I understand why you never wanted to read them. Is it because you were forgotten so much by so many people it was easier for you to push them away, pretend that your life wasn't important to anyone else?*

*He cared about you in those letters, even more so after he read what had happened. The night he found out he called the house. You were still in guarded condition and being questioned by the authorities exhausted you. I couldn't tell him why you did it because I didn't know, only that you were going to possibly need years of therapy and rehabilitation. I wasn't going to tell him about the entirety of what happened, but he already knew. It was so tragic he said. He didn't come right out and say it, but he knew the dissolving of your quartet affected you more than he realized it would. You were the most intense out of all them he admitted, but at times that was what kept your music blossoming. I told him you never blamed him for wanting to go back to school and study abroad. You knew that Europe was the greatest field for a young musician to harvest himself. He never asked if I needed anything. But it didn't matter. All I have ever needed was you and you were still with me in substance and in soul.*

*People go in different directions. To him, it was that simple. You said it was very unfair for him to consider you in his decisions though. You sobbed most of the night when you finally told me this plane had crashed over the waters near Ireland. We were supposed to go to dinner that night and then go to counseling together. You always told me I didn't have to go, that I didn't need to see all your deformities at once, what you felt made you unlovable and deformed. You saw yourself as a monster. I married you because I wanted to experience all you and that included your pain as well. I wanted to be a part of your healing, so you knew I would stand by you. I stayed up with you that night, oftentimes watching you fall asleep on the couch or staring out the window. You stood up after not moving for hours and sat down at the bench of the piano I used when I rehearsed at home. I knew you had taken lessons a while back, but never saw you try to play. God I wished you could understand how talented and rare you were. People spend years, decades learning how to play an instrument and you sometimes learned how to master its architecture in months. It was like being a wild animal tamer. You were able to look into the eye of a beast without fear, without discourse. I never realized that you couldn't do the same with yourself.*

*You pulled out the bench from underneath of the piano and sat down. I knew composers had written pieces for musicians with one hand, but I had never heard any of them. You had researched and then downloaded a few pieces. At first your fingertips moved across the ivory keys as if they were too big for your hands. You pulled your hand back and set it on your lap. I came around and stood in front of you. Your eyes were closed. When they opened you took in such a deep breath and*

103

*slapped your fingers down, punishing the instrument. It was as if you hated it. It wasn't hard for tears to well up within my eyes. The small, personal recital lasted a little more than four minutes. I was never moved more than I was for those, beautiful truncated moments. When you were finished, you stood and pushed the bench back underneath of the piano and came closer to me. You said you would try to learn to speak without music. You asked me to help you, to reconstruct you. I put my hand on your chest and felt your heart trying to tear through your ribcage.*

The rain continued harder and it was the worlds only sound. It was harder to see inside of the bus. I didn't know how to end this. Nothing would change if I turned myself in. I would still struggle to maintain balance, be castigated. It couldn't go on. I closed my eyes. It would have been the only time I would have had courage, killing him. I wanted to get to him so much. I stood and waited for the negotiator to call again.

The beautiful woman was leaning against the glass sobbing. I passed her so I could see clearer outside through the rain. Even if Augustina were out there, she could never convince all those people I never meant to hurt anyone. She would show them the evidence on my brother. She would try to explain to them about my accident and what I wanted to do. I looked at the catalogue sitting in the beautiful woman's hands. There were paintings on most of the pages. The man behind her, in his late 30's to early 40's, told me to let her go. I said no. It would all be over soon. I stopped and clutched the gun tighter. I turned my wrist over and struck him above the eye with the butt of the gun. The laceration opened and blood rushed over his eye. It pooled on the floor underneath of his seat. All I said a man's failure doesn't necessarily make him a coward.

Again I sat down on the floor, watching the rain streak across the glass of the windows. I replaced one earpiece and pressed play, then lifted the gun onto my lap. I moved it up against my sternum then let it settle into the notch in my throat. I put my index finger over the curve of the trigger, moved it back and forth across the thin steel.

*I had a dream the other night, but I'm not sure how you would respond to it if I told you. The bassist in your quartet was here with his two daughters, the ones he adopted with his wife after he quit. We were sitting back on deck chairs, listening to the water trickle from the pond he helped you install. Our son was running through the yard with the twin girls, laughing and grinning, the way we used to as children. You held my hand so tightly in that dream out of passion and love when I awoke I looked at my wrist, hoping to find marks where your fingertips had been.*

*I know you loved children. When we walked around the neighborhood and saw other couples with strollers or setting up lemonade stands, you tried to hide it. But your eyes lit up when you saw them. Perhaps it was the innocence involved in being a child, the lack of responsibility, the lack of self-awareness which sometimes led to self-destruction. Please don't misunderstand what I am saying. You were the most responsible man I have ever known and your accident could never have a bearing on that. No matter what you or anyone else thought. We lived in a modest home I adored and more often than not you always provided what you felt I needed. It was hard for us to vacation together because of our schedules I know. But it didn't matter to me because we travelled to so many parts of the world, albeit without each other at times.*

*I was listening to music the other day, a collection of songs that will forever be echoed in my memory. You bought it for me right before your accident. I expressed such desire to go to see the soloist in concert and you said you would take me. But we couldn't go. It was one of the first times I was actually mad at you. We were struggling for money at that time and you thought it was unnecessary. You were right, but I took it out on you anyway. You would have had every right to be angry with me, but you never were. I wished more people possessed your nobility, your sense of reason. I left that morning while you weren't home and wrote you a note that I was going to spend the night at a friend's house. I was pouting like a spoiled child I know. But I didn't want to make matters worse by saying something I shouldn't have. I tried calling you that night and I let the phone ring once before I hung up. I didn't have the courage to talk to you.*

*It was so late, almost sunset the next day when you pulled up in her driveway and started knocking at the front door. Cars had gone past all afternoon and I hoped it was you, coming for me because you couldn't go another hour without seeing me. But when they weren't you I got upset when I shouldn't have. I expected you to run barefoot to her place and drag me back home with you. We all wanted to be chased. I felt stupid though, like a teenager upset there was no note from that boy she liked in her locker after class. You had a flower in your hand when I opened the door. I let you take me by the wrist and lead me back home. I still cannot believe what you did.*

*While I was gone, our small house seemed to have changed. The front lights were off, but I could see the basket of flowers sitting underneath of the porch light. I bent over to smell them. It reminded me of running through the fields as a child,*

105

the dandelion seeds and pollen clinging to a dress that had yet to learn how to show itself on my body. I wanted to have known you then. I got upset for a quick second, knowing there were things I would never share with you. I wanted them in case we never had a chance to share them now. Stupid things, like your first cut, the first time you spoke, the first time you saw a woman and felt something tingle behind your chest. You raised my eyes to yours and told me to go inside.

Most of the lights in the house were dimmed or off so I let you lead me. I was blind to your wishes. You were my custodian. We moved through the living room and when we reached the doors that led to the rear of the property, you told me to close my eyes. I stepped through the door with your guidance and lost my balance a bit. I singed the side of my ankle on what I knew was a candle. I opened my eyes and couldn't believe what I witnessed. Lining the edges of the stone patio and walkway were small candles floating in clear, oval bowls of water. The piano from our living room had been moved outside and was surrounded by plants and flowers. A large portion of the lawn which was once unkempt and cluttered had been cleared. Across that open space was a large blanket.

A beautiful outdoor bistro table was set up for an elegant dinner, complete with candlelight. In a bucket full of ice were two bottles of wine. You asked me to sit down. I shouldn't have been surprised when you pulled out the chair for me. It was then a man I didn't recognize stepped out from the house exquisitely dressed in a tuxedo. He was holding a hand crafted menu. You told me to take it from him and less than 30 minutes after I did, he unfolded a small table next to us and served dinner. I wasn't sure who made it, but the food was so succulent and amazing. I never saw that man again the rest of the night. You never told me who he was. Everything was so beautiful.

We were alone and I felt so blessed with our life. You kept smiling at me during dinner. It was so quiet in the neighborhood as if you asked everyone to stay away, leave us to swim in the momentary tranquility of our lives. That peace was broken when someone began to play the piano behind me. I didn't turn around until I heard her voice. It was so recognizable to me and I understood how you felt when you composed and played. When I turned around and saw her I couldn't believe it. We were unable to go to her concert, but there she was. The musician I respected and admired the most other than you. It all seemed so natural, her sitting behind our home, playing and singing. You asked me to dance with you.

I held your body against mine, tucked my head in the comfort and security of your shoulder. I felt so exhilarated, so wanted. No one else would have done something like this for me. Part of me wanted to know how this all happened, how she was able to be here, privately with us. We had been dancing for about 20 minutes when I closed my eyes. You asked me if I was okay. I was. I was so okay I wanted to capture this moment in time and never let it slip through my fingers. I didn't ever want you to slip through my fingers either. I told you I was scared. You laughed a little and I had to smile. But when I explained I was afraid there could be nothing after this, that you had created such a strong moment in our chronology that everything which preceded it would be a disappointment, would be nothing more than a wasteland of unfulfilled promises. You touched your hand to my face and pushed my hair back behind my neck. I felt so bad at the way that I had treated you. Tears flooded my eyes and dripped down along my cheeks. When you wiped them away I pulled you closer and kissed your lips, brushed my tongue across your skin. I wanted to thank you but I didn't know how. Before I could say anything, you took my hand and introduced me to her.

The most transcendent night of my life had passed, but you and I still lay on that blanket in the grass. I thought nothing would ever come between the two of us, that we were strong enough to withstand the greatest of storms. When I started trying to undress you, you stopped me and said we should go inside. I pulled at your wrist and made you sit back down beside me. It was so late and I didn't want to leave this place, this oasis you created for us. I stood and slipped off my clothes. We didn't even make love. For a few hours we held one another, let the moon spill its white light over us like water, wetting our intimacy in a unique paleness. You wrapped your arm around me and held me so I thought I would lose my ability to breathe. Your body felt so warm against my back. No one could see us. And to me it didn't matter anymore. I wanted others to see what I had, the man that meant more to me than anything, the man who stopped time for a moment.

The bassist. I know you were upset he told you what he was doing in writing and that he didn't even have the decency and the respect to talk to you about it. It was like your feelings didn't matter, were inconsequential. Nothing you have ever done, especially with me, has ever been insignificant or meaningless. If I have to tell everyone in the world, across the oceans and deserts how important I am in your presence I will, until my mouth is dry and my breath is gone. I know you want the world to see it, that you want to scream with all the power in your lungs. You hoped your music with them would make the world see, make the world hear what you have to say is powerful, that what you feel is as equal as anyone.

Just because you were slight didn't mean you weren't erotic, that you weren't a good lover. I wished you were here right now to make love to me, to take me with torrid, reckless abandon, tear through my flesh and drink me. You could stir my *body because you listened to me when I felt I had something important to say. Even if it wasn't, you felt it was because I was the one having the thoughts, I was the one impassioned about it.*

*I am telling you this as I am going through our closet, looking at some of your clothes. I could smell you on them so much. I want you to raise my skirt and force yourself inside of me, make me remember all the reasons that I fell in love with you. I want you to bite my nipples. I want you to bruise me. But I am here in our bedroom, alone and I have no idea where you are. You once created such beautiful and powerful music, never equaled but unfortunately by some, never valued. Mostly, by yourself.*

~

The things I remembered about her, about that night, the intensity, the sensuality, the smell of the skin on the inside of her elbow where I rested my face I carried with me every morning. But there came a time when those memories began to hurt more than calm. It was hard to avoid, the intense and consistent condemnation of oneself. It was always there no matter what happened, adjusted and motioned under the still surface like bleak water under a frozen pond. It bred. It gave birth. It lingered.

The musical career I desired was gone and the individuals abandoned me, leaving behind a vapid aggregation of audibility and production. I thought about what had happened as I scanned through another series of DAT recordings, imagining her words would change as I had. Soon her praise and her love would become violent and censured. It had to. Mechanical sounds started. It was a recording of a factory that made copper piping. I continued to listen to the abrasive sounds of alarms and machinery. Boat motors. Welding torches. Combines. Presses. Sledgehammers. Explosives used in quarries. That was where the police had discovered the body of the seventh child my brother had murdered, where I had the accident. The intense dissatisfaction and antipathy I carried inside had succeeded that morning in overcoming me. It was that simple. I had wanted to vanish into a forgotten world of tragedies, buried deep in the recesses of the earth. Down in that abandoned quarry I would have rotted, covered in filth, hidden by darkness. But everything changed when I struck and killed that boy.

The police said he lived in a house less than a mile away from the quarry and they weren't quite sure what he was doing there at that time of night. No one had seen him leave. No one could explain it. But it didn't matter and it didn't need to be explained to me. It happened. Understanding the truths behind it was ineffectual and pointless and it wouldn't have changed how I felt. He was dead. Liberating the details didn't make the dead breathe the air of the content and of the conscious. The violence in the collision between the narcissistic manipulation of self and his indelible innocence was gruesome. It looked like he was asleep.

There was a delicate look of stillness across that boy's features, his slight cheekbones ripped through his skin like fragments of broken porcelain dishes tearing through the material of a silk tablecloth. The coroner removed over 60 pieces of glass from his head. It brought everything closer together. The accident report from the police department was exhaustive describing what happened as vehicular manslaughter. I had seen traffic fatalities before, but I never expected his body would move the way it did.

I expected them to have discovered him mangled, his blood splashed over the fluorescent headlights. The car struck him about waist high, flush across his hips and his left thigh according to the report. His pelvis was crushed on impact. Instead of being pulled underneath of the front tires his body bounced off of the hood of the car and careened through the glass. The violence and the physical impact stunned me as he had only weighed approximately 70 pounds. The driver's side door remained ajar. Smoke rose from the engine. I watched the taillights trail off and be smothered by the darkness. It didn't fit, but it reminded me of squinting into the night sky, trying to identify the constellations. It was determined that he was killed instantly. No trepidation. No pain. He never had a chance, the boy.

All things considered, it would have been easier on everyone around me if I hadn't survived. Soot and ash covered my body. Blood poured from the stump where my left arm had been severed when the car overturned. I couldn't see with the blood dripping from my forehead. My head was concussed. Emergency signals stuttered above the hill. Parts of my shirt and pants were torn open. The dirt road underneath my body lacerated the skin on my chest and thighs. I tried to move like a wounded soldier closer to the opening of the quarry. It took me almost nine minutes to move my body only eight feet. I struggled to reach the end, to close my eyes and discover peace in the silence.

Lying there in the hospital bed with my arm strapped to the metal bar because I was considered a danger to myself, I was a misrepresentation of everything I was supposed to be, strong willed, driven, masculine, wanting other people to see something different than what they actually did. It was a horrible thing, being trapped inside a costume of self-hate because a man could run from everyone and everything in the world, but himself. That could never change, the internal essence of what a man felt, what he was born with, what drove him to make the physical and emotional choices that another man wouldn't.

I tried to focus when I opened my eyes and discovered my wife in a chair next to me, her arms folded in her lap. She looked exhausted. That was when I tried to reach out and touch her, but couldn't. The pressure from the straps restricted me and enlarged the veins running through my right arm. I opened my lips, but couldn't talk. There was a tube strapped with gauze and wires over my mouth. It led down my esophagus and into my lungs. One had been punctured by a rib dislodged from my chest cavity. Anything beautiful was at the same moment insufferable, music, passion, the range and depth of disillusionment pressed deeply into the auburn eyes of my wife and how helpless she must have felt. It was an inexcusable thing, disappointing a woman.

That's where the variety of medications had first appeared. I hid them from my wife for months after the first surgery, embarrassed by the absence of emotional strength and biological independence I possessed. Things became more disconnected and less intimate. It was difficult to become aroused. I couldn't provide her with what she needed. A woman needed touched, a woman needed stimulated, physically and emotionally. It was different with her. She needed sensed and embraced, clutched with resolution and courage. It was hard to do that missing a fucking arm. I was an incomplete structure, like the unfinished scaffolding going up on the other side of the river. Whereas that represented progress, I exhibited an industrial collapse.

Everything felt weighted in my chest. It took almost two days before my wife could raise her head to look at me without sobbing uncontrollably. She searched desperately inside of herself for blame. She stared often at the motionless tile under her bare feet; her ballet shoes placed under the chair, listening to the breathing apparatus pump oxygen into my body. Unfortunately, that had become her metronome, the gross apparatus she moved with fluidly. To her, there had to be a reason for what I did. But I never found the right words to tell her.

~

I dropped the cartridge out of the gun, checked its contents and then forced it back into its original position. The world was dark except for the few remaining lights on the bus and the array of emergency lighting outside. It was harder to see. By now someone would understand what I had done. The police department would retrieve my case file. The photographs from the crime scene of my car accident were scorched into the dense scrapbook of my failures. No one could possibly understand with any absolute certainty I felt I spoke the ancient language of the neglected and the unwanted, that I was the steward of the fallen, the broken man. I reached into the jacket again, but there was nothing left. The pills were gone. I stood and turned my back on the other people on the bus and looked out the window towards the highway. I could barely see the entrance to the expressway. Nothing moved on the wide expanse of concrete. It reminded me of things left unsaid and of failure.

It was still raining. The temperature on the bus had become unbearable. I had asked the negotiator outside to bring water some time ago, but it remained stifling on board. I set the gun down on the driver's chair and tried again to open a window. I dug my fingertips hard into the latch on the right side, hoped it held, and then moved to the opposite. The latch kept locking back into place. Both needed to be released at the identical moment in order for the window to open. Defeated, I took the gun from the driver's seat and bashed it several times against the glass. I could see it fracture across the disappointment of my own reflection until it expanded and ruptured pieces of my present and my atonement broken upon the pavement.

I slumped up against one of the seats. I put in another DAT recording. Sounds of laughter swelled around me. It was sound taken at an amusement park. Rollercoasters. Equipment and games. Voices cheered and quieted. A merry go round. Almost all that sightless joy was a composite of what I had taken from that child. In every unique sound, I heard an indiscriminate portion of the life he would never lead because of what I had done. It didn't matter how many decibels it registered or where it was recorded. Even in places he might have never known existed I would hear a noise that made me remember, think about the things he might have wanted to do with his life. Then the sounds on the tape stopped abruptly. All I had ever wanted was to be remembered, not abandoned. I didn't want to be judged. Through all the violent sounds and the frailty, I wanted someone to hear me. And because I believed I was immaterial and insignificant, that no one would listen. I decided I had to make someone listen.

*I don't know what to say anymore. Honestly that's a lie. I do know what to say, but I grow weary of saying the same things over and over again. There are only so many ways I can tell you I love you and honor you before they start to sound vacant, like your recordings. Most of them were so hollow and penetrable, lacking any sort of life or biology. They are lonely. And so am I. I have stood by you when others have not. But instead of loving me more and more, you pushed me away, stacked my warming sound on one of your shelves and forgot about me.*

*I am pregnant now and need you more than I ever have. I am not scared to do this alone, but I don't want to. I know you are afraid to care for this child because of what happened during your accident. But that's exactly what it was. Instead of putting us at a distance where you cannot hurt us, please wrap your arm around us and pull us closer. I spoke to the family of that boy. I know you wouldn't have wanted me to, but you need to understand even they forgive you and they even offered to help you. But they said to me you refused to talk to them. I wish you could forgive yourself for what happened. When I awoke this morning you were gone.*

*Last night on my way home from the studio, I walked past the second-hand music store. People donated their old pieces and most of them went to the local schools to help continue to fund the struggling arts departments. For sale in one of the displays was a violin. It was once played by the same man who left your quartet, the last one to abandon you. He was your partner longer than any of the rest of them. You respected him so much and tried to convince him to stay on. But the day the two of you were supposed to meet, he never showed. It was as if he had vanished, disappeared into a selfish vacuum of distance and apathy. Less than a year later we were in a music store together and noticed his recordings. He had joined a quintet in California, but never had the intestinal resolve to say anything to you. It wasn't fair what he did. The level of disrespect he showed you was unconscionable. After everything you helped him through, his battle with alcohol, his very public divorce and this was how he repaid you, by walking away without so much as a conversation or letter.*

*I could never understand why people never told you the truth about things. Funny because I am speaking into this microphone and am as afraid to tell you the truth as much as they were. Outwardly it never seemed to bother you. You gave so much of yourself to other people, waiting for someone to once give back to you. By the time anyone did, including me, it was too late. All the anger and the hurt you compartmentalized, tucked away into the recesses of your heart and your mind. You buried it under layers of loneliness and doubt. You thought that by ignoring it, it would pass, decay and rot. Instead of destroying it, you made it breathe.*

I let the DAT recorder continue to function and tucked the gun into the front of my waistband. The earpiece dropped to the floor as I stood and walked over to where the beautiful woman was sitting. I grabbed the handle of the gun and pulled it from my waist. I pointed the gun into her unforgettable face and eyes and told her to get up. She looked scared and uncertain. When she did finally stand, she nearly collapsed and I held her up. The barrel of the gun pressed into her skin. We turned around and headed towards the front of the bus. I came up beside her as she stared through the pane of glass attached to the door. Sheets of rain dripped along the hinges and leaked a little bit onto the floor. The gun moved across the desert of skin on the small of her back. The right man could get lost there. I leaned closer to her and whispered I should have let her go and she had been through enough.

Unfortunately I only recognized her a few hours ago. It was her daughter the police found first, in January, afloat in that pool. There were some photographs of her broken family included in the file on my brother. They were both treated as suspects. It mentioned her husband had recently abandoned her, blamed her for what happened. It was a lie, a fabrication created to suppress guilt and sorrow. The same tumult had crippled me, ensuring a vacant and inaccessible existence. Moreover, I undervalued a woman I should have championed. I said nothing more to her and I should have.

The man I had struck above the eye hours ago charged from the rear of the bus and reached out for the gun. Quickly it discharged as I fell backwards and struck my head against the steering column. White balls of light streaked through my eyes. Even with my eyes shut for a moment, I could see the reflection of the floodlights outside cascade against the back end of the bus, penetrate the imperfections in the broken glass and interrupted the solemnity I desperately tried to maintain. But that kind of unbroken innocence, that kind of honest concord never lasts. People motioned at the edges of the street and the sidewalks of the houses surrounding the intersection. I couldn't hear them, couldn't hear their voices tell me I should surrender, save myself, forfeit everything I believed I had accomplished in ruin. There was nothing to gain. That's not why I had done this. I remembered seeing an auction house catalogue highlighting a man's paintings on the floor of the bus. It was covered in blood.

The piercing, red trail of the sniper scope suddenly materialized and danced methodically along the edges of the ceiling, dripping down the edges of the bus and onto the floor beneath me. Movement from the ground underneath the bus disrupted the awkward tranquility I found for a brief moment in remembering what her voice sounded like on those tapes, how her lips never wavered in uncertainty on what words would arouse the tender hairs at the edges of my ears. She tried so hard. It was easy to realize the things that were happening. I didn't even have to look up or talk to someone. I could have closed my eyes and waited for the gunshot to tear into my forehead or rip open my chest. I wondered what sounds I would hear then. They were coming in.

# THE AGENT

I glanced up at the cracked facing of the clock above her dresser. The trains ran every hour. She would be leaving for the lawyer's office soon. After that I would leave as the next bus to the station boarded a couple of blocks away. What happened after I boarded would leave me with minimal contact with anybody, even her. That's the way it always had to be. The department would have a handler on the tracks in Massachusetts. Once he saw me exiting the train that was it. I would be isolated and alone. That man would be the last person to understand or have any knowledge of who I was. Or whom I thought I had once been.

I opened and shut my eyes a couple of times. I wasn't used to the contacts that were placed into my eyes to alter the color. They needed to match the identification set up for me. Details mattered when it came to being undercover. It was difficult at first, pretending, lying, living the truncated biography of a person who never existed outside of a room of specialists and criminal psychologists. One who never had a real address or a legitimate social security number. I couldn't be honest or revealing, even with her. I wasn't supposed to be.

Most career criminals were cautious, not indecisive or aggressive. And once an arrest was made, the person I became, that facsimile slipped into an unmarked folder, locked inside a file cabinet. Sometimes I had to become that same person again and again and again until his identity was breached and he became a liability. Then he disappeared. No matter whom I became, even a husband, in the end I always vanished, hardly leaving any evidence behind I had ever been there.

I stared at the maroon quilt that had covered her body when I heard the handle to the bathroom door begin to turn. The silence thundered across ruffled sheets and the dimmed track lighting. I didn't know what to say after what had happened. She and I hadn't made love like that in months. But it seemed abhorrent, seething of contempt and hate instead of compassion and ardor. The door opened and I could see her reflection in the long mirror against the wall. The hopelessness echoed, like whatever she whispered into the mist she wiped from the mirror with her hand, a small, reflective moment that should have been sublime.

I watched her come out of the bathroom nude, beads of warm water rolling down the inside of her thighs, glistening like morning dew on her pubis. She brushed passed me, her body smelling naturally of pure vanilla. It would probably be the last time the light from our bedroom descended along her unparalleled architecture, the seductive way the silver beams clung to her like mercury, afraid to let go and become lost in the rawness and uncertainty of the dark.

"I feel like a whore," she said, raising her intimates over the subtle curves of her hips. The taste of the skin underneath her armpits at the sides of her breasts was still present on my lips.

"I never treated you like anything other than my wife and I never stopped loving you, regardless of what you think of me," I said.

"I'm not sure you ever gave me the regard you should have. So tell me, which one of you did I fuck this morning?"

*Who was I?*

*William McCoy, convicted arsonist responsible for the deaths of seven people in a row home fire in Philadelphia. Graduated with a degree in chemical engineering from the University of Southern California. Arrested for the first time in 1997 for immolating a building housing an abortion clinic. It was vacant at the time. Released in 2005. No living relatives. Only distinguishing feature, a long, patterned scar on his back from a second degree burn caused by his mother when he was nine. Thought he was doing God's work because the mark resembled the Virgin Mary when looked at in the reflection of a mirror. Believed to be working with other men and women responsible for setting fire to several other women's clinic and at least four other government buildings. Labeled by the Federal Government as an extreme anarchist and domestic terrorist. Currently being sought after in Washington, Montana and South Carolina for questioning on several other fires resulting from circumstances labeled as suspicious.*

"Don't talk like that," I said.

"Don't what, tell the truth?" she quickly responded.

"Please don't disgrace it like that, make it sound so cheap," I pleaded.

"Disgrace what, our marriage? Fucking you?" she asked, stepping into a beautiful maize sundress. "Everything's that's happened between us was depreciated and damaged already. Maybe it always has been and I couldn't see it for what it was. I tricked myself. I hate it every time I let you stick your cock inside of me."

"Then why do it?" I asked.

"Because I've been alone here for so long I needed to feel something," she said.

"You knew what I was and we both knew what could happen," I said.

"You were never honest with me about who you were and what you really did until recently. Were you giving me a way out all that time and I was too fucking naive to take it? Was that your way of putting all the guilt onto me so you wouldn't have to deal with it?" I wanted to reach out and hold her, but fought against it. "It's nobody's fault," she said, her tone becoming more dulcet and subdued. She looked too exhausted to argue, rubbing the back of her neck and allowing her shoulders to lose their rigidity. I moved closer towards her and reached to zip up the back of her sundress. When my fingertips brushed against the small of her back she pulled away.

"Don't touch me," she whispered.

I started towards her as she watched the rains gather strength outside our bedroom window. Her shoulders tensed when I touched them, but she neglected that time to pull away. I wanted to lick the ebony flesh along her throat. She leaned her head back as if to allow me access and then spoke.

"I'm leaving. When you come back from wherever they're sending you, I won't be here," she added, her head cradled on my shoulder.

"Why?" I asked.

"Because I can't do this anymore."

"What love me?" I asked, kissing the side of her face.

"Yes. I can't love you like this anymore," she said. "I won't. What I once felt for you is bordering on hate. It's not right and you know it." She touched the back of my hand. "Somewhere underneath of all the layers of all the people you are, you know I am right. You're gone for months, sometimes a year at a time and no one at that fucking place tells me anything about you," she said. "I've started to find what you do to be selfish, arrogant and cruel instead of noble," she added.

I rubbed her chest, her nipple expanding underneath her dress. I reached inside her bra and cupped her bare breast. "You once told me you knew everything about me," I said.

"I'm not sure I ever did. At times you're a stranger to me, someone who speaks to me as if they know me. But I don't recognize anything.

You're a soft voice, unfamiliar and cold. I was wrong," she said closing her eyes.

"No you weren't," I whispered.

"We've been through this so many times. I can't break now," she said. "I can't. You have to let me go."

"Don't do this," I said.

"Please don't make me," she responded, taking my hand and passing it against her dress. Her lips parted as she guided me across her abdomen and between her thighs. She was beginning to moisten and I wanted her to reach back and massage my stiffening cock. "Don't go," she whispered. "Wherever you're supposed to go, take me with you. Make me into some else with you."

"Do you want me?" I asked. She raised her right leg higher, giving me permission to place my fingers into her, molecules of sweat dripping from the nape of her neck and on the small of her back. I squeezed her left breast tighter. She opened her eyes and examined our images in the closed glass.

"No," she said, with no real emotion or recourse, no sense of repercussions or consequences set upon the air. "Not if you don't stay."

"I can't stay. I love you deeply," I said. Tears slipped down the right side of her face, that angelic face and became lost in the small hairs on the back of my arm. She removed my hands from her legs and pulled away, opening the window in our bedroom. The rain touched her face through the screen. She was quiet for a few moments, so calm and placid I wasn't sure she was even still breathing. I watched her walk out of our bedroom.

There was a painting set behind her, framed on a pale lavender wall. I couldn't recognize it, but it didn't matter who the artist was to me. To her it was everything, legend, history and tragedy all trapped within a flesh of canvas, a skeleton of glue and darkened maple. Noemi was an art instructor at a small institute in New York. On weekends she held a local class at the community college for aspiring painters. She specialized in nudes and close-ups, but struggled to attain a deeper career in forensic authentication and appraisal. I thought she would have gotten rid of it because of what it represented. It was the reason I had been introduced to her, was able to inadvertently brush my hand across the tenderness of her wrist. The slight touch numbed the tips of my fingers.

I listened to her explain what had happened and note the variations in pigmentation. I watched her move her gloved hands across the scratches in the canvas in the right corner of the frame. I noticed the dissimilarity in the amber shades of her eyes. Her left pupil was darker and it made her indelible elegance appear esoteric, unnatural and pressing. It was under incredible duress I first noticed her, the way her gorgeous, backless dress clung to her shoulders, her hair plunging down over the opening. The Prussian blue material contrasted with the background behind her and pronounced the contours of her face and her lips. She had turned her head and glanced down upon a small sculpture. I thought it might have taken me that extended period to isolate all the different angles of light refracted across the piece by the light coming in and her smile.

Years ago a colleague contacted her, questioning the discovery of an abstract unveiled by a collector who purchased a piece in Europe and placed in his attic. Conducting a quick examination, Noemi determined the work was an original by the artist. The authentication of that piece led to its purchase. In reselling the painting it was determined it wasn't genuine. It had sold for four million dollars. Accusations surfaced that the art dealer, the auction house and painter were selling forgeries. The error had not only damaged her reputation within the art community, but there were whispers about her future credibility in the field going forward.

It would have been the first time I had a chance to be someone else. I could have enrolled in her classes, learn. I chose not to. I watched the confidence in her eyes fade into regret and uncertainty. She turned aside. Suddenly the radiant sculpture washed out, the vibrancy appearing to run down the side of the table. It was at that moment I wanted her to teach me everything. It was where I lied to her for the first time. And because of that I had become a nameless, vacant lover who was already dressed and gone when she reached across the sheets to see if I was still there.

~

I did nothing and our world collapsed, dreams and memories corroded, decomposed along the edges of the unoccupied streets, the distant recollections of births and deaths visible in every living thing that took a breath. I watched her open the front door, the rain falling from the rusted gutters and abusing the annuals she planted when we first moved into this house. Most of them were in ruin, wilted stems downturned toward the ground, rotted and heavy with burden.

She didn't turn around at first as she continued down the driveway, evening her stride, a briefcase securing the laptop brushing against the side of her thigh. She wanted so desperately to leave, not allow herself the opportunity to weaken, to vacillate. I'm not sure if it would have mattered. Without an umbrella she waited at the edge of the sidewalk, her shoulders and hands trembling. I couldn't tell if she reacted because of the bitterness in the rain or she was crying. But I couldn't expect her to grieve because of me. Not after what had happened. It was debilitating, understanding my wife would never look at me the same way again, suffocating the endearment that once existed in the rustic, almond color of her eyes.

I stood in the open doorway and did nothing, watched her touch the sides of her face with hers then hide them deep into the pockets of her pea coat. I tried to remember through the rain, the smell of the skin below her throat, the way her laugh transcended through my entire body when I licked her above her windpipe. Minutes later a cab pulled up in front of the house. She was far from an assailable woman, but I would never see her look as vulnerable and as alluring as she did when she turned around and dropped her wedding ring into the water saturated at the end of the sidewalk. The drops splashed up and touched the surface of her left ankle. The bracelet I gave her was gone, no longer clinging to the structure of her delicate bones. The rear door of the cab shut. Please don't. Please don't leave me here, lost in a storm of inadequacy and misfortune, alone and incurable. The earth choked in complete deafness. All I could hear was the sound of running water. Hope had no place in the daily lives of the imperfect.

I walked out to where she had been and sat down on the jagged edge of the curb. I couldn't feel the water soak through my clothes. Some bold auburn leaves, fallen from trees that overhung the street, stamped onto the pavement looked like puddles of dried blood from a crime scene. The bell of a child's bicycle rang out in the distance. If I looked close enough into the street I thought I could see the faded chalk outline of a hopscotch board. I continued to hear the laughter of a group of children playing tag, the hollow bounce of a playground ball banging against the emptiness of the street. I looked around, but saw no one else only a wasteland of debris, damaged toys and opportunities gone. The wind twisted through the branches of the trees, resembling barely audible whispers I didn't recognize.

*Who was I?*

*Johnathan Levin, repeat sexual offender and documented pedophile. Arrested in 1994 for the sexual assault of a nine-year-old girl in Wisconsin. Molested his first victim at the age of 16. Arrested again at the age of 21 for the assault of a college student in California. Incarcerated in mental hospital until the age of 27. Two months after his release was arrested again for the attempted assault of another 16 year old girl in Iowa. Current whereabouts unknown. Repeated violator of Megan's Law in several states.*

The local police department was having difficulty in breaking a case that had been going on since the beginning of January involving the brutal sexual assault and subsequent murders of several children. Their sex and age range varied, as did the resulting levels of violence. That was the part to me most disturbing, the inherent lack of a pattern in the murderer's processes. After discovering more bodies and less evidence, someone at their department contacted the Federal Bureau of Investigation and the Violent Crimes Division requesting assistance.

Local authorities didn't always appreciate federal interference in a case. But the situation was isolated, this community populated by about 900 people. The demographics comprised of largely lower middle class farmers and aged steel workers. Our town suffocated under a depressed economy, unemployment and a lack of industry and technology. A good portion of the population here either commuted to a different part of the state or crossed the border for work. It used to be a beautiful drive, the stretch of highway which led here. Dairy cows and livestock grazed on the fertile grass. Olive green stalks of immature corn stretched for miles, barns and silos built into the hillsides in the distance. Now it only served as a reminder all things, no matter how durable, no matter how unyielding, would break. I thought about her and the alluring way she always turned her head when I called her, listening to the vibration of each syllable passing over her shoulder.

No one appeared to be at fault for the failure to arrest someone or name a clear suspect in the murders of those children. But there were no simple answers. Cases went cold. It was sometimes the natural order of things.

Then the decision was made behind closed doors to involve someone with undercover experience. The initial concern was the possibility of compromising any one of the identities I had by mere exposure. But I had extensive aptitude in sex crimes involving adolescents and was entrusted with all the evidence the department had collected. A large part of tracking sexual predators could be done on the internet through chat rooms, website sharing and photographs.

The only other person attached to the investigation, other than local officials and the coroner, was an industrial scuba instructor and recreational diver. Apparently he was called in after the discovery of the first victim when a certified diver could not be located and the decision was made to maintain some level of forensic consistency by allowing him go into the water if more victims were discovered. In his record it said he had once aided in the recovery of a body after an industrial drilling job.

I felt sorry for him, being a civilian involved in something as disgusting as this. You believed it wouldn't, but it changed you, distorted everything you once respected, manipulated your perspective on love and passion, anything you held dear, no matter how strong you thought you were. Because of what happened, I found being around children anguishing and demoralizing. The unpredictability of consequence was dangerous.

The case file was expansive and well documented. Initially it included photographs of known sex offenders, possible suspects and persons of interest. Then as the murders continued and escalated in brutality, the circumstantial evidence piled up, but never enough to identify a person of interest or establish a clear motive or pattern to the random killings. In the beginning, based on confirmed alibis, at least 50 people within a 200 mile radius were eliminated as suspects. Included were hours of wiretaps, several transcripts, telephone records, but no real physical evidence needed for a conviction. I tossed through the photographs and read over the psychological profile provided by the F.B.I.

*The perpetrator is over the age of 25 and most likely unmarried, but this fact is not to be dismissed. It's possible the suspect is married, but uses it as a cover for the issue of convenience. Look for a past history of abuse as a child by member or members of his/her family. Search for a history of prior arrests if a suspect is identified. He or she rarely socializes with adults, instead choosing to identify with children instead. Establish a pattern if one has not already been discovered of the age, gender specifics of the victims. If crimes continue look for someone who has limited or moreover full access to children; meaning field trips, parties, teachers, babysitters, businesses who employ minors, social workers, members of the clergy, etc. Be wary of stereotyping the above positions. Could be aided by other molesters; i.e., sex rings, trafficking and /or internet profiling. Most likely suspect is intelligent and articulate and should be considered extremely dangerous. Collections of pornography were a beginning. Possible leads existed in published references to child development, deviant behavior, missing children, police procedural and photographs.*

The investigating detective, Daniel Mull had left unintelligible handwritten notes in the margins of the psychological profile. It looked as if it read, "Who was he?" There were allusions regarding public urination, exhibitionism, scatophilia, sadism and coercion. I could read other words such as violent, dangerous, dissociative, costumes, drugs, alcohol and remnants of clothing.

*Who was I?*

*Jonathan Levin. Arrested in May on suspicion of lewd behavior when caught frequenting local playground near a school. Before arrested was seen fondling himself through his clothing before exposing himself to several women and children. Was released less than a month later when witnesses failed to testify and posted bail after undergoing a psychological evaluation. Current whereabouts unknown.*

Pedophiles had a tendency to communicate with one another and frequent places where children gathered. I thought the suspect or suspects lived or were employed locally and had seen one or all the victims at one time or another prior to their being murdered. Even if he or she was stalking their victims indiscriminately, they had to have been watching children. Not to mention the fact a good number of the bodies were in on near areas of water either dilapidated or abandoned. Someone knew the landscapes in precise detail. It would be impossible, but I wanted to search census databases for the last several years for people who had relocated away from the area.

I sat on a park bench and watched a group of children at a playground, focusing rather on the other adults and the environment around the innocence rather than the subsequent children themselves. It all appeared innocuous; children laughing on the swings, playing in the mud, women sharing subdued conversation while fastening child harnesses and shoulder diaper bags. But everyone involved knew something disgusting rested underneath the surface. There was no changing that and no matter who was apprehended, it could never go back to being what it once was. None of us ever would.

~

The flames became impassioned by the latent chemicals in the composition of the photographs, rolled across the discoloring images of suspects and buildings. I accidentally burned a photograph of us at her sister's wedding in California. I leaned closer and tried to save the vibrant colors of the gorgeous dress she wore. Noemi's hair, once a staggering shade of sable, blanched and became dissolved, as she if had aged unnaturally. Within the next 24 to 48 hours an arrest warrant would be issued for a man living a few miles across the northern Pennsylvania border. Most of the undercover surveillance I attained was responsible for his being named the prime suspect in the case. The State's District Attorney was going to charge him with eight counts of murder in the first degree for all the bodies discovered. His public defender would no doubt plead his client not guilty by reason of insanity because of the inherent violent and sadistic nature of the crimes committed.

The child pornography downloaded onto my laptop and the explicit photographs and films shared with suspects, were being destroyed. I had already handed over the backups. In the deep corner in our living room, I leaned up against her leather ottoman and tossed through the remaining grainy images, sick representations of manipulative shadows hovering over innocence. During the case I had seen endless cases of sodomy, abduction, rape, molestation, incest, a horrid laundry list of physical abuse and torture. Photographs, videos, webcam images and sick poetry. The images were parasitic and unavoidable. Most people couldn't stomach it. It wasn't something you ever wanted to experience.

Sleeping had become harder on me. Children embraced by agony and pain occupied my once structured dreams and indiscriminate nightmares. I wanted to scream, the things I had seen pressing in on me. The light from her reading lamp once bled down along the molding and walls and across to the base of the stone fireplace. It moved over the surface of the hardwood. In its reflection I could see partial movements, quick random flashes of light, slights variations in the texture of the floor. I thought I'd look up and see her coming across the room again. Noemi discovered me here several months prior her leaving, obsessing over scene diagrams and evidence, searching for an end and a beginning to everything, unable to determine or recognize one from the other.

"What are you doing up?" she asked. "Is something wrong?"

"I couldn't sleep and I didn't want to wake you," I said, hurrying to hide the crime scene photographs and evidence. There was a distant look of disappointment masked by the intensity of her eyes, even at the early hour. "I didn't want you to see this," I added.

"See what?"

"You don't want me to answer that," I added.

"It doesn't matter if I see them or not. I may not see the photographs or whatever it is, but I feel them every time I touch you, see them in your face every time you make love to me," she said. She crouched down and stoked the embers of the fire. The snap and resulting expansion of the wood echoed across the vacancy of the room. "The colors are all there, in everything. Whatever it is, whatever you're experiencing, it's ruining us," she said.

"I can't do this right now. Go back to bed. I promise I'll be in soon."

"That's what you said last night," she said, turning her back to me. The moonlight sliced through the skin and bones of her spine and shoulders. "This thing has been going on for four months." She wanted me to touch her, open, need her. When I never did, she moved closer to me and rested on the floor on her back, her lingerie touching the sides of my ankles. "It doesn't have to be you." Her body burned in the light as if immolated by a high sun as she lay naked in a field of peaches.

"What doesn't?" I asked.

"The one who ends this, catches him," she said. "Haven't you sacrificed enough for them, haven't we?"

"This isn't for them. It's different this time."

"What makes this case different than all the others? Look at the scars on your hand, your back," she said, holding my hand. "You burned yourself deliberately for Christ's sake."

"It's different. You asked me to be honest with you about what I did. And against my better judgment and everything I learned, I partially was. But I'm not in the middle, out there finding the bodies, struggling with the consequences. I'm only consulting. I'm a voice, a stranger on the other end," I said. "There's no danger in this," I added.

"Look at you. You're sweating and your hands are shaking." She spread herself across my legs and ankles, sympathetically passed her lips over the scar on my leg.

*Who am I?*

*Peter McDonnally, small time con artist. Arrested with three other men for the attempted holdup of an armored car. Transferred to another correctional facility after four years in solitary confinement. Current whereabouts unknown. Last seen living in New Jersey walking with a profound limp after sustaining leg injury from gunshot wound during failed attempt and arrest. No known address. Still wanted in questioning for the robbery of jewelry stores in Missouri, Alabama and North Carolina.*

"I'm worried about you," she added.

"Nothing's going to happen to me," I assured her.

"That's not what I meant. What about us?" she asked.

"Do you love me?"

"You know that I do," she said, moving my legs apart and nestling her body inside mine.

"We'll survive this. It's almost over." I cupped a hand around her chin and leaned closer, perspiration from the humidity in the room falling across her lips. I kissed her hard, violently. She lingered against my face, the delicate nature of her cheekbones melting against the abruptness of my imperfections. I spun her around and ripped her lingerie over her body and explored the muscles in her abdomen. I grew inside her and wrapped her legs around me. In her voice I could hear indistinct screams of terrified children, the light, audible whispers of terror muted by her arousal. In her lips I could taste apprehension as well as desire.

Noemi pulled me through her body and I lost myself inside of her sex, never understanding there were things I could never tell her. That less than twenty minutes ago I was watching a video of a young girl, no more than 14, forced on her hands and knees to suck a man's cock. It was disgusting, being aroused by that violent image and carry on a dialogue with a sexual offender. I hated everything about myself, but not here with her.

I licked her throat, our bodies aroused and discomposed, the recollection of who I was several minutes ago now lost in the violence of

126

the photographs scattered around us, like dead leaves in autumn. Long strands of her hair spread out over a picture of an 11-year-old unclothed Asian girl with her arms tied behind her back by a red sash. There was a story there, in that photograph I could not tell her. There was semen on the girl's skin as well as the inside of Noemi's thighs. I closed my eyes and tried desperately to hide in the tenderness of the skin beneath her collarbone.

"Leave those people. Stay with me," she said, my head then resting across her breasts. I assured her I would and slept for over an hour as her fingertips traced tiny lines over the burn, the imperfections below my clavicle that represented God, but meant something else altogether.

*Who was I?*

*William McCoy, convicted arsonist responsible for the deaths of nine church parishioners in Pittsburgh in 1999. As previously stated, wanted for the destruction of an abortion clinic in 1997. First arrested in 1995 for trespassing on private property with other protestors at a woman's clinic in Alabama. Current whereabouts unknown. Currently on Federal Bureau of Investigations domestic terrorist list.*

The burn inflicted on my shoulder was almost seven inches across and augmented to resemble the visage of the Virgin Mary. That was the way an in-depth psychological profile suggested an agent be introduced to the people who claimed responsibility for the arson related destruction of several women's clinics in the south in 1993. Their motives were based on religious grounds. That same group was also believed to be responsible for eleven deliberate fires in at least eight different states. Initially their actions had only damaged property.

Yet their intentions had escalated to include intimidation, assault and murder. Three people were killed in a fire that ripped through a woman's clinic and ruined an adjacent building which housed painting supplies. It happened over a year ago in Mississippi. Notes retrieved at three of the crime scenes referenced specific passages in the bible written on the backs of religious postcards. The photographs were of paintings. The arsonists believed their actions were based on the word of God and his disciples. Fanaticism bred hate. And that strict disregard and contempt would only widen and burn.

The F.B.I. involved me and decided to manipulate that scar. Attempts were made to use stage makeup, but being around the intense heat of fires made the chemicals run and dissipate. Nothing we tried was believable enough. So we accentuated the existing blemish through a delicate procedure with the advisement of a plastic surgeon specializing in skin reconstruction and graphing at a burn center in Washington, D.C. The Virgin Mary soon appeared on the muscles and skin underneath my right shoulder and I became a domestic terrorist, an arsonist, her miracle visage serving as William McCoy's guide.

Soon William McCoy was arrested at protests in Alabama, Arkansas, Louisiana and Missouri. Whenever I ended up sharing a cell with other protestors and anti-abortionists, I bled out my political views and was vocal when the opportunity presented itself. Opinions became familiar, but not oppressive. I never asked questions about further staged protests or marches, never spoke about hate or retribution. Not right away.

I absorbed information, read their doctrines from pamphlets handed to me at rallies. I blended in. During a protest in Missouri though, that became marred by violence, I was stabbed along my hip with a hunting knife. I never saw who did it. The blade missed any major organs and hadn't penetrated deeply. Large numbers of police were called in to restore order and most of the protestors on both sides of the political spectrum were incarcerated. In the cell, I removed my shirt and used it to temper the bleeding some. People noticed the scar inches underneath of my collarbone and a small biblical passage affixed by a tattoo.

People were always looking for someone else to lead them. That was what made a desperate person the most unpredictable and threatening. It was hot in the cell surrounded by 25 or 30 other protestors. At the rear, I examined the people, wondering if the faction leader was present here with the rest of his or her followers. A woman at the rear of the crowd shouted. It was hard to understand what she was saying as I was lead out of the cell and transported to the hospital. All I heard her say as the doors closed behind me was the word 'hope.'

To the anti-abortionists in Missouri I had intended to infiltrate, I represented assurance the tasks they were undertaking were righteous. The scar and biblical passages altered on the areas of skin below my shoulder only strengthened their determination. When I was released from the hospital and processed, a faction member came to the hotel where I registered. I had been residing there for almost a week. Paid in cash. No receipts. The gun I carried I placed inside an air conditioning vent behind the headboard. Still bleeding through gauze, I reached out to open the door. I grabbed a towel, draped it over my shoulder and pulled at the latch. Standing in front of me was a beautiful young woman, small manila envelopes hanging in her hand.

"William McCoy?"

"What do you want?" I hadn't seen her in the crowd at the clinic or at any of the previous protests. She hesitated for a moment, moved through me and closed the door behind her. Dark blood soaked through my white undershirt. I thought of Noemi spreading raspberry preserves over a fresh piece of toasted bread.

"What do you think you're doing?" I asked.

"You're no good to us if you can't get that bleeding to stop," she said. I switched on the light to the bathroom and glanced up at the mirror. Over my shoulder I watched her. She studied me, uncertain and touched the flesh around the gaping wound. When she pressed down harder, blood seeped out from between the stitches and ran down the inside of my thighs. Leaving me to pull my jeans down to expose my hip, she grabbed the towels sitting on the back of the toilet. Her fingertips moved away from the wound and across my stomach. I closed my eyes. I shouldn't have, but I allowed that woman's hands to explore the muscles below my shoulders. She traced the outline of the scar and whispered something I could not hear. I hesitated and pulled away from her. But it should have been sooner.

"Who are you?" I asked. Besides being alluring she was very composed and self-assured, almost arrogant to a point. I watched her move back into the bedroom and sit down in a chair tucked into the corner near the heater. Some blood remained on her palm. She rubbed them together. I didn't know her name. But I knew exactly what she was. A misguided pigeon and a diseased carrier of false promises.

"Let me ask the questions," she demanded.

"Get out," I said.

"People told me you'd be obstinate."

"People? What people? How did you know who I was and where to find me?"

129

I noticed she uncrossed her legs as she edged closer to the end of the chair. The movement exposed her pale cleavage. "We've been monitoring your activities let's say for almost a few years now. You brought a little bit of attention to yourself at that protest and in prison. But that's not what we would want from someone like you."

"We? What do you want from me?" I asked. In her environment, she had power. It was obvious in the way she moved her body and never searched around the room. There was no nervousness in her actions or mannerisms. Someone had to have been watching the motel for at least a couple of days. At least one or two others were outside somewhere. She watched me tear open the side and slide out a small parchment of paper. On the inside of the envelope were a time and a location imprinted on the back side of a religious postcard. "What's this?" I retreated into the bathroom and laid the bloody towel in the corner of the floor. Waiting for her to respond, I looked into the mirror and examined the wound. It would no doubt leave another scar. At this point I was nothing more than an anatomical map of apprehension and misplaced self-worth.

"Something you can get for us," she said. She remained quiet after that. I had to let the situation run its course. Someone who had been this cautious wasn't going to give me everything here. "It's nothing you haven't done before," she added.

"You don't know me," I opposed.

"Yes I do William," she said. "You were first arrested in 1995 for trespassing during an abortion rally in Alabama. Those were the first 24 hours you spent in prison. You resurfaced in 1997 and were wanted in questioning for the torching of a woman's clinic in Oklahoma. Then you murdered nine church parishioners in 1999," she added. She believed the identity of William McCoy was genuine. As soon would I.

"I don't know what you're talking about," I said.

"Yes you do. Small town outside of Pittsburgh. I saw the police photographs from that church fire," she began, standing from the edge of the chair. "All those sinners. Some of them had their hands still pressed together in prayer. The irony of that situation wasn't lost on any of us. It was beautiful. It took the A.T.F. almost eight months to determine it was deliberate. What did you use? Kerosene? Butane?" I turned away from her and pulled a shirt across my chest.

"Whatever you want from me, believe me. You don't want to know who I am," I said in a threatening tone, taking a few deliberate steps closer to her. I wasn't going to seem eager, hungry. She never wavered, only gripped the envelope in her hand tighter. Ending up only a few feet from me, she traced the edge along a portion of my neck.

"Who are you?" she asked.

Who was I?

"I'm no one," I said.

"No you're not William. You are someone else entirely or I wouldn't be here," she said as she came around behind me and touched the back of my neck. "You're a monster." I had been a criminal so long, kept away from the consistent and tender caress of my wife. Instead of becoming a deeper part of her and our marriage, I retreated, sought refuge in the fragmented identities of savage men I was becoming a part of more and more every day. The door closed behind her and I lingered in the temporary darkness of the room.

Instructions she had given me led me to an abandoned building approximately 25 miles north of the motel. I parked my car behind a gas station about three miles previous and made my way through the woods. The area around the building was poorly lit, but I immediately noticed a rear exit, a small window, the glass broken in. If something happened it was to be my way out. There was an old heating oil tank attached to the building, the side caved in. I took an unmarked handgun out of an ankle strap and placed it inside of the tank. Leading from the front of the building was a soiled path that stretched into the surrounding foliage. It would be another two hours before I would resurface and go in.

There were seven cars surrounding the structure. I noted a few of the license plates before stepping out of the car. Most of them would lead nowhere. In all likelihood they would match different makes and models, almost all reported stolen. One man stood outside. When I approached the entrance he stepped in front of me. Glancing behind me, he squeezed his right hand inside his pocket. It was apparent he had a gun.

"Tell her I'm here," I said and handed him her message from the postcard.

Keeping his attention focused on me, he leaned back and rapped against the rusted metal door. It wasn't part of the original construction of the building. When it slid back, she was standing on the other side. The woman patted the man on the shoulder and he pulled his hand away from the gun.

"He's ok," she said.

The door slammed shut behind me and the echo reverberated throughout the vacant room. Another man stepped forward and patted me down to see I wasn't carrying any weapons. The hope I carried to discover materials and schematics were quickly doused. In all, eight people occupied the space, along with several rusted water heaters and folding chairs. Several were empty. I wondered if there were others that hadn't arrived. It was there I was given instructions. Yet, it was difficult to get additional information. No one talked except for the woman.

"I hope you took precautions to see that you weren't followed. I wasn't sure you'd come," she admitted.

"What do you want?"

"Help. Plain and simple. We need someone fresh, unique. Most of the people in our organization have become too visible over the last year."

"Too visible for what?" It was all I could get her to say. The group needed plans for a local building, sprinkler systems, alarm systems, details of lock mechanisms, construction materials, dimly lit entry points. It wasn't anything difficult to obtain. I repeated my question. After nonverbal deliberation with some of the others in her group, she responded.

"Too visible to be seen in public, at protests," she acknowledged. "Without attracting attention, the kind we don't want or need. Can you get this for us?" she asked.

"You could get this yourself. Most of what you need you can obtain from the internet or local courthouse. It's all a matter of public record," I assured her.

"Our organization would like to have your services," she stated. "Your, let's say philosophy and previous practices have a lot in common with ours."

"I don't give a damn about your politics," I said.

"Yes you do," she said. She moved out from behind a tattered desk and ended up behind me again. Carefully she raised my shirt higher and traced her fingertips over the Virgin Mary. "Wasn't it your mother that did this to you?" she questioned. "She burned you with an iron. The woman who nurtured you singed the delicate pockets of your flesh. Instead of comforting a child, she punished." William McCoy had a past and her people had uncovered all the lies. I never said a word. She was selling, recruiting. And I let her. "She was a regular parishioner at that church in Pittsburgh. How many times did you watch her go into that house of worship before you decided to act, to clean yourself and her of all that culpability, of all that hate? She had an abortion once didn't she? And now you scorch everything you see. It's beautiful."

"I never killed those people," I said. It might have been the last piece of truth I ever uttered.

"The A.T.F., the F.B.I. and several other agencies seem to think you do. Interpol has an extensive file on you. It would only take one anonymous phone call telling them where we found you. Or we could not let you leave this building alive and deliver your corpse right to their doorstep. The thunder of God could crash down all over this place," she said.

"I don't seem to have much of a choice then, do I?"

"Not from the way we see it," she said. "But there's no need to be combative because in the long run our goals are almost identical."

"When do you need the information?" I asked.

"Two days."

"Getting the information is one thing. How can I trust you know what to do with it?" I said.

"What do you mean?" she said.

"Fires are started and less than three minutes later the authorities are still tearing through your doorstep no matter how cautious. It's not enough to make it look like an accident," I said.

"Our group doesn't care about that. Our only concern is the message itself."

"Your only concern should be remaining under the radar," I said. "I don't want caught because one of your people wasn't particular enough. This isn't for fucking amateurs."

"What do you want from us?" she asked.

"The plan of operation no less than an hour before it starts," I admitted.

"When you have the information we need we can discuss it," she said.

"When do I contact you?"

"You don't. I'll find you," she said. She handed me a disposable cellular phone programmed to receive calls, no more. The next morning she did.

Using an accelerant very rare and hard to trace, the vacant Missouri clinic burned quickly, the intense heat of the incendiary fire pouring into the night sky. The beast raged. The dried shrubs around the building wilted. Paint dripped along the walls and appeared as tears falling from the face of a Roman statue. Instead of decomposing, fire sterilized the world of disease and impurity. Moreover, it left nothing behind. It lit up the night sky like a bright sunset spilled from the tabletop of the clouds. She painted a biblical verse on the stamped pavement of the parking lot. In the unoccupied spaces unblemished by ash I observed her.

The winds pulled at the smoke, coiled it, and turned it from side to side. The darkened core of the fire widened, the incandescence eclipsing the pale tranquility of her eyes and transitioning them to something different altogether. I moved closer to the burning building. The heat stretched and embraced me. It felt baptizing, complacent. It changed the texture of my skin. The smoke burned the inside of my throat. She moved closer, cinders settling against the delicate structure of her pallor like patterns in a black snow. The clothes she chose were similar to those Noemi wore the weekend of her sister's wedding. The blouse burned a brilliant sage against the intense oxidization. Portions of the engulfed building collapsed behind her.

Her people scattered as the rest of the building except for a lone wall laid in ruin. William McCoy could be a thing of the past, an abject nightmare recounted in a training textbook. I thought I'd be able to burn down a few more vacant buildings and move on. She wouldn't let me. And for some reason, I wouldn't let myself. I watched her, sweat streaming down her face, her dark nipples pressing through the blouse. She was spinning around in circles like a child, an adolescent of darkness. Sirens began to sound in the distance. When she stood in front of me, she reached up her hands and wiped the sweat and ash from the sides of my face with her right palm. I watched her open her lips and lick away the grime.

"It's time to go," I said. She took my hand and led me to a stolen car parked less than a mile away a member of her organization had left for her.

The next morning she led me into her bed.

~

Soot and cinders escaped the edges of the flames and landed on the hardwood floor of our living room. The small bursts of wood expanding in the fireplace echoed like gunshots throughout. The flames seemed to stop twitching against the stone. I looked out the window, beyond our chronology and my uncertainty. Rain which had been falling against the pavement drifted into an unfamiliar pattern, like it didn't understand its nature, what it should do. Above the fireplace on a floating shelf were shadowboxes, photographs of Noemi and I captured during that weekend her sister got married in Morro Bay.

Time succumbed when she was near, paralyzed into an infinite stillness by the depths of her compassion and her unyielding altruism. Our living room was humid and the confinement choked me. There should have been genuine happiness here, laughter and tears prevalent in her face and smile caused by love and children. She looked so beautiful. Her sundress was a robin's egg blue, offset by patterns of pale yellow flowers. On another woman it may have appeared ostentatious. But hanging over her shoulders and exposing her neckline, it made her demure and unassuming. I remembered how confident she was then, holding my hand, never affected by the impatience I carried in posing for photographs. I never wanted recognized, forever being the cautious handler's care.

The waters behind us on that small island never moved, ceased to even twitch under the boldness of the sunset. It was unique to me, seeing so many empty boats resting on its surface. They were idle decorations. We looked so imposing standing in front of that enormous rock hundreds of yards behind us. For some reason I couldn't get comfortable in the suit she picked out for me, the collar of the carmine dress shirt leaving marks around my neck. Out on the deck of the restaurant a polite breeze blew in off the sea, cooling the cup of coffee in my hand. I moved closer to that picture. The wisps of steam from the cup were seen in the detail. With my back to the water I watched a father hold his daughter against his chest her tiny fingers tugging at his lower lip. I could read his. He asked his daughter who is this. Who is this? We would never have children because of what happened there In Morro Bay.

*Who was I?*

*Johnathan Levin. Arrested in June for indecent exposure when sighted masturbating in public inside an alley located behind a state store. Wanted currently for questioning in the disappearances and murders of several children in Pennsylvania. Considered to be a person of interest in at least two other disappearances. Whereabouts unknown, although reports lead the authorities to believe he is travelling up and down the East coast.*

There were continual neighborhood watches organized by parents. Men and women walked the darkened streets at night with flashlights. It looked like a constant state of Halloween every day. Except no costumes were modeled and people were too frightened to open their doors. The only candy around was a stick of gum in the back pocket of a father. It was so flattened he couldn't remember how long it had been there. I slid back the curtains in the living room and turned off the few lights Noemi had left that afternoon before going to her parents. I locked the front door and called a handler. Although I had to admit there wasn't much information I could pass on to him.

For over a month starting at the end of May after the discovery of a fifth body, I began researching a different angle about the local child murders. Sometimes children kidnapped were sold on-line to other sexual predators. So that's what I had been examining while Noemi spent much of her time in New York trying to restore her stalling career. On weekends she came home to teach, but hadn't maintained that routine in a couple of weeks when she cancelled classes. Dirty dishes looked like fossils piled high in the sink. I missed her. I was no longer the man I promised her I would be.

Wishing to crawl deeper into that realm, I dropped a couple of ice cubes into a glass and opened a bottle of scotch. Leaving the kitchen, I passed through the living room and stoked the fireplace. I missed watching her read in front of the fire in the winter. There were several photos from that wedding in Morro Bay I noticed when I replaced the poker. I longed for the warm glow of the flames to highlight the curves of her body, cast shadows upon the already darkened places I wanted to relearn, rescue and bring back with me into the light. It was the weekend before her sister's wedding the bare thread to the case unraveled and what remained behind was a crumpled and disgusting truth.

Countless of nights I waited as photographs of children for sale flashed across my laptop. The first thing I was looking for were any pictures of the murdered children. It wasn't an absolute certainty, but I thought one or more of them were abducted by someone who lived nearby and then sold to another pedophile. Crime scene descriptions were on a legal pad and reading parts of it made me uncertain. The forensic discoveries didn't match to what I believed happened.

Each scene, each murder seemed too personal to be a sexual appetite spun out of control. Mull believed in that conclusion. But the trauma to the corpses was significant, never an accidental act of malice. It was brutality in its most pure form, not misguided urges of love or passion. Children living in sexual slavery were unfortunately common in other countries, but it existed in a more underground way in the United States. They actually numbered in the tens of thousands. People didn't want to think a parent could sell their child to what I had attempted to become. Not here.

There were so many areas where an individual could go, an individual like Johnathan Levin. Sorting through thousands of photographs of exploited children was unbearable. It was nothing more than an arid wasteland of fetishism and ravaged innocence, an amoral flea market of flesh. The children in the photographs sent to me varied in race and age. One young girl, around 15 was on sale. $10,000. She was dressed in a light yellow shirt, her hair pulled to one side, a man's hand draped across her shoulder. She was scared. It was apparent in the placement of her hands, the subtle angle in which she held her head. Something about her I recognized. There were no names underneath any of the photographs though, only numbers. I saved the file and increased the canvas size. The young girl was under duress. It wasn't clear, but she appeared bound to a chair around the ankles.

In subsequent stills I tried to place where I thought I had seen her previously. A second photograph showed a man's hands raising her dress higher on her thighs, her light colored underwear visible. One individual described the girl as a unique bud soon burgeoning, blossoming. That each one merely needed cultivated. I swallowed hard and stood. Beads of sweat fell into the empty glass at the bottom of the kitchen sink. I thought about calling Noemi in New York. I wouldn't know what to say to her though. It would have condemned her to live in the same filth and corruption I did, suffocated by horrors she would never see coming. And I loved her too much for that. The hand towel I used to dry my face smelled like honeysuckle.

*Each one merely needed cultivated...*

~

Two weeks had passed since I first saw that girl's photograph. It troubled me, unable to ascertain her identity. In grocery stores I would see her pass the end of an aisle or ride off in the passenger side of a minivan. At times she would ride by the front of our house on a bicycle. She never spoke, but I imagined her voice was soft and inoffensive. I requested more revealing images of her. I had also corresponded with several individuals offering to sell or buy a child and provided images given to me. None of the children existed, each fabricated, free of the burden of misuse and neglect. Opposing were the remaining images of that girl in the yellow dress.

There was only one I remembered in excruciating detail. There were actually about 40 in all, but the same reproduction overlapped and bled into the next. Even when she wore different clothes in succeeding prints, I always saw that yellow dress, the ones with the pale flowers scattered across the waist. The girl was on her knees up against a corner in a barren room with little furniture. Paint must have chipped off of the wall. There were flecks of white on the left side of her face. Her hands were bound behind her back. There was a man behind her, his hands gripping her buttocks. He was about to insert his cock into her. There were no distinguishing features about him, scars or tattoos. What made me forget the other photos was the dead lily he must have forced into her mouth after he tied her up. There were tears in her eyes.

*Each one merely needed cultivated...*

There were no judgments issued in a case like this. Some of the things I said in those transcripts frightened me. There wasn't a choice. I thought again about calling New York. Would she understand how it made me feel to tell some pervert I wanted to buy a video of an 11- year-old girl engaging in anal sex? That I got turned on by watching a 50-year old man

138

insert his fingers into a young girl's vagina? I could never tell her how horrifying and crippling it was to pretend to want to fuck a 12-year-old girl and then go to bed with her. I reached out to my handler and passed over what I had discovered, giving him IP addresses and portions of the dialogues I maintained with some suspected pedophiles were being reread. But I hadn't forwarded him everything. Not when I remembered where I had seen her, that girl in the yellow dress.

I didn't establish the connection because the last photographs I had seen her in were taken inside of a small, brightly lit room surrounded by metal tables. Instruments were laid out next to her on a tray. I could no longer determine what color her dress was. It didn't look yellow, but jaundiced. The flowers patterned along her waistline had wilted, ligature marks scattered across her wrist and ankles.

It was her autopsy photo. I discovered it in the back of the file.

Penelope was the third victim found dumped into an abandoned grain silo. I wasn't sure why I didn't hand over that photograph. In some abstract way I identified with her, isolated and abused, trapped by the animalistic nature of the human condition. Or I didn't want her mother to have to look at her child like that, when all the hope she ever had for her disappeared into the inhumanity of another. I sorted through the rest of the file. There were other photographs of her. One taken at her conformation. Another in the room at the hospital when she was born. She was beautiful. It said in the notes when her parents were questioned she wanted to be an agriculturalist. They reported her missing after she never arrived at a friend's house.

I scattered the images captured at the crime scene across the kitchen table. By all accounts the surrounding area was properly searched by a team of forensic experts. I pushed them aside and stared at her naked and stitched like a rag doll. I reread through the autopsy report. Traces of blood, stool and grain were embedded underneath her fingernails. She was penetrated several times prior her death. I dropped the empty glass into the sink and retreated into the living room. More cinders had drifted from the hearth. I leaned over and tried to wipe them away, but they remained, then dissipated. It played out like a crime scene, the shape my fingertips made trying to wipe them up, resembled the ashen color of her body's outline, arms outstretched reaching, but for what I wasn't sure.

~

We were in Morro Bay for almost a week. Noemi believed we needed the time together. Overall, there were 14 men and women working to apprehend a suspect. I left the number to the hotel with my handler if they should discover another body. The place where we stayed was quaint and still considered an active and functioning fishing village. She and I dined often at a small seafood place recommended to us that specialized in local lobster and crab. I could smell the ocean no matter where we went, even in the warmth of that little bakery in the middle of town. At night the atmosphere was beautiful, the sun setting behind that large rock we were photographed in front of. There wasn't much to do except peruse local shops and enjoy the local landscapes. It was quiet and I wasn't sure exactly who to be.

Part of what identified me unfortunately was the noise that accompanied me, a deafening sense of dread and malice disguising itself in the gulls coming with the morning sunrise. As much as I struggled to, I couldn't put the case aside. There was no way to offset the dejection and the suffering that came with it, even here. Noemi went for drinks with her sister and cousins at a pub at the end of the pier. I waited for her to leave and then powered up the laptop I had been using during the investigation. I leaned against the rail of the balcony adjacent our room and opened up a file on the most recent body recovered, the fifth. There was a gentle breeze coming in off of the water.

The violence inflicted on the most recent victim was disturbing, with over 60 lacerations to the face and neck. The coroner couldn't exactly determine what kind of blade was used. No weapon had been found. No trace fingerprints were located on any parts of the body. The victim had been bound and gagged as several ligature marks were discovered around the feet, neck and ankles. I studied the crime scene images. Noemi wanted to learn aspects of photography to supplement her teaching. If she took my photograph I often wondered what she would see. But no matter how deformed and conflicted I felt, nothing from her perspective could ever be unforgiving. It was hard to tell if the body photographed at the edge of the riverbed was even a boy.

Half of his face was gone. There was a large gash below his nose which had split his upper lip like an open zipper. Several of his teeth had been removed, but not enough to inhibit identification. Sediment from the riverbed was embedded underneath his fingernails. It was also depressed into various wounds throughout the body, including in the throat. Samples included traces of clay, mud, sandstone and obsidian. I reopened the forensic files on the first three victims.

Traces of mud, clay and feces were listed in the report as well. The difference in the fifth victim was his body was in the water for the least amount of time, only a few minutes before it was drug to the shore. His body was wrapped in mesh, especially around the neck, which could have restricted his larynx. There was no explanation from the coroner on how mud and soil lined the throat unless it was swallowed during a struggle with the perpetrator or inserted before death, unless the victim was in water previous to the attempts to dispose of the body. I reopened the explicit images of the third victim, Penelope.

I brooded about seeing her in those positions again, but it was the best lead I had. I concentrated on the background of each photograph. There was nothing unique or distinguishing in the rooms. Each had no window, no reflections I could have enlarged. I studied the extremities of her body, especially the feet and hands. Laughter echoed in the empty streets below our hotel room window. I stood at the edge of the balcony. To the right of the railing rested a small flower, planted in a copper container. I reached over and pushed my hand into the soil, rubbing it over and over against my palm with my thumb. Uneasy, I closed the balcony door and looked at that photograph of Penelope, her hands tied behind her back. The image of that wilted lily inserted into her mouth.

*Each one merely needed cultivated…*

I sent instructions to have the sediment retested and compared against plant fertilizers, landscape mulch, seeding, as well as samples taken from the scene. I went into the bathroom to wash the dirt from my hands. The warm water blended gray. With a light bulb missing from the fixture above the sink my features looked darker, burnt. It was if I had been in a fire.

*Who was I?*

*William McCoy, arsonist. Wanted for questioning in the suspicious burning of a government building in Florida. Currently linked to a group of anti-abortionists in Alabama. Last official sighting was over four months ago in Missouri. Listed as a person of interest in the arson related burning of a clinic in Mississippi that killed two people in an adjacent building, a hardware store. The fire jumped as a result of the high winds and engulfed the building. The victims were a man, 54 and his son, 22. The store was supposed to be unoccupied at that time of night.*

I dropped the rubber gloves into a dumpster behind a gas station at the corner. In the distance behind a grove of trees, trails of smoke separated into the strong winds. Headlights flickered in the street from oncoming traffic. I pushed myself up against the side of the dumpster and watched her disappear under the streetlights into an untended field. A second degree burn marred my left hand. I winced as I opened and closed it. Things had gotten worse.

Her group had ended up in Mississippi as part of a protest against a new women's clinic opening in a small suburb outside of Hattiesburg. She brought me along, but gave me as little information as possible about the specifics. All I was told was where to meet her and a fraction of a list of supplies I needed to bring. Once I arrived, there would be an envelope presented to me by one of her members giving me further directions. No one expected me to bring her group in quickly. I needed more names, identities, other possible targets. There had to be more. It would come. But I could only live in the filth for so long before I started to rot. And it all started with the smallest of things.

Less than an hour after we torched that clinic in Missouri, she ditched the stolen car in a vacant lot and burned it. The structure had been completely gutted, but no injuries were reported. Her people had arranged a different hotel for me already registered with another false persona. I wasn't surprised. I had expected controlled or held under suspicion. I dropped my bag at the side of the bed and switched on the bathroom light. I slid back the shower liner a few inches and twisted the faucet. When the showerhead opened up, the warm water stuttered against the cracked tile.

I tasted smoke at the back of my throat. I stripped down and stood in front of the mirror, tapping my fist against the edge of the sink. William McCoy wasn't a god. He was a fabrication, a distortion. I could have arrested her already. There was enough evidence to attain a conviction. It was obvious by her inconsistent behavior the woman was disturbed. Part of me thought she was more dangerous than her group realized. But I never imagined compromising her would lead to the deaths of innocent people.

I wrapped a rough towel around my waist and knelt down on the floor. Looking up, I noticed someone stride past the door. I reached underneath the mattress and pulled out a gun. The shower was still running and the bathroom had begun to be lost behind a thin cloud of steam. The shadows paused at the threshold to the room. An envelope appeared under the door. I waited for the person to walk away then crouched down and retrieved it. There was nothing written on the outside. I sat down on the edge of the bed, the gun still loaded beside me. I opened the envelope. There was a Polaroid picture on the inside. It was an artist's depiction of the Virgin Mary holding a child scarred and burnt in the palm of her hands. Displays of various flowers were set behind her. Blood dripped from some of the stems and covered her legs. Written at the bottom of the photograph was a phrase.

*The destroyer of dreams...*

I stood up and noticed movement behind me in the mirror set above an uneven dresser. There was something unnatural about the way she walked, uncommon, but luring. She seemed to drift through the warm mist circling the doorway to the bathroom. It was obvious she had come here right after ditching the car. Sweat and ash from the fire still touched her body. The hazy green color from the motel's sign made it glisten.

"I don't appreciate being monitored," I said. I showed her the gun.

"How did you know that I was in here?" she asked.

"It doesn't matter. What are you doing here?"

"You represent an investment on our part. If you're going to work with us, trust is earned," she instructed. There was a threatening tone in her diction.

"What makes you think that I trust you or any of your people?"

"I don't see that you have a lot of options. Remember other people would be very interested in talking to you," she said.

"I assume you mean federal authorities? What makes you think I wouldn't turn on your group if you put me in that position? I thought I was an investment?" I said.

"I wasn't involved in recruiting you so I don't care," she said.

"So you don't call all the shots?" I asked. It seemed to bother her I thought of her as a subordinate.

"That's irrelevant," she said, drawing back the curtains and peering out into the blackness. "When it comes to you, I do."

"And what happens if I don't want to follow instructions?" I asked.

She turned from the window and stood in front of me. Assuredly she raised her hands to the nape of my neck, lingered in her decision, then passed her fingertips down across the plane of my chest. The woman's caress was hot and rough, but arousing. She reached into her jeans. When she removed her hand I grabbed her wrist and exposed her palm. In the crux of her fingers she carried a lighter. The flare refracted off of the unique color of her eyes. She toyed with it, rolling it around in her hand, watching the thin strands of black smoke appear and disappear. Playfully she pulled at the frayed edges of the towel. Without warning, she pressed the lighter into the tight flesh of my abdomen.

"Like all those murderers, you burn," she said bending over and rolling her tongue across the red patch of blistering skin. I placed a hand around her neck and pressed my fingertips hard into her throat. She smiled, almost enjoying the violence. When I awoke several hours later, she was gone. The sheets were still soaked with her body's perspiration. In her place was another photograph of a painting. It was again a depiction of the Virgin Mary, standing on a small rock in the middle of the ocean. Floating on the calm waters were children, smoke permeating from their bodies, each one scorched black and unrecognizable. In the distance behind her point of view, flames touched the blurred edges of the clouds.

The politicians of lifelessness will burn.

The water was cold in the shower by the time I stepped in and felt its brutality across my tired skin. I scrubbed the place where she burned me so it wouldn't become infected. I closed my eyes determined not to remember where she touched me, pressed her bare breasts against my chest. I could taste her sweat on the tips of my fingers.

William McCoy was with her group in Mississippi for eight days planning. I was visible at protests with several other members while she remained inconspicuous. I was verifying schematics on building plans, architecture and materials. She wanted her fires to burn and I needed to know the building's construction to decide on an accelerant. It needed to be self-sustaining and emit a higher heat release rate, meaning it burned rapidly. Several of her groups' previous arsons left behind very little if any residual debris for forensic investigators to analyze. Whoever ran her group was educated enough to leave little evidence. The line about politicians led me to believe her group was intending to further their violence to include government buildings as well as other women's clinics. Her intentions were to complete the Mississippi job, then move on to various suburbs of Washington, D.C. I reached my handler and was instructed to continue to be William McCoy, but not to make an arrest until ordered to.

It wasn't supposed to be raining. The barren parking lot of the clinic in Hattiesburg was a river, a black tributary of asphalt and oppression. Winds increased to the point of reaching 30 miles per hour, not ideal conditions for arson. Nevertheless I stood in the shadows of a vacant building and watched her open the front door to the clinic. The alarm was already disabled. Her group was inside for less than eight minutes. I raised a hand to shield my eyes from the rain. Not long after, the front window to the clinic shattered and elongated flames erupted, pushing glass hundreds of feet into the rain soaked lot. The debris smoldered, shards of broken glass glistening against the ground. I never went inside the building.

The fire raged through every corner of the clinic. The vapor pressures inherent in the combustible accelerants made it dangerous. Only particular groups were allowed to purchase large quantities of accelerants, usually fire departments, used in training new firefighters. Most likely she used gasoline. It often ignited easily and left prominent burn patterns. Abruptly a man ran out from behind the building, his body consumed by bright, thick flames. Any screams he uttered became muffled by the sounds of burning flesh and snapping wood. Whoever it was didn't make it more than 20 feet from the building before dropping to the ground dead, his body a lifeless, ashen thing. It looked like burnt furniture.

Water pouring from the aluminum gutters rushed across my feet. It reminded me of Noemi, embracing her in our bed, listening to the rain collapse upon the roof. I remembered the first time we kissed was during a brutal thunderstorm. We had gone out to dinner and talked for so long we missed attending a musical at the high school. Instead I walked her back to her apartment. Our hands dripped, but neither one of us cared. About a block from her place, her umbrella was carried away in the high winds. She started laughing. And in that moment, I kissed her on the smooth, wet underside of her chin.

The swirling winds carried the flames into the trees above the clinic. I grabbed her by the hand and told her we had to leave. She kept looking down at the body. It would take weeks for anyone to identify the remains of her group member. It would give me some time. As she dropped to her knees and I started to pull her aside, the adjacent building began to burn. It was a hardware store. No one was supposed to be there in the middle of the night. With the weather, no one could hear the screams.

~

By the time Noemi came home with her sister I had drifted to sleep. Keeping the lights off, she stripped off her clothes and nestled her body behind mine. I felt her lips find the soft spot below my neck.

"I love you," she said.

"I know."

"You've been quiet since we got here. Is everything okay? I know the place is different," she said.

"It's not the town. It's quiet," I said. "It's been a while since I've felt like this," I added.

"Felt like what?" I rolled over and pulled her across my frame. She rested her head on my chest.

"I'm not sure how to describe it. Calm, I guess." I wondered if she felt the lies on the tender surface of my body.

"I don't make you feel calm?"

"You do. You're the only thing to me that's beautiful," I said. Noemi raised her head and wrapped her hand around and took hold of my neck. In the darkness she kissed me, pressed her tongue inside of my mouth. I should have told her, everything. It was an opportunity where I could have been honest with her about what was happening to me. I fumbled my lips over her naked body and playfully touched her breasts. I didn't want to speak. It was quiet except for the soft sound of her ecstasy. More than once she guided me inside of her, tried to keep me safe from my own vulnerability.

When images of Penelope's rape rushed in, Noemi enveloped the structure of my body, tore at me with tenacity and violence without understanding. When she paused, I asked her again and again. Don't stop. I licked the prone places on her stomach and bit at the warm flesh on her hips. She moved to her knees and I held her hands tight at the wrists behind her back. Noemi begged me to be forceful. Harder. I gave in and penetrated her, as Penelope had been, with disregard and hate. I wasn't even sure who I was, Jonathan Levin or her husband. I didn't even know if I was hurting her.

"You never done that before," she said as she licked some of the perspiration off of the small of my back. I could feel her heart pulsating through my bones.

"What?" I asked. I was questioning what she would think of me, doing that to her.

"Been rough like that," she said, reaching her hands underneath of my body and rubbing my cock. I closed my eyes. I was going to say I was sorry, but I didn't because part of me enjoyed what happened. And so had she. Noemi pressed her breasts against the curves of my back. She leaned closer behind my head and whispered into my ear. "Fuck me again," she said.

We never learn anything about ourselves throughout the course of our lives. Actually, that's a lie. We do. But what is isn't always redeeming. Tendencies linger to repeat agonizing mistakes and painful lessons. There's no getting around it. The men I became changed me. It wasn't difficult to distinguish. The colors on the canvas of existence do though change or fade over time. They don't turn out to be as bold or shine as once promised. No one loves as hoped, nor respects as earned. In the end, betrayal of self was a consistency, a lover always there the next morning. Only you wished they had gone off in the middle of the night, hoping to avoid the awkwardness of the morning when you watched them walk away, unsure of what exactly to say. I thought about it when I let William McCoy bed a sadistic arsonist. I thought about it when I took Noemi. It wasn't the carnality or the passion of the act, but the way it happened.

"It won't happen again." That was all I wanted her to hear.

"Why? I'm asking you to," she said.

"I can't," I said.

"Can't or won't?"

"Don't ask me again, please." I slid out from underneath her body. "It made me uncomfortable," I added.

"Is there someone else?" I reached up and held my hand to her cheek for several minutes. The directness of the question startled me.

"No," I assured her. Hours had passed and we were both still naked atop the sheets. The sea air was intrusive, but soothing. There were dimples on her skin. I covered her legs and stepped into the bathroom. It was late, but I retrieved a razor from my luggage and shaved. In the action I hoped I could step from the unrecognizable into a creature of familiarity. I leaned over the sink and washed hot water over the exhaustiveness of my features. When I went back into the room, Noemi was out of bed, standing naked in front of the window. I went to drape a sheet over her body.

"No, don't," she said. I stood behind her and kissed the top of her shoulders. I pressed my body deeper into hers. She said she wanted to take my photograph. Noemi turned to look at me and touched the side of my face. Her hands traced the full contours of my body, trailed along the sides of my waist, descended across my legs. It felt like she was seeing me naked for the first time, acting as an unfamiliar lover. My body appeared written in Braille. Noemi's fingertips tapped the muscles in my abdomen before massaging my cock, rigid under her caress. I watched her sit on the edge of the bed and secure her camera. I stood with my back to her where she had been and stared out into the water. I wanted to turn around and ask for her help, plead for her forgiveness. She told me she loved me. I wanted to tell her I was disfigured. She told me I was beautiful. It would be the last time she would say that to me in that regard.

"God, you are so beautiful," she said, her voice trailing off behind me. The shutter on her camera opened then closed. The moonlight dripped from the ceiling and onto my body. The graphic images of those children I watched appeared in the dimming bursts of light from her camera. Noemi moved to my right and took another picture in profile. I must have looked defeated because she stood in front of me and licked the patch of skin under my lower lip.

"I want to take a picture of your face, close enough so I can see inside of you," she said.

"The flash won't be enough. It's too dark. Let me turn on the light above the bed." She reached out her hand and interlocked her fingers in mine.

"No. It won't matter. I know the details of your features, your flaws. I can recognize them even in the dark. They're important to me. Everything about always has been." Noemi adjusted her head, nestled against my frame and whispered into my ear. I couldn't bring myself to repeat what she had said.

While I struggled with the decision what to tell her, she stood back from me and depressed a button on the front of the camera. I wasn't ready to live with the weight of the consequences if I told her. I closed my eyes. When she developed the negative I wondered who she would see, staring back at her in reversed and achromatic perspective; a burglar, an arsonist, a pedophile or a husband. Each characteristic, each individual was oppressive to the point of suffocation. I struggled to breathe let alone be whom I was supposed to be. For a brief moment she put the camera down on the edge of the bed and went into the bathroom. The light flipped on and I listened to the pipes cough before the water jetted in the shower. It wasn't long after when someone knocked at the door. I covered up and opened it. On the floor in the hallway was a newspaper. I pulled it back inside and unfolded it. There was a note inside. They had found another body.

~

I could smell her shampoo. The scent was within reach in the bathwater. It dripped across her shoulders and through her hair as I stretched my fingers untangling her curls between them. Her skin felt unfamiliar, foreign. She leaned her head back against my chest. Our bodies were delicate and still, continuous underneath the surface. I never imagined she would have been comfortable in our intimacy after I told her what I did. Noemi rubbed my legs and pulled them across her lap. Her index finger traced circles around the gunshot wound across my kneecap.

*Who was I?*

*Peter McDonnally, small time con artist and serial bank robber. Wanted for questioning in the attempted theft of over $125,000 in jewelry in Los Angeles. Arrest warrant issued in Florida for his participation in the holdup of an armored car. Police have yet to determine how much money was missing. Last seen in the city of Chicago.*

Being involved in the depths of corruption and lies altered the delicate perceptions I developed about humanity itself. Man was barbaric and violent in aspects I never imagined. No matter how much I struggled to, I could never be what I once was to her, unadulterated and strong. The part that got lost in the corporeal components was the emotion, the violent and piercing response to deceit, murder and rape. It caused empathy to burst through every inch of my body. But that was dangerous. And it could kill. I couldn't be weak or compromising, lest it burn through the facades I attempted to manipulate under the guise of what was wrong and what was right. Though the water was warm and clear I could see nothing, but pollution and disease. It was hard to see her like that, so stunning and resplendent, but so close to something unnatural and appalling.

The latest victim was discovered in a pond on a large farm. The photographs of the crime scene sent to me were hard to analyze as a pounding rainstorm had enveloped the area making it difficult to ascertain footprints, points of entry and physical evidence that wasn't compromised. The streaks of rain coming through the temporary spectrum of light blanketed the tall stalks of corn. It was a mess. Forensics was already instructed to go back in the morning if the weather broke. But it would be futile. There was a photograph included of the victim found naked and face up on the water. She was the first person discovered without clothing. I was struck by the horrible intimacy involved. Usually sexually motivated crimes resulted in strangulation, a lurid closeness to the victim, an encompassment or embrace. Opposing was the fact each victim was mutilated or violated by an instrument causing death. It didn't fit the profile. Noemi pulled away from me, reaching for the faucet. The hot water rushed out and I felt the warmth slide through the spaces between my toes.

"What's happening?" she asked.

"I don't know," I said. I told her about some of what I had been investigating. But I still lied to her. Noemi read the papers, but never visualized the brutality, the disgusting details of each murdered child. I never told her initially about Penelope or the other images in some of those photographs. It would have disturbed her to realize I had imagined being aroused by such depravity. And if she would have seen I had taken her in the same way Penelope had been, I would have lost her and all the things we accomplished so far would have faded as her moist fingerprints did from the ceramic tiles. She stood up out of the water and nudged in behind me. I wanted to reach out and stroke the inside of her shimmering thigh, but I didn't. I felt her drip water across my back, her hands falling towards my buttocks, but touching the scar below my shoulder blade.

"Did it hurt?" she asked. The therapist I had seen asked me that same question. The department maintained motivated counselors for its employees, especially those affected by tragedy. Most of the time the discussions were with people who had to discharge their weapons. Besides the internal investigations to see if proper procedure was followed, employees were subjected to emotional ones as well. Decades of exceptional performance could be overshadowed by the remains left behind. Unfortunately, William McCoy's collateral damage was attached to my body, my bones, carried with me wherever I went. There was nothing I could do to get rid of it.

"No," I said. "Most of it was already dead tissue." All my body was becoming necrotic, diseased and broken down layers of epidermis, rough and unforgiving like the husk of a dried fruit. I was a desert. Even the subtle caress of her lips across my flesh would leave her dying of thirst. Noemi told me to turn around and face her. She held my damaged hand. The chemical burn covered a large portion of my wrist and forearm.

"What happened here?" she asked. I tried to pull my hand from hers, but the movement only strengthened her embrace. She closed her eyes and rolled my imperfections across the nape of her moist neck.

"The winds were high and some of the accelerant they used became ignited," I said. The image of my arm raging in umber shades under a drenching rain made me flinch.

"So they were burning down abortion clinics?"

"Yes," I said. Noemi kept looking at my hand and for a brief moment I thought I detected pity in her tender fingers. It wasn't for me I thought, but for the questions it raised. When I told her about William McCoy I tried to leave out opinions or discuss the politics involved. It was my job to believe them, whether I actually did or not. But I still lied to her. Part of me realized I always had. It was difficult to distinguish between what was fact and what was part of the elaborate fictions I had created. I hadn't blurred that line, I became it. It existed within me. Noemi kept staring into the water.

"I have to ask you something," she said.

"Go ahead."

I could tell when she dropped my hand back into the water uncertainty controlled her body now, forced her indecisive movements into a period of momentary isolation. I watched her close her eyes and I thought she was trying to find a gentler way to say what she felt she had to. She didn't ask what I was afraid she would.

"Did you ever have to kill anyone?" she said.

The surface of the water rippled. Her hands were shaking. I grabbed her hands and held them, helped them float to the top of the water. Small tears swept their way down across the smooth contours of her face and cascaded into the water. No matter what I told her, one or three or nine, even if I explained all them, for that moment I would become something else to her. I would have become an animal and a violent creature of customary action, unconscionable and threatening.

"Yes, once," I said. "But it wasn't what I intended to do," I continued. But I lied to her again. I knew exactly what I was doing that night and exactly what it would lead me to become.

"What happened?" Noemi stood up from the bathtub and wrapped a towel around her torso. While she looked into the mirror and brushed her hair, I stood and pressed against her. The tense architecture of my body corresponded with hers, each delicate layer of our skin placed atop one another, a papier-mâché creation constructed by a hardened artist, a man who spent a lifetime abusing his hands, his brown knuckles resembling the petrified roots of a tree rupturing the surface of the ground. Instead of brushing off the soil he would rub it into the strength of his palms. It would take that type of person, that strong of an individual to tear apart what Noemi and I had. What it would take a shipbuilder or mason years to deconstruct I collapsed in the eight minutes it took for that fire to rage and the 11 minutes it took for me to find her in that rain swept field. She moved closer to the mirror and our bodies shifted. In that moment my anatomy seemed to have changed, and my body no longer fit inside the dark contours of her back and shoulders.

*Who was I?*

*William McCoy, arsonist and murderer. Wanted for the arson related deaths of two people in Mississippi. Was last seen staying at the Clark Motor Lodge. Wanted in questioning for the discovery of a body found in the woods less than three miles from an arson related fire. Was seen by witnesses running from the scene.*

My lungs felt compacted with sand. I couldn't stop breathing, exhausted by the tragic truth of what had happened. The outer layer of skin on my hand was blistered and the drenching rain washed some of the blood away the delicate bones underneath were visible. Water from the gutters above me poured into the parking lot and rushed from inside the dumpster I ditched the rubber gloves in. It was hard to see her run into that field. Only two streetlights lined the blacktop at that corner. I took a few quick steps into the alley and grabbed the gun I dropped. When I bent over I cringed and raised a hand to my side.

I pulled my shirt up a few inches and noticed my torso had already begun to bruise from internal bleeding. The section of steel piping she struck me with sat in a small puddle of rusted water and blood. It resembled the color of a summer sunset. I staggered against the rear of a dry cleaning shop and finally came out at the other end of the alley. The lone traffic light swung back on forth in the wind. Running to the edge of the street, I didn't care any longer about being in deeper.

When my feet came down on the blacktop I couldn't keep my balance. It had been raining since we started the last fire a little over an hour ago. Branches from trees aligned the tall curbs on each side of the street. Autumn leaves looked stamped into the pavement. When I crossed the center line I slipped and collapsed to the ground. The side of my left arm scraped across the asphalt and opened up a gash above my elbow. The rain rising from the street made it difficult to see. Suddenly an intense light cascaded through the landscape and I strained to get to my feet. A transit bus was coming towards me through a morning haze of exhaust and mist. I secured the gun in the waistline of my jeans and tumbled onto the sidewalk and rolled up against a wooden rail fence that bordered the field. The bus roared past me and sprayed water and mud across my face. I focused my perspective into the hills. By now she was almost a mile or more ahead of me. I didn't care. There were people still inside that hardware store when it caught fire.

153

I suggested because of the inclement weather her group wait another day or so. But she had her orders, a schedule and an agenda. There was an exaggerated determination in her, a blinding and almost compulsion to her behavior, the way she worked out each detail of a project through the architecture of her mind. When I grabbed her hand and told her we had to leave, she stared at the body of the person scorched in the fire. She fought me and tried to touch the corpse. I struggled to keep her near me. Vapors rose from the body into the night sky like rain striking hot asphalt. A horror novelist couldn't describe the odor emanating from the body in any modern language. She couldn't get close enough because of me and in frustration she started screaming. I never heard someone wail like that and I wasn't sure if it was because of sadness or anger. I didn't understand at that time his death hadn't been an accident.

We started to run from the scene through a one way street and ducked into a closed furniture warehouse less than a mile away. Although it was damp outside, the interior of the warehouse was humid and dense. She immediately went to the front windows and looked around. Quickly she set a small bag down and began rummaging through it. In the distance beyond her silhouette I could see black smoke circling in the high winds. The landscape was indistinct, malevolent in its appearance so much so it looked like mortality itself.

"We have to get out of Mississippi," she said. Although the situation was intense and dire, she showed no signs of panic. It seemed to fit her profile. That's why I was disturbed by the way she acted when that smoldering corpse broke through the glass.

"What the hell were you doing back there?" I whispered.

"Our job," she said, checking to see that the door we came in through was secure behind her.

"It was our job to burn the clinic, not kill one of our own," I said. I grabbed her hand and pulled her closer. "We shouldn't have escalated to murder. It complicates things."

"What about all those people in that church in Pittsburgh that you killed?"

"Who was the man who died, the one you tried to get to so badly?"

"It doesn't matter," she said.

"I want to know," I said.

"I'm aborting the rest of our itinerary," she said. "We're done."

"Who was he?"

"He was a traitor to the cause," she said, her chest collapsing over and over. In a different situation the woman would have been beautiful and seductive. As much as I wanted to resist her advances when we spent the night together, I didn't. There was something raw about her, not necessarily exotic or peerless.

"What does that mean? Are you saying it was deliberate?" I said.

"Yes," she said.

I wanted to reach for the gun pressed against the small of my back. It was the first time I ever felt uncertain being William McCoy. That unnerved me, being at ease using his voice, never planning arsons or meeting her group with trepidation or timidity. "Why?" I questioned. "That kind of action leaves evidence behind. What if someone's able to identify him? It could all lead back to us. You compromised what we were trying to do," I said.

"It reached that when the flames jumped to that hardware store," she said. I was careful not to misconstrue her tone as a representation of guilt.

"That's beside the point," I argued.

"It's not your call to make so it doesn't matter," she said. "There's nothing more that needs to be done here," she said. "It's over."

"Who says? There's more to do," I interjected. When she started to leave through the rear entrance I grabbed her hand and violently pulled her back.

"Let go of me," she pleaded.

"What are you going to do?" I leaned in towards her, close enough to smell the scent of burnt violets on the nape of her neck. "Burn me?" I grabbed her wrists and held her arms above her head. She hesitated then allowed herself to be pushed into the corner at the rear of the building.

"No. Someone like you can't be destroyed," she said. Without fear she gave in and craned her neck, crashed her pelvis against my body. Quickly our bodies collided, a close traffic accident, smooth chassis of flesh and muscle tearing on impact at the intersection of indiscretion and impatience.

"Why did you kill him?" I asked, turned on by her willingness and her danger.

"I was supposed to have killed you two days ago," she said, her lips flashing across my exposed collarbone. There was a hole in the material from the fire, the flesh scorched underneath. She moved her tongue higher along my shoulder then paused.

"Kill me then," I whispered, massaging the dark area between her legs, her burnt garden of displeasure.

"I'm supposed to," she said, her fingertips pressing into the small of my back as she raised her leg high against my hip. "I want to." She was so warm inside. "I can't."

Again I questioned her. "Why kill him and not me?" I held her wrists tighter and rolled my tongue across her throat, her incredible skin coated with her body's sweat. It felt like being in the ocean, the warm salt water rolling across the edges of my lips. Her body could dehydrate the seas and suffocate a man. All I wanted to do was keep her close. God help me, I wanted more.

"Because he was undercover," she admitted.

"What are you talking about?" I released her hands and she massaged them. There were dark red marks around her wrists.

"We found out he was sending message to the ATF," she stated. When I heard her admission I imagined being murdered, right here, felt the quick twinge of a steel blade penetrating the kidney or the lung. She probably had her people close by. Noemi. I missed her instruction, her graciousness. I had lied so much, willing and with such an intense purpose. William McCoy had become a liability, one I could no longer carry and one I could no longer be. I reached around and withdrew my weapon and pointed it at her. I took a step back and told her to get down on the ground and put her hands behind her head, her fingers interlocked.

"You fucking bastard," she screamed.

"It's over," I said.

"You let them burn," she said. "You stood there and did nothing."

"So did you," I said. "But William McCoy was a lie."

"Changing a name doesn't change who you are," she said as I pressed her hard against the wall and patted her down around the waist again. "You murdered them," she said. "Did you sacrifice them to get to me, to get inside me?"

"No," I said. But I knew she was right.

"Yes you did," she disagreed. "Pretend it doesn't matter, those people. Are you married? Does your pretty little wife know you murdered someone with impunity? Do you put your arms around her and tell her you love her or do you smell the dead hiding beneath the surface of her scent? Tell me, does she fuck you like I did? Does she? Does she make your skin burn when she takes your cock into her ass like I did? Does she tear through your flesh when you're hard inside of her and see who you actually are underneath?" she asked.

"You're sick," I said.

"And you're still an animal, no matter what you call yourself. I'm the only one who knows it. Aren't I? Did they tell you to fuck me? Or did I turn you on so much you wanted to that night at your hotel? When your wife kisses you is she going to taste me on your lips?" The discernment in her eyes sharpened from a haunting blackness into a burnished umber as an explosion happened behind me.

I ran into the high sodden grass. Blood and soil streaked my pants and water darkened the ankles. It was hard to tell where she might have gone. But I headed straight up a small hill and into the thick line of trees ahead. It looked like an unattended graveyard of nature, a blighted and dense arrangement of rock and diseased trees. Nothing appeared to possess life except for the various black birds switching from branch to branch.

The trees suppressed the rainfall and the winds and in result, it was easier to see. Nevertheless there was little to behold, a vast chasm of decay and nothingness. Blankets of fallen strands of a pine tree looked like sewing needles spilled from a basket across a carpet. The ground looked rusted and ruined. It took me about 10 minutes to wade through the boulders and disheveled stumps, waiting for her to appear. I knew she didn't have a gun. When she went to check the perspective from the front of the store she must have rigged a charge hoping to tie up loose ends, sanitize who remained of her group.

On the other side of the trees I came into an open expanse of land, several acres of unused field running underneath of an overpass. In the distant mist were several large steel stanchions holding electrical wires. I checked the clip on my handgun and walked out into the plot, searching for her, desperate to stave off her attempts at self-preservation while maintaining my own. The tempered rains started again and thicketed the limited perspective I had.

It was odd, but I wanted nothing less than to strip down and let the rain wash over me, cleanse me. But unfortunately there was some inherent and brutal truth to what she had said. Holding Noemi, caressing her glassy skin wasn't going to change the simple actuality I had indirectly murdered someone. It was the abstruse appraisal we made in some cases, weighing consequences. Sacrifice. Resignation. Consecration. If her group hadn't threatened political members in Washington, I'd probably be asleep by her side, entranced by her elegance, the cadence of her breathing lulling me into a sense of repose. Remembering the violent way her eyes absorbed almost all the light from a room, leaving behind an oppressive twilight. It was then I saw her appear underneath an electrical tower.

She stood motionless, almost waiting for the ground around her to emblazon in vibrant tones of apricot and ginger, scalding, leaving everything a blighted congestion. There was nothing intense and temperate enough that could burn away the traces of culpability and gaucheness in Mississippi. So I ran.

I ran as hard as I could, each muscle pulsing, subtle, kinetic collisions vibrating throughout my legs and ankles. I could feel the acid in my composition course around tendon and bone. Through the constant rain I watched her turn. She should have gotten farther than she had. It wasn't long before I closed the distance between us, but I stumbled several times because of the unstable footing, once striking my head on the ground. When I gathered myself and searched for her, everything had changed into a light shade of yellow, the rain and the trees truncated and indistinct. It had become quiet. The quiescence broke when she appeared again from behind a rusted piece of abandoned farm equipment. Her arms loped along her sides. I could see drops of water collapse along the tip of the blade that she still held.

"Everything we worked for here is dead because of you," she said.

"You're dead already," I said.

"And what about you?" she responded.

"It doesn't matter."

"I disagree," she said.

"You don't even understand what you've done," I said.

"Yes I do. We've done God's reason," she said, moving the knife into a more angular position.

"No you haven't. You've exercised your own hate. Drop the knife and get down on the ground," I said.

"I can't," she began.

"I won't ask again. Put down the knife and put your hands behind your head." Her shoulders slumped in surrender, but her tight hold on the blade increased. Leaves floated in the light winds and collapsed against her body, autumn colors caught up in a struggle of decay. Several landed upon the slope of her shoulders and made her shaded and burnt with vermillion and coral. Suddenly her demeanor changed, the look of depravity and hate seemingly altered by the silence. In that brief introspective moment she came across as vulnerable and alone. But as she struggled to regain her composure the sharp blade flashed in front of me. On my knees forcing air into my lungs I pulled the trigger. Her body came to rest underneath of an electrical stanchion. Still kneeling, I watched her crawl across the ground, her hands spread open, pushing blood and soil higher up on her arms. She tried to stand and failed, dropping back into a prone position and never moved again. The rains punishment increased and crashed down upon the leaves and the grass, undressing me of persona, but leaving most of me surrounded by truth and by failure.

~

Noemi closed the bathroom door behind her. I drained the water from the bathtub and switched off the light. When I opened the door and went back into our room, the curtains parted, struggled against the darkness. I watched her settle into the bed. I climbed in and spooned, tracing my fingertips across her abdomen, a raven oasis where I wished I could vanish without a trace of any of the people I had become, whether they be righteous or criminal.

"Tell me you love me," she said.

"I love you." Nothing I said to her mattered and in the end it was obvious to me she understood that. She bedded and loved a man who murdered someone. And no amount of love could change that and I felt sorry for her. Forgiveness and absolution were faces I never recognized, lost languages I never understood. In that regard, she was my translator. I would lose her. She curved her body and looked up at me. After I kissed her cheek, she smiled. I wasn't sure if she thought it would be the last time I would say that to her.

"It wasn't your fault," she said, her eyes piercing deep inside mine, trying to help me escape, run from an imposed self-imprisonment and rediscover her and us. Because no other suspects other than the two victims could be identified and the arsons subsided, the case was closed. "What you did, that wasn't the man I am in love with," she added. "And it never could be." Once during our closeness Noemi leaned up and brushed her lips across mine. I massaged her breast and leaned in to touch her. As she closed her eyes and sighed, her tongue opening the space between her lips, she pulled away. It was the only time she had ever made me feel detached. It was bruising, being the one a lover pulled away from.

After taking a long shower, exhausted and conflicted, I came back into the room and knew I would have to become Johnathan Levin again. Until a suspect was apprehended it would unfortunately become a constant, the dialogues, the sick photographs, the films and the hopelessness I experienced in everything, even when she stepped out from behind the bathroom door, her naked body glistening under the pale fluorescent lighting, her face alluring, but unexpressive. It was hard to hide. She tried to mask it by turning her back to me, but I could see the disappointment in the way she carried her shoulders, those ink like shoulders I wanted to kiss, I wanted to map with my nervous lips like a cartographer trapped in a charcoal snowstorm, abandoned in an endless plain of blackness.

"Don't look at me like that," she said.

"I don't know what you mean," I responded.

"No I don't suppose you would," she said. She bent over and dropped her head and ran her hands through her hair. When she raised her body and her shimmering locks settled back down over her shoulders, I thought she would never believe in me again. It was something I had watched her do hundreds of times but it seemed unconventional, unsettling instead of being reaffirming and engaging. Instead of battling with her, I submitted.

"Do you want me to resign from the case?" I asked.

"No. What you are doing is noble and I love you all the more for it. I do. It makes me proud, but opposing is a feeling of isolation I guess. I want you to talk to me instead of protecting me all the time," she admitted, lowering her eyes.

"Talk to you about what? Cases? Specifics? You know I really can't."

"What you're feeling. I understand there's a certain ambiguity involved, but I'm not a reporter asking for answers. I'm your wife," she stated with a passion I didn't expect, a sort of aggressive preservation. Understanding I may have wanted her to leave and take the responsibility away from me overwhelmed me with shame, something I approached with caution since I felt I violated her earlier.

"What I investigate most of the time is brutal, violent and disgusting. I live among criminals and the edges of depravity. The only thing that grounds me, reminds me of the man I want to be is you, our marriage, the small moments we spend together. Few as they are. I live for a moment's peace, something as simple as watching you fall asleep on the couch. As soon as I let you into that sad world, make you a part of it all, I'll never survive," I said. Noemi moved closer and turned around. I raised her hair higher so I could clasp a necklace around her neck.

"I'm stronger than you give me credit for," she said.

"But that's not a chance I am willing to take," I said. I turned her around and raised her chin, grazing the underside of her neck. It was the last time she looked at me with an obvious sense of honor and dependence. Instead of being a loving husband, I felt I had become a burden. At the time, she looked so beautiful standing there, a light blue dress settling against the dark complexion of her skin, accenting the smooth curves of her hips. I wanted to tell her she looked more beautiful here in front of me than she ever had. But she pulled away from me before I could say anything when she glanced down at my wrist. She touched my hand and stared at my watch.

It was almost noon and we had less than two hours until her sister's wedding. I should have given her a chance I thought as she pulled my hand to her lips and kissed my wrist as if I were a visiting dignitary and not the intense, romantic man whose head she had pressed against her round breasts only hours ago, a beautiful group of minutes where her scent lingered against my face and intensified the strength in which I held her. An embrace countered unfortunately by dishonesty and fear.

~

The girl in front of me at the wedding had the same dress, Penelope's dress. Not that exact one, but it was so similar for a moment I thought it was. It was the light from the high morning sun that made it look the same in color and pattern; the pale yellow offset by the auburn tone of her hair. Noemi crossed her legs and tugged at the frilled ends of her dress. The girl came down the aisle, holding a small bouquet of flowers in her hands. A light wind ruffled the petals and I was reminded of the perfume Noemi splashed across her stomach before we left the hotel. The aroma changed everything, altered the light breeze escaping into the hallway where I held her hand.

At first the girl moved, her lips parting as if she were trying to remember her steps, her hair pinned behind her head by strands of vermillion silk. She couldn't have been more than nine years old. She was very pretty, in a poised sense. Noemi wanted to have children and we had broached the subject several times, after we made love when both of us were vulnerable to the other. She was the only woman who made me feel comfortable naked. The body I was given was athletic and slender, but the ability I had to blend in with criminals was intellectual. But she had a subtle and sometimes direct way of reminding me how beautiful she thought I was.

The girl began to walk without trepidation, raised her shoulders higher with continued poise and grace. Petals from some of the bouquet dropped behind her.

Each one merely needed cultivated…

The closer she neared Noemi and I the more she became almost imbalanced. Instead of standing straight up, her body began to contort and appear rigid, unfamiliar to her. The prevailing wind changed her skin and it began to dry and crack as if she were a molded piece of pottery. Sand and ash dropped from her limbs and torso, leaving behind an emaciated structure of bones and necrotic tissue. The vibrant shades of the bouquet became oppressive and dull. The hair I admired and found to be beautiful became nothing more than pieces of dried vine, the tied silk clinging desperately. Her shoulders resembled nothing more than a metal closet hanger trying to tear through a dry cleaning bag. Underneath the dulcet tones of a piano I watched her struggle to remain upright.

Pieces of her skin continued to flake off like shreds of burnt paper until there was nothing left. I wanted to go to her, but I couldn't. The stench emanating from her body was indescribable. I covered my mouth. The flower girl toppled over. I moved on my hands and knees to her body as it stopped decaying, laid immobile at the base of Noemi's sister's wedding gown. The sequins in the pearl white dress sparkled in the air, dimmed by the concavity where her eyes had been. Nothing could exist in a place so dark. Each one looked as if they had been removed. Pasted onto the dead flower girl's skull was a look of incredible agony as if she knew what was happening to her and felt the intensity and brutality with each contortion of her body.

I held her in the width of my arms like someone would hold a piece of porcelain or a rare art object, with compassion and grace. And also a ration of fear, uncertainty. There were ligature marks embedded into the brittle bones of her wrists and ankles. Underneath the wedding hymns I could hear her screaming, her desperation reaching into the atmosphere and rippling across the tender wings of migrating birds, causing them to flutter. Tears fought their way across my flushed cheeks as I was distracted from the flower girl's wailing by a cool, startling touch to the back of my neck. I turned around and kneeling over me was Noemi, moving her hands to find mine and gather me aside but in humiliation, not concern.

If I would have waited it would have been clear it was an 11-year-old girl on the ground in front of me, not a 15-year old found murdered and rotted inside a barn silo. I reached out to her. It wasn't her hair that tore from the scalp and ended up entwined between my fingers. The tint was a different color, darker. The girl was sobbing into her palms, confused and upset about what had happened. I wasn't sure what I had done. Noemi's sister took her hand and led her away and I understood she wasn't hurt. Murmurs corrupted the painful silence I endured as I struggled to stand, weighed down by the oncoming consequences and the emotional destitution I had caused. No one helped me, even Noemi. As she dropped my hand, I watched the flower girl turn around when she walked back into the church.

It wasn't Penelope.

~

I closed the file on Jonathan Levin and grabbed the train ticket I was going to need from an end table and stood in the doorway of our living room. It was in here where she discovered Penelope and what had carried

163

her with me to Morro Bay. It was the place where I had been honest with her for the first time when I told her who Penelope was and what had happened to her. And more importantly, whom I was. It would be hard for me to come back here again, to our home, bruised by a lack of direction and compassion. She wouldn't have wanted to see me anyway, not after everything I had done to her. I closed the door behind me, unaware of who I was going to be without her.

I stepped through the door of the bus and took a seat towards the rear against a window. I retrieved a few small notes and went over the identity of who I was going to be again once I stepped foot onto that train. Part of me wanted to be that man and never look back. Patterns of thunder echoed in the distance of the houses. After reexamining the trace elements found underneath of several of the victims' fingernails, we determined all the substances weren't only found in earthen soil, but plant fertilizers as well. When a flower petal was discovered in the latest victim's vagina, I focused on one man in particular. The man whose comments about Penelope resonated in the subconscious ideas I developed while being Jonathan Levin.

There were so many ways I could have told Noemi I was wrong, introverted and unavailable. We were instructed during my training never to tell anyone, including our loved ones, what we did. Part of her understood and she said as much when I explained the investigation in detail to her. What hope I felt we had was lost when she held that photograph of Penelope in her palms, her hands held at the wrist against her lower back. I wasn't sure if she realized at that moment I had, in turn, disrespected her as much when I penetrated her. Instead of understanding it as an act of violent passion between two people who loved each other, I recognized it now as offensive and unjustifiable.

But what I couldn't forget was the emotion that encompassed her face when I told her I wouldn't bear a child with her. If she even still wanted me to after what happened at that wedding, Noemi never said. The investigation and the grief left behind would be a parasite, spread infection to everything. Investigators resigned or quit because of cases such as this, aged and withered due to the dense clarity of the actual conditions. There was nothing here I could ever disremember. But because of the incident with the flower girl, an arrest warrant was issued for a man in his 40's, a florist.

*Each one merely needed cultivated...*

If we were to have a child now, I would break, affected by the truth and the responsibility that Penelope could have been my daughter, hands pushed against her delicate backbone, disillusioned and scared. Sad to say, but a parent couldn't always protect a child. Depending on which criminal I was, no one understood better than I did. I slept with urban decay. It was immaterial, Noemi asking me what she could have done differently. When I heard the bus's engine decelerate, I closed my eyes. All I wanted to do was become who she wanted me to be, walk back into our house and wait for her, relearn all the intrinsic things about her I had forgotten. I would wait as long as I had to. But I couldn't. When I heard the gunshot I stared at the windshield wipers moving against the glass, displacing the obstructing water, only to have it return again, resolute and persistent, like God had personified frustration and failure itself right in front of me.

~

The trees separated in the wind and fractions of sunlight broke through the decaying leaves. Soon the natural light would be gone. No one would see us in here. The handicapped man had dimmed most of the lights inside the bus. Through the rear emergency door though I could see armed men moving into position behind cars parallel parked on the street. There weren't many. Though deserted because of the situation, this stretch of road was usually dense and congested. The expressway would be blocked. People living in any of the houses surrounding the scene would be evacuated or told to continue to remain inside with their doors locked.

An F.B.I negotiator had called to find out the state of the passengers and what the crippled man's intentions were after he stopped the bus. A physical description was provided by the driver when he was released. When the first shot discharged he was authoritative and under control. Now, even as only two hours or so had passed, he appeared uneasy. If that apprehension led to another shot, there was no way they would let him off of the bus alive. A sniper would take him out, no question. So far though, he hadn't injured anyone besides me. It happened so suddenly I didn't have time to react. When I asked him to let the woman go, he struck me above my eye with the handle of the gun and then on the back of the head. I called him a coward. The last thing this town needed was another tragedy. The people and the landscapes here had bled enough. I winced when I leaned back against the glass. The blood on the back of my head had begun to matte in my hair.

It had been an hour since that happened and I wasn't sure if he could even hear what was going on around us. There was an earpiece tucked into his right canal. A recorder sat on the floor of the bus between his legs. I watched him struggle to open a pill bottle. Sweat dripped from his fingertips. In the distance, a police officer directed a postal carrier to pull his vehicle back. The divorce papers Noemi's lawyer drew up would have to wait as we all did. She could have returned, knocking on the door of our empty house. I imagined her not even searching around to see if I was there.

*Who was I?*

*William McCoy, arsonist, domestic terrorist, murderer. Currently listed as most wanted man in the Unites States by the Federal Bureau of Investigation. Sought for questioning after the discovery of a woman's body in a field not more than three miles from the sight of an arson related blaze at a furniture warehouse. Current whereabouts unknown.*

It started storming heavier. There was no noise involved, only brief periods of electric discharge slicing through the unapproachable boundaries. I sat in that damp field for over an hour before I contacted my handler and told them what had happened and where they could find her. I looked over at her inert body and watched the vapor drift out from the gunshot wound in her chest. The warm rain soothed the chemical burn stretched across my hand. It resembled the salmon color of Noemi's lips. I thought about her and what I would tell her. I would lie though, as I always did.

Through the pithy sound of the rain embracing the metal and leaves I could hear the consistent murmur of the electrical towers around me. It sounded loud though, like the noise of a hummingbird with a pituitary disorder. I dropped my gun into the tender grass and looked down. What little light there was around me refracted off of the blade she had carried. I left it there where she dropped it. I couldn't leave behind the absolute loss of integrity and self-effacement I caused by my actions. I stood up and slipped away in the opposite direction through the narrow arms of the uncaring trees when I first heard the sirens.

It was unnerving how quiet it was trudging through the solemn yet vibrant foliage. It was early and the streets were desolate. I stood waiting for the next bus to stop near me and I didn't care how long I would have to wait. It was raining still, the water running along the curb. The handler I called said I should come in. I wanted to run. I could still see remnants of smoke a couple of miles away invading the atmosphere with its rich, artificial blackness. Firefighters and the A.T.F. would be dousing hotspots and searching for a cause. I had let her burn everything. I looked down at the burn on my hand and pulled my arm higher up the sleeve to try and disguise it. I didn't want to attract unnecessary attention. The direct blow I took to my side and kidney was getting worse. But all I wanted to do was go home.

It was the first time in months I had been there, leaning against the doorframe, watching Noemi sleep. I didn't expect her to even be there waiting for me to come home. It was all I ever seemed to ask her to do. There were no lights on. I stepped into our living room, expecting her to have moved things around, made changes. But the fact she hadn't rearranged pieces of our furniture or replaced photographs burdened me with a heavy sense of culpability. Noemi was a woman of unexceptional grace and balance and I had violated that, betrayed everything that we were ever going to have.

Our bedroom window was open and the rain had gathered on the sill. I wiped my hand across the water and brushed it against my shirt. I stared at the delicate bones in her ankle as it moved out from underneath the sheets. I should have woken her and nestled in beside her and explained in unimpeachable truth who I was. I had forgotten how beautiful she was. With pause, I reached out and brushed the back of my hand across her leg.

I closed the door to the bathroom behind me and switched on the light. I stripped down and stood in front of the sink. With tired and sunken eyes I examined my body, the cauterized gashes and the discolored bruise along my hip. The burn on my left hand and wrist was coral and raw. I opened the medicine cabinet and reached in, displacing a bottle of rubbing alcohol in the process. The plastic container echoed off of the porcelain. I grabbed the bottle and twisted open the cap. Holding my hand over the sink I poured the alcohol.

The sensation across my skin was cold and jarring. I reached into the pocket of the jeans on the floor and pulled out matches. I ripped one off and struck it across the thin strip, that dark dividing line between success and disappointment. The sulfur odor invaded everything. I held the match under my hand and watched the pale blue flame roll up my palm and fingers. I wanted it to burn for all eternity, an infinite period of continuance and distance. Alcohol burned so quickly. There would be another scar. I was already covered with them, scars caused by love, by lies, by passion, by guilt and by hate. I pulled back the shower door and turned on the water. It collapsed around me, ripped the grease and ash from my legs and hands. More than that I wanted it to bisect, strip away all the biology that manifested and all the places where I had given that woman access.

It should have disgusted me, what I did. In contrast, as I leaned up against the ceramic tile, I thought about her more than I was comfortable with. That night in the hotel room after we set the first fire, I pressed my fingertips into the soft spot of skin along her throat. I leaned in and licked her windpipe. I should have strangled her. But I wanted it to happen, wanted everything about her. Dangerous and luring, she pulled at the buttons of the shirt I wore and tore at the seams with wanton, violent abandon. Her lips pressed against my chest. I wanted to close my eyes and remember who I was. I had a chance, I did. But I couldn't.

Instead I noticed the indirect movement of her pelvis, the fullness of her lips against my deficient flesh. She took my hand and maneuvered it between her thighs and my fingertips penetrated her warm insides. I held my breath as she pulled me closer. With heedless and perilous abandon she and I suffocated one another's idealism that night. It wasn't the circumstances involved, our bodies conjoined, colliding, the perspiration soaked into the thin threads of the sheets. It wasn't the firmness of her breasts or the hardness of the developed muscles across her abdomen. It was the hard, brutal verity I wanted more, more of her instability and more of the sweet taste of the dark area between her legs only hours after she had gone.

The hot water from the shower dripped across my back and shoulders. I knew there were imperfections there, imprints made by her rough nails as they descended along my longitude from the cusp of my neck to the axis of my backside. The thought of what happened that night made my cock harden. I wanted absolution. Not McCoy or McDonnally or Levin. I did. The door to the bathroom opened and I knew it was Noemi coming in. Embarrassed being aroused in this condition, I turned around and pushed deeper into the corner. I could hear her voice behind me as she stood outside against the door. I fought against asking her to leave and breaking through the glass.

"I tried to call so many times looking for you. No one would tell me anything," she said.

"We've been through this. No one will talk to you about where I am, they can't," I said.

"All this time I thought you were never coming back. I thought you were dead," she said.

"It would put me in danger if people knew who I was, where I was," I said.

"What you did?" she asked.

"No," I said, looking over my shoulder, wounded by her insinuations, even though I knew I didn't possess the right.

"Tell me what it is exactly that you do," she said. "Please."

"This isn't the time," I said.

"When is it going to be? I don't ever want to put you in danger, but I'm in danger every time I am sitting here, worrying about you," she said.

"I know. All I can say is that I'm sorry," I said.

"I need you to say something else."

"What do you want me to say?"

"Say anything to me. Say everything to me. I don't care what it is," she pleaded.

"I love you. I love you so much that without you I lose sight of who I am anymore. It's all I have the strength to say right now," I said. When I responded she slid aside the door and embraced me. I didn't stop her. She was still wearing an unassuming piece of lingerie. The water merged with the pale blue material and soaked it. I could feel her breasts, her body mesh with the intricacies of my spine. When I winced she retreated and noticed the burns and utter degradation.

"Oh my God. What happened to you?" she asked.

"It doesn't matter," I said.

"I need to know," she pleaded.

"It's okay," I said subdued.

"Look at you. It's not. Stop trying to keep me at a distance. Please tell me what happened," she said, the water cascading along her curves. It couldn't still be warm. In that isolated, compartmentalized space, so close to one another's susceptibility and weaknesses, she and I were separated by fathoms of oceanography. "I don't know what you do. Not really. I know I am trying to understand what keeps you away from me. I wake up in the morning, so fucking angry I can't talk to you about the simplest of things. It doesn't matter what they are. You listen to me. No one else ever has. I see people in the streets, when I go out shopping trying to find a dress I could wear when I saw you again and someone always asks how you are, where you are. And I don't have any answers, so I lie. It makes me hate you for such a quick, fleeting second, having to do that. It's not who I am.

"So I come home to this pathetic, lonely silence I am always immersed in. I stand in front of the mirror, sort through my clothes to find my sexiest bra, draw my hair to the side over my shoulder, and slide into the dress I bought anyway. It's the color you said I looked so what, lissome in? Yet all those concave things you said to me vanish as I wait for you to come up behind me and take me away from all this detachment. Everything is so vacant here so I leave, go to dinner all dressed up alone. I sit outside because it's cool and calm. I look for you in the people on the street even though I know you're not going to be there. The waiter feels sorry for me. I can see it in his eyes when he pours me a glass of red wine. I don't even care he can see my breasts in that dress. I want him to touch me, ask me to stand and take me right there outside, in the peaceful breeze. The hard truth I want another man, a stranger to fuck me so I can feel something, feel like I am not wasting away makes me hate again. And I don't want to think about you like that," she said. "I missed you so much," she admitted. I turned around and ran my hands through her hair. There was a sadness immersed in her. Noemi watched the water cascade across my chest and fall to the floor. Her fingertips reached out then drifted, hoping to learn me again in subtle apprehension. I couldn't hide the fact I wanted her to touch me. When she dropped to her knees and moved her lips over me, I sobbed.

~

The light rain still came through the window and dripped onto the floor. Noemi was slumped over my legs asleep. Her body rose slightly when she breathed. It was hardly noticeable. Those were the things that made her beautiful, the passive, unimportant movements she manufactured, the unintentional seductiveness in the way her hair fell across her face. A little over an hour ago we had made love. It was intense and vehement, our anatomies researching our different mathematical equations. Nevertheless there was a sense of indifference in our passion now. There was a proximity that once existed in our marriage, a closeness of organism and mind, dense with candor, longing and indispensability. Yet there was a distance here, a radius of doubt and incongruity I never noticed. I didn't want to wake her, but I had to leave soon.

I had contacted my handler again, but not until the sixth morning after I had arrived home. The department was disappointed I hadn't come in already. William McCoy was dead. According to police records, his body was discovered at the scene of a fatal arson fire approximately two weeks ago. The arson and domestic terrorism case I investigated was closed, the deaths of the two men in that adjacent building ruled an unfortunate accident. No criminal charges were pending. Three of the suspected arsonists were dead. I was going to be psychologically evaluated and then reassigned to a different investigation or put on medical leave, depending upon the outcome of the review. It wasn't something I wanted to do. The idea of becoming a regular man, ordinary and abiding disrupted me and carried with it a compartmentalized function of rejection and impracticality.

I watched Noemi's body move and I slipped out from underneath her. Leaning up against the headboard, I opened up a sealed file describing the case I could be assigned, but only on a consultant basis. Most of the photographs inside were of children. Any leads or specifics were preliminary. Only one set of crime scene photographs were included to this point. Instead of immersing myself further, I closed the red file and opened another.

I searched through all the evidence, names and substantial leads I had gathered as William McCoy. Included was an autopsy report on the woman I had killed. There were no records of her fingerprints in any of the federal agencies, including Interpol. No one could establish with any direct certainty who she actually was. Noemi rolled over and opened her eyes. There was never going to be a proper or right time to tell her about the things I did, the fractured characters I had become. I existed only in a false, morality play she would never sit in the audience long enough to see the ending to. Written across the bottom of the coroner's report, attached on a separate piece of paper, was a question directed to me about the woman I killed. *"Did you know when you shot her she was pregnant?"* I no longer had relevance or citizenship in the lives of others.

~

The crippled man stopped the recorder and dropped the earpiece into his lap. The gun swayed in his hand. I couldn't see his face. His head was down between his legs. After a few minutes he rose up and looked back at the three of us in our seats. He set the gun on the seat next to him. I thought he was going to surrender himself. Instead he rubbed his temples and my eyes followed his outside. The emergency door was close. I could do it.

I understood I could die because of what I did. It stayed with me every day. The wrong address or information in an undercover operation and I'd be dead in an abandoned rail yard or dumped on a barren road behind a building. Strangled. Shot in the head. Noemi couldn't accept I was willing to sacrifice everything, including her, to protect strangers. What she failed to understand was I was migratory. An immigrant. It wasn't fair to ask that of someone else. But it was something I had come to terms with. I couldn't determine whether what I did was sympathetic or irrational.

Was she there outside in the streets, hoping she would see me descend the bus's stairs? If I did see her when it was all over, I would quit and struggle to become what I should have always been for her. There wasn't much sound coming from outside. Inside, I could hear the crippled man begin to sob. Whatever he had been listening to seemed to burn into what resolve he had, the way William McCoy torched that clinic in Missouri and repeatedly took an anti-abortionist into his bed.

That autopsy. It wasn't my child. It couldn't have been. There had to be other men. The possibility I had murdered a child I conceived encumbered me with such coldness and anguish. It was something I could never tell anyone, could never tell Noemi. I loved her, but I struggled to balance the lives of the men I had become. The husband in me longed to hear Noemi speak my name in a gentle undertone, feel her tender hands brush across the small of my back as she walked into our bedroom, naked, her wedding ring still housed around her slight finger.

*Who was I?*

*Anthony Bariole*

No wait.

*Who was I?*

*Peter McDonnally wanted for the brutal beating and robbery of three people on a commuter bus. Items taken from the victims included a platinum watch, a wedding ring and cash. Witnesses said that McDonnally threatened one man with a handgun, then beat him unrecognizable with a fire extinguisher. Was spotted leaving the scene after he escaped though the emergency exit. Current whereabouts unknown.*

No wait.

*Who was I?*

*Johnathan Levin, wanted for the sexual assault of a woman on a commuter bus. Was said to have exposed himself to the other passengers as well. Witnesses said before the attack occurred he was mentioning something about school children attending their first day of school next week. Was heard saying aloud he could smell innocence in the cheap material of the seats. Samples of semen were discovered in the general vicinity. Was spotted leaving the scene after he escaped though the emergency exit. Current whereabouts unknown.*

No wait.

*Who was I?*

*William McCoy, wanted for the arson related burning of a commuter bus, three other passengers killed in the blaze. The bodies were charred beyond recognition. Was heard by witnesses on the scene outside of the bus that the world was a cruel, apathetic existence and should burn in the fires of industry and guilt. Remained at the scene for several minutes after the bus immersed in flames and shouted flesh would singe, change for the better and be carried way in the arms of the wind. Current whereabouts unknown.*

I stood from my seat. I could be murdered here, my body lifeless and without meaning. I would be less than a name written on a toe tag, less than an elongated shape stuffed inside of a black bag. There would be no one left who could identify whom I had been.

# THE MODEL

I stood frightened by the cold isolation of the faded and dried colors imprisoned in the splintered flesh of your wooden palette. In a certain aspect of light, from a distance, it resembled the skin of a man, one experienced, mature and damaged. The darker chemicals absorbed into the grain mirrored age spots. I thought you would have taken it with you, for it no longer had use for me and I was no longer a stimulant to the physiological depths of its artistic temptation. But as much as I wanted you to leave after what happened, I wanted you to stay, even though I knew it was for the wrong reasons. That it would be a mistake. All along, I thought I was stronger, thought I could overcome the faded hope I held onto.

In the apartment you had left me a hand written note, the sentences structured and complete as if you had given no hesitation to the definition I would retrieve from its insensitive vocabulary. Things were too far gone you said and I remembered how insipid you could be with your tone when I disagreed. I shouldn't have compromised so easily. You must have dropped it through the mail slot of the apartment when I wasn't here. By avoiding me you made me feel like I had done something wrong, that I had violated our marriage. That alone I thought made you out to be a coward.

I didn't see it at first, the note, hidden underneath of an unopened moving box wilted at the seams because of the rain that dripped from the roof. It missed the bucket I must have misplaced during the night when I couldn't sleep. I thought I heard you rustling about for your brushes, the ones you used to keep in the hutch I refinished. That hutch remained, timid in the distant corner opposite the kitchen in the living room beside a bay window. Its' shelves were in need of care and the glass doors remained unfastened against the wall. I didn't have the desire to reattach them. The albescent moonlight poured through the cold glass and spilled across the floor like milk from our child's table. I missed cleaning up after her, our Jennifer. I missed all the things that at one point made me angry and irritable as a mother.

It's odd, the situations you long for and the circumstances you wish could endure again and again, no matter how cursory and no matter how painful. Part of me wished to be arguing with you again, so I could put my hands on your chest and feel the intense heat of your opinions tear through your flesh. And when one of us submitted, anguished and regretful, I understood why our chemistries sometimes counteracted.

The last time I remembered your hate washing over me was when I walked away from you. I never had before when we were disagreeing, like a boxer continuously punched to the abdomen, but refusing to lower his hands in defense. I walked into your studio and tore away at a blank canvas. I should have directed the hurt at a finished creation, but I wanted to take something away. I wanted to ruin an uncreated mural that might have graced its skin. You came in behind me and when I moved, ripped that Prussian blue sweater at the shoulder I adored. It ripped on the seam and exposed the delicate joints and bones. I wanted to hit you, pound hard with desperation and torment at your chest, but instead I grabbed a jar of brushes. Each one collapsed to the floor after striking the wall behind you. When I turned to run past you and leave the room we collided and I fell. The color can I landed on spilled across the drop cloth. It was a tone I had never seen before and on the skin of my hands and wrists it was exhilarating. You noticed and I knew you would.

I removed the torn sweater and stripped down, watching you grab your brush. I rubbed some of the loose color across my abdomen and hips. You pirouetted around my body, telling me not to move, then to move, then not to move again. Hold. Please. I'm sorry. It might have been the only time you ever said that to me. God, I love you. You grabbed more of that exquisite color and as I bent over at the waist, my leg stretched across an end table, poured it over my back. It was cold and dense. I spun around and slapped you. You responded by licking my throat, the only region on my body not bathed in that pigment. I watched you drop to your knees, and then closed my eyes when I could no longer differentiate between the cold color and your lips washing over me.

We have been apart for a little while now, but I still recognize you in everything I see which is unfair to the originality I wanted immersed in. You taught me angles and lines and I noticed them in comparison to light and dark. It doesn't matter where I go. Sitting in my unfinished dining room I folded and assembled my napkin to show its texture and possibilities. I could hear your voice telling me not to focus on the object, but to spaces between the dark and the unseen. It didn't matter what you told me at times, I wanted to hear your wisdom echo its way through the unseen and the dark. I wanted lost in its uncertainty and whatever definition it might have held. But at times I thought when you painted me you never noticed me at all, just the atmosphere around me. You wouldn't have known I was even there if it wasn't for my chest pulsing and the beads of sweat that dripped to the floor. I stood and walked into the living room, the light pooled around my ankles like saltwater foam, remains from the broken crest of a wave.

You painted me once naked, my extended belly bulged like ripe fruit toppling from a basket. You said my skin tasted like peaches. The dimmed streetlamps outside corrupted the light and bathed my shape in a salmon tincture. You stopped me to turn my body towards the left and guided my shoulders, plunged the slope of my collarbone with your fingertips warm and gentile against my swelled breasts. Your hands moved across the plain of my rounded stomach. It paralleled a pumpkin, a yellow-orange squash seeking comfort from the sun under a patch of darkened leaves. I remembered I first understood I loved you as you picked them, pumpkins, stretched their vines and pried their tired arms from the secured comfort of their dirt womb.

I loved autumn, the smells and the arrogant attitude of the nature I was born within, the security and confidence she possessed in allowing the entropic destruction of what made her beautiful. Your color, the intensity of your hair appeared born from the leaves of the beautiful sugar maple tree above your head, dripped from the sloped branches onto the edges of your skeleton. The McIlheny's sold organic vegetables and other products during the various seasons and each time welcomed the township onto their property.

Large, decorative hay bales were sold out of the back of a rusted pickup truck. Children stood at the banks of a small lake behind their house watching for small frogs. A pair of empty overalls was given substance by mulch and leaves that spilled from the wrists and ankles like unkempt hair. An older man gave children slow rides on an enormous tractor, his large wicker hat casting shadows against the stalks of corn. If he hadn't moved, he would have looked like a withered scarecrow, an aged protector of crops and vegetables stood propped against two cracked and uneven pieces of wood. The tires of that tractor were so tall to the children they must have seemed like skyscrapers, the light kicks of their sneakers causing no effect on the hard, compressed rubber. I passed a display of gourds and felt sympathy for their sometimes grotesque appearance, maligned, twisted, unwilling victims of a degenerative disease. They were like lepers; separated from the beautiful, the elite, cast aside by others as stricken denizens of a once close community.

And there you were, seated on a fragile wooden crate turned on its side behind a picnic table, a row of small glass mason jars highlighting different colors laid out in front of you. One by one you painted unique characters onto a child's pumpkin, flicked your brush over its sturdy rind, allowed the lobed leaves to recede back into place. You moved them aside without cause, like a woman tucked a wayward strand of hair behind her ear. I picked up a misshapen gourd, a golden piece of deformed fruit and held it in the palm of my hand.

"I feel sorry for them," I said aloud, not expecting you to break your concentration and listen to me. I don't know what made me say it.

"For what?" you asked.

"These poor pieces of melon," I said.

"Why?" you asked, setting the tip of your paintbrush into a small jar full of what I assumed to be warm water. The pale blue color escaped from the harmless clutches of your brush and swirled between the molecules, that delicate balance of hydrogen and oxygen. I never saw anything so beautiful, but I was searching too hard for someone who would love me. Droplets of water hung at the edges of your fingertips. It caused me to notice your nails. They were smooth and rounded, like a woman's.

"Because no one seems to care about them except when the leaves have fallen. They're cultivated to be a slave to our fortunes of autumn. And tomorrow we'll clean up the remains of their bodies like soldiers fallen in battle, who they were and what they'll never be remaining behind in the colored stains on the cement of sidewalks and front porches," I said.

My sympathy.

No, my pity.

178

My childish pity for a sad fruit had brought together the tenderness in your eyes and the violent honesty I could not hide from them, could not suppress behind language and thought, things that were once blankets of immunity that hid me from the diseases of ambiguity and consequence. I should have retreated then, receded back into the isolation of my career and remained alone. Instead I allowed myself to move closer towards you, towards your existence and polite apprehensiveness. I was already hopeless and lost.

I wondered if you could see it when you dropped the letter off, through the front window, could still see the remnants of your fingerprints settled into the dust. None of your instruments took up space upon its frame any longer, the set of palette knives, the different length and style brushes scattered around the lip of a cracked and stained coffee cup. The only thing that occupied the solidarity of the unfurnished, stuffy room was the distributed pieces of our truncated marriage and the now pathetic, colorless silence that accompanied them. As well as photographs of our daughter Jennifer.

I turned on the faucet and watched the inconsistent stream of water rise to the rim of a glass. When I held it up to the light, aged, colored swirls showed through. I hadn't washed it so well. I had done it on purpose, kept some semblance of your existence behind I could measure and cherish, like I had Jennifer's. I had to unwrap it. It was still packed and I stepped on the newspaper when I sat down at the kitchen table. One of the small articles mentioned your upcoming retrospective and auction in New York. That advertisement was placed months ago and I wished I would have forgotten about it. The sound of the paper seemed to echo throughout the vacancy of an achromatic existence, a place where honest colors became emaciated, starved of their nutrients by tragic circumstance. Everything after was lonely and everything created by the new morning was stillborn.

I pinned your note to the wall with a pushpin. It stated your attorney would contact me when the divorce was finalized and you had signed the papers. You made arrangements at the bank to have 50% of the funds garnered at the auction from your works placed into my account. I didn't care about the settlement. Somehow you knew I wouldn't be there. Somehow you knew I wouldn't go to New York. I hated the presumptiveness in your arrogance and I despised myself for letting you understand so much about me I should never have.

~

I was alone here at the local community college's art department, unable to even glance into the sullenness of my own reflection, examine any of the paintings from past students that adorned the sterility of the dressing room. It's hard to trace back and understand where things started to bend, where passion and pride shifted against the immobility of my own sense of reason. I had disappeared into the collective ravine of forgotten objects, like articles of clothing or a damaged painting, slipped to represent an unprofitable body of work.

I laid a robe over the small dressing screen behind me and struggled to unfasten the white buttons of my blouse. I pulled down on the delicate straps of my bra, slid each one over my shoulders, and exposed my breasts as if I were going to be alone with a lover, allow the sometimes awkward, but tender intimacy of the moment to acquiesce me. I raised my legs and stepped out of the shelter of my intimates. I touched the deserted wasteland of my stomach and sensed my daughter Jennifer, her loss through the retrospection of her feeble legs struggling to kick at the comfort of my insides, your hands rushing to my extension to understand and all the more, take part in her joy. That joy should have lasted longer.

My skin was so insulated, no longer soluble to the tendencies of the supple pressures in the esoteric, but didactic movement of your hands. I rubbed my shoulders as if they were unfamiliar to me. There was blue ink on my neck above the collar of my blouse. I moistened a cloth and wiped away the unwanted flaw off of my skin. Should I have left it there, the small, foreign imperfection as a reminder that everything beautiful inevitably collapses into a cold chasm of ruin and extinction, a perfect example of disillusionment? No. It was up to them out there to baptize me in the colors of the corrupted. A bell chimed in the empty hallways. It sounded distant, like a ship lost at sea, trying to find its way back to the shores of a loved one. The first art class started soon.

The hue I was saturated in from the fluorescent lights of the dressing room rolled across the veracity of my shoulders as I continued to rediscover them, trickled down to the edges of my water colored anatomy. I was undressed by your actions and the actions of others, abandoned and pulled down into the most unprocessed of emotions. I felt raw and scared, like a child missing in a blinding winter storm. I removed my wristwatch and set it down on the edge of the sink.

The process in which I once loved you was bleached, scorched and whitened by the savageness of your infidelity. You painted me once in a room like this one, before I rinsed my body in the shower after jogging, in the most introspective of dyes. There should have been nothing spectacular about it. A simple woman, baptized in her body's perspiration, undressing after running outdoors. It wasn't listed in the catalogue of your retrospective delivered to me, which I had brought here without my knowledge. There was also one outside among the textbooks and easels here. I tossed through its first few numbered pages and struggled to understand who the woman in those pieces was, why I couldn't recognize the characteristics in her face and cheekbones. The first painting surprised me. It represented more of our ending for me, or the beginning you may have wanted all along. *Page 3.*

It was easy to see the cutting discontent for our life together you had painted, placed so unevenly in the subtlety of the leaden representation of color, insinuated in the cruelty and the brutality of the winter's commonness. I always thought the painting looked incomplete, that there was more you wanted to say, but didn't. I never gave you the chance. You disguised suspicion and pity in the impracticalities of the inherent disorder of undertone. You chose not to paint more into that landscape.

I remembered the day, the morning after that snowstorm. It was so cold. You painted everything around the house on that canvas so dark, so raw with complete apathy and indifference. The bleak unhappiness you must have felt because of me reached the outside edges of the withered canvas. If I reached out with my hands to touch it, bits of moisture would have formed on my fingertips and rested there until I moved them closer to my lips. It reminded me of the time Jennifer licked her first icicle.

You were helping her build a snowman. It was the first time she had seen snow that wasn't captured on paper in one of your photography magazines or art history books. A little bit at a time you helped her mold his shape, but not too tall she couldn't reach his face. You tried to teach her how to shape it, use proper technique and distance, to not put the old carrot straight in for his nose, but to maintain the right lineage so people could see what he was feeling by the way the shadows moved across his face when the sun passed over his button eyes. She had taken each one from my sewing basket, spilled them across the floor of the living room. It didn't matter to her what color she picked, but I watched you crawl beside her and talk to her about what size and shade she used. The purple scarf she later pulled out of the closet that belonged to me was way too big. But she took care not to let it rest on the ground before she wrapped it around his neck.

The tips of the trees looked like indistinct fingers, extended and yet stunted by the characteristics of curiosity as to what went on in the warmth they could never be a part of. It gave them strength, the brutality of the oncoming seasons. At that moment I wanted to join them, feel the chill come through the window of the back door. It made me think there was warmth inside you kept to yourself. I felt like running to stand in front of their legs, the trees, waiting for them to lift me as if I were an infant in desperate need of their embrace, their guidance. I would sleep in their arms until spring, look down from atop their shoulders and wait for the bulbs to become impetuous, disregard their normal, exacting patience and push through the hungry soil like a newborn bird wailing for food from its mother. Never once did I remember you sculpting flowers with your fine brushes. There were no vigorous orchids or bougainvillea, nothing to give hope to the landscape change would come after Jennifer's death. That our purpose to one another could endure.

I wondered if you had felt that way through the aggregation of our marriage and my giving birth to Jennifer, misplaced and disinterested among the impetuous debris in the incomplete foreground and the illusions of gratification carried like particles of frost in the wind that slept underneath the ledges of the windows. You painted the distinct loss so casually, so matter of fact, the evaporation of autumn with simple discernment, such scorn and such misguided waste. I was immured in the fragile mythology of your silent winter. It bothered me I couldn't recall the name of the elderly couple that lived in that house behind us. I wondered if Jennifer were still here if I would have looked at that painting differently.

Not only were most of the paintings I inspired written about and dissected in the catalogue listed, but some of the preliminary sketches as well, nothing intricate fledgling designs and ideas, some actualized and others discarded. I wondered if you had kept that first painting inspired by me or if you were going to auction off our complete emotional wealth. Those precious colors always appeared to be at the end of your fingertips, staining the underside of each rounded nail smeared across the emptiness of my own canvas. They rested, confused in the indifference of the ceramic tiles along the walls, the intricate patterns of sculpture on the floor beneath my feet. They felt so cold in the delicate pockets of my skin.

I opened the door to the classroom studio, covered in a vermilion robe and walked into the center of the room. I felt cold even though the atmosphere was conducive to causing sweat to form on the small of my back. I shouldn't have been nervous. Exhaling, I pulled on the sash of the robe and let it collapse against the top of my feet, the material irritating the skin on the side of my ankle. I raised one leg and stood on a small pedestal, a wooden box draped with a satin cloth cut too long and spread across the floor like a beautiful, raging weed in one of Monet's paintings. I stretched my torso and admired the definition of my stomach. The long, raven hair you often lost the tips of your fingers in spread across the crest of my back and toppled across my wrists. I raised my eyes and studied the other artists, their concentration, and the way they appeared sad, elucidating on the pensive sultriness I tried to convey. They shouldn't be looking at me this easily. I should have been a privilege to them, a discovery. Instead I felt worn.

I looked down at my ankle, fixated on the scar that adorned the small, round bone, one the size of a child's, pressing against the extended outer muscles and tendons. The color always seemed pretty to me, the light pink lemonade shade of the line, the color of bubble gum. My bubble gum ankle. It itched when I remembered how it happened, when I watched the small trail of blood fall across the fleshy skin between my toes underneath the front porch. I broke from my statuesque position and arched my body back, my arms reaching toward the light coming in through the window. The movements gave my breasts a more defined shape, tightened the architecture of my abdomen and allowed the construction of the bones in my ribs to become exposed. The instructor told me to stop there and hold. Look at the hope she said as she traced her hands across my stomach.

Look at the hope she again whispered, her soft voice colliding against my flesh. That's what I wanted to hear.

What they painted here though was a forgery, a clever reproduction concealed by untold truths and silence, no matter how pure the intimacy in the representation turned out to be. You had a rare chance to experience the fragility of my undertones, the characteristics that individuated who I was, who I had been, but would never be again because of Jennifer's murder. The fresh colors dripping on each one of their palettes intended to seduce me. I wished I could tell them my secrets. I wished I could tell them I could not be inveigled, I could not be reconciled. I spread my fingers to envelop the boundaries of my neck and throat and swallowed hard, letting the delicate muscles undulate underneath them. I closed my eyes and allowed the recollection of your touch to overtake my basic movements.

It was as if you stood behind me, tugging on the material of the sash around my neck, trying to understand the perspective of my body, your chin nestled in the small pocket of my collarbone, taking hold of my thin wrist and passing it though the soft space between my breasts. I thought grains of sand were embedded into the concentric swirls underneath my thumb as it irritated the pale salmon flesh of my nipple. The instructor depressed a light switch behind me and suddenly I was blind, except for a small spotlight highlighting my upper body.

As I stopped and they began to study me in muted darkness, each instructed to examine the contrast of darkness and light in representation to the human muscle and dense bone of my body. I could feel the short hairs of your paintbrush collide against the inside of my thigh. The seconds passed beside me, behind me and underneath me. I felt like a prisoner, interrogated under that perspective, tortured with the violent instruments of your unparalleled talent. The seconds passed and I thought I saw you, trying to hide amongst the neophytes, critiquing their work, individual and distinct colors staining your skin, the light on your face changing, each time more arousing, each time more sensual. As those seconds disappeared and the vibrant paints dried and scattered like pollen from a Van Gogh flower, I was alone, your visage beside me, behind me, inside me. For the first time I noticed it was raining outside.

~

*Breathe.*

*Breathe.*

*Breathe so hard your lungs tear like tissue paper under the weight until what's left behind is unrecognizable and grotesque.*

I could smell your arrogance in the water, as if it fell from the muscular contours of your body. God I hated you because of what happened.

The water from the ceramic basin in the bathroom spilled across the countertops as I allowed the faucet to run, poison the dryness of my hands and forearms and rinse my body of the charcoal the instructor spread across the back of my shoulders. I wanted to pull away from its climate, like trying to avoid the tides on the beach, the numb feeling of the sand and the salt pulling between your toes. Your hands were once like beaches, soft, warm and familiar, reassuring me as I watched you create our second watercolor, now displayed next to your biography in the catalogue I wanted to scorch with the accelerants of loss. *Page 5.*

I listened to your affluent speech collapse along the edges of the permeable ocean and waited for the ashen clouds to rupture, the instability of their contents spilling out over the peacefulness and onto the sands. We sat together on the shoreline huddled and isolated within the boundless latitudes of our exoticism, but frightened and unsettled by the ease in which we became compromised with one another. I loved you without regard of consequence or reparations.

At times you were the most selfish man I had tasted, driven to levels of perfection and regard by your hubris, your innate need to succeed and conquer. Sometimes Jennifer and I were secondary. I bent, refracted like the fractured light that bounced off of the skin of the water in the painting. I was drowning in the fascinating moisture of your boldness. But inevitably it would dry out, evaporated by the distillation of the trust I endeared in you. I should have recognized the dissimilarity in the colors you had placed upon the tips of your brushes, the misguidance in the structure of their bound fibers. I laid in your arms thinking about the subtlety and the fragility of our covenant. It was so humid the sliding glass door frosted over with mist. I could see the steam rising from your body. I knew then it wouldn't last. It was too arrogant, too angry. There shouldn't have been spite in our mouths, in our fluids. It was something that couldn't sustain no matter how much we tried.

Later, I sat down on the beach alone and sipped from a glass of wine while you spoke to a potential client. A light wind pushed passed my shoulders and became lost in the trail of reeds and ocean grass behind me. The seagulls that graced the sand were gone and the only thing remaining was the intimacy of the water. The waves climbed the shoreline towards me and then retreated to their womb. It made me think you always knew you were going to leave me at some point. I should have respected and understood that. Like the water.

Its molecules changed. If I were to walk into its vast domain now, it would be colder. I would not be able to experience the elation of its more temperate nature at a better hour, when the orange sun watched over her. Earlier when we made love, your flesh was hot to the desperate touch of my caress. I stood from the shore and ran back to the hotel room. I wanted to know if I coaxed you into the shower and only allowed cold water to collide with our clinched bodies, if your skin would still feel the same to me. When I opened the door to our room, there was no one there.

But what makes a woman stay with a lover when she understands she would be irrevocably abandoned, left alone with delicate questions never answered? And I believe now that is why you often painted the world and us in such quiet and exquisite retrospect, ignored what I considered to be the significant details of our violent time together and the scenes that should have been vivacious and impassioned. The intrinsic value of an object is often attained by the acceptance and the evidence of its rarity.

~

I opened the main door and sat down inside the entranceway against the wall, seeking shelter from the brazen color of your eyes that appeared in the soft rain falling, clinging ever so slightly to the high grass, the petals of the vibrant tulips in the garden across the street. Their color would fade soon though. The few remaining students in the class walked passed me, unable to notice the light tears gathering their unique shape in the corners of my eyes. The early light from the streetlamps made them look like pieces of melted sun falling across a pale, barren desert. A desert of salinity. I wondered what those students would see if they looked long enough and close enough. Savage beauty or violent imperfection. When I dressed inside in front of the mirror my reflection held a haunted look, a look of isolation and collapse, a theme you termed in your paintings to be *'gentle ruin.'*

I wrapped my arms around my thighs and pulled my legs closer towards my body. The air was rude and bitter. I didn't want to go back into the genial, but distant, warmth of the classroom and listen to them subjugate, watch them rinse their pallets and hands, charcoal smudges resembling bruises on their knuckles, admire the paintings that didn't mean as much to you, to them, the remains of your life here that you left behind hanging on the walls. One of your smocks was still perched in the corner.

The creased pages of your catalogue were noticeable from the contents and leather material of my bag. My black dress slacks had risen higher up on my calves and again I noticed the imperfection on my ankle, my little pink scar. I took the heavy air into my lungs and held it. It felt as if my insides were going to collapse under the weight. The smell that hung in that air reminded me of rotting fruit left inside of a wicker basket in the summer as I hid underneath of the front porch of my childhood home.

I had only hid there a few times before that afternoon, from the lies and the secrets, the struggling ambiguity, the betrayal of adolescence. I once slid my slender body under the loose sideboard and pressed my flush cheeks against the arid soil. There wasn't much room to move around. It looked as if no one had ever been under there since the house was built. I wanted to dig under the roots of the trees and see if anyone had left things behind. There was nothing underneath me except an unknown history of soil, decay and assorted stones. I wondered if my father knew where I disappeared to sometimes.

That first summer day I chose to go there, the temperature rose and I sweltered in the intense heat, listening to the transistor radio my father had, the jazz music echoing through the floorboards. The person on the radio said the names of the artists after each song. I never heard of them. The salt from my sweat moistened my lips and made them turn into a light shade of salmon. The glass of lemonade I poured for him was perspiring, soaking a perfect circle into the wood. He took a long sip from the glass, the ice cubes sounding like church bells, and replaced it in another spot, closer to the gap between the boards. Some of the condensation fell through and I reached out my hand, balancing the coldness on the tips of my fingers. It tasted lonely, like the bitter, hard taste of metal.

Even with the consistent static and the distant hum of neighboring farm equipment, the landscapes and he were quiet and tranquil. Under that porch, I hoped he would whisper aloud his secrets, share them with the stars and the moon. There were so many things I never learned from him. He never talked to us much, my sister and I, never talked to us as young women about our intricate and delicate biology, never talked to us further about our mother, who had abandoned us when she died. He never talked about her. When anyone approached him concerning her, he sighed and altered the course of the conversation.

People called him stoic and I couldn't understand what they were talking about so I went to the library once to look it up. It meant indifferent or unaffected by pleasure or pain. I stayed under that porch, oftentimes for hours sometimes falling asleep in the dirt, in some abstract way to be close to him, hoping on some occasion he would need me. Need us. But he never opened up to me and never said a word, sipped his lemonade and rarely moved, occasionally stepping out of the rocking chair to water some pansies. He took exceptional care of them, nurtured them. The tint of their petals resembled the hue of my mother's skin, the tender palette of flesh on the inside joint of her elbow. That's why he gave them such unadulterated care, trying to keep a part of her present and close.

I inched closer to the opposite end of the porch, below the window leading into my older sister's bedroom. There were sounds coming through the break in the glass. All I could hear were slight moans, repeated in my sister's sometimes harsh voice. I couldn't tell if she was joyous or scared. He was in there again. There were times I know he abused her, but he said he would never hurt her. I heard him tell her he loved her. She said she didn't want anyone to hear them. *Let's runaway. I don't want to talk about it here. Let's leave right now. We can't but I want to be with you. But what about your father? He doesn't care about me. We could be careful, leave when he's at work. I don't want to talk about it right now. What is keeping you here?* I wanted her to say it was me, that I was the one person who mattered to her. The words I wanted to hear never came, even as she parted her lips and kissed him. All I heard her say was she loved him and nothing would change.

She was four years older than I was, but remained more immature in some respects. I was only 14 but I wanted to become a woman, have her help me, become worldly and mature so I could understand how someone so much in love could disappear, could give up all she had, everything she had given birth to. There was so much anger I brought about when I thought of our mother, why she died, and moreover, that she wasn't there to tell me what to do now. I was afraid if my sister was gone, I would be incommensurate as a woman, unable to differentiate between love and contempt, intimacy and proximity. In part I wanted to give my father the regard he lost, sculpt anew from what he had had become. A shapeless and vacant carcass of water, organs, blood and bones. But a person should never grow up suddenly. Sometimes it made them audacious instead of circumspect.

I thumbed through some more pages in the catalogue. On certain ones there were discussions on lighting, shading, what brought about the themes either hidden behind the colors you chose or seen in the bold, oftentimes pained images. Things I would have never told anyone were mentioned in passing, as if they possessed no deep meaning for you. You told the world our secrets, instructed them on how to gain admission to the most private and intimate parts of me.

Although my name was never attached to any individual painting, I was there, visible in the stunning cobalt blues and tender grays. Tears developed in my eyes when I read your words telling strangers where to touch me, where to arouse, what promises made the tiny hairs rise on the small of my back. I hated your for that, but more so for another piece. *Page 8.* You never showed this one to me. I recognized the distance of the trees behind the house and how they looked like thin colored pencils pressed into the ground. There should have been a small wicker basket on the corner of the porch. It would have been so miniscule and insignificant I couldn't tell what rested inside of it. But you removed it although it would never change what happened. I could see the bleached areas within the paint of where the porch structure attached right above the front door. I wished I could have asked you why you failed to include it. It wasn't until now I regretted telling you what happened.

~

The rain searched its way through the aluminum gutters, dripped onto the edges of the concrete and into the grass. It sounded like a thousand fishing lures breaking the surface of a lake. It reminded me of the fisherman you painted off the coast of Maine in that secluded boathouse purchased by your parents before Jennifer was born. I would watch you scrutinize them every morning while steam rose from the cup of coffee at your feet. The mornings when you painted them, sometimes before dawn, were so tranquil and still. I would watch you through the open window, the curtains drawn, trying to entice you to come back into our bedroom and make love to me. You never wavered in the intensity of your concentration, testing the uncertainty of some colors on the edges of the canvas. If you would have broken and turned only once you would have seen me standing there, the breeze coming in off of the lake nudging aside your favorite red dress shirt so that my breasts warmed in the sunrise.

There was nothing there now, dried supplies, some spoiled groceries and toys she used to play with. A portion of the clothes she wore. You appeared to punish me for what happened by putting most of her things there where I could not touch them after she left, could not handle them and remember her gentle laughter and curiosity. You wanted me to forget about her. I could see your reflection in the water of that mural and I wanted to reach in and disrupt its equanimity, drink from the bounty of its ingredients.

But the inexperience of nature there was tainted because of our failure, the water virulent to the composition of my lips, obstructive to the economy of those elderly fishermen, whose struggle you once captured in such unique plainness. I could always see them when we were there, through the neglected glass of the windows, reeling in their catch before the sun rose, removing the rough, tempered line from their catch. I hardly slept during the nights even after you had made love to me, gave me your passion, knowing all along your body was holding back. Sex with you had begun to make me feel alone and insufficient, but I never stopped you from entering me because I wanted loved by you. By someone. Needed. A lover always knew what the truth actually was, especially a woman. There wasn't a need for me to question it at all, deconstruct it. I needed assurances that seemed too inappropriate for your body to give to me any longer.

I wondered when that other woman had touched you, where she had first discovered the complex substance of your canvas, your fingertips still stained with the complicated resins of the paint's base. You had stretched out the tree line from a stranger's perspective in that third painting, distancing yourself from the obscure background. And I was lost there in the relationship between the bay and the stone at the base of the lighthouse. I didn't remember it in proportion to the boat you said we needed that sat abandoned, tied to the edge of the dock like a wanted criminal. In your note you said I could look after it now. There was little I knew about boating. I would go up there once more, clean the property, scrub the molded edges of the walkway to the dock with bleach and let everything drown. I could retrieve some of Jennifer's things and place them here. I wondered if those fishermen were still there, voyeurs to the coming sunrise, wading waist high in the unpredictability of our subsequent gallery, waiting for me to return to them.

The rains continued to dampen the morning. Burdened by the denseness of emotional complexities and failures, I moved through the memories raised by each painting. I turned the pages of the catalogue hesitantly, like a child tenses in reading a ghost story by flashlight in the dark. Beyond the light sounds of thunder and the faint screams of past tragedies, I could hear the distant engine of a bus coming down the street. It sounded muffled, like a child crying under a blanket, our child as she nursed from the comfort of my tender breast in our cold bedroom.

I wiped the rain and tears from my eyes and tried to distance myself from the art and the uncertainty and the awkward intimacy of the relationship between the students and myself. Another student left the building, the intrusive wind fighting its way through the small space between the frames, further tossing aside the pages of the catalogue. *Page 24.* I stared at the bones and muscles in my naked back, strands of my dark hair cutting the tender plane of alabaster skin over my right shoulder.

The water in the cast iron tub stuttered from the brass faucet. I pushed opened the door and stood above her crib before taking a seat at the edge of the bed. I barely had the strength to remove my own clothes. Steam slipped into her bedroom like a thief. I watched it move along the edges of the baseboards then disappear. The tight, black slacks I wore to go to dinner still cradled the shape of my hips, my legs. You never came home. I removed my bra and stood in the doorway, moving closer to the tub. I undressed further and raised a leg and placed it into the water. It numbed me and it shouldn't have.

Till the water was cold and unfamiliar I sat on the rim of the bathtub, waiting for you. Doubt was a close lover. I cupped some water in my right palm and dripped it over the right side of my neck and collarbone. It was clear, but you later added small pieces of black cinders into the painting, especially around my face, as if my tender fingertips could break the surface of the world to scorch everything. As if I was pestilence. I pulled the drain from the bathtub and listened to the circular waves of dull water collapse through the metal screen and rush into the pipes. The sound was hollow. For some reason, it made me feel impermanent.

There were no words spoken when you arrived home and woke me. I had fallen asleep, calmed by the light breathing of our daughter on the monitor. I wished I could sleep as she had, closed my eyes and dream. The pressure from your body shifted me closer towards you. I tensed when the fine fibers of a small, detailed horsehair brush traced across the curves of my back. I soon asked you what color you were using and you answered as you kissed my shoulder blade and spine. It was ashen, a hue you often used to symbolize failure and fear in your portraits. I asked you if that's what I reminded you of, pain and loss, the attribution of uncertainty and decline.

You placed the brush in another spot harder and whispered across my flesh I was beautiful, but fragile. Inside hid an intense and tender woman terrified and afraid. That is what you saw in me, your lover, and the mother of your only child. Apprehension. Aversion. Timidity. I opened my body to you, uncovered my breasts and stomach, turned towards you, my slender legs rubbing against one another. When I remained untouched by your body I understood. There was someone else. I should have been honored and I should have been valued. I wondered what words scrolled along the architecture of my back and shoulders.

As I neared the edge of the road, the bus was now less than 200 feet away. I couldn't go to New York. But I knew I had to see you once more. I could never let go of you or Jennifer. I placed a foot onto the first step and when the pneumatic door opened, allowed the man in front of me to enter the bus and asked the driver if he was going to New York. He said there was another bus I could transfer to. The colors from your paintings seemed to be noticeable in the structure, the dingy shade of the gray tires and rims covered in brake dust and oil. They streamed and poured down the sides of the smeared windows, clashed with the clear raindrops and spilled onto the black street, the morose tones invading the broken branches and bleached curbsides, masking the colored chalk the kids scratched hopscotch numbers with, destroying the evidence that innocence was ever there once.

When I reached out and grabbed onto the interior handrail of the bus I retreated, overcome by the oppressing odor of burning wood and grass, paint thinner, blindsided by the still drying images on canvases that followed behind. It all seemed threatening instead of calming. I realized how dangerous seeing you again could be. As much as I wanted reconstructed by never seeing you, never hearing your voice, I wanted ruined by it all as well. There were only a few other passengers inside, but I took a seat towards the rear of the bus away from everyone else. A few of the overhead lights were out. My footsteps sounded hollow on the metal floor when I passed by a handicapped man and another gazing through the window, running his fingers across the inside of his elbow. The interior was humid, uncomfortable and condensation appeared on the panes of glass.

I touched my finger to it, the sweat and longed to lick the salt from the back of your neck as you painted the plush, endless green acreage behind our home on an easel, the sun punishing the skin on your back. That mural appeared out of place in the inventory. *Page 7, upper right.* It wasn't as detailed and intense as I once remembered. It was the only painting you hadn't titled. It was 5 a.m. when I discovered you alone outside, the sun imprisoned behind your interpretation of mornings' early struggle. The grass was high and the blades touched the sides of your ankles, dampened the bottoms of your shoes. I wished you would come inside and leave tracks on the kitchen floor so I felt I had a purpose. Your purpose.

There was no hiding her, protecting her within the sullen blue colors splashed across the invariable range of her sands, like dark coral on the ocean floor, drowning in salinity and destitute amongst the sunless depths. I wondered how long she would have been able to sustain when your paints, your inspiration poured over her, the deepest colors of the world seeping into her pores. But she was too beautiful not to see. Once she had opened, stripped herself of all her inadequacies and her sanctuary, barren amongst the structure and colors of your wasteland, the small fibers of your brush tracing along the definitiveness of her sex, you were her messiah.

Was it the first time you had seen her with that much passionate detail, seduced by the fervent tenacity of one of God's elegant reproductions, lying there on the floor of your studio, her flesh and body agitated, but aroused by the placement of your hands across her breasts, molding her into what you wanted her to be? Or did she seduce you with the gentle promises of passion and understanding about what had happened? The thought you might have let her conquer you through the weakness and vulnerability about our daughter's murder made me sad and angry as well.

I never saw you that way, almost pathetic and pitiful among the ruins. Did she let you sob on her smooth shoulders, tears of misunderstanding and disillusionment finding their way downstream along the banks of her neck and throat then pass through the caverns of her bones and breasts? No, you ruled her. I was sure of that. With your persuasion and your exoticism she broke in the presence of your will, your persistence and the innate need you had to recreate everyone you came in contact with. How many times did you paint her, tell her how stunning and alluring she would be on a pale white canvas, surrounded by various pigmentations that only spoke one thing, the truth? The truth about the emancipation she would feel as a woman, inapprehensive and raw on a drop cloth, watching you reconstruct her lines and her lips.

Should I find solace in your omissions regarding her or had you been careless in removing her sense of touch and her countenance again, bound to your linear perception by the collapsing of her lungs when you touched the tender cavity inside her smooth thighs? *Page 7, bottom right.* When you used me, there was always criticism behind each depiction, each direction. It lingered on the backs of my bare shoulders. It affected me, your judgment in how I moved, how I pulled my hair across the nape of my

194

neck to expose the clandestine areas of those shoulders. But could she move, slide her body across the areas you wanted her to, turn her head at the proper angles, her eyes pure pools of Chinese blue liquid? You never painted me in such stimulated regard without severe analysis, never opened up my blouse and discovered the geography of my body, standing over me as I posed nude, the wax from a candle dripping, shaping, the composition of the fluid changing, reacting with me.

The morning after you admitted your "misconception" as you called it, you left me alone, the rationalizations a woman expected to encounter repeating with the desolate walls of my self-loathing. You weren't even there to allow me to descend into indignation and doubt. I should have been allowed to become angry, been given the respect to first grieve and then salvage. The guilt your judgment about Jennifer induced upon me was disfiguring. But did they see it in that classroom, those artisan neophytes, as I lay nude and effortless before them, motionless among their questions and their criticism? Was my once indelible, tender body now wretched and poison to their erect canvas, causing their vision and colors to hemorrhage? The speckles of rain coming through an open window in front of me on the bus gathered in the small pocket between the bones of my shoulder. I wasn't as beautiful as I once had been.

I did admire how that small painting in your retrospective resembled a worn photograph, the small scratches at the bottom of the critic's point of view, contrasted by the advection of the morning atmosphere concentrated over the sagging shoulders of foliage. The representation of the isolation I felt was so vibrant, so dense with my pain and instability as if you were experiencing affliction through me, through my uncertainty. In the painting I couldn't tell if it was raining or not. The bus stopped and idled at the next traffic light.

I could almost see you on the opposite side of the street, seated on a wooden overturned planter box at the edge of that foreclosed property, dipping your paintbrush into an empty vase full of water, the mailbox disproportioned and rusted over your right shoulder. The flowers that once occupied that space had fallen into the kitchen sink, their various colors scattered and stained across the nicked, porcelain basin. Some of the intensity of the petals faded, as if you had spilled bleach on them while washing dishes. When you stood and moved beside the incomplete canvas to change your perspective, I saw that woman's lithe, naked body emerge from the woods, our daughter chasing behind, her fingers fumbling to gain access to the inside of her palm.

Once reached, she gripped her bones, terrified of abandonment and insecurity. For a brief moment our daughter turned towards me, her eyes sullen and disconcerted. Ashamed. I haven't been able to sleep for days, exhausted by the heavy images of your body crossing over the unexplored sands of her desert. I was a hostage, blindfolded, tortured by the very man I had once promised everything to. I wondered about how you would react when you saw me come in to the auction, her arm wrapped around your elbow and then reaching up to brush her fingers across the nape of your neck to remove a speck of dirt or a hair out of place. She might have even kissed you there as I once had, allowing her lips to linger along the stratus of your throat, the indecipherable map of your flesh.

~

I removed a pin from my hair and allowed it to drop down across my shoulders and cover the water falling in one me from the window. It deadened the intensity of the oppressiveness inside the bus. It was quiet sitting alone, a bit desolate like walking through a desert or a silent film, except for the mechanics of the bus starting and stopping. No one else had gotten on at any of the last few stops. It was like no one cared to understand I was there, see me. That was all I wanted, to be remembered, to leave something behind other than colors and murals, images no one but you and I would ever understand. Jennifer was supposed to be that innocent admonition. I turned to another page in the catalogue. *Page 13.*

I rubbed my shoulders and understood how much I hated that concurring painting on that page, the truth it beheld in such rich and stunning arrogance. I stood and shut the window as the rain changed its rhythm. The handicapped man closed his eyes when he turned and saw me. In the distance was a side road, a stretch of over 600 feet, where inoffensiveness and aggression had led to everything, isolation and tragedy. My hands trembled as we neared the corner of Washington and Garden.

The lucidity of that street was constricted by the claustrophobia you induced through your intemperance and insensitivity of light. The leaves on the line of trees were bleeding, severed by the edges of decay in the once plush garden of our marriage. You made the branches burn with the indecency of garnet, seared and fed by the relentless breath of the wind. It made everything appear pernicious and promiscuous when it shouldn't have. Autumn was her favorite time of the year.

I must have told you that countless of times when she wanted to go the McIlheny's farm for Halloween. She had your appreciation for boldness and color. You were too busy to understand her or had you forgotten, to be later consumed by your narcissism and selfishness? For some reason the intensity of the undertones in the painting made me sad we would never have any more children after the accident. That was something we shouldn't have classified it as, an accident. Everyone knew it wasn't, including the local police. But no one knew for certain until her autopsy results were released. When given specifics of how she died, I was devastated. And for some reason you blamed me.

The waters that had gathered in the greens after that storm carried the blood of those leaves and our daughter across the asphalt roadways in front of that house refracted the indecision you and I harbored afterwards. We had been there so many times with Jennifer when she was younger, watching her ride her tricycle in and out of the puddles that hovered in its unevenness. There was a trust with them, an understanding nothing would happen to her. She loved going over to visit them, swim in the backyard pool, especially after school. We never had a chance to report her missing. She was seen leaving school alive and unconcerned. The horrid phone call came the next morning.

But I couldn't tell when I looked at that watercolor, gained no sense of loss or destitution through those bleeding leaves. It was as if you constructed the view as a character actor, a charming and credible player who was hiding his demons behind proud colors and desire. Instead of being lured into a sense of faith and promise, I was ambushed by actuality, crushed and undone.

No one could see the regret behind your counterfeit as you held my hand when told the news. I had wanted you to clutch it tighter, provide some inherent meaning to your actions. All you responded with were words that bled hollow, down the contours of your arm and across your fingers and into that street. You loved and trusted the canvas more than me. Everything would eventually wash away and it angered me you found encouragement there, as if you slept upon her blackened and rigid body, the sidewalks her alabaster arms embracing you.

There was nothing more we could say to each other when the police pulled her body from that pool. What were we supposed to do now? No one told you, not the police or their psychologists what to do after your child was murdered. In place of anger, I embraced guilt and culpability, personified in the details and shades you painted. Especially the perspective, the distance between the far edge of the street and the camera's eye. The leaves in those trees were insulting and irresponsible. Did you ever include her? There was no mention of Jennifer on any pages. And I was glad.

As much as I missed her I could have never glanced upon her on canvas, seen her grace paralleled in angles and enamel, a sobering reminder I was childless and I was vacant. You used what happened there, the death of our daughter, as an excuse to seek abdication from the grief we should have fought together. Instead you laid in ambush in the undressed and protective shape of another woman. The emptiness and the lack of clarity in the water in the foreground was a misrepresentation of hope, something you took from me and misplaced.

The bus began again and I watched the street pass by behind me. The rain and what had been happening here made the town look tarnished and dull, like unpolished silver. The winds carried a small blanket from the front porch of a house onto the grass. It remained there untouched. I watched it change colors almost immediately from the transparent blue of a robin's egg to the shade of pale winter frost. It would take tender care to heal and clean, caressing the stains until they soon faded over time.

I imagined it belonged to a young girl, given to her by her grandmother. She was supposed to save it for her wedding day, place it across her shoulders over her dress under a cool evening breeze. Or bring home her newborn baby within its tender construction. But somehow she had misplaced it, allowed it to remain unattended on the front porch. It made me sad. I watched the blanket try to move, weighted down against the soil by the wind and the rain. My fingertips pressed against the glass. Everything appeared so unconquerable. I wasn't sure why, but I started to sob, pulled my fingers down along the window, leaving distorted impressions behind. The deformations gathered on the glass and resembled those left behind on the panels of that lighthouse. Page 16. It was the one less than a mile from our boathouse by the bay, where I should have remained and should have taken her away from you.

I climbed the old steel ladder that led to the crest of that lighthouse once and I sat there for hours without thinking of anything but the way the shape of the water changed when the winds moved across the concavity of the bay. But things became so motionless, stilled under the dim light of a shy moon. You should have brought the definition towards you more when you painted it. The way you cast the light across the rungs made them look immaterial, so fragile like tissue paper and if I were to climb its heights, I would fall into the arms of the water and the cavernous, jagged rocks below.

I wrapped myself in that old, tattered quilt your mother gave to us on our wedding day. Do you remember? She had said it belonged to your grandmother. I wasn't sure what I should do with it anymore. Even though it was you who had betrayed us, I felt like my skin was damaging the delicacy and simplicity of the hand woven fibers. Your mother telephoned after she found out what had happened. She tried several times to get in touch with me. I leaned back against the crudeness of the white brick, listening to the fabricated, mechanical sounds coming from inside the lighthouse. I thought she was careful, but deliberate with the words she chose, never blaming anyone in specific, but also never absolving me from my responsibilities as a wife and a mother. I hoped she spoke the way she did that she didn't want to offend me. She was right when she expressed her concerns over the difference in the inexperience of our separate but beautiful youths.

The rains had diminished and all the sounds inside the bus became suppressed by pain and illness. I closed my eyes as chills passed over my arms and legs, numbing the senses I once held exclusively discomposed. Selling the images and murals should have unburdened me. In place, each one's disappearance suffocated the independence I thought I could sustain. You tried so hard to maintain a dictatorial hold over the shape of things around me, seduce the precious elements of my topography. You measured yourself as a water-colored alchemist, an intelligent handler of chemicals and dyes and now the very substance of oils and resins in those paintings appeared to enshroud me, choke the warmth and blanch the suppressed colors of my now destructible femininity. I was your map, a place where you could live, a place where you could conquer.

~

Months must have passed before you had painted that street again, the solitude of that small, white house where Jennifer's body was found, masked by the fragile security of the thinning pine needles. *Page 11.* What made you revisit the tragic surroundings of her murder so soon after what happened? Was it an act of catharsis or did she become consumed by your grief and beg you to rid yourself of that violent purgatory? A place where she was too scared to walk, to pass through for fear of reminding him someone else loved him once, cherished him even for all the things he once hated about himself. I had wanted to touch upon its doors in the months after you had gone. I wasn't sure how many times I walked along the deadened silence of that street, waiting for our daughter to come running out of the trees, shouting with excitement she was fine, she was hiding and wasn't hurt. It was all supposed to be make-believe, pretend, like we were plastic pieces of her giant dollhouse she could dress talk to, place wherever she wanted and love.

The woman who had found our daughter's body lived in that simple house. I had no idea what to say to her and her family all the times I looked into that white house, watched through the front window, sometimes noticing the polite way she placed food upon her dining room table. I thought at first, as the authorities did, it was an accident and she had fell and struck her head, leaving her unconscious. But it turned out someone had placed her body in the pool after the fact.

I never feared for her safety because you were always with us. To a child's eyes, a parent is unconquerable and secure. And our daughter adored you, the comfort you provided for her when she awoke in the middle of the night. I sometimes went to her side, but she always wanted to hold your hand, as if I were too feeble and inefficient. It was wrong to be jealous and hate you for that, but I did. When it happened, she most likely thought you would be there. No one could ascertain with certainty where she had been murdered because of the condition of the environment around her. Apparently water washed away a lot of physical evidence. The police also had said her body was battered. I always hoped it was after the fact. I couldn't imagine our daughter going through that. I didn't want to know.

The painting was so sterile though, the wires and tress all in their places. Nothing was even disturbed. You acted as if nothing had happened there, that innocence and joy were still living in the cut grass and painted traffic lines. But nothing existed there that was happy or naïve. I couldn't find any resemblance to the peace you had duplicated in the stillness of the almost colorless milieu. It made me think that there was nothing for me, no reason or motivation to continue with this irreparable journey of self-discovery through color and remembrance. It had the coldness of mortality. You painted that woman's house on the vast edges of the canvas, so far removed from the truth.

I must have stood in front of her door at least four different times since. Once I even found the resolve and strength to walk up the driveway, wondering what to say to her. I had so many questions, most of which I understood within my heart she would never have the answers to. I wanted to know if she reached into that pool and brushed aside her hair, tried to help her. I never spoke to her even with the knowledge she might have been the last person to touch our daughter with care, with compassion or with sincere gentility.

After being on that street for hours the last night we lived together, I gathered some of my clothes while you were gone, the sudden unfamiliarity of everything around me deadening. There were some of her things on your dresser, some strands of her hair isolated on the dull bristles of a hairbrush. I could see them in the reflection of the medicine cabinet mirror. How I had been replaced, without vacillation, without balance. , I hoped we would reconcile, pardon our misgivings. Would you have designed our reunion on canvas? Or would you have ignored our chances and remained by her side, forever debased by her power? You didn't even have the decency to hide it from me.

~

A small girl peered out from behind a set of curtains from one of the houses. She could have been her child. I could see because of the lights on behind her, that her hair was long and dark, touching the blades of her shoulders. You would have sculpted her with your brushes to further resemble our daughter, changed the tint of the shades to match the furniture your muse picked out. The bird bath in the front yard of the house was shaped in a dingy, faded stone. In your mural, it would have been clean, polished, small droplets of water clinging to its lips, patterned after the ovals rolling down the rear emergency door of the bus. The colors might have been different, the brazenness in the dogwood tree, unattended and decomposing along the edge of the sidewalk.

Behind the house was a large, tilled over field. There were hundreds of spooled hay bales, wound in large circles. It was usual around here, archaeological relics of unsteady agriculture. Scattered birds milled around the ground, dipping their heads into puddles of water. You most likely would have forgotten them, failed to attract the watcher's eye to their baptismal ritual, absolve them from the criticisms of our perspective. I wondered if the little girl in that house ran around those huge bails, joyous underneath of their overwhelming size which cast shadows over her body. To her it would have been like climbing through mountains, gripping her tiny fingers into the strands of hay to reach the top. And what would she have done when she got there? I couldn't remember what I did when I conquered. When I looked back at the window, the little girl was gone.

In her place was a broken flower, a lily, the soil spread across the window ledge. The richness and color of the soil seemed to absorb itself into the frame, darken the textured wood and individual grains like a parasite. Like rot. Things were disappearing. The glass pane dissolved into bits of white snow and fell onto the ground. The destruction was acidic, seized every corner and angle of the house. It bled into the ceiling beams. Tiles adapted into small birds. Some were able to take flight and others drifted towards the ground. They were so black, ones that didn't make it. They looked like were refugees from an oil spill.

Too heavy for flight, some plummeted downward into the naked trees snapping frail branches. Abruptly each branch crumbled into millions of grains of sand, pooling at the base of the tree. A vast desert of sand pulled away from the stump and in its place was you, naked and bathed in artificial light, surrounded by the discoloration of water. The ecological evidence that had once existed in the plane of your habitat had been washed away by the violent attrition of the tides crashing around your ankles, the coming and going of the strange water eroding the delicate chemistry of your materials. A lone seagull remained in front of you, a scavenger of unfulfilled dreams and anticipation, feasting, gorging on my naked bones, leaving me to rot, to become a petrified deposit lying under the surface of the loam.

Suddenly voices were raised when the handicapped man stood and held a gun over his head. Oh my god! Bordering on sobbing, he pulled the trigger. When I tried to cover up, the catalogue dropped from my bag sitting next to me and onto the floor. The pages had spread out. It was odd, but I thought about that piece. Page 34. When I saw it, the volatile essence of everything around you, no matter how transitory, how unimportant erupted. It wasn't violent though and at first I wasn't sure why I concentrated on it so singularly. Nothing could remained unharmed though on our easel, people and dreams soluble, absorbed and washed away by our selfish will, our slight breath carried on the cusp of the wind.

It was so gorgeous the morning after her murder and I thought how cruel the world had become, how our only child could be removed from us. Where the colors I felt were bitter and damaging, but incredible lines of warm, gold leaf could pour down from the heavens upon the fragile fragments in the sand. I stood there unseen and crying, the water from the mocking sea cascading across my toes and ankles. People walked past me, but it wasn't up to them to notice my despair. You should have.

It should have been you who discovered my body lying embracing the tides, the warm water rolling over my shoulders. Our exhausted appetites were obsolete because of what happened, deteriorated and no longer retained that phosphorescent brilliance, like the albescent foam which appeared to dissolve around the seagull's feet and mine, corroding along the shoreline like acid. I wondered if it was then that you decided I could not be changed or altered by you. It wasn't what you wanted anymore. I wasn't.

But you couldn't wash me, cover me with a different color or mask the imperfections in my muscles and bones. You were stubborn, like a prized pugilist, weathered by age and erosion who believes he still possesses the fixity of purpose and dexterity to defeat younger and undisciplined opponents. You made the world look like bent glass, fractured and twisted, the water itself asphyxiated by the dispersion of oxygen. I grieved. Unfortunately I would never be as close to you as I am through color.

I wasn't sure what was happening. Instinctively I searched for you in the landscapes, the depressed shades of olive and ash overtaking the grey streets. Would you have painted her there in one of the windows, a look of concern and empathy blurred across her face? Or would you have tried to protect her from the disruption and disorder going on around me? I was sure I would die here alone, imagining you and her having a child, the one you denied me. You had painted with such repetitive lines of conjecture and indifference throughout your noble culminations, masked what you knew in the artificiality of the suppressed imbalance of reality and what I believed through your promises. I had long given up on the unsteady object of hope that lingered in the hurt of what you had left behind.

~

The handicapped man wouldn't let us open any windows after he let the driver off. The emergency lights from the ambulances in the distance, along with the humidity inside the bus reddened my eyes. Each one itched, and I was terrified to close them, exhausted from crying. Members of the police were standing behind yellow sawhorses I also knew even if I needed help, you wouldn't come.

Someone on the outside might have called you, told you what had happened. But I doubted it. I wouldn't have wanted them to. Oftentimes you only cared when you needed something from me. When you did call, in the background, I could always hear her laughter, her joy and your happiness in her. That broke me. That you never had enough respect for me to understand how difficult it was, losing Jennifer. You should have had the decency to leave me alone or talk to me without her there, where I couldn't trace the scent of violets in the air around me, her smell travelling past your lips and through the world.

I leaned back against the window and wiped away some of the condensation. But then I lowered my hand. I didn't want him to think I was signaling someone. It was hard to tell what people were doing outside. There was so much movement and all seemed scattered and haphazard, no shapes, no substance, a sad crisis of circumstance painted by Jackson Pollock. There were fire trucks, ambulances and other emergency responders. I thought I could make out a local news van raising equipment that looked like a satellite from the roof. The man holding us here sat at the front of the bus, tapping the tip of the gun on the floor. The sound scraped at my head, like car brakes grinding. He had been doing it for almost a half an hour. The rain had lessened.

Underneath one of the bus seats about two rows up rested the catalogue. I could make out one of the pages when the lights rotated through the glass. *Page 26.* The edge was covered in blood. It came from one of the men, the one with his head buried in his hands. There was blood on them as well. The handicapped man had struck him above the right eye on his temple. A siren bellowed beyond the trees behind me. I looked down. The colors on that page dripped an anguishing history across the floor of the bus. I remembered feeling this hopeless once. I had looked at that painting about an hour or so ago after hearing the gunshot. I could smell the chemicals saturated into the delicate filament of the canvas and how their stench impeded the maturity of the air struggling to continue its journey across the coastline.

Summers along it could be tepid throughout most of the day. At least until the sun went down. It wasn't often I could get you to sit on the beach and ignore your work, listen to the whimper of the dying waves pour out across the cooling sand. The footprints of children making castles had long digested into the stomach of the sea. It wouldn't be until morning that people walking there would step on seashells and dried seaweed. It was another empty canvas for you to fill.

Seagulls sounded like ship horns. A small shop around the corner rented bicycles. They were odd shapes, tall, like ones from an advertisement in the 1920's or props from a circus. The restaurants were all closed except for one place, 'Norah's', a quaint café where they rented out blankets and picnic baskets. Most of the time when we were there, I ordered a bottle of wine and a late dinner we could enjoy on the sand. Waiting for you once, I stood at the edge of the dune and took in the atmosphere. A new hotel was being framed about three miles in the distance. To my left was a handcrafted furniture warehouse built in the 1940's. I shielded my eyes and turned facing the water. It was then I understood why you painted so much, why it was hard to get you to focus on one singular objective when so much passed around you.

A few weeks before the fire we sat close together on a cobalt blue blanket and watched the stars turn on and stun some of the blackness. It was one of those times where we would walk home a little drunk, hand in hand along the thin sidewalks, wishing some of the shops would open up. Sometimes we stayed there all night and watched the sun rise. It was nothing extraordinary. The sun rose everywhere. But it was different here for me. You understood that and I loved that about you. I didn't have to make you see the world like I did. You accepted it, made commentary about the tint mixed within the horizon or how you would have changed the direction of the wind. Our time there was my page from a coloring book and you never strayed outside the lines. At least not then.

That night we barely made it through the front door before I had to touch you. The light was still on in your studio which was constructed from a converted garage. Tall racks held dozens of colors of paint and brushes, some thick and hairy, others thin, like an underdeveloped moustache or the hairs on your forearms. White tables housed discolored jars of water and newspaper. The faint smell of turpentine shattered through the wine running its course through my blood. On top of one of the shelves was the pumpkin you painted for me when I first met you. You were more beautiful now. There was no question. Half empty tubes of watercolors rested on a smaller table below the light switch. They weren't as harsh as some of the tones you often used. A huge roll of butcher paper stood in the corner. It weighed so much. I stopped you from turning off the light.

Still numb, but certain, I let you embrace me and lay me down onto one of the large tables. It was where you had started another large for the wall of an elementary school in town. Local kids had sprayed graffiti on the back wall and instead of covering it up you thought if it was more beautiful, people wouldn't abuse it. Make it ugly or unapproachable. The outline was drawn in pencil and only partially filled. None of the paints had dried completely. I pushed your jeans down to the ground and removed your underwear. There was paint on the inside of your ankles.

It was so humid. But I wanted your stench all over me, soaked into the pores of my hands and lips. I took your swelling into my mouth and cleansed you with my tongue. You fucked me there, my naked body absorbing the colors of your spectrum. I was a beautiful stencil. I grabbed your open hands and told you I wanted another child, even so soon after what happened to Jennifer. All you did was lean in closer and lick the side of my neck, sweat beginning to form underneath of my arms. The moment took your caress down past my breasts and reached my belly. Without you, I would be dehydrated and barren. Two weeks later the fire happened.

The intensity of that fire burned so much so days later I could lean against the frame bordering the deck some 300 yards away and feel the temperature feed on the cold sensitivity of my flesh. I touched my fingertips to the charred wood. Pieces of it broke loose like artist's charcoal. It got deep into the lines on my hands and stained them. The odor was suffocating if I took too deep a breath. I must have washed my hands until blistered and it never went away.

I spent that night alone at Norah's, waiting for you to come home from finishing that project. You thought I'd stay home in the boathouse. The air was bitter because of a cold wind coming in off of the ocean. The water was stunning, but it could be ignorant as well. Even alone though, I adored coming here. The flames of the candles fixed inside tin lanterns on the counter stuttered. You had been gone for over a day, working on the elementary school project about an hour away. It was when I decided I would walk home and begin to read a book and watch the sunset that the explosion happened. At first it sounded like a loud collision. I turned away from Norah's and saw the spouts of flame rise above the tree line to the east, where the furniture factory was. No one was sure how it started. I extinguished the little candlelight at the restaurant and watched in horror with other residents.

When the local radio station announced the impending evacuation less than an hour later, all I wanted to do was find you, clutch to the tendons in your forearm, feel your lips through the angelic woven masks the medical personnel were placing over everyone's mouths to protect their lungs from the unknown contaminants. The factory stored stains, paints and other materials considered hazardous if inhaled in large quantities. The luminescence burned on the current of the water like a napalm sunset. If I stood there I thought the water would move closer, pour through the wind and the trees and burn me till there was nothing left. I felt alone for a moment because all I had was you. Without you or Jennifer, no one would be able to identify me.

I walked down a side street with other people, past that bakery where you could smell the bagels every day at the waking of dawn. They made everything from scratch. Police had begun to block off entrances to the oceanfront and some streets. Some remained calm while others ran by reaching for the fleeting hands of their children. Another fire alarm sounded. I turned around and watched the factory burn, the thick, black smoke blanketing everything. The anxiety of seeing you in the embrace of another woman as you were escorted out of a local apartment complex blighted the already decaying forest of my ego. I didn't understand what was happening.

A different woman stopped and handed you some of those white masks. She clutched at the side of your arm above your shoulder. Her body ended up supported by your embrace. People bumped into me as they hurried by and a man knocked me over completely. Bruised and hurting, I raised my body higher and leaned against the side of closed store. At the end of the driveway, you grabbed her hand and started running away from the chaos, running further from our life. You even possessed the artistic and emotional audacity to personify her there, in the lower right hand corner of the painting, giving her mystery by concealing her, cloaking her in privacy and excluding the intricacies of her countenance. You made her devoid of any tangibility. Again I wasn't sure if you were shielding her or if you were trying to protect yourself.

~

Someone from the outside called the handicapped man. The cellular phone inside his pocket rang about 11 times before he answered it. At least I assumed it was a man. It could have been a woman. Considering the circumstances around us though, it was probably a hostage negotiator. It made me feel sorry for him in a way, sitting there wondering if there was someone reaching out to him, like I wanted to reach out to you. He studied the phone for a minute and then held the receiver up to his right ear.

The man only said a few words and I couldn't hear what he was saying in return. I stole a quick glance and watched him place the gun across his lap. Any emotion he possessed at that moment was lost in the

208

interminable tension that made my skin pale and unattractive, the aridness causing beads of perspiration to trickle down to the small of my back. It was difficult to tell what he was feeling because he remained immobile, the muscles in his face never wavering or changing. I knew he wasn't listening to a woman who loved him. It would have been clear, obvious in the passive color hidden behind his eyes, the intake of breath through his lips and down into his throat. Because of a woman, a man changed for the better, whether he recognized it or not.

The handicapped man closed the phone and set it on the seat next to him. No one else was moving. We were all sitting in different seats, waiting for something to happen. At least I was. The man rubbed his shoulder where his arm was missing. I held in doubt what had happened to him. Could it have been noble or was he a criminal, praying on the prosperity and emotional philanthropy of others, bound to torture with impunity and malice? I imagined how you would have painted it, seen what you would have wanted to see in his movements and his architecture, cautious to represent his flaws without ridicule or scorn. I wished I would have been granted the same respect.

In one mural he would have been an aged soldier, running through the chaos and tenacity of battle to save several men of his company. Yet selflessness was a color I wasn't sure you could ever recognize. Being naïve, I hoped his condition had been the result of a romantic tragedy, his body forever changed because he was living abroad, hoping he could convince the woman he loved to emigrate, runs from the oppression and dictatorial landscape consuming all passion, all clemency. But I ruined all things good, all things virtuous when near you, with your inclination to use somber colors and no voice to express your turmoil, your soul.

After Jennifer's murder, you never talked to me except what you could say through fucking watercolors, whose culmination was laying in blood out of my reach like a newborn child, our child. But she was never helpless even as an infant, unyielding and blind, lying in the security of my forearms wanting to be on her own. Her tiny muscles often struggled to get away from my protection, willing her to break free and be independent when independence was a concept she couldn't even begin to understand.

Looking beyond the uncertainty and the disorder, I thought I saw her running up the street along the side of the bus. Her hands were moving in front of her face, a button falling loose from her dress. I would have to sew it. It looked like the one I tore hiding underneath of that front porch. With the bus immobile, she grew nearer. I stood up from my seat and closed my eyes. When I did, the handicapped man told me to sit down. But my daughter is there, don't you see her? Can't anyone see her curly hair bouncing upon her shoulders? I stepped back into the space of my current canvas and pressed my hands against the window. There was no one running along the side of the bus, the streets vacant of people I coveted.

It was like I was a muse again, regardless of brush or gun, sitting there, exhausted and thirsty, moving my body left than right. No, raise your head a little and tilt it back. Put your hand up, like that. Please cup your breast with your hands. No never mind, with your fingertips. God you're beautiful. That's all people could ever see. It made me hate myself. I was a delicate, fragile thing, flawed and torn. I wanted to wail as loud as I could. I wanted to live in a place of no structure, no color, an achromatic landscape where the beauty in everything would suffocate and collapse. All things being equal.

The catalogue was farther from me now. I must have sat down in a different seat. It caused me pain, but I needed to hold it, search through your murals and find peace in one of them. The handicapped man had studied me since I stood up. It didn't bother me. With seeming interest, he came closer and kneeled over a few rows in front of me. He picked up the catalogue and sorted through some of the pages, balancing it against his chest. He didn't even notice all the blood on the back corner. On one occasion he paused in his search and looked at me. I couldn't help but wonder where he stopped. Surprisingly, he closed the cover and handed it to me. All he said to me was that he was sorry.

The handicapped man sat back down in a seat at the front of the bus and placed two small, black buds into his ears and pressed several buttons on some kind of recorder. It was like nothing I had ever seen before. The cassettes were larger. When he placed the gun across his right thigh, he closed his eyes and exhaled. He didn't remain that way for long. Slowly he raised his head and moved his hand across his face. It looked as if there were tears in his eyes, but I wasn't sure.

I wiped some of the blood from the catalogue on my jacket, which I removed hours ago. The shades of red and umber I used to smear across your palette when you tried to teach me to paint showed themselves on the fibers of the coat, reminding me who I was or warning me. Some of the pages had stuck together because of the moisture and the blood. I pulled them apart. I looked out the window beside me and watched an ambulance turn down a side street. Still, no one stood within several hundred feet of the bus. I grew weary of all the continuous, flashing lights, brightening up the sky. There was no way you could know what was happening.

There was so much humidity inside the bus with most of the windows closed. It made me long for rain, for winter, to wander the fields of infinite white, pressed in by the latitude and longitude of glacial cold coming in across the plains and the brittle nature of my own skin. You only ever recreated winter twice in our marriage, the second being that painting. *Page 4.* I studied it, waiting to be released from the suffocating confines of grieving, passionate turmoil. Then I would be worth something. I could see your breath trail in the winds of her voice whispering to you.

You always said to me you hated most of the parts of winter except for the tranquility, the muted voice of the grass and the dirt, muffled under a light coating of cold and ice. But here you painted a school, the grounds virginal and unmolested by children or nature. It wasn't our daughter's school though. Did her children play there, in that field obscured in the arcane background you had washed on with such personal and private gentility, as if you had already been there, held them against your chest, felt the uninterrupted course of their breath crawl on the underside of your chin? What would you have told them and what promises did you provide to them? Had you already crossed that uncovered passage into their playground, trapped in the vertiginous echoes of their unblemished innocence?

I thought of all those nights at Jennifer's open houses, talking with her teachers about her intellectual dreams and what she wanted to do when she was older. I never found out what her adult aspirations were nor would I ever have the chance. I began sobbing, stricken by guilt I did not know what our daughter wanted to do with her life. It was something a mother should have known. But what difference did it make now? Had I

211

taken enough time away from you to understand her, listen to the things she had to say? Was I so greedy with my hunger to be touched, to be consumed by you, I pushed her aside? I tried to suppress my momentary self-hatred by turning towards the window again and placing a fist over my mouth. I could see the reflection of the man sitting a few rows behind me in the sweating glass. There was still a sizeable line of blood trickling down along his cheek. It reminded me of you, wiping paint from your face.

Once I tried to wash it away. We were sitting on a bench, similar to the one I stared at that sat unoccupied and alone at the intersection behind the bus. I couldn't remember where we were going. In retrospect, it didn't matter. Because even when we were reclusive and content, you made me travel the world with you, whether it be through a textbook or a painting someone else had mastered. Sitting on the couch together in front of the window watching it rain, I was actually struggling to keep up with you backpacking through the arid deserts of Bahrain. Hours later when I drifted asleep in your arms you were actually carrying me across a glacier in Iceland, the bitter cold unforgiving and infinite. When I awoke, my flesh was so cold it was as if I were besieged by frostbite.

I went everywhere with you and it never mattered where. As the wind pushed through your hair I reached up and tried to wipe away the red paint from the spot of skin above your left ear. It reminded me of when I first met you, the nervousness in reaching out to touch you, wondering how your skin would feel underneath of my fingertips. You pulled away. Sometimes you said you left it there until a particular painting was complete, free of indecision and partiality. There was still paint on the underside of your arms as well. I stared at the bones in your neck and throat. There were marks there as well. We missed our bus twice because we were arguing. All I wanted was for us to have a day away from our lives. I wanted so much to be more than a muse. I should have been content with being the mother of your daughter.

You painted a bench in that winter creation. Had you and she sat upon that bench like you and I, your faultless indiscretions clouded in the snowy mists that landed upon the anxious surface of her skin, the wool scarf around her coat concealing the condensation crashing into the plunging softness of her breasts? Did you let her see your unwashed colors, trapped upon the surface of your skin and allow her to wipe them away? Did she moisten the tips of her fingers and pass them across your delicate bones or did you grant her access to your privacy? I turned away from the window and the man behind me, wishing I could be isolated and safe instead of surrounded by harsh concepts and indignation I could not run from any longer.

~

I kept trying to find any semblance of clarity, even the faint orange glow of the burning tip of a cigarette to discern what rested on the axis around me. The handicapped man had his head down, not paying any attention to what was going on. He was still listening to whatever was on those tapes. I stood up from my seat once and asked him if I could have some water. I watched his hand flinch and for a second he reached for the gun. At times it shook uncontrollably. When he raised his eyes it felt like he thought I was someone else. It wasn't like he was looking at me, more through me towards someone I couldn't see. I didn't know why I had that feeling. He asked me to sit back down. He dialed a cellular phone and spoke to someone. Sometime later, a man came up to the door of the bus and rapped on the glass. The handicapped man secured the gun in his waist and opened the bus door. He told the man to turn around. Using his one arm he patted the young man down. Satisfied, the handicapped man stepped back a few steps and told the man to slide several bottles of water onto the floor and retreat into the darkness.

The handicapped man passed out several bottles of water, starting with a man in his late 20's or early 30's. His hair was cut short above his ears and high up on his neck. I hadn't heard him say anything since the bus stopped moving, a few seconds after the first shot. Earlier, when everything happened, he was wearing a long sleeve shirt. With it being so humid I was surprised he was still wearing it. He looked worn and exhausted. Sweat dripped from his brow and onto the floor of the bus. When the handicapped man stood in front of him with a bottle of water I wasn't sure if he even noticed him. When the cold bottle broke his plane of vision, he was rubbing his arm across the inside of his elbow in contemplation. He pulled his sleeve back down and accepted the bottle of water.

Instead of enjoying its purity and its relief, he twisted the cap off of the bottle and poured the water onto the floor. It pooled momentarily and then drifted its way to the lowest point and quieted. I was so irritated and thirsty I wanted to get down on my knees and cradle the fallen fluid into my palms. The handicapped man leaned in closer and placed the barrel of the gun inside the notch above his sternum. All I could hear him say was not to do that again.

Without looking, he reached behind his body and told the other man on the bus to take a couple of bottles. I thought that man would use the distraction to reach out and take the handicapped man's gun. But he didn't. He took four bottles and set them on the seat beside him. As patiently as he could he tore part of his shirt and soaked the fragment with water. Then he applied it to the laceration on his scalp and above his ear. I wondered if he had medical training. In a matter of minutes he had cleaned the wound and used another section of his clothing tempered with water as a compress. I hoped it worked. The blood from his head had been turning darker. Instead of asking him if he was alright, I waited my turn for water.

It came, but not without imbalance. The handicapped man stood in front of me longer than I had hoped. He reached out his hand, the gun tucked into the belt of his pants. I took only one bottle. He asked me if I wanted more and I whispered to him that I was fine. Thank you. I wanted to burden no one with my hunger, with my distress, even the strangers who kept me here. The handicapped man stared out the window for a moment. Standing there, he braced the bottle of water against his left hip and turned the cap. Because of the angle, half of the bottle spilled onto the floor and across my ankles. In his eyes, I recognized agony, a similarity, a fleeting reflection of my own misery and undesirability, obvious in his structure and his voice, his sad voice.

I asked him how he lost his arm. When I said it, I meant it with tenderness. Instead of lingering or punishing, he turned away from me and I thought I heard him say over his shoulder he was never complete before the accident, so it didn't matter. The water from the bottle still dripped across my ankles and it was cold and startling, like paint, your paint. Swallowing the water, I turned and looked out the window when another ambulance pulled up in the distance. I wondered if the people

214

outside thought something would happen inside this bus. The handicapped man hadn't been violent or abusive, mostly reticent and withdrawn, hardly a man who had shot a hole through the roof and detained us. But it didn't take much to turn a person into something they never thought they could be. There was no way of knowing beforehand though what direction that turn would go.

I glanced at the catalogue and again wanted to prove to you how much that painting was a lie, where your recreation was flawed and unfair. *Page 8*. It hadn't changed since I looked at it last and I wished more than anything that it had. I thought this was as close to you as I would ever be again. Sweat dripped from my forearms onto the pages. I wiped my palm across the page. Nothing could be as close and stifling as hiding underneath of that porch, not even waiting here, waiting for the disrupting and indistinct colors of death to enshroud me. I couldn't see any color outside, no sea greens or ochre, no carmine reds. The world was blank.

It was beautiful out that night, but you painted such a raging storm of clouds and rain instead, a reckless and blind array of charcoals and lead dripping down the slope of the roof and pouring into the rusted gutters. There was no place to put all the water as it absorbed into the ground and the whole world above reflected in the pools of pale silver. But it wasn't that way. I remembered the sky being bolder, ablaze with alternating lines of umber and scarlet. The heat was oppressive, almost bullying in a way throughout the morning and well past sunset. You corrupted the peace and silence I beheld by changing landscapes with watercolors and stained ego. In no uncertain terms, lies.

I must have slept for hours underneath of the porch after pulling tomatoes from their mothers, examining their ruddy flesh for imperfections. Most of them were ripe, exquisite pieces and I imagined pressing my lips and tongue through the skin, the small seeds invading the spaces between my teeth. Yet you had crafted most of them as pale, inexperienced children, incapable of existing without the guidance of their elders. Was that again how you saw me? Was I a blind, infantile woman who could not speak, muted, and could not form the words to express the images that haunted me, like beautiful phantoms pulling at the tenderness of my body? I was much more than you ever understood, ever painted and drenched in the common colors of your misguided spectrum.

You were wrong. But it was something you thought you had accomplished through the didactic nature of experience. When I opened my eyes all I could see was a legion of fallen fruit, their flesh torn from body, heads crushed, fluids spilled across the arid dirt. There was a small indentation on the side of my collarbone from a rock pressing in. Toppled from the basket you masked with indecision were the tomatoes I had pulled. I thought they might have tumbled off of the porch on their own, eager to escape a predetermined fate. I heard enraged voices coming from the house. I want you to leave. That's not happening. I don't love you anymore. It doesn't matter. Please leave. Instead of led by the individuals and scene around me, I was forever being torn.

It wasn't long until someone stepped out onto the unstable beams of the porch and across that battlefield of fallen agriculture. I pressed myself deeper into my private darkness and held my breath. You tried to mimic the tension I felt in the obstructed background and barn, hide their witness behind a blurred glare and the absence of detail. My chest tightened inside of your ideas. The imprints left in soil were too small to be his. In your colors you left no evidence than anyone else had been there, as if I had covered up a crime, bleached your canvas of fingerprints and genetics. As if I could silence the perspective and voice of nature, suffocate its cruel intelligence and vision. It had to be her, my sister. Would you have crafted her as she was or how you thought I saw her? Again, you told people I had been alone.

It wasn't fair to her, the woman who should have helped me become someone else, assured and resolute. But you should have helped her become more, through your brush, bathed in elegance and fortitude. Instead you chose apathy and promiscuity. You would have been able to feel the silken touch of her fawn hair on the canvas.

You never painted her stepping off of the front porch, her jeans ripped behind her left knee, exposing her thigh. Weighted down by anger and uncertainty she struggled to regain her balance. Sweat dripped from my lips as I recessed deeper near the house. *You said we were going to leave here together, that you loved me. I can't leave. What is it your father? I don't owe you anything anymore. The hell you don't. Fuck you.* You didn't show her turning and running into the vacant barn. Timidity moved with the streams of perspiration across my arms and legs. No one could see her hide behind some kerosene barrels. I could see him move behind her. You can't leave me. Stop! Torn by silence. Abandon by tinted saturation. You never painted him as I saw him, running into the barn behind her, slamming the old pine door, the hinges still shrieking afterwards when it tried to remain closed. When I heard her scream, I closed my eyes, hoping he would leave. We were alone and I wasn't sure what to do.

I started to slide my awkward body out from underneath the porch. I was wearing one of her sundresses and I liked the way it clung to my body, even though it was a size too big. Behind my neck I had to pull the dress tighter by using a safety pin. I repositioned my hair to cover it so she wouldn't see. There was so much dirt penetrating the cotton I would have to wash it before putting back in her drawer. I almost had my slight frame away from the house when I felt something grab at my ankle. It scratched away at my skin between the straps of my sandals. When I reached back to grab hold of my leg and pull it closer to me, a steel nail split the patch of skin woven around the bones in my ankle. It hurt so much I bit down on my lip and tongue to keep myself from crying. The blood trickling down across my toes was ticklish. I rested my head on the hot ground and sobbed. You could never have made what happened beautiful, no matter what colors you washed on.

The only nobility I could see between the lines and colors in that painting was your vagueness, the absence of specification and circumstance. You knew what happened to her inside of that barn. Yet you painted it off of the edges of the canvas, saved what she unfortunately experienced behind those kerosene barrels. I had confided in you what I felt, the feelings I encountered hiding underneath of that porch. We were drinking at home and Jennifer was with your mother. I allowed the mixture of wine, guilt and regret to assimilate into my bloodstream. You were across the room, sketching my body in profile sitting on our couch, gazing out the window at the night sky, the stars stuttering against the black. I pulled my jeans up to scratch at my body. You whispered to me to tell you what beast could have damaged me, laid violence to my delicate ankle. If you would have asked me any other day I would not have answered. I never told anyone else. But you were my husband and lover, not my foil.

Putting as much pressure on the wound as I could, I slithered out from underneath the porch. There were no sounds coming from anything anymore, the shifting of the structure of the old house, the faint buzzing of equipment from the neighbor's field. It was dreadful, listening to such vacancy and emptiness. I took careful steps towards the barn, shifting my body to try and see through the small spaces between the boards. All I could see was the light coming in from the other side. There were no voices. You would have painted me a little farther away from the barn than I was when the door opened. I didn't know what I was going to do if it were him. She pushed aside the barn door and staggered out.

Her body moved as if all her bones had been replaced with those from others, a sad sampling of disjointed and discarded femurs and shins. Less than 15 feet from the entrance she fell to the ground, her lips marred by blood and dirt. I covered my mouth when I wailed. She lifted her eyes, watched me start towards her in her sundress. It was ruined. It looked funny on me because it came down past my knees when it wasn't supposed to. Her legs were longer and more golden than mine. I looked down at them, one bent at the knee and a long trail of blood decorated the other. It was a couple of minutes before I sat down next to her. I ran my hands through her hair, the smell of kerosene absorbed into the concentric swirls at the ends of my fingertips.

I closed my eyes and let the cold water pass over my lips, the bottle suspended above the bridge of my nose. It rolled over my cheek and chin and followed the contours of my throat. I spread the water through my hair. Drops fell and washed over the catalogue. The painting began to bleed. I could smell gasoline.

You never painted anything else again in my life that existed before you. I missed her. God help me. That's what I thought love was, intense and passionate, nevertheless imbalanced, full of oppression and hate. And you helped obscure what should have separated them, the tangible moments where my body experienced your undying passion and your infinite abomination.

~

The handicapped man had been talking to someone off and on for the last hour. A third ambulance had taken position behind the bus, beyond the barriers. Things appeared bleak. I would have expected the man to have surrendered already. There was nowhere to go. But, he never made any demands from me or anyone else. He barely even looked at me after I asked him what happened to his arm. The consistent emergency lights circling outside had stopped about 20 minutes ago. When the first squad car pulled away he stood and secured the gun in his right hand. It wasn't long before he came towards.

You always got up early when you were painting landscapes. The morning after you first made love to me I awoke to find you gone. But I calmed when I saw your keys still sitting atop my dresser, your jacket tossed over the arm of a recliner hidden in the corner. I picked it up and ran my fingertips through the collar and held it under my nose. I liked waking up after seeing you, my body invaded by your scent. It meant more in those few private moments I had alone before I noticed you out of the corner of my eyes. The world was still dark with small patches of light encompassing the easel you stood in front of. I moved towards the window and took you in, admired the way your hands moved, how the tips of the long brush you worked with conducted the orchestra of colors. It was the first time I had watched you paint something other than that pumpkin. The one you painted stared up at me from the windowsill. Its eyes were wide and sallow.

I stepped onto the lawn where the grass was wet with residual moisture from the dawn. There was coffee by your ankles, the steam rising from the circumference of the mug, drifting into the atmosphere. You hardly even looked at the canvas while you were splashing on color, kept your perspective on the landscape. I moved up closer behind you and sat down in the grass.

So naïve, I purchased a book on the composition of paints that afternoon after you left. I learned about binders and pigments, solvents and emulsion. I wanted to learn as much as I could about the world that you often existed in. I didn't notice it at first, but on the front steps of my apartment you left me something. I never expected you to see me again. Inside a small box was a shell. In such unique handwriting you said that it was a 'painter's mussel,' a freshwater mussel artists sometimes used as a dish. I believed you when you said it belonged to your grandfather, who grew up as a painter in Europe after World War I. You talked about him a lot when we were together, the roughness of his hands, the fact his paintings were so authentic you could smell the breath of the people linger while it sat asleep on the easel.

The catalogue was ruined and the only pages not steeped in water were the last. The painting listed there shouldn't have been the final one sold. *Page 39.* Its definition was too saturated in violence, too unpropitious. The inclusion of its canvas, in the end, made me frightened. It was claustrophobic, that painting and I always felt pressed in by its truth, by the blatant way you made my body look so blemished, yet disguised my emotions in pockets of blacks and grays. It was another lie, another fabrication. Did you tell anyone what happened or was I made out to be the one who betrayed you, your sensibilities and your vows? I thought you would have wanted to not recreate that failed moment of emotional restraint, the only time you hit me in our marriage. We fought so many times towards the end, even before Jennifer was murdered. None of our friends ever seemed to notice. It was introverted, hidden underneath of all the lines you always tried to make me see in paintings.

It was a couple of days after the fire where I saw her with you, arm in arm under all that panic, loneliness and distress. I was so reticent in my behavior, the truncated responses I composed to you when you asked me what was wrong. I broke down and I told you I saw her. With improbable eyes and trepidation I saw her, the sultry, long curly hair cascading down past her shoulders, the look in her eyes she held. It was as if she knew she could count on you right away to help her, to save her from uncertainty. That was something that took me almost a year to possess, the absolute, the mathematical probability I meant more to a man than another and I was worth an eternity to someone. It wasn't you, although I wanted it to be.

You hid the bruises well in that painting, pulling my dark black hair down past my face towards the bed, blending it into that quilt. Someone took great care when they made you, took their time to fashion a man of ardor, a man of rough integrity who balanced and encompassed tenderness. All that was still there though, layered beneath the infidelity and the contempt. The thing I kept asking myself was where did we go from there? Was there any way to remove the stains of the subjugation of that painting and find hope in the wreckage underneath of it to begin again, forgive one another for our pertinacity?

Using darker tones and shadows you highlighted the outer edges of my body, made my muscles look taught and confident. I looked provocative and erotic. Yet there was a touch of censorship you placed upon my body, never letting me rise up above the repression of my weakness, of your vulgarity. But in all, I couldn't understand what I had done to drive you to her. I admitted to having a tendency to seek a definition in everything around me, your words, your actions, but most of all your work. You taught me that. You taught me to see through every object, to analyze beyond its color and its physicality.

I said such horrible things to you. I had cause, but I never should have said those things. In my heart I knew them to be out of character, but it felt like you were trying to blame me and I caused our difficulties. When we moved closer to one another I began sobbing. I began slapping you, pounding my clenched hands against the breadth of your chest. I kept asking you if there was something wrong with me. You didn't say anything for a couple of minutes, just stood there and let me pound on you. You closed your eyes and said I was unlovable, I was cruel. But even through it all I still loved you and wanted you to make love to me.

Instead you grabbed my wrists and nestled closer to my neck so you could whisper to me. I felt your warm breath attack the territory of my shoulders. I knew what I wanted to hear. I wanted you to ask me to have another baby. More than anything I wanted your resignation, the brutal and violent naked truth we could somehow build upon the ruins of our daughter's murder, reclaim the sensibility and the happenstance we often found in one another's vivacity. You said she was already pregnant. It was going to be a girl.

I tried to pull away from you, but you grabbed my forearms tighter and pinned them behind my back. You whispered no man, no artist could ever make me beautiful again. You pressed your lips against the small area of flesh underneath of my earlobe and said it should have been me hanging dead inside of that barn, instead of my sister. You said you hated fucking me.

I gazed out the window of the bus. I couldn't see into the field of the farm I examined earlier while waiting here. The barn had recently been refurbished, the clean, white roof mirroring the slight skin of the moon. I wondered what objects I would find inside if I ran from the bus and into its unfamiliar stomach. There would be no traces of violence or despair, only inoperative objects and stability. It's what I longed for more than anything else, besides seeing Jennifer again. More than the smell of your body and the feel of your brush against me, establishment, and balance. I felt like I belonged in one of the fragile panoramas you painted, a rotted tree convalesced in the marshes, unable to reproduce even the slightest of leaves, seeds, children, unable to stay rooted to the ground. I thought of what you confessed to me, that she was having your child. Yet somehow I felt joyous for her, carrying what I could not. Even so, there was no absolution for the last thing your body, your essence said to mine. The last words I heard from you should have been softer, kinder, something a woman wanted to hear her husband say to her.

I felt betrayed when I thought about that painting again. *Page 8.* But there were fewer details in the colors for me to be wary about, since the barn took up so little space upon the canvas. I remembered there was a small pane of glass facing the viewer, a window you could see through, straight out into the plains of wheat and grass in the distance. Did you omit that vision, that clearness because you wanted to save her dignity and mine? Or was there a point where you stopped listening to me when I told you about her, when I told you about anything at all I deemed necessary and important?

I remembered waking up very early, almost an hour before the sun would rise that morning. I stepped through the hallway in front of her room, not wanting to wake her after what had happened. Our father has been out of town for a few days attending the funeral of a close friend. It was so quiet, but not the sort of calm that put me on edge. I felt it to be relaxing after what he did to her. I headed outside through the back door. There was dew glistening on the handle of the pump to the water well.

We hardly used it anymore, but I didn't want to rattle the aging pipes inside by running the faucet. I was going to fill a bucket and tend to her wounds, wash that dress. I was afraid the blood would soak into the stitching. I set the bucket down next to me and raised my hands over my head. I felt like standing there until the sun came up beyond the wheat and the trees and enriched my body with patience and virtue. After a few minutes, gold rays blazed over the tips of the dying wheat, set fire to the few animals still sleeping between the rows. Soon it made its way to the edges of my bare feet and glided across my ankles.

I looked down at the few traces of blood still there. I tried as best I could to hide it from everyone, didn't want anyone to know what I saw. I kept waiting for the sunlight to burn away the remains, but it never happened. It didn't work out that way. Nothing could ever pull all the hate and the pain from the deep recesses of the soil and the crops, not even the perfect blend of colors from your 'painter's mussel.' The artistic guile and wisdom of your grandfather was inefficient and dry.

I soaked her dress in the warm water. I held it under. The lime stains on the inside of the pail changed the texture and the color of the water. You never painted that, my kneeling in front of the other worshippers, hidden in the agriculture, ringing her dress, squeezing it as hard as I could, hoping that I could change what happened with the unsubstantial strength of my fingertips. There were so many details you would have captured with your threaded horsehair and fiber. The movement of the sun across the glistening metal construction of the water pump. The unending, fallen infantry line of crushed vegetables still strewn across the dirt near the porch. I tried picking most of them up last night after she fell asleep, but I couldn't. My hand kept shaking and I often became imbalanced, sometimes falling to the ground, looking out into the darkness, praying the barn I couldn't quite see wasn't there. Nevertheless it always had been its placement and construction poignant because of the way the sun refracted off of the worn shingles, the washed out paint. It was what led me to her.

When I stood and went to tend further to her, I toppled the bucket. The gray, dingy water spilled out against my feet and ran down the slight slope towards the field. The dress I tried so desperately to correct spread out in the water, sodden and soiled by my carelessness. Defeated, I retrieved the dress and started towards the barn. I was going to hide it there and wait until I could go into town and purchase her another one. When I opened the barn door was when I saw her, hanging there.

Someone should have been there to help me. All those years I had forever wished that it was you.

I should never have come on the bus. I recognized that hard truth as I watched the streams of sweat roll down his forearm, connect with the barrel of the gun and drip down from his fingertips and onto the floor of the bus. I should have never allowed your note in my apartment to lure me, to seduce the cognitive aspects of my wanton reasoning. Everything now was directed at me, his anger, his seclusion, his despondency, your hubris, your brush, his gun. I felt suffocated. He leaned over closer to me and told me to stand. I hadn't for so long then I did I stumbled and nearly collapsed.

The handicapped man grabbed my shoulder to support me. When he did, the gun pressed hard into the soft underneath tissue of my arm. It made a small indentation in my skin, like falling asleep on top of one of your brushes. He directed me to go towards the front of the bus and stop at the door. The tip of the gun pressed against the small of my back and darted across the bones in my vertebrae like a metronome.

The handicapped man said he should have let me go hours previous and I had been through enough. I didn't understand. I had tried so hard to change, be the woman and the mother I should have always been. We all see things in one another that aren't there, including ourselves. It all happened so quickly I never was able to recover.

"I am sorry about your daughter."

The words he said made me cold. Through them I could smell the turpentine you used to clean your brushes. I never had a chance to stretch and pull at his words, mold them like warm clay into the shapes I wanted them to take. The man at the rear of the bus rushed closer and reached for the gun. I wished it would have been you, driven by a fractured sense of nobility I thought existed in your gifted hands, in the delineation of your murals. The gun discharged through the small of my back. My body lunged towards the ascending stairs and slammed against the door. I landed on my stomach, my face flush with the top step. Blood seeped from my abdomen. I wished it was that brilliant vermillion shade you used in most of your paintings. You were always very good at hiding it so no one ever knew it was there.

All the colors of your world became an amalgam, a sad array of blues and olives, alabaster and umber, pulling away from my hands, colliding with the steel architecture of the bus. It was as if you tipped your palette and allowed the vibrant psychological primary colors to coalesce, withhold from each of them their unique passport. I was nothing more than a failed restoration, an undesirable piece of unattainable art, once priceless and original. I was so cold. I understood what the handicapped man was listening to. The earpiece he used was pulled from the recorder and I soon heard a woman's voice. I wanted it to be your voice asking for my forgiveness, trailing through the deteriorating whispers of promises and hope that passed over my skin. Your colors were gone and I was alone, asleep on a bleached canvas, frightened and neglected.

# THE BALLERINA

A small ray of light cut across the hardwood floor and for a fleeting moment, I thought the sun had come out. It lacerated the lithe curtain hanging above the window and refracted off of the wall length mirror I stood in front of. As I leaned against the handrail, I watched it reach its pinnacle of prominence, then retreat. It passed over an extra pair of my ballet shoes. They looked like they were ripe with flame, burning. The glare belonged to a lamp outside. Each one had turned on when it darkened. Sadly, it was still raining.

I sat down on a small bench on the other side of the room and untied my shoes. I craned my neck to the right and then left, noticing the time on the clock framed above the door. It was nearing noon on a Saturday. The light music echoing in the background faded and left the room maudlin and silent. Usually more people were here now of day, particularly on the weekend. The inclement weather must have kept others indoors. I pulled a few layers of tape away from my swollen, raw ankles. I slipped the rest of my belongings into a shoulder bag and said goodbye to the pianist who usually played for me during rehearsal. I had been practicing my counts for a fledgling production our small company was trying to get made.

Stepping out into the rain, I looked up and let the water discover my lips and wash away the perspiration and inconsistency I had struggled with inside. The details left behind by the choreographer and artistic director were specific and dense. They were both in New York trying to convince an artist to help them with sketches about costume design and color. We needed help, hope and were struggling to find it, even in the most transparent of places. Attaining funds was turning out to be a political and difficult process. No more complicated than the movements I supposed. Fundraisers we held previously had failed. The township was already strapped economically and always had been. Even more so because of the investigation. And then there was everything else.

I crossed the vacant parking lot and sat down inside of my car. I moved, hindered now by uncertainty and abject aversion. The rain pelted the windshield with an increasing veracity. For a moment I thought I could see the lights go off in the building. Then I closed my eyes.

226

Everything once in motion, was now still. I didn't want to move, even breathe. How long could I go on?

I sat there listening to the rain, waiting. I switched on the radio to drown out the solemnity, moreover the reminiscence that accompanied it. I turned the dial until I found something antique, more classical. The notes dripped from the speakers. It was a string piece. I thought about the first time he touched me with his cello bow as I sat at the edge of the tub, gliding its delicate fibers along the longitude of my back. He once told me my skin, the subtle intricacies of my flesh resonated notes, made music and I was a tender, beautiful portion of a composition, a symphony, an andante. I lowered and moved my hand from the steering column down across my belly. Everything was changing though. We were having a child, a delicate and difficult composition all its own.

~

I opened the front door to our home without pause. It was always so quiet since his accident. He never played music in length afterwards, at least when I was around, only fragmented pieces, nothing more. Incomplete notes, never carrying any real weight or emotion. Maybe he did inside of his sound room, but it was difficult to tell at times. I couldn't hear unless I was in there with him or the door remained ajar. That antiseptic room was clothed in such an intimidating artificiality. I wanted to stand in front of its simplistic authority and fracture the glass, break through its strength and its apparent sanctuary, one I used to believe in and understand. Yet now, I wanted to shatter its quietness and determination, erase all the hardened and inanimate sounds he collected. Those digital audio tapes for his time with OSHA. Nothing about it was beautiful. I set my bag down on the floor next to the dining room table and headed into the kitchen.

Nothing was cleaned up from last night. I reached into the cold water several inches deep in the stainless steel sink and loosened the drain plug. Reaching into a drawer, I removed a large dish towel and spread it across the counter. I pulled all the soiled dishes out and set them on a kitchen block behind me. I thought about being with him last night and what had happened. It wasn't going to be easy. What I told him should have been celebratory, that we were going to start a family. Instead of overwhelmed by exhilaration and pride, he reacted with castigation and doubt.

Reservation. Recrimination. I placed a good portion of the silverware and some glasses back into the sink. I turned on the faucet and let the water begin to rise. It was warm and encouraging to my cold, distant body, something he should have been yesterday.

I was liable for his lack of receptivity, the uncertainty and disillusionment I had about our future, conspicuous in my movement and speech. I couldn't hide it as much as I struggled to, the honest disappointment in our marriage. Part of me was regretful he was the father of my child, in as much as it pained me to confront the inherent and brutal truth in that. I turned away from the sink after turning off the water and headed towards our bedroom. I stopped in the middle of the hallway when I saw the strewn glass on the floor.

I stepped around the broken pieces and paused in front of his sound room. The thick, glass panel on the door was broken. Careful not to cut myself, I secured the handle and pushed open the door. Part of it had loosened from a hinge at the bottom. Wood splintered. It looked like it had been kicked in repeatedly. I moved inside and immediately noticed his desk was askew, the digital audio tapes he had archived for OSHA for years, in piles across the floor. The once organized shelf had been pulled from the wall. Sheet music lay torn in piles. I moved out of the room and back into the kitchen. I never looked inside any other room. I grabbed my cellular phone and called the police. I described to them what I believed had happened, instructed by an operator to go to a neighbors. Was anyone else home? Did I believe that the perpetrator was still inside of the house? The thought never occurred to me someone else may have been there.

I went outside through a door adjacent to the kitchen and ran into the backyard. The rain had lessened some. It didn't appear anyone else was around. I stepped behind a short row of bushes and moved through a small fence into the neighbor's side yard. I ran to their front door and began pounding with my fist. It seemed feeble. No one was going to hear me. For several minutes I stood there, waiting for someone to come. I retreated into the corner of their front porch and slumped down against a wall to their house.

Where was he? I pulled out my phone again and scrolled for his number. The device trembled in my hands and tumbled to the concrete patio several times. There was no answer. I hung up and dialed again. It rang. I dropped my head. When I began to stand several minutes later, I heard sirens.

A police officer parked in front of the house and started towards the front door. Another went to the rear. One had his flashlight drawn. I became anxious. It was so quiet around me even with what was happening. After what seemed like hours, both officers came outside and one headed towards their car. He reached through the window and spoke into a radio. I stepped off of the porch and into the grass. When he saw me coming he asked me if I was the woman who had called. I said yes.

"Did you hear anyone moving around when you first entered the house?"

"No, I didn't," I whispered.

"Was your front door locked?" he asked.

"Yes. I had to use my key to get inside," I said as if I didn't have verbal permission to go into my own home. I wasn't sure why but I felt like a scolded child.

"Did you touch anything inside before you called us?" he asked. I explained to them my precise movements when I walked through the door. I went to the kitchen sink to wash the dishes, but stopped. I then went into the hallway leading to his sound room and our bedroom when I noticed the broken glass. "What did you do then?"

"I opened the door to the sound room and went inside," I answered. I told them I only touched the handle and the door was already dislodged.

"Did you go into any other rooms of your house?"

"No, why?" I questioned.

"You didn't go into your bedroom or your bathroom?"

"No. I never had the chance to," I admitted.

"I need you to come with me please and try not to touch anything. We're going to need to take fingerprints in your home. We'll also need to capture yours and anyone else who may live here for process of elimination. Okay? It's a routine procedure," he added. "First, I want you to come inside and another officer will follow you through your home. I need you to determine if there is anything missing while I make another call."

"Was anyone supposed to be home this morning?" he asked.

"No," I said.

"You're married?"

"Yes."

"Have you been able to contact your husband at all? Do you know where he is?"

"No," I admitted. Help me. Help me reach him. Help me make him understand I need him now more than I ever have. I said I could do this alone, but I didn't want to. Please tell him I'm sorry about what I said.

"I need you to start towards the front of your house, the living room, and see if you can determine again if anything is missing," he said. "Can you do that?"

"Yes. Excuse me. I need a glass of water," I said.

"Someone will get it for you. Please, sit down." I slumped onto our couch in the living room and closed my eyes. Where was he? I needed him. I glanced down at the facing of my phone again. The officer sat down on the edge of a coffee table and handed me a glass of water. It was warm. My lips felt so numb I didn't care he didn't put any ice into the glass. It was all insensible and muddling.

"Do you keep anything of value in your home? Large amounts of cash that someone may have known about? Jewelry?" he asked.

"No. I was wearing my wedding ring. We don't own a lot of jewelry," I said. "Whatever we had we sold most of what we had a couple of years ago," I admitted as I glanced down at my wedding ring.

"May I ask what you do?" he said.

"I'm a ballerina, but most of the time I teach personal lessons," I said.

"What about your husband?" I wondered how long this man had been a member of law enforcement here. Almost everyone in town knew what happened to him. Maybe he was a replacement, covering for someone.

"He works for OSHA. And he's a musician. Was a musician I mean," I whispered.

"Is there anyone else you can call who might be able to help you, come by and be with you until we can locate your husband?"

"No. I need a minute." I felt nauseous and invalid.

"Would you like me to call for an ambulance? You seem pallid." Upset, I still appreciated his concern.

"No, I'm fine. I recently found out I'm pregnant," I said.

I stood from the couch and began searching our living room to determine if anything was missing. I couldn't find what might have been taken. Nothing challenged me. Everything was pristine and organized from what I had seen so far. The officer followed me into the kitchen as I set my glass of water on the counter. We were going to examine more of the house. I paused in front of his sound room and stared at the broken instruments, the tattered sheet music and the quiet chaos of its broken existence. An overwhelming dread leaned upon my shoulders and burdened me with a weight I thought would crush my delicate bones.

"Do you know why someone would have wanted to ransack this room in particular?"

"No. None of the instruments have any real monetary value. Just personal," I said. "Everything else was his work," I added. "Artificial. It meant nothing to anyone. It didn't have any value."

"Excuse me for a moment." The officer disappeared around the corner. I realized my clothes were lying disheveled on the floor of our bedroom. The sheets were still tossed aside, rumpled. I could pursue our bodies' migration in the fragmentary cotton linen, the regions of whiteness and impressibility where we had made love. It was never difficult or abstract guiding him inside me because of his disability, moving, changing and transitioning. I loved him so much despite everything, his unblemished assembly moving across me, behind me, under me, caressing, placating, renouncing. For all too brief moments we were happy and I was his goddess.

I heard the front door open and rushed to the window. I hoped it was him, coming for me. One of the police officer's sat down in the front seat of his cruiser and began speaking into a radio. Satisfied with what he heard, he stood and retreated back towards our home. I heard mumbling, incomprehensible questions coming through the walls. I stepped into the hallway at the same time the bathroom door opened.

"Could you come in here for a minute please?" an officer asked.

I didn't know how to process what the police discovered in our bathroom. All I saw at first was the empty pill bottle sitting idle at the bottom of the bathtub. When I moved my perspective to the floor I saw dozens of photographs and documents spread out across the tile. I felt their stares and pains punch at my chest. Each one was miserable, with a haunted resonation that echoed throughout the vulnerability of the room. They asked me not to touch anything.

"Do you know how these photographs got here?" he questioned.

"No. I've never seen them before." I crouched down above the faces, the blurred innocence reviled and the violent images disturbing.

"I need you to look at them, tell me if you recognize anything. But please don't touch anything," he said.

Crime scene photographs.

Dead children.

The contents of the file were confidential, police property. I could see portions of an ink stamp on the outside of an envelope identifying that. They asked me again if I had any idea how they could have ended up here. No. One of the officers stepped out from the bathroom and into the hallway. All I heard him say was that he needed to speak to Detective Daniel Mull immediately.

~

The rain picked up some again. They ushered me back into the living room and asked me to remain there until someone called for me. I watched them walk past in a steady procession inside and outside of the house. Through the bay window I could see one of the officers retrieve a camera from the trunk of his car. I understood they were going to take photographs of everything, assuredly the bathroom and his sound room. I wondered where the remnants of that police file had come from.

Another vehicle pulled up in front of the house, fitting against the curb. With an umbrella extended at its current angle, I couldn't see who the person was. With cautious pacing, they approached the front door and stepped inside. Water dripped along the entrance-way. I would have to clean up so much.

Where was he?

When the umbrella wilted like a black, dying flower and struck the floor, I recognized him immediately. Mull asked the officer who had come to the front door to guide him through the scene.

"She's the woman who called 911, reporting a possible break in," he added.

"I'm Detective Daniel Mull. I understand there has been some damage done to your house," he said, easing into what I believed would be a harsher conversation because of those photographs. I braced.

"Yes. I came home from a ballet rehearsal this afternoon and found it like this," I began. I rubbed my hands together, trying to remove a stain that wasn't there. I kept pushing my right thumb into my palm.

"There's no need to be nervous. I understand that you're pregnant. Congratulations. Can I get you anything?" he asked.

"No, thank you," I said.

"About what time was it when you arrived home?"

"A little after noon I guess. I left practice a few minutes before noon, but I didn't come straight home," I confessed.

"Did you go anywhere else? The grocery store? Did you need gas? What time did you leave this morning? It might help us determine when your home was broken into," he said, writing constant notes in a small, black tablet. A tablet of history and tragedy I assumed.

"No. When I finished practicing I sat in my car for a few minutes, listening to music. Then I came here. I'm not exactly sure what time I left this morning," I acknowledged. "But I was only gone for a few hours."

"What time did the dance studio open?" he asked.

"Nine. But I have a key. I usually have access to the building whenever, since I teach. My schedule varies depending upon the students." I leaned back against a pillow and tried to stretch my legs. Mull asked if he could have a glass of water. I complied. I stood from the couch to get some distance from what was happening and rummaged for a clean glass. God the dishes. I plugged the sink drain and let more warm water puddle inside the basin. My lips quivered.

"That leaves only a few hours. I understand that you haven't been able to reach your husband. Was he still here when you left this morning?" he asked.

"Yes," I said. Suddenly it occurred to me he had ransacked his music room. I don't know why. All that history, promise, technique and talent and he tossed it all aside. The resolution and the disappointment covered my face. Mull noticed, I was certain, but he didn't say anything. He would work his way up to it. It was obvious. Besides, they knew what had happened to him. Everyone here knew he was a fractured man. It made sense. But nothing explained the photographs. I turned off the water in the sink, but didn't turn around. Instead I watched the rain cascade against a bird house sitting broken at the base of a small tree. It was a gift he had bought for me from one of the local craft fairs. I became transfixed by the scene. We had a romantic dinner in our yard once, a sensual tenderness permeating the grass and the lilies that I planted. Everything had fallen so hard since then. I closed my eyes when Mull began again.

"Come with me please," he asked, ushering me by placing his hand on the small of my back. I took passage in front of him and stopped when we got to the broken door of his sound room.

"You said your husband was a musician," he stated.

"Yes. But you know that already," I said. "Your name is on his accident report."

"Yes it is. It's inconsequential, but why did he stop playing?"

"I've asked him that almost every day since his accident," I said, languishing in an aroma of skepticism and ambivalence.

"What was his answer?"

"I never got an answer to many things, that being one of them," I said.

"May I ask what was kept in here?"

"Nothing of value. The instruments he used to play. His old cello. Some musical compositions, notations and some sheet music as well I suppose. His data tapes were stored on that shelf there, the ones for OSHA. And a recorder. That was the only time he usually came in, to catalog them or add to them for his work. I only came in here a few times," I said.

"Why?" I turned to look at him when I answered, knowing full well he wouldn't understand.

"Although nothing had a real voice, everything in there was always so loud it frightened me," I said.

We started down the hallway towards the bathroom. Mull whispered in the ear of another officer and nodded his head in agreement. On the floor were small, yellow plastic triangles with numbers stenciled on them. They started at one and went up to 13. Someone was placing the photographs with small tweezers into plastic bags.

"There's an empty prescription bottle resting in the tub. Do you keep large quantities of drugs in your home?" he asked.

"No, not at all. They're my husband's. Painkillers. Antidepressants. He started taking them after his accident. Sometimes he gets depressed because of what happened. Perhaps he always was. I knew he was still taking them, even though he tried to hide it," I said. "I never told him I knew the truth."

"Why wouldn't you approach him about it?" he asked.

"What could I say to him after all that he has been through?" I said. "He's a deep man detective. It's hard to reach him," I said. "I thought I used to know how," I whispered aloud.

"I understand. But I have to ask you a more direct question. I need to know how this confidential material from an ongoing police investigation ended up here on your bathroom floor," Mull asked, his posture turning a bit more rigid and severe.

"I don't know. I've never seen it before," I said.

"Are you absolutely certain of that?" Mull asked.

"Yes. Why would I want to look at something like," I stammered. "Like that?" Looking pallid again, he took my arm and moved me back into the living room. On the table at the edge of the couch was a cellular. I picked it up and glanced at the display. No messages. No one had called.

"Please sit down. What I'm going to tell you is confidential and I cannot address the seriousness of it enough. What we found on the floor in your bathroom is the police case file concerning the children who were murdered in and around here this year. It's sensitive property. Although I was removed from the case towards the end, nevertheless, it does constitute nine months of our investigative material, crime scene analysis, photographs, dates, locations, names, transcripts." Mull said.

"I don't know why it's here," I said, shaking with reckless abandon. I was becoming nauseous again.

"I do," he said. "Do you recognize this name?" he asked, handing me an index card with a name written in ink on the reverse side. Mull had pulled it from the breast pocket of his coat.

"Yes. That's my husband's brother. Please. Tell me what's happening here?"

"Augustina, I need to know where Tobias is, right now," he said.

~

I watched water rush down the side of the tree and topple the birdhouse. The gutters and the rain applauded the sudden failure. I leaned back in the bench and raised a cup of warm tea to my lips. Why was all this happening now? More men were coming here. The detective said he needed to search the rest of the house and the surrounding property because of what was in our bathroom. He asked me if he had to return with a search warrant. No. I granted him permission, even though he had probable cause. Go ahead and rummage through our belongings, dissect the carcass of our dissolute marriage, diagram and label the pieces and remnants found in our bedroom, clothes, photographs, our lives and place each one into small plastic bags. In that plastic safety, instead of remaining fresh, our memories, our successes and failures would never move, rot, grow stale. Evidence we surrendered, without reservation and without battle.

Two men wearing light raincoats stepped into the grass behind our home, resembling modern reapers, gilded and menacing. Each one was holding a flashlight, a metaphorical scythe, bringing with it the truth, bringing with it death. The death of the town's innocence. The death of what innocence we had left. I didn't know what that was anymore, innocence. In sections, they examined the perimeter of our yard, beginning behind a small, inconsequential garden at the rear. I had only planted a few perennial flowers. By the looks of things, they were all decayed, defeated and lifeless in a wasteland of sodden soil and neglect. There was nothing there. There was nothing anywhere.

One of the officers moved closer to me and asked if there was a key to the small, wooden shed behind the garden. I told him where it was inside of the house. Not long after, he retreated further into the yard. The low wattage bulb hanging inside the door I knew was broken. I should have said something to him. I had dislodged it from its housing a few months ago when I began recording over portions of his DAT tapes, hoping through those manipulations, he would someday hear me again. It was an isolated place where I was unhindered by his harsh sounds or even louder despair. After several minutes the officer closed the single door, but never replaced the lock. They found something they wanted to question me about or re-examine. The door opened, pulled by the arms of the wind. They would want to listen to what was already on the recorder hidden in the shed. I could hear the pauses and wailing sobs on that dulling strip of iron oxide echo throughout the desolation and taper off into the past.

I felt guilty, but I wasn't sure exactly of what. I resented the way the two men beheld me, as if I was a criminal, as if I had buried the corpses of tragic secrets deep into the recesses of the softened earth they muddled though. Everything about Tobias and our life together in this small community was public because of his accident, the articles and recurring questions, the funeral of the boy he struck and now this. Those poor, murdered children. I could never again have a moment of isolation, a moment of soundless reflection where I wouldn't feel the tremendous weight and depth of a thousand stares. Our child would now be susceptible to all the entropy of our existence.

I set the warm tea down on the porch between my feet. They were sore from dancing and repetition even though I had been treating them with lamb's wool before I performed. I reached over and rubbed each one. I should have gone inside, but instead I pulled an afghan tighter around my shoulders and my neck. There was a chance I would be detained until Tobias could be located. Indirectly, he had made our child and I accomplices, but to what I wasn't exactly sure. Perhaps he didn't understand the situation I would be in. Or care.

I grew colder, anxious at the impending idea he no longer loved and cherished me, valued our marriage, all the wonderful things we told each other we stood for. I stood and in doing so, toppled the tea at my feet. I watched the pale, amber color move under the ugliness of my toes and hide itself in the cracks of the porch, disappearing into the dark expanse of landscape underneath. It looked like living, breathing rust, the once unique color of his cello. It reminded me of the first time I had heard him play.

I exhaled as the ruptured pipeline dripped beads of water pooling upon the edge of the stage in New York. A few stagehands around for practice scattered. My clothing pressed in on me. So many times during that rehearsal I wanted to admire him, become transfixed by the way his hands were so still when he began to play. Yet all I kept thinking of was repetition and placement. Technique. Balance and fluidity. I am liquid movement, I am water. I wanted him to drink me, drown in me. He played, sustained by a composure and an intensity that should have feasted upon one another and left a mangled carcass of talent and technique behind. His music was calculated, measured. I could hear people behind me, their instructions soon muted by the repetitive placement of that Pernambuco bow and horsehair. Nothing else moved, people and nature trapped in atrophy, only the peerless sounds of his music echoing upon the lingering landscape. I took the night air into my lungs and exhaled, then paused. It was all so beautiful. When his cello quieted, I turned and ran behind long, lavender drapery hung behind me.

My hands trembled as I stood in front of a tall mirror, trying to unfasten one of the buttons on my blouse. I couldn't grip them well. When I looked up, I could see for the first time my nipples darkened against the light material. I wondered if he had noticed and thought differently of me because of it. I parted the drapery and watched him, riddled with water and emotion. He was still seated in a chair, leaning into the high curves of the cello. It was against the side of his face, his lips moving. It was as if he was communicating with the instrument, was the luthier who crafted it, shaped it, instructed it on how to age, to learn, to grow. As if it were a born child in need of security and nurturing. I noted how with tremendous care he returned the cello to its case. I wondered if he held a woman in such regard, with grace and fragility, careful not to damage her. He stood and looked out from the empty stage, ignoring the water surrounding him. It continued to sway back and forth against his ankles. I wondered of what he thought, what images occupied the stage of his challenging mind. I wished I could have remained there longer, in solitude and retrospect, admiring the disarray of the colors of the night that made him look so uniquely beautiful.

~

I closed the porch door behind me and placed my vacant mug into the sink. The dishes still sat there, ignored and insignificant. I pulled the plug from the drain again and watched the water disappear into gravity's oblivion. It felt like everything was, the inertia grabbing, pulling me under and leading me further into despair. I again felt nauseous. An officer moved through the kitchen and bumped into me. My stomach pressed against a cabinet handle. I reached down and placed my hands across my abdomen. I thought about the doubt I had in his inability to protect us, be strong when we would need him to be. Not physically, but emotionally,

238

being supportive and calming. When situations worsened, would he endure? All because of a slight, accidental nudge by a stranger.

"Are you alright?" Mull asked.

"Yes, I'm fine. I don't understand anything of what's happening here," I admitted.

"We're trying to figure that out as well," he said. "I have to ask you again. Are you sure you have no idea how those photographs ended up in your bathroom?"

"No, I've already told you," I sobbed. I dropped my face into my palms. After several minutes I looked up. My eyes were red and swollen. "Excuse me please," I said. I moved down the hallway and paused at the bathroom. Two people were inside. "I need to use the bathroom," I said.

"Of course," someone said. "I am sorry. But we need a few more minutes to document things."

"I understand," I said. I wandered down the hallway and collapsed inside of our bedroom. My body felt shapeless, formless, devoid of stability and continuity. I moved further up onto our bed and laid down in the space where he slept. I could smell his musk in the fiber of the sheets. I retrieved my phone again and dialed his number. Nothing. I tried four times. I closed my eyes and buried my face into the duvet spread across the terrain of our isolation.

How had we come to this?

I moved my fingertips into the private places where we had been. I wished I could go back to those silent moments last night where I believed we were an unblemished union, closer than we had been since his accident. I could still taste his skin on the surface of my lips. I had moved his hand away from my stomach. I made sure he remained asleep and opened the door to his sound room. I should have gone outside to the shed. There was already a tape loaded into his DAT recorder. I leaned against the wall so I could see into our bedroom, notice if the darkness blossomed into light. I depressed the record button and listened to the sound of my own voice. I rewound the DAT tape when I finished, closed the door to the sound room and went into our bathroom. I closed the door, in hopes of his remaining asleep still and at peace. I rubbed my abdomen. Lost in images of abject apprehension and uncertainty, I sobbed.

I climbed into our bathtub and felt the cool wind brush across the back of my neck as it intruded through an open window on our evening, one that alternated between passion and aversion. The water pooled over my tender ankles and I closed my eyes. I didn't know how to tell him we were having a child. With all our marriage had been through since his accident, I thought this development would bruise him, inflict more damage upon an already fractured soul. All because of the consequences of his attempted suicide. Not long after I climbed in, he rapped against the bathroom door. I thought about locking it, but that would have caused deeper insecurity on his part, the sudden inaccessibility to me. Things were going to be emotional and crippling enough when I told him.

"Is something wrong?" he asked. "Did I upset you?"

"No, you were wonderful, dinner was wonderful. Everything was beautiful. I love you. I'm a little tired and sore from dancing," I said, covering my belly underneath the water as if I were showing already and I could hide our coming child with the simple placement of my hands. "I have something I have to tell you?"

"What's the matter?" he asked, sitting down on the floor, his back against the bathtub. I reached out and ran my wet hand through his hair, miniature tributaries of water cascading along the curves of his neck. Tiny rivers turned down his left shoulder and fell into the space where his arm had been. I thought about kissing him on the back of the neck, but I didn't.

"I'm pregnant," I said.

"What?" he asked as he shifted. It seemed insignificant, reflexive. Though with me, movement always had a purpose and a definition.

"We're having a baby," I said, looking down at myself through the displacement of the water. I moved my hand upon the surface, the ripples of the water stirring.

"Are you sure?" he asked, never turning his head around.

"Yes," I said, a little more in defiance than I had planned.

"How far along are you?" He leaned forward and grabbed at his ankle.

"Roughly 12 weeks. I had an appointment with my obstetrician yesterday," I admitted.

"When we're you going to tell me?" he said.

"I'm telling you now. That's the only thing that matters. I wanted to have some tests done before I said anything to be sure. The doctors thought I was having problems with my gall bladder," I said.

"What are we going to do?" he asked.

"What do you mean what are we going to do?"

"Are we going to keep the baby?" he said. I stopped touching him and slid down into the tepid water and closed my eyes, hoping and praying I had misheard him through all the questions. When I surfaced, I ran my hands through my hair and wiped the warm water from my face.

"How could you even ask me that question? We've discussed having children before, remember?" I said, with no resentment, no harshness.

"Things were different then. We can't handle having a child right now," he said. I watched him turn completely around. The unvarying calm and passiveness expressed in his voice was almost violent in a way, like an animal devouring wounded prey, feasting on the recognizable smell of blood.

"You mean you can't handle having a child," I countered. The burgeoning resolve in his eyes collapsed into recollection and ambivalence. Something that would forever be behind his eyes, his mannerisms, his speech and his love making. "It wasn't your fault what happened. It was an accident. I don't know how many times people, including myself have to tell you that. Our friends have. The doctors all have. But I'm starting to think you like playing the martyr," I said.

"Almost every artist does at one moment or another. It helps to give birth to creation, but that's got nothing to do with it. I don't deserve to have a child after what happened. Selfishness breeds consequences, sometimes ones you cannot ever leave behind," he whispered.

"What about me? What do I deserve? I'm very happy in our life together, regardless of what you might think or feel. You're my husband and I love you, all you, everything that defines who you are, overwhelming joy or failure," I said. "Please. I need your help in this. I'm scared in a way. I'm not sure what I am supposed to do," I pleaded. "And whatever it is, I don't want to do it without you."

"What can I do? How am I supposed to hold her, console her? Should I wipe away her tears with such artificiality? A plastic resin hand?" He mimicked moving his arm. All I could see was his shoulder flinch.

"What's going to happen when she grows older and starts to see things, determine things on her own? How will she see me?" I smiled inside at his consistent mention of a daughter.

"As a man, a father, someone who is honest, passionate and loyal. You're not anything else and you never have been," I concluded.

"We both know that isn't true," he said, turning around again and moving his body away from mine. Lying against the opposing wall, I watched him close his eyes, lower his head and rub his temple hard. A lavender towel became rumpled against his shoulder. It reminded me of when I first fell in love with him. To me, he was as beautiful now as he was holding and playing his cello that night, even more.

"Look at me," I said. "Tell me Tobias, what are you? What are you besides a talented and beautiful man, a man I love and a man that I've always valued?"

"Please don't," he said. Tears began housing in his eyes. I stood from the comforting water of the bathtub and stepped onto the cold tile floor. My nude body was trembling as I always did when I neared him. He was such an impassioned and caring man, intelligent, courageous. I stood close enough to him that he could reach out and touch me. And he did.

"Don't what?" I said. I placed my hand on his face and raised his head.

"Don't remind me of who I used to be," he said. Tobias rose up on his knees and moved closer, wrapped his arm around my waist and placed his head against my belly.

"You're still the same man I fell in love with when you were cradling that cello. Standing on that stage, you were the most beautiful thing I had ever seen, determined, passionate, a bit withdrawn. Regardless, I wanted to know everything about you the second your bow caressed those strings," I admitted.

"Why? There's nothing special about who I am," he said.

"I disagree," I whispered as I leaned over and kissed the top of his head, cradled his neck in my hands. "Don't silence who you are, the music, the beautiful sounds," I said. "Even without those things, even if you never try to play again, you're far from worthless. And if it takes all my life to show you, I will," I said.

"Everyone else has gone. You should have been with someone else," he said. "Someone who could provide for you better."

"Don't say that to me," I whispered. "It's not fair and you know it. You've been trying to push me away ever since your accident. Why? I've stood by you when others have gone, abandoned you in everything you feel makes you who you are. Our child will want to know who you were, who you are. It may be easier being alone, but I'm not going to let you do it," I said.

"Any semblance of that man is gone," he said, moving his shoulder higher. For a moment I could feel his missing arm touch me. It was the water trickling down my hips. It gave me a sudden chill.

"No," I countered. I sat down on the tile floor, maneuvered my body into the tender places of his perfect architecture, as I studied it, the completeness of his muscles and abdomen. I nestled my back against his chest and placed my head against his shoulder. I placed his arm across my breasts and inhaled. I loved him so much, despite everything that had happened, despite his wavering courage, his consistent inability to be bound and secure. I leaned closer to his sensitivities, his melancholy and reached up, kissed the underside of his chin. "I've never loved anyone else," I said.

~

I exhaled and turned, moved my body from the distant comfort of memory into the vexation of close uncertainty. I glanced at the ceiling and thought about closing my eyes, falling asleep in the images and sounds I desired and cherished the most. Those wondrous things would grow old and decay as well. I made my way into the bathroom. There was no one around, but the small, yellow markers notating the remaining evidence. I closed the door behind me and stood in front of the mirror above the sink. I ran water in the basin for several minutes then drowned my hands in the cold element. Through the consuming dread, I could hear the rain outside. Some of the water's flight clung to the window screen. From a distance it looked like a spider web, trapping everything in its unusual perfection.

Finishing up and washing my face, I moved into the hallway, glancing again at the evidence markers. Things always remained behind, remembrances and visual inscriptions taunting, always lingering and never leaving. The past was tenacious. The sudden images I had seen were gone. The unfortunate children in those photographs on the bathroom floor had vanished into an overwhelming and staggering realm of tragic statistics. Studied, then written down in the detective's notebook.

The men who remained behind in our home whispered in a suspicious hush when I approached. Their implications of their glances saddened me. I hadn't done anything wrong. I regained composure and stepped out onto the porch again, the rain worsening, punishing even. The sudden cold blindsided me and I shuddered, more in worry instead of discomfort. The shed door opened and I could see inside. The bulb had been replaced and a man was moving around, Mull. Quick and sudden bursts of light stuttered throughout the humid structure. More potential evidence, including fingerprints, were catalogued and photographed. Through the now stinging rain he raised his hand and gestured I come along. I grabbed a Henley sweater and marched across the sodden grass in our yard. It was Tobias' sweater.

I could sense his love and his anguish in the delicate wool construction. I always loved the color. As I walked, I could see the places in the grass where we made love once, made promises we would be now challenged to hold. In the dense atmosphere I could smell his cello burning, the scorched cinders staining everything with an odor I could never remove. Isolated places in the grass were barren and would never grow again. The sudden reflection made me move my hands across my abdomen. When I reached the building, a photographer exited, holding his camera inside of a bag to protect it from the rain.

"Please come in," Mull said. The shed was small, windowless and arid, almost disquieting. When I was in here previously, I searched through his belongings, wishing I could discover a reason, some clinging hope why he was so depressed, so fragmented and unreachable. That was when I inadvertently shattered the bulb, plunging any possible answers I wanted to find into darkness. Not that they would have been easy to see in the warm comfort of the light.

Mull closed us in some by pulling the door closer. It wasn't much, but I appreciated his regard for privacy, the slight gesture of nobility blemished by the hopelessness of the situation. Detective Mull was glaring over my shoulder. On a small, worn, empty leather instrument case was a second DAT recorder. The lone tape that accompanied it was around each spool, unlabeled. When I discovered the apparatus, I thought it would be recordings of his music, his unfinished compositions, hidden, buried like a forgotten scroll of an aged religion. I had pressed play and heard silence evaporate upon the shed. It lingered longer than I expected and I began to believe the recording was empty.

Soon after, I heard light rumblings of sounds, faint, then harder, rude almost. OSHA. I closed my eyes, opened my auditory senses and listened to the sounds of an accident, a collision. I stopped the tape. Had he been listening to this recording alone where I couldn't hear his perceived failure? I pressed play again, but remained apprehensive in continuing to listen to the recording of a car accident. The horrible sounds looped over and over, so much so, I could smell the scorched rubber in the shed. I began sobbing.

Those irreversible consequences were so unbearable, evenings alone in a hospital, wondering why he chose to attempt suicide. I had never felt so useless or so barren. Hollowness abounded me, wandering achromatic and antiseptic hallways when I was able to, the dull silence and loneliness only broken when a surgeon or nurse would whisper something in my ear. After a while, nothing they said resonated with me. Those days lingered, days where I carried and wore a continent's weight, all its people's strife upon my slight frame. No one else ever came to see us besides police and there was no tenderness in their approach, questioning anything and everything he once did and said. A fragile sense of hope comforted me during the intense weight of those horrible hours. The one man I needed and wanted was unavailable, alone and imprisoned in a sad land of utter stillness. Mull reached out and touched my shoulder, freeing me from the instability of recollection.

"Understand because of what we found inside your home, I have to ask you about this recording," Mull began.

"I assumed as much," I said.

"Did your husband place the recorder here?" he asked.

"No, I did," I said. "We purchased a different model."

"Do you remember when?"

"Almost a year ago," I said.

"Was this tape already loaded or did you put it into the recorder?'

"No, it was already loaded," I said.

"Did he come out here often, sometimes alone, spend time listening to his work?"

"No. He dealt with all his OSHA materials in his sound room," I said. "But he has remained distant at times from everything, so I can't be sure when and if he came out here."

"Did he play or record music here, without your knowledge?" Mull said.

"No. He respects and adores sound. This small space would only suffocate the beauty he used to find in it. If he did play, it would have been in that room. But even separated by oceans, I would have heard him play," I said.

"Do you know what is on this tape?" he said

"Yes," I began.

"I'd like to play it, to be certain it's not a recording belonging to our case, although all the others submitted into police evidence were labeled," he said. "I doubt it's anything related to what's happening, but I wanted you here alone, in case it was something personal. We're invading your home enough, your belongings, rummaging through your marriage. I'm sorry," he concluded. As I reached to press play, a man opened the shed door wide and whispered in Mulls' ear. His identifiable gestures turned incomprehensible.

"Excuse me Augustina," he said. The men ran through the grass and I listened to the sound of desperation that accompanied, the quick placement of bone and tendon, the kinetic ballet of muscle. I wished I could dance again in the damp grass, close my eyes and turn in circles. I moved closer to the DAT recorder and pressed play. The voice sounded unrecognizable, devoid. It was mine though. I wasn't even sure it had changed a single note since then. When I had pressed record, I paused on several occasions, unresolved in which sounds would reach him, a whisper, a sigh, a laugh. I exhaled and began whispering, promises, lies, memories, any sounds that I could.

*Tobias, can you hear me?*

*Do you still love me, a woman who cherishes you, honors you in fragility and in strength? Who am I to you now, as I listen to the sound of my own voice echo in the arid darkness, away from you, away from the richness of your touch, your consideration? I struggle to understand why you wanted such a tragic ending to everything we struggled to attain, more so our love, which will always endure.*

*Am I unbearable, impatient or distant? There are so many questions I can compose, but wonder if you would even hear me. My body is overwhelmed by apathy and rage because you excluded me so often in what made you sad, made you, as you once said, fractured. I do not know where to go from here.*

*The sterility of everything around me makes me want to drown in a pool of your music, if your music could transpose into a pure fluid. I would suffocate, allow the golden water to fill my lungs, take my breath the same way you did each time you walked into a room. Like the notes you stopped playing, you were a classical man, renaissance, cultured and beautiful. You captured my heart the moment I saw you and no matter what we have said to each other, after everything that has happened, I will never stop being yours. The ballet shoes I wore that day, I never wore again. I could have danced to the world's greatest compositions and wouldn't have cared. It was the most perfect moment of my life and nothing will change that. I love you more at this moment than I ever have. I wanted so much for you to play again, so I could have a reason to hold those shoes, place them over my skin, and tie them around my ankles. Something I once respected inside of you is missing, lost in the unfinished symphony of our lives...*

The words coming faded as I moved around in silence. Some old garden tools hung, immobile and useless. Behind a neglected spade was his prosthetic arm. I walked over to the artificial limb and touched the fingertips. Even through the molded resin I could still feel his unique touch, the incredible way those pieces once cascaded down the structure of my spine, the purfling of his cello. Things I recorded previously resonated and I grieved I had even rehearsed each phrase, each horrible word, as if I were composing a unique ballet. I never placed that DAT tape into his raw collection of sounds, hoping someday he would discover how much I needed him, without reminders, an idea born inside himself.

Even in anger and regret, I loved him. I removed the prosthesis from its noose and cradled it against my body, remembering how he once held me. We danced upon the grass outside, when that musician was here singing, the places where the steady rainfall was having trouble finding a home. So much has changed. Now, our yard was barren and subdued, jostled by the sound of sirens in the distance. The water from the continual rain caressed the footprints from the detectives vanishing in the grass. I closed my eyes, holding prisoner the assemblage of tears that sought escape from the dictatorial regime of my body.

I pulled the sweater tighter around my shoulders and closed the door to the shed. Mull had been gone with the other officer for about ten minutes. I tread through the yard and stood on the porch for several minutes, eventually sitting back down. The spilled tea stains were still visible, yet to blend into the grain of the splintered boards. The afghan I used to warm myself was still tossed over the arm of the bench. I slid it up over my body and under my chin. The rain worsened again. Regardless, I didn't want to go inside, become surrounded by passive, still objects and the fragmentary remnants of murdered children.

The intrinsic, small movements of peace and happiness I desired were missing. Leaning back I closed my eyes and listened to the rain cascade along the slope of the building and settle in the gutters. Some water pooled up in the cluttered leaves and debris and ran over the edge of a drainpipe, landing in the artificial embrace of a forgotten plastic bag. The sound scared me, made me recoil some. It echoed throughout the eerie silence, without any semblance of grace or sympathy. I was rescued from the cold grasp of remembrance and regret when the police siren's wail ceased, very near. I heard doors closing. I closed my eyes, hoping Tobias was safe, a valid reason why police evidence was in our bathroom and our home. No more hardship should occupy our stage, the tremendous depths of our marriage already played out upon a cruel stage where everyone could see. Moments later, the man who had whispered in Mull's ear stepped out onto the porch, a grim demeanor pressed into his features.

"I'm afraid I'm going to need you to gather some of your things and come with me," he said.

~

It was growing humid inside of the police car. I inhaled as deeply as I was capable and rolled down the window, the rain rushing across the windshield, along the side doors and through the opening. I leaned my head against the glass and sobbed, letting the rain touch me. Why? We were so close to understanding one another once again, changing the perspective on what track our marriage had been on. Or at least I believed we were. There were so many things I became discouraged by early, his vulnerability, his inability to persevere when hindrance prevailed in his music. Tobias did struggle daily, his perfections and imperfections waging a war upon one another where no solider could remain unharmed or unchanged, come home and begin again. There was a place I carried him when he worried, reassured him he was indispensable, handsome, admired and loved in his uniqueness. No man could ever challenge me artistically as he once had. I made such progress helping him since his release or, believed I had, when our lives changed, a change I felt subconsciously I had to force. I touched my abdomen.

We were heading along the main road through town, leaves and debris immobile aside curbs and hooded parking meters, taken hostage by radical terrorists' ages ago. Some businesses were open and witness to their abduction, yet many had unfortunately closed. A bridal shop. A loan building. A second-hand music shop. I pulled a hardly used shoulder bag, hung over a coat rack by the door, closer onto my lap. I couldn't remember the last occasion I had used it. I slipped my purse inside it though as we were leaving. My dancing bag was still full of clothing and shoes, sitting on the floor in our room. I wished I had it with me. It gave me some sort of comfort. The only thing I would be dancing with here was unpredictability and sorrow.

The car idled as I glanced down again at my cellular. No calls, no messages. Nothing. How I ached, longed I could hear his voice, his uncommon, sad melody echo upon the suffocating nature of the car. A flower shop had placed a terracotta vase along the edge of the sidewalk, adjacent a streetlamp. Raindrops collapsing from a falling gutter dropped into the display. The flowers wilted under the weight of the steady stream of water, pulling on the clutching fingertips of the soil, desperate to keep them secure, keep them safe. It was impossible though, to keep someone from harm when the rapidity and the intensity of the violence came from underneath the surface of their own lives.

We had soon pulled into the rear, municipal parking lot behind the small cluster of closed businesses we drove past. The building in front of the car was an abandoned real estate office. One could still see the main road, the lone intersection I could see, depressing and desolate. In the distance, past the lone railroad crossing, the connection to the interstate. A side door to the building down an alley had been propped open with a cinderblock. Some of the lights were on inside and a man was busy replacing some burnt out bulbs on a small ladder.

This area was hit hard after the housing market collapse and some of the properties devalued and remained abandoned. The creation of agriculture and jobs was always difficult here. I leaned back in the impersonal seat. This was the realtor we brokered with when we purchased our house. I didn't even remember when they closed. I could hear sirens fading in the distance. I grabbed my belongings and stepped out of the car. I walked beneath a rusted fire escape that led to an efficiency apartment above. Through the rain I wanted to shout in despair and in impediment.

"Is this about my husband?" I asked. The officer who had driven me here came over and placed his hand on my shoulder. "I don't understand. Where is he? What is happening?" The raindrops had trouble finding me in my doubt.

"Please, come inside," he pleaded. "Please."

I stepped onto the disheveled and dingy hardwood floor and waited by the entrance. Portions of the boards had expanded from water damage. I could see the shape of his old cello, the curves, the once beautiful luster and sheen in the rotted and bowing construction. The ceiling above me was missing tiles and I noticed a slight stream of water falling from certain sections of the copper pipes in the corner of the building. Deep inside, underneath all the ambiguity, I found it alluring and rhythmic, encouraging in a way. I closed my eyes, imagining Tobias here, holding me, guiding me, dancing upon the broken floor. The music I heard inside me was some of his early classical recordings, ones he had disowned long ago. The mood and quick images were soon severed by a man, pulling at large sections of the sheets of beige paper that covered the inside of the front windows. It resembled in color, the parchment Tobias used to compose music upon, the tender balance of staff and chord, held together by intellect and skill. Amongst the separate panels and markings, I saw the notes waving as the man pulled more sections of the paper aside and caused them to fall through the air and to the ground. Obviously they weren't there. But I saw them anyway. They were like small, beautiful particles of hope. The room silenced as I stepped over the threshold of the building.

"Can someone please tell me what is happening?" I asked, frustrated by the lack of clarity and the total absence of any apparent empathy.

"I'm not the one who should be telling you why you are here because I don't have all the information. The last thing I want to do is mislead you or make the situation worse," he said.

"What do you mean by situation?" I said.

"Please. When Detective Mull arrives, and he is on his way here, I will send him in," he said. I dropped my head. "I understand you are pregnant. Some men are here to straighten up the apartment upstairs. There are some things the previous tenant left behind. There's a sofa as well. We want to ensure you and the others are as comfortable as possible," he said. Before I could question him on his response, he moved outside. I listened to his footsteps crash against the metal staircase leading up to the apartment above.

I moved to the far corner of the building, away from the dripping water, the constant traffic and chatter of men, women and police radios. I held my cellular so tight my fingers turned bone white. I wished I knew where Tobias was. There was a chair near the rear exit of the building. I pulled on the furniture and drug it closer. I leaned forward in the chair after a few minutes and buried my face into my palms. Not again. I felt more alone and barren than I ever had, even after everything else that had happened. The stains in the tattered section of carpet runner broke my attention away and I took in my surroundings.

There was still a desk pushed into the far corner, behind the entrance door near where I came in. A file cabinet rested against an open electrical panel. The various colored wires protruding from the steel box looked like deformed strings from a broken instrument. Someone had left a ladder behind. Or it belonged to the man changing bulbs. Next to the exit where I retrieved the chair was a bathroom. I stood and stepped in, shutting the door behind me.

I tried to turn on the light, but there was no bulb in the socket. I took the phone out of my shoulder bag and used the minimal light from the display to see. Everything was crumbling, the old, dingy tile floor, the porcelain sink. I became nauseous. I slumped to the floor, resting on my knees and vomited into the toilet. There was nothing to describe how I felt in that moment, sobbing on a disgusting, broken floor, wiping saliva from my lips. There was a slight knock upon the door. After several minutes, I opened the door and when the light finally intervened from outside,

251

Detective Mull was pulling into a space in the front of the building. I regained my composure and held the phone again. I watched him pull the collar of his coat tight across his neck and cough into the crook of his arm

"Augustina, please come with me for a minute," Mull said, placing his hand upon my back and leading me towards the alley next to the building. Asking me to go first, I stepped onto the staircase and went up to the efficiency above. Whereas the real estate building was cold and rude, the apartment was stifling and humid. The few windows were frosted over and there were no curtains. I could see the couch the other officer mentioned earlier. It was still in very good condition. Some folding chairs were stacked in the corner as well as a square table, its metal legs still collapsed. A large roll of wire was astride it all. Mull gestured for me to sit down. After asking the other two men behind him to leave, he exhaled and spoke.

"Augustina, a little over a mile from here near the interstate exchange is a bus sitting idle in the middle of the road. We have a substantiated report the vehicle has been hijacked and a gunshot has been fired," he said.

"What do you mean hijacked? Why would someone hijack a transit bus? That doesn't make any sense," I said.

"That's why other officers were reluctant to say anything to you in detail, until I had a chance to visit the scene and speak to you. Have you heard from your husband?" he asked. His leaden eyes took in scribbles from his notebook before fighting their way higher against what I thought had to be a mountain of exhaustion to meet mine.

"No, I haven't been able to reach Tobias," I said. "I've tried, but it just rings."

"We believe that your husband is on that bus," he admitted.

"What? Is he all right? How do you know that he is on that bus at all? Have you spoken to him?" I said.

"The driver of the bus was released by the hijacker shortly after. Although he has a medical condition and was being ventilated, he provided us with some very specific details about the other passengers, who else was on board, before taken away by paramedics. Luckily, there weren't that many passengers on that route. One individual matches the description of your husband," he acknowledged.

"I don't understand," I said. "When I left this morning he was there in our home. What is he doing on a bus?" I dropped my shoulder bag on the sofa and focused on the wet footprints underneath me on the floor. Odd, but there was a pattern to them I discovered, an abstract method and vocabulary to their placement. As they faded, they decreased in ratio, became the size of a child's. I searched for Tobias's fleeting reflection inside of them, any remote semblance of hope I could caress. "Why am I here? People are standing here. Why isn't anyone doing anything?"

"At the moment we are doing what we can to ensure no one is injured and no further shots are fired on that bus. Our job foremost is to get everyone off alive. We have very little to go on I'm afraid," Mull confessed. "The man who commandeered the bus hasn't said anything, made any sorts of demands or even asked to speak to anyone."

"Who is he?" I asked. Please tell me all this is a mistake, a practical farce, a rehearsal. And Tobias will come home to me, even if he was the same man whom I left this morning. A man who was ready to abandon the responsibility of our child in earnest. We would push on as we always had, persevere, have our child and change when we could, when we needed. I loved him regardless. He was all I knew. For a moment, I wondered if that made me weak.

"Augustina, the man who took control of the bus and fired the gunshot is Tobias," Mull said.

"Oh my God," I whispered, falling to the floor so gingerly I appeared suspended in time, in atmosphere, falling from the sad colors of a photograph, waiting for someone who looked upon me to unfold their hands and cradle me in the gentle valley of their palms. Pressed against the floor, I moved my fingertips against the wooden slats, as if playing an instrument.

After lying on the floor sobbing, Mull guided me back onto the couch. He excused himself and I listened to his footsteps on that metal staircase echo throughout the vacant apartment. Soon he returned with a bottle of water. It was warm, but I didn't care. Most of the water rushed through my esophagus, but other portions made their way down the outside of my throat. I closed my eyes and for all too brief a second, remembered the identical way it studied me on the precipice of that stage when I danced and he played.

"Augustina, we are doing everything we can," he began.

"It isn't enough," I said in a whisper. "I'm sorry."

"Do you have any idea why Tobias would be doing this?" Mull questioned. But all along I felt, believed he knew.

"No," I said. "No."

"Other officers are at the scene, stationed around the perimeter, far enough away to not antagonize Tobias, cause him to make any sudden moves. As I said, our goal is to end all this peacefully. The roads are cordoned off in both directions. We're trying to maintain the scene as best as we can, so I ordered people remain on lockdown in their homes or businesses. The weather is helping," he continued. "I haven't spoken to anyone about what was found when officers arrived at your home this morning. For now, it's going to stay that way. It could and will cause complications later. I'm going to go back to the scene to see what I can find out. I need you to stay here, in case we need you for anything," he said.

"You mean in case you need me to talk to him?" I said.

"It's unfair to ask anything of you after what has already happened. You've both been through something I cannot begin to imagine. Uncertainty. Guilt. The strength you have standing beside him is staggering. I'm not sure anyone else can understand him, listen to him the way you do. Because of that, you may be the only person he may covet." I dropped my head into my hands and wept roughly, wept a disturbed ocean's fateful swell. An officer knocked on the door frame and asked to speak to Mull. All he said aloud was the rest were on their way.

"How many people are on that bus?" I asked.

"We're not confirming anything, but including Tobias, four," he said. "There is a woman downstairs who is a police psychologist. She's going to stay here with you until I come back," he said. Through the floor I could hear the voice of a woman. At that time, an electrician entered the room and went over to the junction box. "We're having the power and water lines turned back on so you and the others will be as comfortable as possible, given the circumstances. Let's go downstairs for a moment. I want you to understand everything about what's happening and what we are doing," he added.

We walked down the staircase and re-entered the real estate building. A table had been set up as well as a few folding chairs along the side wall where there were no windows. Several power strips were being plugged in to the wall. I watched Mull move to the front of the building and speak with the man uncovering the windows. They both stared through the glass towards their left.

"Why was he peeling away the paper earlier?" I asked.

"We're trying to get a better line of sight on what is happening," he said. He gestured for me to come closer. I stood beside him as he pointed. "There is another officer stationed in the building across the street, quite visible from here. Going left, he is about two or three buildings down. Do you see him? From where he is, he will be able to relay to us what is happening through a radio. He is receiving his information from an officer who is on scene near the bus. We want you close in case we need you, but not where some harm may come to you or anyone else. It's routine procedure." Routine. I knew that because I studied it every day. A prescribed and detailed course of action. Also something common, unoriginal.

"Why is this happening?" I said.

Mull exhaled, paused, then turned around and touched my shoulder. "I have my suspicions, but it wouldn't be right to suggest anything at this point. I don't know Augustina," he confessed. "I have to go. Arrangements are being made to deliver some essentials, food, water, blankets and bathroom supplies. I've requested several pillows as well because of your condition. There will also be a few EMT's outside as well. I've been assured the electricity will be on shortly. In the apartment upstairs there will be places to charge your cellular phone, in case Tobias calls you. I need you to keep it charged Augustina," he said.

"I understand," I said. The female psychologist set down her purse. She was tall, a purple scarf looped around her neck.

"Is there anything you need before I go?" he said.

"Is she here to talk to Tobias?" I asked.

"We don't have anyone on staff who has any real experience in hostage negotiations. We've contacted the federal authorities for assistance. Up until January, I would have said none of this kind of stuff would ever happen here, this situation, the murdered children and the collateral damage. That we're supposed to go on somehow after all this," Mull said.

He pulled his coat up on his shoulders and tighter around his frame. "She's here to listen, in case anyone wishes to talk."

"Do you think after everything, all his struggles, Tobias would talk to her?" I said.

"No. No I don't," he concluded. Mull turned and instructed another officer to escort me upstairs to the apartment.

"Thank you. I want to lie down for a little while," I said to him. I never even heard anyone go upstairs. There were several bottles of water on top. I knelt down onto the couch and peered behind to see if there was a power outlet close. Seeing there was, I placed my unfamiliar shoulder bag on the end. I rummaged through the small purse inside for a charger and my phone. Still, no one had called. The electricity had been turned back on. I could hear the light humming of the refrigerator. The unit was older, had no central air and old fashioned radiator heat.

I heard light footsteps behind me. It was a police officer and a man who I assumed was the electrician. They excused themselves for intruding and carried the remaining spool of wire, a small step ladder and a box of equipment downstairs. I was alone. Again. I felt deserted. It was so stifling and oppressive, like held down in the middle of a desert. It was as if I were in the sound room when Tobias was gone, struggling to find reason, searching for disclosure in those instruments and tapes. The quietness and stillness of that room was painful, almost violent in a way.

The last time I went into that artificial grave of sound and fury, was to return the last DAT tape I had recorded over. I replaced the earlier ones where they had each been, with measured exactness and certainty. Sometimes I wished he still cared for me in the same manner, with such an intense, categorical precision and vigilance. I moved around the room cautiously touching his past. For some reason I was afraid he would catch me in here and by having intimacy with the articles of his history, I would give them presence, life, allow them to breathe in the fresh air of the forgotten. And in turn, he would have to remember them, see who he was and always would be, no matter how caustic it was to him. I paused in front of his cello and as always, waited for it to speak.

The smudges were still present, archaic, yet identifiable. They were Tobias's. There was a fine layer of dust gathered across the cello's neck. With the white, fluorescent lights dimmed, hanging overhead and the shades drawn, it looked like the instrument was outside during a snowstorm. I kept waiting for the cello to thaw, the once rich, amber color to dissolve into the delicate flooring. I moved a lone fingertip along its construction and pushed some of the neglect onto the floor. But regardless if I removed it from its cradle and tended to it, I would never be able to give it back its original brilliance, the shimmer and magnificence it once had.

There was so much history, a chronology he chose to bury deep within the sounds of industry. In the corner we had placed a small, antique chest, which housed some of our wedding memories, nothing expensive, pieces I valued. Photographs. A wine glass. Flowers, pressed inside the pages of a music book. Resting at the bottom of the trunk was a hand crafted, leather journal of parchment he once composed upon. I was sure he hadn't opened it for some time. I had cycled through those beautiful pages of sheet music, studied his musings on pace and pitch penned in the margins. The flowers were always in the rear, after the last several, clean pages. Some pages were missing. I understood the journal would never be finished.

On several, different pages I could read the name "Augustina." Each time he seemed to scribble it a different way, with different writing instruments. Once his penmanship appeared nervous, another time eager. I liked the apparent randomness behind his written gestures. All that promise, all that musical intelligence was gone, became nothing more than a tossed pile of debris when he ransacked that room. Music, passion, love and ideals. Each one mutilated, beaten until it became unrecognizable. It made me think of the photographs of the children on the floor of our bathroom. It was all so sad. I realized I never moved deep enough into the room to see if our wedding memories were undamaged or if they too had become broken.

I slid one of the folding chairs in front of the window. Before sitting down, I struggled to turn the latch so I could open it. The curved metal pinched at the inside of my palm. When it finally turned, I lifted the wooden frame up. It was heavier than I thought it would be. The cool air and rain rushed through. It felt wonderful, the atmosphere rolling over me, the sudden chill stimulating the hair on my arms. I could see a few

257

officers go into the building Mull showed me. I wondered how far away everything was happening and who else was on that bus.

Please don't hurt anyone Tobias.

Please don't leave me to do this alone.

Through all this, I was saddened as well for the community here, good people whose sense of innocence and existence was ruined. I sat there for a little while, watching the small town we were a part of become like a dissected insect, ripped open and studied, internal secrets exposed and scrutinized. Its history and biology questioned, almost violated in a way. I closed my eyes and listened to the sound of the water. I wondered if Tobias would even notice that it was raining.

If I made noise, mimicked the sound of a hard, manufactured object, he would hear me. I thought about grabbing a glass, carrying it out into the street and smashing it, hoping the decibel waves would shred through the solemnity, the rain and reach him. And he would understand the tones, the sound it made and even what it meant. I wanted to walk to him, dance along the barricaded and closed road and reach him, put my hand to his chest and tell him to come home, please. Listen to softer sounds, other sounds. Place your head against my belly and listen to the music of our child, the notes emanating from its instruments of speech and movement. The world around me, the sodden grass and the cold asphalt would crumble underneath of my feet if I even attempted to sense, perceive any measure of hope and try to hold it. In dejection, I closed the window, readjusting my feet and pulling them closer to the chair. The area of the wooden floor where my feet were looked as if scorched from a small fire. Everything I danced upon seemed to turn to ruin.

"Excuse me," someone said. "Detective Mull instructed we bring these to you." I turned around to see an officer holding several pillows and a few blankets. I moved closer and lent him a hand.

"Thank you," I said.

"There are a few of us downstairs if you need anything," he said. "Don't hesitate to ask." I wasn't sure what to say or how much he knew about what was happening. So I nodded. I glanced at my phone. There were still no calls, or messages. I never asked you to give up anything in our life before. Your hopes, your dreams, your music. Please give up

Tobias, lay down your anger and your despair and surrender. Please come home.

It was hard to get comfortable here, waiting, understanding nothing of what was happening. I thought of our child, how soft their skin would be, how their feet and tiny toes would redden as mine did. I placed a pillow on the end of the couch and stretched out, worn and beaten by uncertainty, the silence and false peace a rigid and uncomfortable blanket I couldn't ever wash and soften. The quilts in our home were soft, downy. Last night he watched me sleep atop them, my back towards him. I knew he was there, leaning against the doorframe, his deep breathing revealing his position. I so wanted him to curl up behind me, say he was sorry, say he would try to be a father and we could begin again. And again. And again. I wondered when it would all stop, the continuous hardship and the interruptions.

I almost turned around to see the contemplation in his eyes, but I didn't want him to see the adolescent tears, the small orbs of regret and concern roll down across my face, cloud and stain our quilts with even more emotional turmoil. I could hear his feet change position on the floor at times, retreat and attack, as if engaged in an abstract ballet. I heard the door to the sound room close.

As I drifted into sleep, carrying with me the futility of resolution and conviction, I placed a hand on my abdomen and exhaled. The couch in the efficiency was unfamiliar, but I appreciated the respite regardless. My muscles and spine were sore from dancing, rehearsing, at times carrying the dense weight of our marriage, his faithlessness upon them. Yet I still loved Tobias. And I forever would. As angry as I could be because of his inherent failure to see hope in anything, I remained obstinate in my refusal to give up on him or us.

Everything inside my body was anesthetized to the point of atrophy. Going deeper into a fleeting sense of peace, I remembered Tobias giving up his physical reticence, his restlessness last night and nestling behind me atop our quilts. He maneuvered his body behind me, his fingertips touching my spine, the small of my back. I waited to hear the notes he would play along the instrument of my vertebrae. All I could hear though was his breathing, labored by his restlessness and the consequences of our earlier conversation. I had to tell him. And now that I had, I could not

259

break, could not falter. When he pressed against me even closer, somehow his body felt different. But that is what I needed him to be, different, stronger and more decisive. I needed him, now more than ever, to be my husband and the man that I married.

"Are you okay?" I asked.

"No," he said.

"What's the matter?" I raised his hand to rest against my breast. The back of his knuckles brushed across my nipple. It expanded slowly.

"Are we going to do this?" he said. "Raise a child?"

"Yes Tobias, we are," I said, gripping his hand tighter in mine. I kissed the back of his hand and exhaled.

"I'm not sure I can do this," he said. I felt his lips kiss the back of my neck. Even the lightest of touches from him, even now, made my body shiver. As would it always.

"You can. You will. We will have our struggles, moments where we aren't sure what to do. But that's natural. We will do it together, as we always have," I added. I bent my knees and moved my body closer to his, pressing against his pelvis. For a moment, I felt his breath stimulate the back of my shoulder. I wanted to make love to him again.

"Don't," he whispered. I stroked the back of his hand and moved away from him.

"Don't what?' I said. I braced for his response.

"I just want to lie here with you," he said.

And so we did. I spooned with him for several hours, smiling when I realized he had fallen asleep against my body. Inside I was dancing to the rhythm of his kinetics, the movement of blood and oxygen through his organs. From where I was lying, I looked around the room, wondering where we could set up space for the baby, here with us. We hadn't even talked about a name, even though it would be a little while until we were able to tell the sex through a sonogram. It didn't matter to me what we had. I wanted him to try, stand beside the promises we once made to one another. Once that night, I thought I heard him whisper my name in his breath. Whether he said it or not, it was a sound I would carry with me.

I stood up from the couch and walked over to the entrance to the apartment. A loud sound shook me from my memories. At first I thought it was thunder, yet when I paused for a few moments, the room remained even and still as no more rumbles followed. Down through the staircase I could see police ushering a woman into the real estate building below. I wondered who she was. Even here, there were already so many strangers.

I raised my hands above my head as high as they could go, stretched and tried to loosen up my body. Dancing every day was arduous and soon I would carry a partner. The production I so wanted to be a part of would elude me now and I would have to take part behind the scenes, even if we did dance. I hadn't thought of that before, that I would be replaced. I would be able to choose the dancer who would pattern and learn my marks. Deep inside, I knew that the funding would never come regardless. I wasn't one to give up, allow circumstances to lessen me. I looked around then moved closer to the old refrigerator. I opened the door and put a few of the water bottles inside. Nothing else was in there. They would never get cold enough, I thought. We would be home soon. I held one in my hands.

Next to the refrigerator was an older radio, unplugged. I wondered if it had been here previously. I grabbed the cord and was setting it on the kitchen counter when a voice interrupted me. When I turned around, the same police officer who drove me here was standing next to a woman. I assumed she was the one I saw through the staircase. Draped across her forearm was a jacket. It covered the straps of a bag she was holding as well. The same expression I had earlier, she equaled. One of indecision, one of puzzlement.

"Please," he began. The officer gestured that she enter the room further.

The woman set her things down in the room, near where I placed the chair to look out the window. She leaned down and stared through the glass. I didn't recognize her. I felt I should have, but after Tobias's accident, we didn't go out socially as much as we used to. He had always been reclusive, driven to spend more time on his music and the study of sound, rather than engage people in discussion. It was the only way he knew how to survive. Our town was small, but most of the people I had contact with were dancers, musicians or other artists. Even with her presence, the apartment seemed to become even more desolate, colored in silence.

I removed the cap from a bottle of water and gulped the fluid into my throat. It was warm still, but at this point I didn't care. Anxiety had corrupted my taste buds. I wanted to take a shower, rinse everything that had happened down the drain, allow it to remain unaccompanied into oblivion. I stepped into the small bathroom and closed the door behind me. I stood in front of the basin and turned on the faucet. No water came out. I collapsed to the floor, the muscles in my legs failing me when I needed them most. I pulled my legs closer and rubbed at my feet. Part of me hoped I wouldn't be needed here. I wanted to talk to Tobias, but I knew I couldn't yet. What could I say? I leaned against the door and used a fist to muffle the barbarity in which I wanted to wail. I wanted to scream so I would fracture the building, the glass, right down to the foundation. I had chances where I could have left and divorced him. And all this would be behind me like a closed production. I would have had freedom. I didn't know what to do. As much as I denied it, I wasn't sure I could carry myself with the strength and the resolve I believed I needed anymore.

I exited the bathroom and exhaled, hoping I could remain vigilant in what I might be needed for. To talk to Tobias. To possibly lead him to his inevitable conclusion and destruction. I was supposed to reach him, penetrate his fractured exterior and have him release everyone and surrender. The other woman smiled when she saw me, but said nothing. She moved her bag onto the floor atop her coat and sat in the chair I had placed in front of the window. I wondered how much she knew about what was happening and why she was here.

I thought of all the things I said to Tobias on those DAT tapes, the lonely mornings and anxious evenings recording over portions of his collection. There was so much more I could have said. What if I didn't get that chance, the honest opportunity to tell him although I doubted him at times, I did love him? There were things so beautiful about him others would never know. The gentle way he held me when I needed to be. The raw and undervalued honesty in his eyes, ones so expressive and deep. The tender selflessness in his romanticism.

I closed my eyes and listened to the rain on the roof of the building. I imagined it sounded like a thousand different piano keys crashing to the ground. I stepped through the apartment and stood in the empty bedroom. There was nothing there. No sense of comfort or familiarity. The window was open. I crossed my arms along the ledge and rested my head. There was one ambulance parked in the lot out back. I hoped Tobias hadn't injured anyone. It all looked innocent from this perspective, a young woman glancing out a window at the things and people surrounding her. As I reflected, another emergency vehicle pulled up. It left me with a sense of dread things were going to become worse. I didn't know why. I could hear muffled voices. What I wouldn't give to listen to him tell me how beautiful he thought I was, the sound echoing, then getting lost in the vacancy of the spaces between everything formed and everything ruined.

I moved back into the front of the apartment. The door to the efficiency was open. It was still raining. I moved over towards the staircase and watched as Detective Mull came out from the real estate office with another woman. I couldn't see what was being said as he stood in front of her. On one occasion he placed his hand on her shoulder. I stepped down the stairs to pass them and as I did, Mull took hold of my wrist. The woman walked behind me and ascended into the apartment above. It was the art teacher from the local school. There was nothing vivid or artistic about what was transpiring, all the pain and tragedy. Nothing remembered, nothing valued. The colors were uninspiring and destitute. I wondered why she was here.

"Are you okay? Is there anything that you need?" Mull asked me.

"I'm not sure anyone can grant me what I need," I said in a whisper. "I am useless sitting here. You have to do something." I fought to hold back an endless river of tears.

"I understand how helpless you feel. I do," he said.

"Tell me, why is he doing this?" I said. "What is happening?"

"Enough confidentiality has been breached already. It wouldn't be prudent for me to say so," he said.

"Tell me one thing about my life that has been confidential? Almost everything about our marriage and what we have gone through has already been public. You should see how people look at Tobias when I'm with him. I see their discernment. But he's so much more than any man I have ever met. Aren't we entitled to some semblance of privacy and isolation?" I said.

"Augustina, anything I would say would be conjecture at this point. I'm sorry. Look, I know this is difficult, but please be patient. We're doing our best to bring an end to this as quickly as we can. Then we can sort through everything, pick up the pieces afterwards."

"How am I supposed to be able to do that? I'm pregnant with his child. If you can get him to surrender, will he be arrested?" I said.

"Yes," Mull said. So again, I would be going at our life alone. "I'm sorry," he added. "But we can try to get him the help he needs."

"Do you know what is happening?" I asked, gesturing towards the other building where officers were gathering information as well. Mull took my arm by the elbow and moved me aside.

"I'll be honest, I don't know what's happening on that bus," he admitted in a much quieter manner than previously. "The weather is affecting our line of sight and there's no lights on in the bus. We believe he has broken the bulbs or removed them to make it harder to see inside. And it's only going to get darker outside the longer that this continues," he added.

"When is all this going to be over?" I said. My meaning went much deeper than what was happening on the bus.

"That may be up to him Augustina. We haven't spoken to Tobias. We have his number. We've been trying to contact him, but he isn't answering," he said. "I have to assume at some point he will want to talk to us."

"If you do get a chance to speak to him, are you going to tell him I am here?" I asked.

"Honestly, I don't know," he admitted. "Not in the beginning, but at some point I may have to," he added. "I wish I knew how he would react if I told him straight away. It might change things," he added.

"So do I. A part of me is afraid to talk to him, especially now. I told him last night I was pregnant." The expression on the detective's face told me I didn't have to elaborate any further. "Who are those women upstairs in the apartment?" I asked.

"They're the same as you in a way," Mull answered as he turned away. Without care, I walked towards the entrance to the parking lot where we came in. Shielding my eyes from the rain, I stared up the street. All I could see was discouragement.

I stood in the raindrops for several minutes, thinking about how it smelled, old and damp. Like grief. I could detect turpentine and oil. It was the same odor as when Tobias burned the cello. The color of the flame drifting from the instrument shouldn't have been that beautiful, the light hue of the orange points flickering in random directions. I remembered how it looked touched against his body, that gorgeous spectrum of light underlining his structure, his inherent vulnerability. It was what made me fall in love with him over and over again, that kind of naked openness.

It was cold then, the warmth of the burning instrument changing the texture of my skin. Tobias was brooding, reticent and never spoke. I lashed out at him, struck him across the face, neck and chest. And then I unfortunately called him a cripple. I remembered collapsing to the sodden grass in withdrawal. When he kissed me underneath of my chin, I wanted to scream, but I allowed his lips to moisten the tender patch of skin. We argued so much that night, even after a brief respite, deep into the early hours, exhausting our souls in a tireless struggle of futility and misguided pride. That should have been the beginning. I should have broken then and given up on us.

I moved inside as the rains increased. We were all so quiet, in that vacancy. The woman driven here last was sipping from a bottle of water. I exhaled and sat down at the edge of the couch beside my pea coat and phone. Oh my God! Tobias could have called. I stood and began touching the phone. Still, nothing. I grabbed my shoulder bag and rummaged around. I hadn't used it in so long I wasn't quite sure what was inside. I found some make-up, a few pages of ballet moves, sketches and a pair of nylons. Underneath all the ballet instructions was a section of our wedding flowers, still pressed and fragrant. I wondered how long their violet color had held without light, succumbed to the cotton darkness of the bag. I held them in my fingertips.

Deeper inside, I discovered several folded pages of his old music journal. Each one was rough, creased, torn from its bindings in obvious haste. I could see his handwriting through the parchment. The radio began emitting static. The dial was being changed. One of the women here was trying to find a station. A clear signal came through the band and took command over the encompassing silence.

I began reading the pages, none of them dated. The voice of the beautiful artist who played for us during dinner so long ago, ages, began singing on the radio. There were no words on his pages, only musical notations. I moved my reddening eyes across each note, each bar. There were no markings underneath any symbol to dictate its corresponding alphabetic definition. But I could read music fluently. That artist's compelling and soul crushing voice echoed throughout the stillness and uncertainty of the apartment. Her words lingered, haunted all my movements. My hands began trembling as I read his composition further. Tears rushed in freedom along the contours of my face and settled delicately on my lips. I could taste the salinity in his loneliness and pain.

No one else could understand how much I loved him. In an indirect way, he was playing music again yet without sound, without audience. I raised a hand over my lips, hiding their quivering appearance, embarrassed by my own frailty. What Tobias had composed was sad, reflective and seeped in finality. That beautiful woman's voice cascaded over every living thing, around architecture and form. Reading the remaining page my hope and my heart finally fractured. It looked as if Tobias had composed this section separately. The script was quick and smudged. I could see whorls of his fingerprints in the smeared graphite. The bones in my feet gave way and the remaining structure of my body pulled along, down onto the floor, as if I were dancing pas seul, afraid and unaccompanied. I concentrated on the artist's silken voice, remembering Tobias' touch when we danced, the unique way he spoke only to me. I parted my lips. No sound succeeded. I wailed mutely, unable to express the deep anguish in which I read his composition in sound. A sound which he could hear regardless, one which only he could understand.

# THE DOCUMENTARIAN

I could feel it deep within the recesses of my tissues as I pulled my knees closer to my body against my breasts, the thin cotton sheets rumpled around the edge of my ankles. The thin straps of the yellow slip I still wore kept sliding down my shoulders. I felt I could see the marks on my skin where he had touched me, too lightly as to what I wished for from him. I rubbed my shoulders. I could feel it, the guilt. The guilt in what happened was causing my body to become necrotic, diseased and perishing tissue. It made me want to scratch through my flesh and disrupt the construction of my bones underneath. I turned and exposed parts of my bare back to the closed bedroom door. The side of my breast was still visible. It had only been a matter of minutes since he left. I so had wanted him to stay. I had been crying since then.

I had tried desperately to seduce him again, shame him almost into taking me. I was embarrassed by my lack of clarity for the situation, only now understanding I was only pushing him further and further away, into a place where I could never follow. Back into the uncertainty of the water. The rains changed direction against the glass of the window in front of me. It looked like it would never stop. When I pushed the covers aside and started towards the bathroom, I avoided my own reflection in the mirror when I moved inside. Shame caused me to feel imbalanced. Usually after he left, the bathroom was covered in a beautiful mist, small, delicate ovals clinging effortlessly to the shower door or the inside of the porcelain sink. It was my material evidence he had been there, the unattended residue of water. That he hadn't left me. That he was still a part of me. But instead, everything was quiet, dry, white and flawless, without the subtlety of imperfection.

I pressed my palm against the glass door of the shower and massaged the handle several times with my fingertips. Not long ago, Kelvin was in here avoiding me. Perhaps washing me from his flesh, like a grime that carries with it an odor of distaste and sadness. No amount of water could wash off what had happened to everyone here, especially the families of the victims. All those poor, murdered children. I placed my fingertips atop the frosted glass where he had leaned against it on the other side, wishing

I could have touched him this morning, even for a moment. Instead, I manipulated him. I wanted him to fuck me so I could feel something, anything, but this chasm of regret and ambiguity. I so wanted absolution and again become a composed and impressive woman. The woman I used to be. I should have said something different to him before he left than what I did.

Instead of opening the shower door, I turned away and knelt down in front of the claw foot tub we hardly ever used. I couldn't remember the last time we held one another within the warm water, my head resting against his chest. I tapped my knuckles against the rim of the tub. It was very heavy and cumbersome. That's how I felt, weighted down and oppressed by my own self-loathing. The tile of the floor was cold on my skin and pinched at the area around my knees. I leaned over the chipped edge of the tub and maneuvered my hands over the brass faucet, unfamiliar as it was. Water frightened me. At first I only wanted to wash my hair. Yet it was hard to wash out the horrible stench of infidelity. I moved closer and cupped water in my hands and splashed it over the back of my neck, rubbing it into the roots of my hair. Long strands of auburn color broke loose and fell down in front of my eyes. But as puddles of soap gathered on the circumference of the drain, I began to sob again.

Defeated and fatigued, I pulled the straps of the lingerie down over my shoulders and along my arms. There was a small scar that would never heal below my breast and one to the right of my breastbone. I let the article of clothing fall to the floor and the water dripping from my hair started to alter its color. It seeped out across the material, like despair had on our once innocent community. I still couldn't understand what had happened. And Kelvin was in the middle of it all. I wished he would have walked away from the investigation. I turned the faucet to a more moderate temperature and decided to let it rise inside the tub. Turning aside, I pulled back the door to a tall cabinet and pulled some medical tape closer to gain access. I outstretched my arm and looked at the section of gauze clinging to the inside of my elbow.

I sat down against the wall beside the cabinet and peeled off the adhesive tape concealing the needle mark. Instead of tearing the tape, I meticulously pulled at each fiber clinging to my skin as if the action would allow me to relive the circumstances of its birth. Experience an infinite loop of indictment. A penance. I bit my lower lip hard to avoid sobbing further. I bit so hard I thought I was going to taste blood. Underneath the sound of the steady stream of water crashing against its porcelain prison, I stood up and closed the cabinet door. There was still soap hiding in the back of the locks of my hair.

I let a pair of scissors roll into the sink. The noise sounded hollow and separate. I'm sure that's how Kelvin had felt when he pulled me from the water. Detached, isolated and alone. Afraid. God, what have I put him through? The water level was nearing the rounded edge of the tub. With a washcloth over my hand, I twisted the faucet off and stepped into the clear water. Instead of gathering, adhering to the desperate pores of my flesh it withdrew, frightened and repulsed by the displacement of my body. It knew and understood what I had done to him and ignorance and solitude were my corresponding infliction. Eventually the clarity of the water blanketed around my hips and legs. I leaned back against the corner of the tub, the washcloth behind my head and closed my eyes, the monotonous, wan and antiseptic tone of my surroundings pasteurizing. We should have painted it a different color. Something more hopeful. If I could have changed my own arrogant and selfish color to something a little less bold and delineable.

The room reminded me of winter. Not the light, delicate sense of nature that calms in admiration. More the violent, selfish side of the changes landscapes endure, what's left on the other side. The water around me started to carry such a dense weight. It pressed in on me, made it difficult to breathe. I clutched at my chest and pressed my fingertips deep into the area where several of my ribs had fractured after the accident. I wasn't sure it was fair to call it that anymore. An accident is an undesirable event, one rooted in chance and fortuity, even one drenched in logic. It would be a lie to call it that because I had desired the circumstances that had led me there, to that cold and dark abyss in the river.

The sterile details of the room had begun to reconstruct, decreased in exactness and familiarity. The area of the water increased, opened into a rush of unease and unyielding perspective. The clarity in which I existed when I stepped inside the bathroom had blurred. It was as if I was blind and wading in the infinite oceans of helplessness, an angry current fighting against me. The distance and the water became unmanageable. I felt the lithe touch of sand beneath my feet instead of the grain of the tub, yet its constitution lacked in any sort of comfort or sustainability. The water covered me and I was drowning. I lunged up and punctured the surface of the water. It had seemed so depthless and indistinct. I gasped deeply for air. I rolled from the tub and collapsed roughly onto the tile floor.

*Water could frighten you if you let it.*

Again I grabbed at my sternum and tucked my body into a near fetal position. I screamed releasing the anguish imprisoned in my body. Through the small opening underneath of the door, I could hear the rain begin to strengthen against our bedroom window. For all too brief a moment, it sounded like something artificial tapping against his regulator. But I knew that sound and I understood with unbounded certainty that Kelvin was gone. Puddles of water seemed to move away from me, move across the floor as mercury did. With a purpose, a defining clarity. I closed my eyes and sobbed. I was so tired. I wanted to sleep the sleep of the dead and of the condemned.

~

I made tea, the frail mist encircling the circumference of the cup. I grabbed it with both hands. Sipping, I closed my lips for a few seconds, then allowed the warm liquid to pass through my throat. I set down the cup on the edge of the counter and grabbed the recycling. Moving through the kitchen, I opened the garage door and dropped it next to some of his diving equipment. I went down the steps and sat against the last one, moving my hands on the outside of an empty air tank. The older steel tank was beginning to rust. When I moved my fingertips across the cylinder, some specks dropped off onto the floor. He wasn't using one when he pulled me from the river. He had held his breath. Near the tank were several damp towels and a tattered dry suit. I couldn't remember which body he had pulled from the water when the zipper tore. I rose and placed them on top of the washing machine.

Caught inside the bundle of clothing was a regulator, which when attached to the proper equipment, allowed Kelvin to breathe underwater. I held the object in my hand and placed it in front of my mouth. I wanted to taste his breath. But I couldn't embrace the water like he did. Not anymore. We would never have that in common, going forward, after what had happened. As I repacked some of his loose things into a duffel bag, I realized we were now nothing more than aimless, migratory lovers avoiding and traveling away from each other. Always coming and going, always opposing.

He spent so much time in the water, even more so after the accident. Sometimes I would wake up in the middle of the night and notice he wasn't nestled beside me. Often times, I found him asleep in the living room on our couch. We had talked previously about his needing time, space to regain perspective because of what had happened. More to the point, what I did. But his body, his clothes were always damp and sodden. He found solace in the water, the kind of serenity and clarity that he used to find with me, in my arms. I thought I could smell salt even now on his body from being in the sea, even after he showered. But I hadn't gotten close enough recently to his body to actually testify to that fact. There was a set of keys on the floor. He taught children how to swim at the local YMCA as well and always had keys to the building. I picked them up and held them in my hand. I wasn't sure what these were to. Once I drove out to the building in the middle of the night when I awoke and found him gone.

The parking lot was desolate except for his car positioned in the rear of the building. It was raining. It looked so beautiful and gentle outside. I parked behind the dumpsters and walked up to the side of the building and stole his image through the window. There was very little light inside. In the lane furthest from where I stood, I admired his stamina and persistence, but I couldn't understand what was behind the intensity and determination he moved through the water with. I never asked him if it was because of hate or if he was trying to put measured weight and distance between us. His body was still somewhat sleek and toned, even though he stopped his regular training regimen about two years ago. Yet the resistance and persistence of the water continued to try and mold his shoulders and chest nonetheless. I thought he looked more beautiful than he ever had. He never gave me reason to do what I did. I thought what tenderness we shared suffocated now because of the consequences of the water.

I never watched him swim so desperately and violently. The rapidity in which he glided within the water was symmetrical and elegant. In succession he would reach the end of the pool, tumble underneath the surface to turn and begin again. In the fractured streetlight cutting through the glass his arms outstretched in almost beautiful, but brutal repetition and consistency. After executing a turn, he disappeared. I waited in nervous anticipation for him to burst through the darkness and the uncertainty. It was getting colder outside standing there. I tightened a light scarf around the nape of my neck, then pressed my fingertips against the glass.

We used to go into the water together when we first courted. I longed to be in the water with him, awed by the way his body actuated through the temperature, space and distance. But I couldn't get near him now, not when surrounded by that translucent and fluid collection of molecules. It intimidated me. There were too many memories beneath its surface. It reeked of death and helplessness to me, now more than ever. I wondered for a moment how many of the children murdered swam here. There was no intimacy in the audacity and the guilt of redemption.

~

The collection of still photographs I had archived rolled from left to right across the screen of the laptop. I transitioned from page to page and underneath of the barren landscapes and the hardship in them, I felt persecuted by their countenance and their voiceless rhetoric. Perhaps behind the sepia tinted remembrances and deterioration laid some type of amnesty for me. I had to find it.

All the material I had gathered since March for a documentary seemed to reintegrate and shape into the room around me, became demarcations on an enormous, living map. I could touch my finger to the wall. I was there I thought as I touched a shaded space, shrouded by the illegible readings penned on pieces of rotted pulp paper, a South African postmark branding one corner. I moved and vanished among the coordinates of a blinding desert, greeted by the sands of culpability that roughened my skin and no one else's. I often hid behind the tired, sad people in those photographs, their lives and ones brandishing the same regard. More so now than ever before. Especially after what had happened along the river.

I thought about how none of the photographs or images I collected now contained water.

I touched my chest as if I couldn't breathe. Sometimes even now, I had to minimize my breathing, pace my intake of the atmosphere. The burdensome thoughts of abandoning my current project robbed me of breath and function. I couldn't finish the documentary, not now. The strenuous rehabilitation I started after the accident put me in an awkward position. The producers wanted to schedule its release by the end of the year, but I balked at their persistence and frustration. With everyone, a curtain of sympathy covered me, even though I was the one responsible for the pain and for the pity.

I moved further along into the file and couldn't find the things I was looking for. I was going to hand some of my documents over so they could keep pace with their own deadlines. Now more than ever, I needed to take a step back from filming, writing and research. The items in particular I wanted should have been there. I pushed the laptop into the center of the kitchen table and headed down the hall. I paused when I passed our bedroom, but I couldn't ascertain exactly why. I knew he wasn't in there. I dropped the impending uncertainty and opened the door to the den.

The room was lit, the only shadows cast from the oblong shape of a lamp set back upon a small, cedar table. The curtains were drawn together and only partial, broken scissor like slants of light ever came through. Oftentimes I used the room to screen portions of what I had filmed, but it became an editing room where I pasted together the sometimes tragic chronology of other people's lives. I pulled the curtains aside and waited for the sunlight to pour through, but it was still raining. I wondered if he was going to go back into the water.

*Water could teach you humility if you let it.*

Each time this year he went into the water, he brought death and finality out with him. At times, Kelvin acted like it hadn't changed him. But it had and that fact made me worry. It shouldn't have been his responsibility, retrieving those children. He was a scuba instructor, a teacher, a swimmer, not a member of law enforcement. The panorama of the riverbank played in my mind and the thought chilled me. I tasted the consistency of mud in the back of my throat. I moved aside several manila envelopes on the desk and a small sofa that sat opposite where I stood. Each one was labeled, signifying the months, days and years the material inside was either ascertained or created if a date could be determined or authenticated. I searched for the folder dates from March of this year. After retrieving it, I pulled the curtains closed again and sat down at a light table.

I opened the envelope which only had a few things inside. There was a small index card that listed its contents attached to the outside. The negatives of the photographs I captured fell out into my lap. I took a few of the strips and laid them out on the facing of the light table. Cupping a small, ocular glass reader, I leaned over and examined the negatives, ensuring I found what I was looking for. I would need to order reprints to be on the safe side. I rushed through the other strips, but stopped when I got to the last few. They must have gotten put into the folder by mistake.

I held one of the negative strips a few inches above the light table. It was a profile shot of Michael Dyer, the other man I had slept with. I had taken the photograph before I even knew him. Tears washed over my ducts momentarily. Kelvin had been the one to pull his lifeless body from the river after his car careened through a guard rail. God, what he must have felt, seeing me with him in that state. I wasn't in love with him, Michael. It was a regrettable fascination, a temporary and enticing distraction. We all needed one because of what had happened here.

I was taking photographs, as I always did when beginning research, when I saw him going into a coffee shop. He had a presence, a style about him. I went through the same door and sat a few tables away from him. I strained to listen to his voice, hear what he had to say. He stood from his table and grabbed a napkin from the counter. In returning to his seat, he noticed me. I should have looked away, but I chose not to. Soon, we engaged in conversation, about anything and everything.

At that moment, I didn't care about marriage, about Kelvin or about the children he pulled from the water. Leaving the shop, we walked around the corner and as he hailed a cab, I felt his stubble brush across my lips from the side when he leaned closer. I liked the roughness of his skin, the foreign nature of his eyes. I held onto the negatives of him to make sure I didn't put them back amongst my material. I would toss them into my shoulder bag. I wanted to get rid of it outside of here. I didn't want Kelvin to see them.

I remembered the original letter with the South African postmark wasn't there. I had relocated it to a different place. It was the most important piece to me. Satisfied with what I discovered, I tucked negative strips into the breast pocket of my blouse and resealed the envelope. When I replaced it back into the proper box I nudged it, moving it out of position. Underneath, at the bottom, was a photograph of my husband and I. We were so young. We were so different then, naïve I guess. Or I was at least. I looked at the image of Kelvin. No one ever has looked at me with such tenderness, yet such a barbarity of purpose.

I pushed aside the guilt that always manifested itself like a shadow on the wall, even in the dark, and reached underneath of the desk. There I had hidden a small, metal document box, the kind that prevents damage from fire. Using the miniature key, I turned the lock and raised the lid, reaching into the blackness of its belly. The plastic bag which contained the South African letter was there. I was removing it to place it into a safety deposit box so it would remain undamaged by physicality or my own misguided ambition. For some reason, I didn't want anyone else to have it. The words inside comprised one of the most gut-wrenching and beautiful stories I had ever read. The ending was so poetic, so sad. It made me think of how Kelvin looked when I first saw him after leaving the hospital. It was something I would never forget, the haunted appearance of his face, his body pale and gaunt. It looked as if he hadn't slept for days or even eaten. I wanted to touch his chest. I wondered how I would feel about our ending, content with its fate. I didn't want him to leave me. It was becoming harder for me to blame everyone else, especially the water.

*Water could tell you the truth if you let it.*

I closed the door to the room and stood in the hallway, looking at some of the framed images adorning the walls. There was so little here to add definition to what we were to each other. In almost all them we were alone, wrapped in solitude with achromatic skin. I liked the inherent honesty in a black and white photograph. All the vibrancy in the surrounding landscapes avoided us, our bodies shielded, shunned from the light. I stopped in front of a photograph of our wedding. We married so quickly after we first met. He was such an intensely powerful man, driven, caring and tempestuous, which was bracing at times. I was surprised though by the simple ability he had to remember almost everything about me, no matter how insignificant. It all mattered. That was what made me love him deeply, he listened and I was important. And I disrespected that, took it for granted. I murdered our developed sense of trust. His understanding of my needs and dreams once absorbed me. For a brief instant, I thought the water in the background of the photograph moved closer to him with the tides.

It was unseasonably bitter when I first admired his shape given birth by the sea. I was taking photographs for a documentary article in an environmental magazine I was co-authoring. While I was setting up a tripod on the dunes, an oceanographer was capturing measurements and notating changes in a small notebook. The measurements I had difficulty understanding at first. We had very little financial backing or funding. We had started preliminary work over two years ago. If I never saw Kelvin again it would take me longer than that to forget him, his sleek form moving through the water, gliding through the demanding attrition of the tides. He appeared to move against the current and the winds, his extended arms serrated, cutting through the water as if it were blue tissue paper. The truncated sunrise shimmered across the breaks, collided with the sinewy muscles in his back and shoulders. The lines, the pockets of light recoiled, shattered upon the tenderness of the shore. I rotated the tripod away from the oceanographer and watched him walk along the sands through the extended lens.

At times his body moved too quickly to stay in focus. I noticed the way that he seemed to move above the dunes and up the decaying wooden stairway that led to a small parking area. The worn, leather strap attached to the camera irritated the back of my neck when I removed it from the tripod and stepped away. I wanted to step towards him, but instead I retreated. I zoomed in to capture images of something I could remember him by, something I could take with me. I noticed his hair was darker when he was out of the light and away from the water.

I sat back down in front of my laptop and began to gather what I needed. I draped a jacket over the arm of a chair and searched for a phone book. After I made the call, I knew I had about ten minutes before the cab would pull up. That would give me plenty of time to get ready. The cellular phone on the table vibrated, but I never answered it. I didn't recognize the number, although I hesitated initially. It could have been him calling from the police station or a phone booth outside of the hospital. I knew that he was getting frustrated having to go there so much. And now that the doctors wanted to increase his visits, Kelvin was growing weary and I wasn't sure he was going to stay with me any longer. I had to tell him chances were we wouldn't be able to have a child. I couldn't lie again. I wanted him to call, to talk so much so I could explain again why I did it, beg for forgiveness. I wanted to fall into exhaustion, listening to his voice tell me everything, anything. But I knew he wouldn't call. The tea I had made not long ago had grown cold. I placed the unfinished cup into the sink, the metallic sound of its settlement artificial and obnoxious. It resonated like the sound of his equipment. I fought against the spasms of grief.

The phone on the table rang again. I let it ring, praying it was him and I could hear his voice leave a message. Tell me he loved me, that he wanted me to stay. There would always be things I wanted him to say that would echo inside me. Remembering what it was like telling him in exactitude what happened at the river made me tremble with indecision and distrust, even though his lips never moved in the beginning. It was all measured and clarified by the voice in his eyes, the harrowed language I used to be able to understand with such intention, such clarity.

"Kelvin, I'm sorry," I said, after released from the hospital. When he didn't come to see me after I was admitted, I believed he would be gone when I arrived home and I would be served with divorce papers. That's not what I wanted. The house was stone quiet, almost like a graveyard of random objects at the bottom of the sea. As I moved deeper into our home, I could hear the sound of water. I found him there, under the water, sitting in the shower. He said it had been running for a little while. I sat down beside him, cradled his head in my lap and listened to the rhythm of his body and the water crash upon mine. He could see the bruises under my eyes.

In careful voices we listened to one another, impressed with the calmness in which he spoke. It had been a few days since he was able to come into our bedroom, even see me in the slightest stage of undress. Since that endearing moment in the shower, we had hardly shared words.

I was changing a bandage in our room when I heard him come in behind me. Over my bare shoulder I viewed him, appearing vulnerable, yet dangerous. Kelvin never judged me initially, although he could have. And he would have had every right to. I never gave up on loving him.

"How are you feeling?" he said.

"The pain is less," I answered, trying to change a dressing near my collarbone.

He moved closer. "Here, I'll get it." I handed him a clean bandage and inhaled as he touched me. I held my breath.

"I'm sorry," I said.

"What was his name?" he asked.

"You know what his name was," I whispered, ashamed to even repeat it in his presence.

"I want to hear you say it," he said, without any semblance of anger or conflict. That frightened me more than anything, his apparent lack of disdain.

"Michael," I whispered.

He replaced the bandage and touched my shoulder, ran his fingertips down the side of my arm. I shivered in both excitement and trepidation. "Were you seeing him long?" Kelvin asked.

"No," I said.

"How many times did you see him?" he said.

"Three times," I whispered.

"Why were you?"

I closed my eyes, still leaning against a small table in front of a mirror. "I don't know," I responded.

"There had to be a reason," he began. "I've thought of all the things I have said and done over the last few months, trying to put some definition to it all," he said. "I wanted to figure out if it was my fault somehow. The only thing different in our lives lately is the bodies, the dead I swim with. My involvement with the police department," he added.

Tears challenged me, but I stood my ground. "You have been different since all this began. You do bring a small part of them with you whether you realize it or not. I can hear it when we talked about having a child. I can feel it when you touch me," I said. I watched his movements in the glass. "But that's not why," I said.

"Did you make love to him?" he said. Telling him that I did, that I let him take me two different times would crush him. But fabricating more than I already had would be cruel. The way that he phrased it made my heart weaken. Did I make love to him? Not the other way around.

"Yes," I said as I closed my eyes, fearful of what I would see if they were open. I exhaled and turned around. He was sitting with his head in the comfort of his trembling hands on the edge of our bed.

"Hannah, do you still love me?" he said. I hadn't expected him to ask me that.

"Yes Kelvin, I do. I am still very much in love with you. What happened was a mistake. Mine and mine alone," I said.

"I love you," he said. "I want to so much," he whispered.

"Want to what?"

"Touch you," he said. I had never seen him vulnerable, never until these last few days. I closed the bedroom door, then stepped towards him and reached out my hand.

"I'm right here. Touch me Kelvin," I said.

"I can't," he said, pulling back from my reach. He stood and moved to look out the window of our bedroom. I came up behind him and nestled my head on his back. The streets were empty yet watched over by an objectification of malice and ignorance. It existed in the shadows of the trees and the faces of the houses. I wondered, for a minute, if there was another body out there somewhere that he would have to recover soon.

"I'm sorry. We can get through this. We're strong," I said. I ran my hands through the back of his hair and asked him to look at me. I reached up and pulled his head down towards my face. Leaning in, I kissed his lips. It felt different somehow.

"I can't do this," he said.

"Yes you can," I said.

I unbuttoned his shirt and rubbed his chest. The action caused his lungs to expand. I tugged at the belt loops on his jeans and pulled them down to the floor. I brushed my hand over his stiffening cock. Kelvin touched the bandage on my shoulder and traced his fingertips across the slip, the material soft and silken. As I pulled his shirt over his shoulders, he whispered he had wanted to drown, sleep under the surface of the water when he rescued me. Push me towards the surface then not come back up for air. I closed my eyes, imagining what his death would have done to me. I never would have been able to reassure him that I was who he married. That what had occurred would never happen again. I kissed his throat with force, an extremely intense ardor. The kind of ardor that changes the direction of the wind. Kelvin pulled me down on top of him on the bed.

"I-----," he began.

"Shhh," I whispered. In the uncertainty of everything around us, I guided him inside of me. Our carnal struggle was passionate, almost violent in its beauty and technique. We devoured one another and the sadness and the regret I carried, for one brief moment, relinquished its hold on me. And him I thought. Would it last? I let him baptize me with his lips. I kissed his shoulder, kissed his face. I had always been in love with him. The fear of losing him right now, here in our bed was debilitating. I closed my eyes, holding back oceans of tears willing to crash upon our shores and interrupt our passion. I put my hands against the sides of his face and stared into him, pressed into his flesh. It hurt my shoulder, but I didn't care. I whispered his name, sometimes aloud, sometimes privately. Saying it over and over again. We held one another for hours after. Lying naked under the sheets, his lips caressed the small of my back. I reached back to touch him, light coming through the window. Kelvin was beautiful. That night though, our sex changed everything. It turned out to be damaging when it should have been magical.

*Water could inflict pain you if you let.*

He said he had been asked to do something he wasn't trained to do. And I was his shore. Now he felt he had nowhere else to go. Those children could have been ones he taught how to swim at the YMCA, how to breathe and manage the water. We both had wanted children, but were in no rush to do so. As I stood up and stepped into the bathroom, the house phone rang. It hardly ever did. I let it go. Not now. Retreating back into the hallway, there was a knock at the door. I wrapped the jacket around my shoulders and grabbed the materials. When I opened the door, I started to hand the cab driver my bag. I looked up when it remained stationary in my hand. The man had on a thin, black jacket and I watched the rain drop from the gutter and bead against his shoulders. He was brandishing a badge. It was a police officer. I dropped the bag to the ground.

"Hannah Cohen?"

"Yes," I said.

"I'm afraid I'm going to need you to gather some of your things and come with me," he said.

~

The first image that came across to me was he had gone in to retrieve another body and was injured. Or drowned. But the water was his mother and would have carried his body across the oceans to lead him to dry land, to safety. The water cleaned him when he was dirty, cradled him when he was sick. It raised him when he fell, comforted him when he was sad. It would never hurt him, or at least I had thought so. It should have been me, doing that for him. All those things. But I forfeited that right and honor the moment after he pulled me from the water, if not before.

I leaned my head against the window of the police car. It was raining heavily. I glanced down at the fresh gauze taped to the inside of my wrist, covering the infected needle mark. We were going to a class on infertility tomorrow morning to understand what our options were, if any. It was going to be difficult to bear children. All because of what I had done.

When I slept with Michael, I had contracted a sexually transmitted disease that wreaked havoc on my reproductive tissue. In turn, I had passed it on to Kelvin as well. I don't have a concise answer on why I felt attracted to Michael. It wouldn't have lasted. It would have been transitory, selfish and subsequently I would have broken. I loved my husband and I was as scared as I ever had been, sitting in the back of a police car, uncertain on what was happening or where I was even going. The officer that arrived at the door wouldn't tell me anything, except there was a situation in town and I could be needed. Someone would fill me in soon with all the pertinent details.

What if something had happened to him in the water? The way we parted this morning was so tense and rife with resentment. I didn't know how to survive from day to day anymore with this weighted sense of guilt and sorrow. I needed his help. What if I didn't get a chance now to tell him how much I loved him? And I was sorry, so sorry for all the pain I has caused, the grief I could still see manifested in his sullen eyes. I wondered if I could live alone with the recrimination and the consequences.

The streets were barren and melancholy. Everything had changed since winter began and Kelvin started going into the water. All those poor children. The tragic crimes had taken such a toll on an already struggling community. The stop light we passed through was blinking a steady yellow. It appeared as if everything was in slow motion, trapped and muddled in atrophy. I began crying in the back of the car. Soon we pulled into the parking lot of a closed real estate office. I could see some people inside on the first floor through a window. Most of them appeared to be police, judging by the uniforms. I exhaled when I didn't see an ambulance around, yet remained frustrated nonetheless. Maybe no one had been injured. Maybe he was safe.

I moved into the building on the first floor and was told to stand in a corner for a moment. Several men were conversing on the opposite side. I had no idea what was happening. An electrician was flipping switches inside a panel on the wall. Someone was standing on a ladder changing several lightbulbs. There were some laptops plugged in on a table. There was a woman talking on a cellular phone in front of what looked like a closet, but I wasn't sure. I liked the scarf she had draped around her neck. It was such an intense, but polite shade of purple. A man noticed me standing motionless and walked towards me.

"I'm Detective Daniel Mull," he began. His voice was hoarse.

"I'm Hannah Cohen," I said.

"I know who you are. Your husband has been working with us," he said. I understood the real reason he knew me was because of the accident at the river. His features gave away nothing of what he was thinking. That uncertainty was punishing.

"I know," I said. I wanted to tell him I hated what the water had done to him. What pulling those bodies from the river and other places had done to our intimacy and sense of purity. The man looked tired, his face heavy and lined, stretched, like dried clay.

"I asked one of my officers to bring you down here. I cannot tell you everything, but I want you to understand some of what is happening," he said. "More importantly, why we brought you down here." I appreciated his honesty and his apparent directness. But it didn't change how I felt about his department, how I felt they were using Kelvin, asking too much of him. No man should have had to do what he was doing.

"Who are all these people?" I asked. The voices inside the room were overlapping and becoming louder. He gestured for me to follow him outside. We walked towards the rear of the building and out through the back door. There was a small overhang. We were able to stand together without getting rained upon. The water tried to find me regardless.

"Not long ago, we received word a transit bus a mile or so from here was hijacked. One gunshot we know of was discharged. And we believe no one on the bus was injured. The driver was released by the perpetrator apparently due to a medical emergency. He was able to give us some preliminary information though. We understand now with certainty your husband is one of the passengers on the bus," he said.

"Oh my God," I said. The fault garnered in the hands of circumstance was my own. I placed my hands over my mouth and tried to remain composed. It wasn't working. I leaned against the rear wall of the building sobbing. The rain gutter above me was dislodged and hanging down. The water rushed down the brick and mortar and across my shoulders. It was so cold it stung. It reminded me of the water in the river the day of my accident. Cruel. Malicious. Suddenly, I felt nauseous. Mull took me by the crook of my arm and led me back under the overhang. All I wanted to do was dry off.

*Water could shame you if you let it.*

"Believe me when I say we are doing everything we can to have this situation resolved, without any more shots being fired. Everyone's safety is the only thing we are concerned about at this moment," he said.

"Can I talk to him?" I said.

"We have yet to make contact with the hijacker, but we're working on that. I'm not sure if he'll let those on the bus speak to anyone else though. If he follows a usual pattern, he'll seize their cell phones, but we don't know for certain. We brought you here in case we have that chance," he said.

"Why is this happening?" I asked.

"We have an idea for the motive, but it's not something I can comment on or discuss at the moment," he said.

"What am I supposed to do?" I asked, beginning to feel myself fracture from the inside out. Mull turned, leaned over his shoulder and whispered into the ear of another officer. He nodded his head in agreement and turned back towards me.

"Right now, we need you to stay here. We have officers across the street monitoring the situation as well. There's an efficiency apartment upstairs we have commandeered for our use. It's been vacant for some time. We are in the process of turning back on the electricity and having some necessities brought in so you'll be more comfortable," he said.

"Thank you," I said.

"I know all this has been difficult." He paused before continuing. "Hannah there's a woman you saw on your way through here. She's a licensed psychologist. If you need to talk to her about anything, she'll listen," Mull said.

"What would I say to her that could matter right now?" I said as I shook my head. I believed I knew what he meant, but was afraid to say it. But not bringing it up didn't mean it didn't exist.

"I don't know. That's up to you. We called her in because she's local and might be able to help you and any of the others get through this," he said. "If we're lucky, the hijacker on the bus will want to speak to someone," he added, nodding in the woman's direction. Mull ushered me through the chaos and uncertainty downstairs. He directed me outside through the front door and into the alley entrance where we came in. There was a metal staircase leading up to the apartment. I took to the staircase slowly. I stepped awkwardly into the apartment. Inside, there was another woman. I wasn't sure what to say to her. She appeared familiar to me. Although the town was small, there were pockets of isolation. There was a chair placed in front of a window to my right. I set my belongings on the floor in front of the chair and sat down for a moment.

The room was uncomfortable and humid, despite the window being open. The inherent silence and stillness was horrifying. I looked out into the afternoon gloom and exhaled. I wondered how far away Kelvin was, what he was feeling. If he was thinking about me or if was thinking about Michael and I being together. Please don't let that be your last thought, I whispered aloud as if he could hear me. Please don't think about what happened. Broken lines of rain spit through the window and across the ledge. I ran my fingertips through the drops, hoping I could feel him in the molecules. It was then I realized that my cellular phone was on our dining room table.

I grabbed my belongings and whisked through them, in the off chance I had grabbed it before leaving. No. I closed my eyes and wondered if I would see ever him again. The bandage on my arm was soaking a frail pink. I removed it slowly. I reached into the bag again and grabbed a fresh, small square of gauze. I pressed it hard against the needle mark. Inside the bag, underneath other small packets of gauze was the medical information on what I had contracted during my sexual intercourse with Michael Dyer. Some mistakes you kept paying for. I read those terrible pages several times already, became familiar with symptoms, side effects and any possible treatments. But the prognosis wasn't good. Unfortunately, there was no literature I could find telling me how to cope and overcome the circumstances that led to it.

We had made such powerful and intense love that night, when he asked me what happened with Michael after released from the hospital. For all too brief a moment I supposed, everything was quiet and contented, with an accent of normalcy. It was only days later I first encountered pain. I didn't think anything of it initially because of the accident. The doctors had said I would still feel pain for weeks, even months because of the severity of the trauma. I would be able to manage it through precaution, care and the prescribed medication. When I checked in for a routine follow-up appointment was when they discovered it. Oh, God! I left the doctor's office sobbing and drove around for a little while. Everything appeared haunted anymore because of the murdered children. Even the once elegant cherry blossom trees seemed menacing. Their incredible color and quick passing allowed to that fact. Everything beautiful, in the end, dies.

*Water could erode you if you let it.*

I pulled into the parking lot of an old park and playground, one children rarely occupied even before the murders happened. It was situated in an isolated part of our community, away from the small farms and family owned businesses brought about through generations. How was I supposed to tell Kelvin about what the doctors said? Whatever

285

progress we had made, if any since, would be crushed when I told him we might not be able to have a baby. And why. I got out of the car and walked through the frosted grass, the tall blades needing care, brushing against the inside of my ankles. It made me think about all the things we would miss out on, the little moments of joy and pride. I sat down on one of the swings regardless, the water soaking through my jeans. I kicked forward a little from the ground, noticing the sandbox in front of me was empty. There was no sand inside its boundaries, only dead leaves and debris. It looked like an image from a crime scene. What were we going to do now?

The rain made popping sounds as it struck the top, hollow rail of the swing set. As I rose then fell, I glanced around at the backs of closed businesses, an empty storage facility. What happened here was tragic, cruel and unfortunate. It used to be so tranquil and idyllic here in town. The world here was dying. Inside, I was dying. It was easy to see why no one played here anymore. It was a place of nightmares. I couldn't remember when it last looked beautiful. When I got back into the car to leave, I looked ahead at the swing I had been on. It kept moving back and forth, pushed by the unseen arms of the wind.

I pulled into our driveway sometime later. My hands trembled adjusting the rear view mirror. My heart palpitated. I began coughing. The air I tried to breathe in appeared made from iron. It reminded me of nearly drowning in the river. I wondered for a moment if I would have had the courage to tell him about Michael if someone else had pulled me from the water. I opened the front door and placed the medical information underneath a book sitting unread on a small table. I didn't want him to see it first thing. I had to be the one to tell him, regardless of what happened afterwards. I could hear him in the garage. Moving through the kitchen, I could see through the open door, Kelvin rummaging through his diving gear. There was a small tank to his right. I closed my eyes, scared he was going into the water again. If so, that meant they had found another child. I wished all this would end.

"Are you going into the water again?" I asked, shaking. I placed my arms at my side and behind my back, trying to hide it.

"No. I'm just checking some of the equipment," he answered, preoccupied. "Just a precautionary check in case I'm needed. But I might do some light swimming. I haven't quite made up my mind yet." He was wearing a deep blue turtleneck. He looked so handsome and commanding. It seemed every time I thought he looked his best, I was getting ready to break him.

"Can we talk for a minute?" I said. He never looked up at first, kept his head down and continued to tighten something on that scuba tank. I waited for him to answer, understanding everything would have to be on his terms for a while. Whatever right I had to dictate situations or conversations, I lost. When he raised his head, I could see moisture in his eyes. I wondered if he had been thinking about Michael and I. He was trying very hard not to appear fragile, maintain his strong convictions. I could see it in his hands. "I went to the doctors today because of the pain I was having. They put me through some different testing this time," I began.

"Are you alright? Is it residual from the accident?" he said without seeing me. Maybe it would have been easier if he didn't. But I wanted him to look up at me.

"No, it's wasn't from the accident," I said. My shoulders shuddered and I began sobbing. I couldn't stop and it made it hard to pass the words through my lips.

"What else could the pain be from? Did they say?"

"There's a problem, an unexpected complication. I'm so sorry. When I was with him, Michael, I contracted something. It's a communicable disease. It's very serious. The doctors aren't optimistic about our chances," I said.

"Our chances for what? What does that mean exactly?" he asked.

"We might not be able to have any children," I said. Kelvin dropped the tool he was using and I could see the anguish in his eyes and in his mouth. It existed in all the parts of him angry and loving. I continued to sob. The grief in me, for him was tormenting and burdening. "I'm sorry. I know there's nothing I can do to make it right. I accept the fact you may never trust me again and I'm willing to wait as long as it takes for that to change. I don't know what to say. Please, help me. Tell me what to say," I pleaded, warms tears rushing down the sides of my face.

"I'm not sure what I'm supposed to say," he said in a whisper, although I could still hear his voice crack.

"Kelvin, please talk to me," I said.

"Hannah, I -," he began.

"Tell me you hate me," I said. "Please."

"It would make it all easier, wouldn't it?" he said. He paused. "I don't," he said. "I should. I want to. I want to see you and not feel the way I do. I want to tell you how broken you have made me feel, how vulnerable and alone and helpless. Yet all that's buried underneath the love and the genuine affection I have for you. I see you standing there, completely alluring in your vulnerability. I know during the course of the investigation it's been difficult for you. I've been distant and reticent at times because of the things I have seen. I'm never going to excuse what you did, because I don't understand it. I'm not sure I ever will actually. Unfortunately, I love you, although right now I wish I didn't," he said.

"That's something for me to hold onto," I said. I went over and stood in front of him, reached down my fingertips and touched his wrist. For several minutes I stood there motionless, waiting for him to raise his head and look at me, see through me like he once used to. See everything inside me that said I always would love him and I never should have been unfaithful.

"Do you need something like that so bad?" he said. I raised my hand and touched his face, made him look at me. At first he pulled back, then gave in and allowed my palm to cup his cheek. For all to brief a moment he closed his eyes.

"Yes. Because for a while I don't have all of you," I said. My hand was shaking. Kelvin moved his hands across mine and steadied me. The warmth of his tears collapsed down his flesh then changed direction to follow the curve of my hand. It was the only water that hadn't run from me recently. When Kelvin ended our embrace, he was inconsolable. It hadn't lasted long enough. I watched him grab a small bag full of some equipment and clothing.

"I'm going into the water for a little while," he said.

"Where are you going?" I asked.

"The only place I am safe. Hannah, please don't follow me," he said. Kelvin grabbed an old ten-speed bicycle he used when he was training and started off. The rain didn't seem to care. I watched him pedal down the driveway and fade into the distance. Something inside of me felt smothered. Thinking about losing him made it difficult to breathe. I wanted to follow him regardless, keep him close, but I wasn't sure where he was going. I thought for a moment he wouldn't come back. I went back inside the house and through the kitchen. The keys he had for the local YMCA were missing. I started towards the front door and remembered where I had placed the medical information. I removed it from underneath the book and put it into my bag. I closed the door behind me. I thought I knew where he was going. I was wrong.

When I pulled up alongside the river, I expected him to be swimming in the cold waters. I don't know why. I imagined Kelvin tearing through the water as if he were trying to change the history of what happened here, moving faster through the current. Changing the direction and path of the water, thereby changing everything. I sat in the car for several minutes, afraid to move closer. The truth was a violent tide. I stepped out of the car and over the still damaged guardrail. Pressed into the ground I could see tire tracks. As the rains continued to fall and the grass grew, the evidence would vanish. But the scars, the memories would forever be prevalent. I leaned against the nearest tree and rested my head. I closed my eyes as I could hear the water talking. I wished I knew what it was saying.

We were in the car, Michael and I, coming from his home. Kelvin thought I was doing research for my documentary. I don't know why I went there, to Michael's. Whatever thing I felt I was missing or wanted I could get from him was transitory, an illusion. We had planned on going out of town, anywhere away from here, the metaphorical land of the drowned and the dead. Part of me, at the time, didn't want to come back, never look across the bridge again and disappear. Become someone else. But I couldn't exactly ascertain why. I stepped closer towards the river. The bank was sodden and damp. I grabbed at my chest. I nearly died here, pinned under the surface of the water. There were footprints patterned in the mud. I thought about Kelvin being here when shot at after pulling that boy's body from the river. I mirrored some of the steps already imprinted.

*Water could change you if you let it.*

Michaels' body was recovered not far from here. It was sad, what I caused. When the car landed in the water with such velocity, I was rendered unconscious. I looked out towards where the body dropped in the river near the small bridge. So much tragedy and sadness. I placed a hand over my mouth, forcing myself not to collapse. Kelvin would have seen everything when he went under the water, the closeness of our bodies in the car and Michael's apparent state of undress.

When I finally regained some semblance of awareness after the crash, I was in an ambulance transported to the hospital. I'm uncertain, but I think I said Kelvin's name over and over, the lone word falling upon deaf ears. It wasn't until a police officer entered my room later I understood what had happened. Kelvin never came to the hospital. When he didn't, I thought he was gone. I watched broken pieces of tree branches float along the skin of the water. It made me think of the murdered children, wading in the water.

When questioned at the hospital about what happened, I was glad that Kelvin wasn't around. To see the features in his face change when I spoke would have caused me to hesitate. Their initial interview was direct and I was instructed to be as descriptive as possible. With solemn patience I had to tell the police where we were going, what rate of speed the car was travelling and why, when the body of Michael Dyer was pulled from the water, was he undressed from the waist down. I understood full well they had to establish a cause for the accident. I crouched down in front of a tree and noticed scarring in amongst the layers of bark. I touched my fingertips to the area, then to the notch below my throat. I stood up and walked closer to the water, imagining Kelvin diving into the pool at the YMCA, the gentle warm water collapsing across his raging body, the anguish in his heart.

~

I leaned back in the chair and continued to watch the rain fall out the window. Several men had come and gone over the last few minutes. I only noticed a few people moving anywhere near the street and the intersection. Our community looked abandoned, evacuated. My legs were beginning to weaken from being in the same place for so long. For some reason I was scared to move. The other woman here in the apartment with me seemed distracted as well. I could see honest pain and fear in her eyes, something I knew I was most likely projecting as well. She was rummaging through a bag, looking for something. I leaned over and seized mine.

Underneath all the gauze and medical information, I discovered the negatives of the few photographs I took of Michael I wanted to destroy. I held one of them up into the light. Next to the profile shot was one I captured of him looking out of the window of his bedroom. Nothing complicated. A quick rush of wind forced its way through the opened window. Being here, I felt the same way I did the first time he and I were together. Isolated, scared and anxious. I sat at the edge of his bed, restless and uncomfortable, but incapable of leaving. The room was warm and pressing. I felt the bed move when he sat down behind me. I asked him twice to please turn off the light, as if I could hide amongst the secrets of the dark and somehow be less culpable. The only light that came through the window were tiny cracks of moonlight. I watched them change places on the floor when he closed the drapes.

For several hours I let him explore the architecture of my body, gave him access to the same tender places where I allowed Kelvin. When Michael kissed me, I was a different woman. Not better, different. And that unique woman was someone whom I could no longer be. Lying against his bare chest, I told him that, drawn back into more kissing and awkward discovery. When I lifted up my head and kissed his neck, I tasted his sweat. It reminded me of the salinity of the ocean and the way the water moved when it was restless.

I stood up from the chair in the apartment and nearly collapsed. My legs were so numb and I felt nauseous again. I stepped into the bathroom of the apartment and turned on the faucet. I leaned against the sink as the pipes trembled and coughed. I let the water run in continuous circles, but never placed my hands underneath the stream. Listening to its voice, I thought of what Kelvin must be going through on that bus. I wished so to talk to him. The police needed to end this peacefully. I closed the bathroom door and headed towards the rear of the apartment. Outside of the window I could hear voices and a ceasing siren. An ambulance had pulled up, causing me to wonder if something had happened. I moved closer to the window and looked out. An emergency responder was standing over a steel barrel, lighting some wood that rested inside.

I left the apartment and started down the staircase above the alley. The steel construction was insecure and as I stepped, I slipped and had to grab onto the railing. I finished the decline and walked along the rough and uneven sidewalk to the rear of the building. Behind the real estate office were a few trash dumpsters, the ambulance and several parked cars. I walked over to the burning barrel and dropped the negatives of the photographs of Michael into the sporadic flames. I watched the chemicals of the negative, the emulsion emit a smoldering amber color. I welcomed the ruin. It looked like the color of my birthmark. I imagined Kelvin kissing that blemish, with the same vigor and intensity he did before all this had happened. I thought when we made love he avoided kissing the tender terrain of my neck. The rain was still coming down. Standing underneath an umbrella was Detective Mull. I hoped his being here again meant everything was going to be over soon. When he wheeled around to talk to another officer, he saw me shivering under the water.

"What are you doing out here? You should be inside," he added. "Is something wrong?"

"Yes, everything is wrong," I said.

"I know this situation isn't ideal for any of you. I'm sorry. We are doing everything we can."

"Have you been able to make contact with anyone on the bus? Is Kelvin hurt?"

"As far as we are able to determine, no one appears to have been injured. We've gotten the hijacker to speak to us, but only briefly," he admitted.

"What did he say?"

"I'm afraid I'm not at liberty to elaborate on that. We don't want to do anything to jeopardize anyone's safety, including your husbands," he mentioned, his concern expected, but at the same time welcomed. He moved the umbrella so it rested above my head. I watched the water run down the lines in his coat. It looked like tinsel.

"What am I supposed to do? I'm sitting here and the longer I do, the more anxious I become. What if something happens to him now after what happened?" I said.

"Nothing is going to happen to him," Mull answered. "There is an end for all this."

"You don't know that," I countered. I looked around at all the activity going on in our town. It all started when Kelvin went into the deep end of that backyard pool. Not only did he bring out a child's body, he drug the soiled carcass of chaos out with it. "You should have let him walk away from the investigation months ago, replaced him with another diver and told him you no longer needed him" I said. "I don't want him going into the water again."

"I understand your frustration in his staying onboard during the scope of it all. The investigation has taken a toll on everyone here I'm afraid, not just him. But he was a valuable asset and our resources were limited at the time and they still are," he said.

"Are you going to need him to go into the water again?" I said.

"I'm afraid that's not up to me anymore. I am no longer in charge of the investigation," he said. "It's under federal jurisdiction now."

"He doesn't see it, but he brings it home with him. Kelvin goes into the water when you tell him to and that coldness and despair soaks into his body. It's in the clothes he leaves behind in the house. They never seem to dry. I feel it when he touches me," I said. "The water here has changed everything. Nothing here will ever go back to the way it once was. Especially the trust between him and I. But that's not your fault," I admitted. I paused then spoke again. "How do you do it?"

"Do what?" Mull asked.

"Forget about the things that you see?" I said. "What's happened here. How do you keep all the death and the sadness from getting into bed beside you?" I asked.

"I could lie to you, tell you it's easy. The truth is, you don't," he said. "In all honesty, some things are too strong to let go of."

"You should have lied to me," I said in a whisper. I watched Mull turn aside and listen to the words of another officer. He turned his back to me and started towards the small tent being set up and then came back over to me.

"You'll have to excuse me. I'm needed back at the scene. Please, get out of the rain and go back upstairs into the apartment. It'll all be over soon. If there's anything you feel you need, go downstairs into the real estate office and speak to someone. They'll make the necessary arrangements." Mull strode off in the rain. I watched the water cling to the edges of the umbrella. Some of the drops hung there, suspended, like icicles in winter. I walked towards the front parking lot of the building and glanced up the street. Everything felt like it was changing again. I exhaled in the rain and let the water continue to soak my clothes, hoping somehow I could feel Kelvin's touch in the falling precipitation. At the moment, I didn't care about anything else.

I climbed the staircase and stepped into the apartment, brushing past the other woman. I smiled at her and the sorrow in her eyes crushed what resolve I was struggling to maintain. I turned away from her and sat back down in the chair by the window. It seemed to be getting colder. As I slid the window down a little, someone else entered the apartment. It was another woman. She looked apprehensive, standing inside the staircase. I recognized her as she taught art here. She seemed poised, but I could have misread the announcement in her beautiful features. I wondered why she had been brought here as well.

The apartment seemed even more compressed by silence. None of us spoke to one another. The art teacher walked past me with her head down towards the kitchen area and closed the bathroom door behind her. The other woman was quietly sitting on the couch, still searching for something in her bag. I closed my eyes and listened to the rain still falling outside. Because it continued to, I knew that Kelvin was still alive. The water never would have fallen without him.

*Water could wash away hope if you let it.*

I stood and crossed the room, stopping to retrieve a bottle of water from the refrigerator. It was warm, but it didn't matter. I sat back down near the window and opened the bottle. After opening my bag, I grabbed a painkiller and swallowed the bitter pill. When I took in deep breaths, my body still winced from the injuries. I took out the medical information again. No matter how I understood the words, the end result wouldn't change. Even going to the infertility classes would be inconsequential. Too much damage had already been done. The chances were we would never be able to have children biologically on our own. I sipped more water, but coughed repeatedly. In doing so, I dropped the bottle onto my lap. It soaked the shirt that I was wearing even more. The smell for some reason reminded me of the clothing on the floor of our bathroom, ones corrupted by menace and by the water.

There were some of his clothes in the corner of the bathroom this morning. I sat down after getting out of the bathtub not long after he had left me behind. A pair of his jeans pressed up against the base of the toilet.

There were several tears in the fabric. Holding them closer, I could see blood stains in the fibers. Kelvin had injured himself retrieving the body of another child. But he never told me. I noticed the slight limp and the unease in which he moved around our room. When I tried to seduce him this morning, I sunk to the floor, defeated when he refused me. After he reached out and touched my face, I could see the dampened marks on the leg of his clothing. The distance between us was expansive, untenable and insurmountable.

In regarding our fractures, I watched the art teacher close the bathroom door behind her, move into the kitchen area and turn the dial on an old radio. Maybe, by some miracle there would be news on what was happening. I thought they would go on only telling us so much. I overheard someone outside say a newspaper photographer had arrived near the scene asking questions. I closed my eyes when the biting noise of static kept interrupting. I flinched at its repetition. It reminded me of weakness and incoherence. If I closed my eyes, it mirrored the sound of running water. It was useless to forget its touch and rhythm the first time Kelvin and I were in the water together.

The water was so warm there, in that natural park, towards the end of summer. It was August. The trees were sewn with leaves so bold and vivacious in color. I was awestruck that something so beautiful sustained. We had been together for only a few weeks. I still got nervous around Kelvin then, although stimulated by the freshness of learning about one another, discovering the things unlearned. Something like that could only happen once. The first time I heard his voice say my name. The initial occasion where his fingertips brushed across the private places on my body. The one time I first heard his laugh or saw him smile.

It was a Tuesday. We held hands, strolling through the wonderment of the mountainside, waterfalls so clear and lucid they appeared suspended in air. We were walking on a wooden bridge that stretched across a small creek. I leaned over the edge and listened to the water. It sounded relaxing. Kelvin came up and wrapped his arms around me and kissed the back of my neck. It was warm under the sun, but his action made my body tremble. Along a hill behind us, a freight train rolled by, approaching the entrance through the mountainside. Underneath the bridge, the water tumbled. I touched the back of my neck where I remembered him kissing me. Things were so much different then.

Persistence and time had worn down the environment and created natural water slides along the once unpassable and dangerous landscape. Kelvin was wearing black shorts. He looked ruggedly handsome, the reflecting sun shining across his angular face. I sat down behind him in the water, apprehensive, but eager to follow as well. Quickly he leaned back, propelled by the rush of water along the narrow rock channel. The passage ran on and opened up into a small pond of water, large enough for others to swim in. He broke the surface, stood up and I watched the way the water descended down his body, accented the musculature of his abdomen. I closed my eyes and trusted the water to carry me to him. And it did. I came up beside him and felt him pull me higher, his hand under my forearm, guiding me to stand. I looked intensely at him, his eyes wide, smiling. I reached my hand up and touched his face, wiped away the water from his mouth. I stood up on the tips of my toes and kissed him eagerly, a hard and commanding kiss, one I thought would cause time to splinter.

Surrounded by fractured, black rocks, the water's sheen made everything look like oil. The cascading waterfalls gave the surface a light mist, one I could feel brush against my legs as we walked hand in hand. That park was the most beautiful place in the world, our world. I wanted to go back there after all this was over. Move away from here. Begin again. But no matter how many times I stood upon my toes and kissed him, it would feel different, poisoned somehow because of what I had done. I looked back out the window at the vacant street, the leaves nothing like they were once before. Autumn was such a singularly graceful season. The only imperfection with the beauty of fall was that it was forever changing. The unequal static from the radio soon disappeared and the ethereal sound of a woman singing swept through the room.

The woman on the couch suddenly slumped to her knees on the floor, holding several papers in her hand. It looked as if she was reading something. She began sobbing as the sounds of the song on the radio faded underneath of her final wail. I thought it was so violent and honest it could be heard endlessly, across the oceans and the continents of the discouraged. The woman psychologist from downstairs came into the room with a police officer behind her. They helped the poor woman up from the floor and led her down the steel staircase. She was still sobbing uncontrollably.

I turned away as if I was witnessing something too personal, something I had no right to. I rose from the chair with my bag and stepped into the rear, empty bedroom. I watched them sit the woman down inside the back of an ambulance through the window. Someone placed an oxygen mask over her face. She reached up to hold it closer. Her hands were trembling, still clutching what she was reading. The breath gathering on the inside of the mask looked like a light morning mist. Fighting back tears I closed my eyes. I couldn't help but think something had happened on the bus.

I slumped down against the wall in the corner and cupped my hands over my face. Why was all this happening? I wiped the moist mascara from my eyes. Outside the ajar window, I could hear the detective's voice above everything else. It was deep, commanding in its presence and resonance. Michael spoke like that, deliberately and with conviction. At least it seemed that way. I thought about that night, the first time we were together. When I made love to him. The voices from outside entered the room, lost in the light mist that fell into the open spaces of regret.

It was unseasonably cold, waiting in his house. I was standing in his bathroom, the only light a small stutter coming from a candle. I couldn't undress in front of him. My skin was cold and unfamiliar. I washed warm water over my face and neck. I closed my eyes, unbuttoned my blouse and rested it on the floor. I continued undressing. I soon stepped out of my intimates and opened the bathroom door. The bedroom was dark and I could see his naked silhouette standing a few feet in front of me. A very dim light made him appear magical. As I stepped tentatively towards him, my body trembled. I nestled closer, wrapped my arms around him and pressed my lips into his neck. His body was warm, dry. I stayed that way for several minutes and waited for him to lead me, guide me into his bed. I didn't want to be the one to do it.

We embraced underneath a warm quilt, the material soft against my skin. I asked him not to speak, not to complicate what we were doing with words or promises we would inevitably break. As he licked the nape of my neck, I closed my eyes and let him discover me, only partially. I was scared to let him in, yet for selfish reasons. His skin was like a rough desert, a mesa of mystery and risk. I enjoyed the uncertainty in his terrain, moving my fingertips across his chest and thighs. I awoke early before him the next morning. I moved around the room.

As I uncovered the remoteness of his belongings, I displaced some of his things from a waist high dresser. Some documents, mail and photographs fell to the floor. I knelt down and began picking them up. Most of the photographs were of his family and his one child. I didn't want to see the details in their respective smiles, their happiness. I replaced what I had knocked to the floor. There was still a newspaper pushed underneath of the bed. I picked it up and held it in my hands. It was several months old. I saddened when I read the headline, the bleakness apparent in its words and subject. Below the text was a photograph that accompanied the article. It was taken at one of the crime scenes, the pond where the local children skated and played hockey, where the second victim was unfortunately discovered.

The landscape beyond the photograph looked so peaceful and serene, the trees asleep under their icy cover, the field immersed in an envelopment of snow. At the forefront of the frame was an emergency technician and a police officer. Their backs were to the camera. To the right, there was the detective, his hands in his pockets. I recognized his jacket. In the background of that grim and cold image was Kelvin. I could see him, standing at the edge of the frozen ground alone and isolated in his sorrowful responsibility.

I listened to Michael stir in the bed behind me. I turned my head over my shoulder to look at him. The quilt that once covered us was strewn to the side. I noticed sections of his naked body. In the faint morning light, he looked different somehow, less authentic. I looked back down at the photograph in the newspaper again. Kelvin seemed so far away from me. The encompassing snowfall blurred portions of his face, but I thought he appeared afflicted.

I could see the hole in the ice where he had gone into the water. The article mentioned some specifics of what occurred. What Kelvin must have seen under the surface. All those nights where he came home to me damp and disenchanted and I declined him. Reading through some more of the article, the depravity of the crimes disgusted me. Such innocent children. I couldn't help but wonder how Kelvin had felt, breaking the darkness of that frigid water. It must have been so cold, so surreal and horrible. As I sat down on the edge of the bed, Michael moved and slid up behind me. I tensed when I felt his fingertips collapse along the curvature of my spine. I felt guilty, allowing him to change the texture of my skin from placidity to arousal while Kelvin was swimming with the tragedy of the dead. It wasn't the only reason. Yet so much more had happened since February.

I stood up and moved in front of the window again, the rain continuing to cloud everything with anguish and aversion. People were moving around outside with purpose. I closed the window then stepped back into the front of the apartment. The music silenced, disappeared into the echoes of that woman's grief. The other woman, the art teacher, was going down towards the rental office. I watched her go down the side alley, then stepped onto the staircase, inhaling the dense air. I clutched at my chest and descended. I peered into the real estate office.

*Water could teach you loneliness if you let it.*

Some of the people inside I recognized. A few were volunteers that helped to search the woods on the McIlheny's farm, where that young girl's body was discovered in a pond. Volunteers were called on to go through the rear of the property, in hopes of securing evidence. Initiated by the local police because of the expanse of the farm and the denseness of the woods. It wasn't uncommon. We had been there, Kelvin and I, on their farm more than once. Everyone who lived in our community had walked through its corn stalks, picked fresh vegetables and gone on hayrides. Kelvin swam in the pond's cool waters several times, always looking more handsome each time. I wondered what he looked like afterwards, when he came out of the water, her body in tow. I never went into the water there.

It was surreal, standing with other members of our community, so we could spread out in groups and search the surrounding woods. Some people were using their cellular phones for light. It had been storming on and off for most of the day and the ground was a mess. A man stood at the front of the group and gave instructions on how to search, where to look and how to move through the landscape. If we did discover something we thought to be of interest, we were to call out to a member of law enforcement. That person would, in turn, mark the area and record any relevant information. At times, we would even have to get down on our hands and knees to search between rocks and fallen debris.

I didn't stay long to help. It was so difficult to see anything. I slipped and fell once, stepping between some branches. The rain beads on the trees and rocks glistened in the spectrum of the flashlight. It looked like stars had fallen and broken open over the edges of the moss covered stone. It would have been beautiful anywhere away from here.

I stepped out into the parking lot of the real estate building, the water beginning to gather in the soiled places of our once innocent community. I stood at the edge of the street and walked across. Inside the building on the corner were more police. I stood in the open doorway. I couldn't see the detective anywhere. I wanted to talk to him, tell him I knew it wasn't his fault. That Kelvin could have walked away from the investigation, yet chose not to. For a moment I wondered what that revealed about me, about our marriage. Everyone appeared busy, engaged in conversations, the room though drowned in meager gatherings of whispers. At that moment, I wondered if my name passed through Kelvin's lips with a murmur.

I walked past the front of the building and stood at the intersection. The water was rushing through the streets along the edges of the curbs. I walked closer to the road. There was debris settling on top of the drain. I crouched down, listening to the water echo across the opening. It sounded like someone gasping. I changed my perspective higher, looking out into the barrenness of our community. Barricades paraded across the streets and sidewalks in the distance. As I stood up to walk away, I saw an object floating on the surface of the rainwater.

When it drew closer, I could see it was a child's moppet. The cloth doll was facedown upon the stream of water passing by. Startled, I stumbled backwards and struck against the building behind me. For a brief moment, I thought it was the body of a child. My body slid down the brick façade. Resting on the backs of my heels, I closed my hands over my lips and screamed. I watched the doll wash down the street, dirty and sodden, waiting for Kelvin to pull its delicate little body gently out of the water.

# THE PAINTER

Color.

The visible aspect of things caused by different qualities of light.

Various hues were used to represent almost anything, happiness, despair, uncertainty and even death. The death and decay of almost anything once living, once vibrant I often described using color. Most often in grays or blacks. Black is the mere absence of color, yet it was oftentimes necessary in painting. It still carried with it a quality of identity and perspective, although somewhat limited and bleak. When looked at as a whole, black was concluding, black was finality and black was motionless. Black, in a way, was atrophy. I thought of the end of all things, sitting in the train car, watching her drift to sleep, her body slumped over against the window. I had placed a small blanket across her lap. There was a black beauty mark on the small pocket of skin between the bones of her right shoulder. It looked like a small ingress, a place with no gravity, a small place where light or darkness could never reach.

The rain rushed across the glass in bloated lines as the train wavered across the tracks. It had been raining for several days, staining everything with a dull gray, an effortless and indolent shade. I saw everything in color, understood how I could transition them, change their appearance to represent anything by altering the areas around objects and sometimes people. At times I felt you got in the way of that, saw the things you wanted to instead of understanding what was visualized. Or even said. In essence, the truth. Yet you were the mother of my child and a woman I had once loved without regret and without hesitation. You were once my muse and my goddess. And now I was beginning again, selling some of our historic and tragic murals as I had handed the conductor our tickets. Quickly. Silently. Most, but not all them, were listed in the catalogue sitting next to her on the seat across from me. I knew you wouldn't come to the auction in New York. I sent you an invitation regardless. But in as much as I may have wanted you to come, seeing you again would indeed change nothing, the emotional and physical damage already dispensed, autopsied and buried. As was our daughter Jennifer, the first of a series of children murdered, her body discovered in a backyard pool in January.

I painted you so many times, in so many different colors, some of which seemed to be born from your beauty, from your architecture. Each pigment couldn't have existed without your flesh, would have remained clear and unimaginative. Idle. The train passed by a small farm in foreclosure. There were far less economic issues here in the Northern part of the state. The farm was much smaller than the McIlheny's and lacked the same character, that prideful sense of belonging and community. That desperately needed sense of peace. That poor acreage would never again be a place of happiness because of what happened there. I wondered for a moment if anyone else had looked upon a woman on those golden acres of tilled grain and corn as I once had you. You were so brooding and gorgeous, your albescent skin burning with the sun and the faceless, orange pumpkins around your ankles. It appeared as if you were engulfed in a painless fire, blighting everything near you. You were that strong of a woman and I thought at the time, that sad.

It was evident in your mannerisms and moreover your voice. When you approached and placed a gourd in your hands, you spoke about isolation and loneliness without using either word. Dipping a paintbrush into a Mason jar, I stirred the color as your naked honesty moved me. It was rare I thought, for a person to express that much depth and isolation. After you replaced the gourd, I watched you move through the landscapes away from my table, your fingertips brushing across the tops of some grain, pulling the color of the cereal grass into the air and staining an already vivid sky. The wind carried them. It looked like the horizon beyond you was littered with little, brown bees. Jennifer was so allergic to them. She used to have to jump growing up to reach them, the tips of the grain stalks. If things had been different, she would taller than them now.

The sun had set long before I finished delighting the local children by creating small moments of joy on autumn's temporary canvases. You were still there, leaning against a wooden fence post near a small bonfire. The reflection of the flames made your cheeks look like peaches, plush and bountiful. Part of me wanted to brush my fingertips across them, feel the fine texture of their brilliance. I turned around the crate I was sitting upon and began sketching you in black charcoal from afar. I should have used a different color. It was a close up of you, your dark hair falling frontwards over your shoulder, colliding with the nape of your neck, the rest strewn down your back. I still had that simple sketch. I hadn't realized how haunted you looked in black and white, your eyes missing the strength and the soul I fell in love with.

Looking back in remembrance, they seemed porous and undefinable, your eyes. Affected. It was easy to get lost in the darkness of your locks, something I could always reproduce from memory. With intricate detail I could paint every strand, understood how it would move when I ran my hands through its mystery. How the ends always curled up as if beckoning, pleading for lost intimacy, lonely in their color. Regardless of our separation, it was something I would always hold dear.

When I finished, I folded up the sketch and placed it in my bag with the remainder of my painting supplies. I moved closer, ending up beside you. I never shared that sketch with anyone, including her. Later I stole that peach color from the past and painted you in a stunning and gorgeous dress. The heat from the bonfire was fading, but it still interrupted the ease and calmness of my skin. It was as close as I had ever been to fire, until that night, when you saw me with her. I grabbed the catalogue and opened to a photograph of that painting. *Page 28.*

It wasn't how I wanted you to find out about her. I should have been more open about how I was feeling, even before our daughter's body was retrieved from the water. Suffocated. Vacant. Yet even with technique and subtlety, I couldn't hide what was behind that painting. She and I had made dinner together, enjoying the subtlety and quietness of such a simple action. With her, there were no questions, no interrogations, no desperate need to feel acknowledged. A blank canvas that had yet to be altered by color or tragic circumstance. We were on her rear balcony, sipping wine and saying nothing to each other when the explosion occurred.

I wasn't sure what was happening, but then we saw the dense, black smoke rising over the roof of an adjacent building. It wasn't long before paramedics, fire fighters and police began evacuating everyone. We rushed from her place, a place of simplification and hope back into a chaotic scene, people screaming and uncertain. So much fear, so many different colors. They handed us white masks to wear. Even then, I thought it felt like your body brushing upon my lips. I supported her, held her in the midst of doubt when I should have been holding you. Talking through our differences instead of ignoring them. I never saw you coming out of Norah's. I wished I had. I wished now I had the strength, had the resolve to be more forthcoming and less secretive.

The train rounded a distant corner and she opened her eyes, took me in for a moment, smiled and then closed them. It had to be uncomfortable for her to see our history revealed and sold as well. Understanding there were parts of me she may never reach, achieve the intense depths into my being you once had. I could paint her in the same colors and indicate the same theme and it would forever be a reproduction. Some elements would be pure inspiration, but inside, I would be bringing back something that could never be. Some sort of artistic necromancer. I hadn't thought of that until now.

I reached into my inside jacket pocket and grabbed my cellular. Nothing. Reception was difficult here along the train lines because of the mountains. Yet I had given you no reason to call me. Admittedly I had been selfish and impulsive concerning your regard. And for that, I was sorry. I only ever knew how to communicate with you through color as words were hollow and couldn't hold the intense weight of what we had to say to one another. Oftentimes I would unintentionally hurt you. Or intentionally. It had gotten so I couldn't tell the difference anymore.

In about an hour or so we would reach our destination in New York. I would attend the auction as even I was becoming scared the memories of what happened to our daughter would come tearing through the barriers I had constructed, some represented in the catalogue. That they would never hold. That they would free themselves from their artistic, canvas prison. The true colors I chose would dampen the pages, begin bleeding out. Then they would terrorize the boundaries of the sanctuary I now chose to live in with another woman. Without our daughter. Under each painting auctioned were minor notations. I wondered if you had tossed through its pages and remembered how wonderful we used to be together. I held the catalogue in my hands and fought back initial tears when I looked at the winter painting. *Page 3.*

The thing I remembered most vividly was how cold it was, the bitter air shredding through my gloves. The trees appeared to stare voyeuristically into our landscape. The snow that still remained on the darkened roof looked like decaying marshmallows, or the skin fallen from a cloud. You were inside and I could see you through the window. Although it was difficult to tell because of the glare, you looked troubled. If you had stepped out, you would have gotten lost amongst the delicate, but albescent beauty. I wouldn't have been able to rescue you from the cover of winter's beautiful cloak.

I helped our daughter create her first piece of art there behind our home, her first snowman. Although I tried to teach her how to shape the element, use it to the benefit of her creativity, it became a valueless exercise. She was so much like you, passionately intense and impulsive, even at that age. Yet you stood still longer for me than anyone else ever had. The silence in watching you stand there, looking at me painting you was serene, heartbreaking in its simplicity and tenderness. Perhaps I took advantage of that. I wondered for a moment if you were still in place, standing still, waiting for me to tell you how to position yourself, where to look, when to breathe and when not to. Still holding on to me, to us, what we had.

When Jennifer went inside, I followed her, eager to see what interested her. I was learning, as you were, what made her angry and what made her cry. I laughed when she overturned your entire basket of extra buttons. They spilled from the sewing accessory like marbles, scattering off in different directions in our living room. I should have painted them, in retrospect, captured their various colors and sizes in disarray in a small mural. It would have looked wonderful hanging on the wall above the bed in her room.

There were over one hundred buttons seeking freedom. I got down on the floor. She laid down next to me and I talked to her about what size and shade she should use. I tried to tell her different colors could mean the snowman was happy or sad, lonely or even laughing. But it was something an artist experienced alone at times, that sort of perspective and it couldn't always be understood. I should have painted all those buttons, small or large, black or red. I should have picked them up one by one, remembered how they felt between my fingertips. I could have replaced each button back in the basket and through association by color, named aloud a reason I was in love with you. Those one hundred buttons would be a kaleidoscopic collection of our affections.

I exhaled and looked down at the sleeve of my white, cotton shirt. One of the small milky buttons was coming loose from the threads that held it in place. That was all it took sometimes to change things, a tug at a loose thread. I thought about the small, black buttons on the clothing she was buried in. I still cannot believe what happened and it never should have. And the fault lied in the recesses of our souls. The fabric of our marriage and our beliefs ripped at the seams, pulled apart at the very stitches of innocence. That brittle line between love and chaos. Our daughter's murder represented that slight tug of the thread.

The train's horn sounded multiple times passing through a brief stop by a now abandoned station. It had been built in the early 1930's, damaged by fire, rebuilt and then burned down again within the last few weeks. I glanced at the partial structure. What had been constructed with steel and stone still remained. There was a scorched beam leaning up against some fallen metal. It looked like an easel had been set next to the building then set aflame. I thought about what could have been painted there by that train station if that was my studio.

I looked out upon the area to the left of the station. The trees and the landscape reminded me of the lone trip we took to the mountains. I could almost see our daughter running across the grass, stopping to pick up a branch or two, a rock or small pebble. Sometimes she was in such a hurry she toppled over. I could have painted the branches onto a canvas, the corresponding color pressed deep into my memory. I would have placed the rocks she picked up and held in the palm of her hand somewhere at the forefront. It would have given them more importance, although a fleeting one. I listened to her tell me what she thought they looked like as she handed me each one. Sometimes small castles, sometimes princesses turned to stone. I turned around then as the winds changed. You had stood off to the side beside a small creek, by the water's edge, somewhat aloof to her imagination and her discovery.

It's sad, but I can't remember how old she was then. I could describe, even now, in infinite and minute detail how the sunlight reflecting off of the water made you look angelic and purposeful. It would be easy for me to reproduce the spinach color of the moss on the stones, the sad gray of the base of the mountainside. You and I hardly shared interaction then. Yet those are the intrinsic things I could recall, without struggle or strife.

There was no reason I should have been unclear on Jennifer's age. After all, those are the times and experiences I should have recognized and remembered, appreciated for their simplicity and happiness. I again took in the fall of the station. Secured to a broken pole with a chain was an old newspaper kiosk, distorted and reshaped by the intense heat of the fire. It looked like melted clay. Some things insisted upon being a prisoner, a helpless witness to their own destruction. Perhaps we were the same.

~

I had lulled myself to sleep for only a moment, the depressing weight of decisions and regrets boundless upon me. She was still asleep in the seat across from me. The auction house catalogue had slid off onto the floor. I reached over to pick it up and brushed her ankle. I thought about the scar on your ankle. One of the corners of a page had folded over. Flattening it back out, I looked at the painting of the fisherman. *Page 10.* I loved that painting, with its genial nature and tranquility. Yet there were things hidden underneath as well, below the surface of the aquamarine water, within the deep greens of the trees. It rested at the bottom depths of the water. It was in the repetitive gestures of the fisherman, their unseen faces off to the right, blended into the background. It existed, no matter how much we struggled to deny permission it did, that hidden sense of foreboding something ominous was coming.

The weather was gorgeous that day. I had gone up alone while you were doing some modeling. I welcomed the long drive up in silence. Coming back here had always been wonderful and fulfilling. Now, I dreaded the isolation and the memories being here would conjure, like an odor does, or a sound. It stimulates the very core of the skin, the body. I wasn't planning on staying long or even painting. When I reached the house, I made a strong cup of coffee and sat down by the water's edge and reflected. It was barely hot enough, but the steam coming from the liquid reminded me of spoken whispers. I wondered now what they would say, what they would tell us we were responsible for. Any even what we weren't.

I stayed by the water's edge for a while, thinking about the touch of your skin, how it was almost like being surrounded by the light breath of angels. Yet at some point, that feeling, that comfort had faded. I painted you here once if you remember. It was the last time we had come up here before Jennifer was born. I was frustrated by the lack of imagination and inspiration in a mural project. You most often had a way to calm me down some, slow the stubborn process of my passion and imagination. It was a blessing, one I would never experience again and one I undervalued.

I understood how controlling, manipulative and intense I could be when I painted. I was planning on dinner, wine, listening to the water's current crawl over the contours of our feet and ankles. I had prepared everything as I hoped you would like. When you arrived, I was oddly nervous, as I was usually arrogant in your company, assured I would conquer anything and everything when needed. You looked the house over, then said you were going to change. I stepped outside onto the deck and waited. It reminded me of the first time we made love together, that imbalance in my chest.

You were wearing an orange, silken dinner dress, the thin straps clinging on the bones of your shoulders. I never could have painted someone so staggeringly beautiful, someone whose slight movement could turn the world of off its axis with the same compulsion. You were the pinnacle of beautiful chaos. The night was so enchanting, sitting next to you, watching the moonlight reflect off of the surface of the water.

We danced, our bodies engaged in an attempt to find their place within one another, without the struggle of art or creation. Quietly in a way. I kissed your shoulders and used my fingertips to slide the dress from your body. The moonlight was coming in through the window. You moved towards the glass and pulled the shades. Your elegance and your naked body made me feel worthless. We kissed each other. We made love late into the night, our bodies altered by brilliance and dedication. I had loved you without regard for consequence or reparations. Our daughter was conceived that night, brought into our pastel universe with love and pride. And now, I would shutter away her memory, her light, trap it in the recesses of the dark.

I went to the car and began bringing in some boxes of our daughter's belongings. We couldn't keep them in the house anymore, although you wanted to. It pained me to see you sitting on the floor, holding some of her clothing and sobbing. You tried so hard to hide it through stillness and movement. There were times I thought you wouldn't be able to stop and your body would decay right there in front of me. There were photographs, keepsakes, some of her music and schoolwork. I stepped into the small den she used as a room when we stayed here. The bed remained unmade. I pulled the sheets from the bed. Things had to change, be in some semblance of motion. It was like painting, I couldn't stop sometimes to consider how the inspiration began. Only where it would end.

I sat down at her small desk. There was a photograph of the three of us together, taken at a beach not far from here. Next to the frame was a Mason jar filled with seashells. She always had so much joy in her while running in the sand. I remembered the morning when she discovered them, while you and I were holding hands, our feet brushed by the retreating of the tides. She had sand on her hands and fingers for what seemed like days. Off in the distance, above the water, a storm was developing. I thought at the time we were far enough from the temperament and the winds. I was wrong.

~

I stepped from the car when the train stopped at the next station to pick up other passengers. It was still raining steadily. I stood underneath of an overhang and glanced at my cellular. There was only one call from a number I didn't recognize. I cleared the call history and replaced the phone. I wondered where you were at this moment, what intensity of light might have been collapsing across your neck, the sides of your face. Regardless of what you may have thought, I still cared about you a great deal. But it was never easy loving you, despite the credibility and ease of your features, the altruistic depths of your tendencies. Yet our marriage became so cruel, so violent. I thought about whether I would have still been able to paint you, what color or tones I would use. A man and a woman several feet away were whispering to one another, cautiously, but deliberately. It made me think of my infidelities.

I entered the train and sat back down in the seat across from her and listened to her breathing, the rhythmic swelling and collapsing of her lungs. I wanted to nestle beside her and allow her body's movement in sleep to carry me along. I leaned into her body, resting my head on her hip. It was like being asleep on a boat, the water holding hands with the underside, the oars. Our daughter used to love being on the water. Prior her murder, I rowed our small canoe out to the lighthouse and the rocks.

*Page 14.* I must have sat there for hours, trying not to contemplate on anything, art, color, abstracts or the guilt that manifested itself in the darkened colors of that painting. I scrubbed hard to wash all the paint off from underneath of my fingernails after I completed it. I could still detect traces of umber and coal.

She used to play in the lighthouse with you, running up the small set of spiral stairs to reach the top. I used to think there was nothing more beautiful in the world than seeing the apricot sun set behind you and our daughter looking out over the expanse of the water. The way the light refracted off of your dark hair, your lip gloss made everything else beautiful in the world seem unappealing, appalling. Somewhere amidst the arguing, the passion and the colors, that light, that uniqueness disappeared, became something violent and disturbing instead.

I climbed down from the rocks and sat back down inside of the boat. There was a series of colored stains resting on the bottom. It was from Jennifer. She had tried painting different type flowers on the bottom of the canoe once. I had forgotten about it. After I reached the small dock in front of our home, I went inside and grabbed cleaning supplies. I sat back down inside the stillness of the boat and scrubbed the stain. My knuckles kept scraping against the rough wood. I scrubbed harder. As my hands began to turn a bone white and my knuckles bled, I sobbed. The color remained, undaunted and sadly vibrant. As did much of our daughter. Almost everything we had, everything we shared was worthwhile only because of her. I could see her pale complexion in the small pockets of soap that rested on the bottom of the canoe. I moved my hand over top of the white bubbles. The shape that remained reminded me of the ones that escaped from her lips as a baby.

I turned away from the window of the train. I felt like I possessed so little of who our daughter was, the things that made her smile and made her laugh. What frightened her? What else besides being near you made her smile? Looking back I lost hold on all those things as well, concerning you. The phone vibrated in the seat next to me. I ignored it. The things I indeed possessed were generic, unsubstantial and fleeting. There should have been more I could hold, more I could share. I kept thinking about the colors on the bottom of the canoe. I was never able to remove it all. I held onto the catalogue and stepped out of the train car.

I sat down alone against the window in a small café car. Some short distance trains still offered dining services. I ordered a cup of coffee and exhaled. It was still raining outside. When the coffee arrived I held it in my hands and let the warmth send shivers through my extremities. You used to do that to me, alter me and change me. The train rounded a corner and passed by a small mountain range. I looked out through the glass. One of the formations looked like the architecture of a woman's back. I thought of yours, refined and delicate. All consuming. *Page 18.*

Our daughter was still so small then, tiny and vulnerable. When I came home you were sitting on the edge of the bathtub, your underwear piled on the floor. Black looked so transcendent against your milky skin, especially in the dimmed light of the room. The tub was rustic and very artistic. It was the first time I had started to see flaws, small pockets of imperfections in our marriage, in you. I saw them and painted them in the uncorrupted depths of the water, in the droplets sliding down the slope of your shoulders. With your head turned towards the right, the way your hair hung across your arm was beautiful. It looked a shade of cobalt blue under the light.

It had started as a pinch, a nagging sensation we were struggling to connect on any level, barring physical. I enjoyed the destructibility of our tenderness together, how I could dispose of its strength, turn on you and feast on your skeleton. Yet there was a place in you I could not reach. I kissed the back of your neck and abandoned the both of you. I wish now I had stayed, held our daughter in the corruption of my hands. Perhaps things would have been different. I had gone down to a small studio where I painted sometimes. The room was humid and used to be a garage to a neighboring apartment. I turned on only a few lights and stared at a blank canvas, wondering where to start. I placed a long sheet in front of the canvas on the floor. I sat down upon the material and exhaled, looking up. I painted what I felt, what I believed at times was the truth. The rest was subterfuge.

I stood up, grabbed a brush and moved a couple of Mason jars on a rolling table beside me. I seized some tubes of paint and a palette. As I opened a tube, there was a knock at the studio door. When I opened the large, garage style door, a young woman was standing there, wearing a raincoat. Her name was Eula. She was a 27-year old Greek art student at a college near the New York border and a blossoming model. Upon shuttering the door, she stood in the shadows of the studio, against a brick façade wall. I didn't say anything at first, because most oftentimes I didn't have to. A woman always knew how to move, how to give impetus. I stood back from the canvas and moved a lamp closer to me. When I switched it on, the young woman was wearing only a white, cotton sleeveless shirt and nothing else. I pointed the lamp in her direction and told her to lean back against the wall. I stepped towards the canvas and dipped an angled brush into a jar. I only had to tell her to move once or twice.

An hour later I had finished the painting, somewhat minimalistic and unemotional. The young woman stood next to me and reached over, interlocking her fingers with mine. I ripped the shirt from her torso and studied her construction. She was angular and thin, the bones in her hips and shoulders tightly wearing her skin. I ran my hands down her body like a tailor, measuring the distance between her underarm and the top of her thigh. I knelt down in front of her. She pulled me astride her naked form and I wrapped myself in her milky flesh. I wanted everything and at the same time, I wanted nothing. It was the first time I had slept with another woman since we were married.

I came home and found you lying on your side in our bed. You were topless. I studied your body quietly as you were asleep. I woke you, inspired, but driven and consumed by the memory of another woman's touch. I kept thinking about her originality, the ripeness behind her lips. I found a small horsehair brush and wet it with paint. I began penning cursive on your bones, your spine and the small area of flesh below the soft underside of your kneecap. I kissed your shoulder blade. I had moistened it hundreds of times. It felt different now with her saliva on my lips. You asked me what color I was using.

It was a random mixture of black and grey and some tints of blue. I used it in paintings where I felt solemnity or neglect. It symbolized to me, fear, uncertainty and oftentimes, failure. Contrary, it wasn't something I saw in you, but in the environment around us. Not pain, not loss. But ignorance. I moved the brush down your arched body and paused at the small of your back. A man could get lost in your architecture. I said aloud I thought you were fragile. You turned your body over, facing me. Your breasts were round, your nipples rising in anticipation. You rubbed your legs against one another, your toes on your right leg tracing lines along the inside of your left thigh. The curve of your stomach around your navel was shaped like a painter's mussel. I could have pooled any color on your abdomen and made history. Your stomach flattened out and I imagined all that color running over the edges of your body and onto our bed. In those fleeting colors rested on the sheets I would see only apprehension. Your eyes begged I take you, reassure you I loved you, desired you. I slept beside, but never touched you.

I exited the small dining car and sat back down in the seat across from her. She had risen and was leaning against the window. She saw the auction catalogue in my hand, then looked away. I looked down at my phone. Nothing. I couldn't deny some ambivalence on what was happening. I thought of it as I tried to see through the increasing rain and winds. The train rounded a corner and passed through a small tunnel carved into the hillside. The car went dark momentarily. In that darkness, I thought about where her body was and I thought about how she looked. When the train ran through the tunnel and out the other side, there were several maroon leaves, pressed against the glass, motionless and serene.

That once idyllic street where her body was discovered would never be the same, at least not for me. *Page 21.* I painted those leaves burning with the indecency of garnet, seared and fed by the relentless breath of the wind. The waters had gathered in the street after a rainstorm, refracted the indecision I harbored after Jennifer's murder.

Autumn was her favorite season. That much I knew. As a painter, I held it in high regard, for its vibrancy and at times its decay. You had sent her to a friend's so you and I could be alone. I was distant, distracted by an art show held the next day. I was trying to decide which paintings I would highlight, which ones I felt would move people, initiate commissions. We were struggling financially again. You made me dinner. And when we made love later, I was disengaged, vacant. I brushed you aside as easily as changing colors or cleaning a palette.

When our daughter couldn't be located, I was the one who convinced you we didn't need to call the police. Sometimes we smothered Jennifer, never giving her space or allowed her to make mistakes, all a part of adolescence. You became hysterical when she wasn't where she was supposed to be. There had to be an explanation. When the police finally did call and break the news to us, I blamed you for what had happened to her. Your need to be loved, reassured was an intense burden at times. Perhaps I was as indulgent. I didn't recognize what color I had painted myself in. Things should have been different.

I reached out to touch the glass on the window of the train. I kept my fingertips pressed opposite those fallen leaves. I thought I could pull their tint, absorb the color and aspect of their suspension through the slight imperfections in the glass. Some fleeting light passed through their autumn skeleton. I could see the venation in the dampened and dying epidermis. They looked like the dead veins in our daughter's neck. I still noticed them when she was lying motionless in a coffin during her viewing, despite her disposition. You were holding my hand, so your fingernails cut into the creases of my palm. You're never ready to bury your child. Ever. She looked so lonely surrounded by such harsh objects incapable of comfort or tenderness.

I stepped back and dropped your hand. You were wailing. I didn't know what to do. I leaned up against the wall in the hallway and shut my eyes. What were we supposed to do now? All the solvent ever created couldn't rinse or wash away the colors I was seeing right in front of me, take the tainted and spoiled canvas that was our daughter and reconstruct her joy and her innocence. You were still on your knees in grief helpless. I stared at your prone and inert body. Our daughter's hair was as silken as yours. The bones that shaped the construction of your shoulders and the back of your neck were the same color as hers. White. As if made of chalk. Our daughter's sad face mirrored yours as you continued to be inconsolable. Her cheeks were sunken, giving her a haunted, gothic look of sadness and despair. Yours were hollow, abandoned. Our daughter's hands, inert at her sides, were as small as yours. It was at that heartbreaking moment I understood each time I looked upon your body, your beauty, and no matter how slight, I would see Jennifer lying dead and alone. I would see her in everything incorruptible and sweet. So I abandoned you as much as I was capable. A priest knelt down to help you up and comfort you. The colors I was seeing now would change if I solaced you, held you in my arms. I didn't think, at that time, I would be able to paint anything beautiful again.

I had surrounded myself with as much beauty and color as I could and it wasn't enough. I should have been content with our life together, but I could never get comfortable. I tried to suppress everything, the emotions I encountered through color and spectrum. Instead, I should have revealed and discussed the hesitations I had. I looked over at her, still drifting in and out of sleep and wondered if I would end up doing the same thing to her. Opening up to her, painting her, studying her, then abandoning who she was and everything she was ever going to be. She was pregnant. All the things I would learn about her, I would someday destroy. I had cheated on you, my wife and the mother of my child, but I hadn't with her so far. With you I had reached a conclusion. I was a person who would always hurt others and meant to be alone.

I painted that street again, where our daughter's journey ended. *Page 27.* That house was on the far right. Months after what happened, I found no happiness, nothing resembling hope or beauty I could paint. Instead I painted from the worn luggage of our tragic memories. That painting was so sterile, the wires and the trees all in their places as if nothing had happened, as if innocence and joy were still living in the patches of cut grass and painted traffic lines. But something had changed.

I couldn't hide it amongst the spinach-colored trees and the moist, pine needles. Her death, her end existed in the distance and perspective of the shadows. I couldn't deny its presence. At times, it made me think there was nothing for us, no reason or motivation to continue with our irreparable journey of discovery through color and remembrance. At times I wondered why you would want to remain with me, swimming against the raging currents in a diluted ocean of infidelity, strife and resentment. Too much damage had already occurred. The only vessel we had to reach our secluded islands was our daughter. Our art, our passion would never be enough.

The phone vibrated in my pocket. It was the same number as before. I held the phone up and answered this time, but the call dropped. The train pushed on regardless, through the tunnel and past a few more open fields and undeveloped acreage. We were entering the edges of another small town, the population similar to where we once resided. I could never go back there or walk past that house. I wanted to burn it down, scorch the earth with the colors of cinder and flame, render it forever a part of some unremembered past. It was an unsold painting removed from its canvas and rolled up, never seen or studied. A mural left to suffocate within the arid intestines of an unfinished attic.

It was then I gathered some of my clothes while you were gone, the intense and sudden unfamiliarity of everything around me overwhelming. Yet I had been gone for some time and vacant. Some of the remaining things that belonged to our daughter were on your dresser, some strands of her hair isolated on the dull bristles of a hairbrush. I wondered if the person who found Jennifer in that pool had brushed aside her hair to see who she was and tried to help her. We should have done so much more for her, guided her, supported her wants and the things she didn't. We were selfish and misguided, egoistic and fallible. We failed to protect her from the indecency of the world. I wondered what color, if any, would have painted us in a better light. I wasn't sure if such a tint existed anymore. But ultimately, we failed to protect her from ourselves.

I looked hard out the window as the rain continued. Everything appeared quiet outside, subdued, even with the motion of the train on the tracks. I still couldn't believe what had happened. I wondered if there was anything I could have done. I never knew the color of malice, how to shape its face and hands. Torn and isolated by my own grief, I forgot about the other victims, the other families now torn by the murder of their children. Yet it felt narrow and weighted because Jennifer was the beginning, the first victim. Why her? I never expected there would be so many after. Neither did anyone else.

Soon though I would have another child. I moved from my position and sat down in the vacant place beside her. After reaching for her hand, I kissed the back of it and rested my head against her swelling belly. We were having a girl. I listened to her light gesticulations, her gentle movement of limbs. I could almost hear her infant coo. I closed my eyes. In months, I would have to paint her bedroom. As the mother of my child, you deserved to be told what had happened in a different way. When you saw me with her near Norah's, the fire had escalated so quickly. I lied in color, plain and simple. I had become charmed by her, lured by her indifference to recognition that obsessed you. She was more amiable and less impassioned. Whereas your beauty was violently intense, hers was placid. I got lost in that placidity, swept away by the calmer movement of her tides.

For days you had been distant, spending time alone at the art department, modeling for some students. I hadn't painted you in a month. When we finally slowed down enough to talk to one another, you told me you saw her with me, evacuated post the explosion. It hurt, but more so when you said seeing the concern and care I had for her simply by holding a white cloth to her face. White, the color of maximum lightness. With our barriers up, we said such awful things to one another, things a man and a woman should never say. Especially ones once so in love. Not long after we exchanged barbs, you began sobbing, moving your body closer to mine. I thought you were going to yield, ask me to hold you. On a rare occasion, we could almost stop time when our bodies touched, slow down the perpetual motion of the world's rotation, topple life from the point of its order. Yet at times we were disorder and rot personified. No more so than what that painting represented. *Page 39.*

As you moved even closer, you reached up to touch my face, then struck. The blows came repeatedly to my chest and face. I could imagine the shade of red that would surrender against my skin. I stood there, watching you batter me with all your tumult and failures. The things you said to me I deserved. Yet you and I crossed lines we never should have, slinging vile brushes and tints at each other's damaged and torn canvases. We were only going to be able to heal alone, away from the conflict and the derision we harvested. We were two continents shifting against the currents and against each other, our lands colliding. My body shook as it continued to absorb your anger. All it couldn't have been from me and what pain I had caused or what you believed I was responsible for. There had to be more. Then I said you were unlovable and I hated fucking you. That no man or artist could make you beautiful again. It wasn't true. You were the most beautiful woman I had ever seen.

But in that beauty lay misdeed, your soul like an underpainting where all the colors of sadness and hubris clung. An alabaster pallet of grief. When you came at me again, I slapped you. Your body collapsed upon our bed. And in that collapse I found some semblance of grace and eloquence in the aspect of regret and shame I carried. Your raven hair spread out across the bed, a lonely hand trying to pick up the pieces. The muscles and bones in your neck and shoulders were overshadowed by obscurity and a dark color I never used again. I couldn't. Artists were always searching for an image, a concept. More often than not, I seemed to perceive beauty in sadness, the natural decay of time and existence. I painted a watercolor of violence and resentment. And it pained me. Whoever purchased your pain, would never know the watercolor's reason for birth. What's the old saying? The devil is in the details.

She ran her hands through my hair for several minutes as I still listened to a life growing inside her. I had the opportunity again, a chance at some semblance of redemption and honor. I'm sorry I failed to engage in reciprocity. We couldn't have a child after what had happened. You often thought and even said to me once I exploited you, used your pain for the betterment of my art. But the colors of pain are the ultimate inspiration, as bold and as vivid as anything else. Pain, longing, loss, these were the tragedies that moved us. Inspired us. You were not at fault in what happened with our daughter. With what we know now, after the other children, it could have occurred at any point or in any place. It was circumstance out of the realm of our grasp. Please don't dwell on it. Heal. Grieve. Allow the canvas of your new life to dry before coloring it with another. If hating me helped you heal easier, then tend to your wounds and think of me no more.

The train slowed down going through an intersection. I stood up and looked out the window as she excused herself. Her legs were numb in her being so stationary. I asked her if she wanted me to walk with her for a little while and she nodded no. The front of the train emitted some exhaust. I watched it cling to the side of the cars, walking its way along the wheels and track rails. It swept past the window like a morning fog, dense in its grayness and lack of any semblance of transparency. Slivers parted off and wrapped itself in circles around the telephone poles and cable wires. It resembled the morning advection I had painted once previously. The area in that watercolor though was more desolate of construction and technology. An open field of thick, unkempt green grass, a thin line of thirsty trees standing watch. *Page 20.*

I had created that painting without showing any aspect of your beauty. There was more to that painting than captioned in the catalogue. It seemed so innocuous, capturing what appeared as a calm and introspective moment post dawn. But it was the things unspoken and unseen that always cast the truest reflection. We had been arguing again, almost throughout the entire evening without pause. You said everything you did for me, it was never enough. It was the first time you had ever said to me I had exploited your history and your pain, for emotional and artistic profit. There is inspiration, but no profit from turmoil or tragedy. I can paint it, color the canvas with technique and style. But it's an illusion, a mere concept of optics. When I painted it, Jennifer had been dead for about a month.

When you stormed out of the rear of our house, I watched you move like a ghost through the morning. The warm fog pooled around your ankles like murky water, moving aside with each gentle step that you took. It was as if you were walking through a mill pond, ethereal and haunting. You moved deeper into the background, your fingertips swirling around the flesh of the fog. The thin dress you were wearing seemed almost transparent as I could see the shape and length of your legs through the material. You stood motionless in amongst the quietness of nature, your hands running through your hair. It was one of the most beautiful things I had ever seen, the poise your body graced itself with, even in hurt and indignation. I wanted to tell you to be still so I could paint your essence, show everyone how beautiful you always were, no matter the circumstance. I remained hushed in silence by your grace and by your vexation.

It seemed hours had passed when you turned around, defeated in your attempts to injure. You were crying. I could see the tears rolling down the curves of your face. The mist appeared to ripple like water. It was as if one tear gleamed down your body and broke through the surface of the mist, altered by your simple pain. Some drops of water fell across your chest. I could see the firm shape of your breasts. You looked up at me, still hurting from the things I said. It was painful. Even now, watching the smoke from the train dissolve into the atmosphere, I experienced changes to my skin, my body. When everything cleared, you were nowhere and everywhere at the same time.

Still pressed against the window, reflecting upon our misgivings, the phone rang again. I let it sound. I couldn't answer. In the distance, hidden behind a piece of farming equipment was a small cemetery. From here, it looked disheveled and ignored, the grass and weeds grown tall enough to cover up someone's name. I thought of our daughter. With our parting, who would be her keeper? Who would look after her during the seasonal changes, brush leaves from her marker? You would be responsible now as I was running. Running from the things that once made me brilliant, vulgar and at times cruel. I glanced down at the auction catalogue. I had used our daughter's death as an instrument, as a paintbrush. The freedom I longed, I unfortunately found in her obituary.

~

I stepped out of our car, looking for her. I strolled through the cabin of a few more connected cars and found her sitting at a table sipping tea, where I had come alone earlier. I could smell cinnamon. I sat down in a chair across from her. She reached out her hand across the table. I took it and held it within my own. There were tears forming in her eyes. She turned aside and looked outside the window of the train. History was moving past us, the history of the structures outside, the history of what happened in our small community of the broken and the shortened history of your innocence. Your past was littered with sadness and adversity. Wherein all our supposed problems lied. I remembered when you told me what had happened when you were much younger, with your sister. I reproduced some of your chronology in color. Page 8. That antiquated farmhouse was worn by age. I had painted a small sign on the door. It read "do not trespass." We should have heeded that warning and not trudged over the corpses of our individual memories together. Yet we submitted, anguished and regretful, our chemistries counteracted, a collision of audacity, lust and selfishness.

I was across the room when you told me, sketching you and our daughter sitting on the couch, gazing through the window at night. She was at my mother's. I would add her in to the painting later. The stars on the horizon stuttered against the black. I changed the perspective, removing you describing images of sunlight and summer smells and replacing each with torrents of rain and desolation. I couldn't have further corrupted what happened. It was impossible to make despair appear anything, but its truest definition.

In sad and precise detail you explained to me about your sister, about her assault and impending collapse. As you delved deeper, I set down the pencils and charcoals and listened. It was the only time I truly heard you, wasn't invested in what was in it for me only creatively. There had come a point where I had stopped listening when you spoke, when you told me anything at all that you deemed necessary or important. You used such vividness in your words, images and colors dripping from my ears. It was quiet, but not the sort of calm that eases someone. I couldn't see the scar on your ankle from where I was, as the dimmed lighting was losing the war, fighting to keep your body visible to me.

You said that you had fallen asleep underneath the porch. When you opened your eyes, all you could see was a legion of fallen fruit, their flesh torn from body, heads crushed across the arid dirt. Toppled from the basket I masked with indecision were the tomatoes that you pulled. You thought they might have tumbled off of the porch on their own, eager to escape a predetermined fate. I should have painted them there, been more supportive of a circumstance that shaped so much of who you would be. In the darkness of our living room, I could hear you sobbing.

The next morning you were up early, dew glistening on the handle of the pump to a water well. It was hardly used and rusting, but you didn't want to wake your sister. The sun was coming up beyond the wheat and the trees, golden rays blazing over the tips of the dying wheat. Soon it made its way to the edges of your bare feet and across your ankles. Your ankle. There were traces of blood still on your leg, failed in your attempt to hide it. You said you kept waiting for the sunlight to burn away the remains. But nothing could pull the hate and the pain from the deep recesses of the soil and the crops. Not even the perfect blend of colors from my painter's mussel. I should have removed the barn in that painting, ignored its placement and construction, the poignant way the sun refracted off the worn shingles. You switched on a lamp in our living room behind you. You raised your pants so I could see your scar. You touched the bone.

Someone should have been there to help you then. All those years, you said, you wished it would have been me. Submerged in your past I thought of our daughter. All I could see were the details of her death. In listening to the things taken from you in your youth I understood, even though someone else murdered Jennifer, that we were the ones who had taken life from her the most. Neither one of us was giving enough in our marriage. We never stopped long enough to pause, to hear one another. We listened, yet we didn't understand. There was so much now I wished we would have done.

~

The train stopped at a station. I stood up and allowed her hand to fall against the table. I stepped from the dining car for a few minutes and verified where we were. The phone rang again. I stared at the incoming number and did nothing. An employee came in and said the train wouldn't begin again for several minutes. I went back over and told Eula she should go back and get some more rest. That we would be there soon. I helped her back to our seat and touched her face. I closed the door behind me and stepped off of the train at a junction between the cars.

I walked through the rain now falling a little lighter. Passing through the station, there were several people waiting inside. I kept going and stopped in front of a broken window next to the restrooms. Brushing some grime away from the fractures, I noticed a small elementary school in the background. I remembered our first parent, teacher night, one of the only ones I attended. Jennifer was such an engaging student, always helping others when they struggled. She was a quick learner and an avid reader. I'd give anything to be holding her hand again through those innocent hallways, admiring the adolescent works of art adorning the classroom doors. I painted a school once, the outside of one, in the winter, not long after she was murdered. It wasn't our daughter's though. I thought about all the children unharmed, that would have to gather again to learn, trying to understand the consequences of the barren seats, the empty desks. *Page 30.*

The snow in that painting had such an incredible tint of blue, a simple and passive shade which soothed and secured. Only a small strip of asphalt was cleared at the time. It made the rest of the painting look still. The tips of the trees held what particles of snow hadn't fallen, moved or placed somewhere else by the almost indeterminable winds. There was an empty ballfield on the left, set upon the background. You could barely see the fence. A small bench remained abandoned, its uselessness apparent in the light tips of the brush strokes, its lack of presence. The horizon looked like it was overcome by smoke. Smoke was like grief, it could move and

322

pass through anything. It was the strongest thing in the world besides the movement of water.

I did regret certain qualities of winter, the harshness of its temperament, the bone chilling grip it had that held everything still. Yet it possessed such a fragile and unstable beauty. From the perspective of a cold bench, I exhaled on my hands, watching the snow fall, waiting for her to arrive. The school was where she and I were first drawn to one another. I was leaving after discussing a mural project and saw her, walking through the high grass behind the trees. I watched the winds move the blades aside. I remembered it being quiet waiting for her, my breath disappearing into the morning. She had heard about our daughter. I sat there on that bench, the intense cold soaking into the muscles of my body. In the distant, light movement of the trees, I could Jennifer's laughter.

When she arrived, she sat down next to me and held my hand. I had taken off my glove so I could experience her warmth. It didn't feel real, our daughter being gone. Being witness to those unique, blue shades she held me as I struggled to understand what had happened. I should have been by your side, but instead I was with her. She kissed the back of my hand, then pressed her lips against my face. She helped me up, the tears I made pressed against the quivering softness of her lips. When she turned to the side, it was like she had kissed the night sky, the brightness of stars clinging to her skin. The snow was so dense on the surface we barely made footprints in the quiet whiteness.

I stepped away from the window and exited the station. I boarded the train, exhausted by the debilitating weight of having buried a child. I could see failure in the faded colors of the fixtures. Our failure. I entered our car and took a seat across from her. She was lying down again. She saw me, smiled, and then laid her head back down. I bent over and touched her face. It reminded me of moving the hair away from our daughter's when I said goodnight to her in her room. I tried to remember the last words I had spoken to her. Part of me didn't want to remember the possible guilt in understanding they were hollow or insignificant. Why couldn't I remember? I should have. Out of the train window I could see several children waiting with their respective families. There were seven. I felt intense grief for the others, their lives altered by the savage brutality of man. I wondered what the other parents had whispered to their children in the last moments before they went missing or were abducted. As the train began again, a siren signaled our departure. It sounded like someone screaming.

The rains changed, now falling harder. It was difficult to see out of the window. The movement of the train reminded me of being on a roller coaster. Jennifer loved carnivals, the genuine amusement in games, and the light, innocent rapture. I smiled in remembering how aggravated she was when she wasn't tall enough to ride on some of the attractions. She had your temperament. I wished I still had the caricature I constructed of the two of you. We had so few photographs of all us together. Why? I started to cry. I had done so many things wrong. If I closed my eyes and inhaled, I thought I could smell warm funnel cake, the confectioner's sugar pressed into the creases of her fingers.

I held the auction catalogue and stared at the cover. I remembered that morning, how the ocean sea smelled, the biting, acrid scent of salt permeating everything. I turned to the page that discussed the painting. Page 34. It was one of the most peaceful times we ever had, brought about in incredible lines of warm, gold leaf I captured in the fragile fragments of the sand. I painted the water so blue it appeared measureless, stretched out for thousands of miles beyond the canvas. It made the few people standing on a pier in the left corner seem insignificant. The clouds looked like enormous balls of cotton pulled apart. We both laughed when she reached her hands up, trying to grab pieces of the material with her fingers. But the ecological evidence we had been there, together and united as a family was washed away by the violent and repetitive attrition of the tides. I symbolized it there, innocuously in the sodden, beige sand turning gray.

Nothing could remain unharmed on our easel, everything innocent and welcoming absorbed and ruined by our narcissistic will. I painted in a lone seagull walking in the water, a scavenger of unfulfilled dreams and promises that waited to feast on our bones, leaving our bodies to rot, lying under the surface of the loam. It appeared to dissolve around the seagull's feet, corroding the sand like acid. I always thought I could paint anything. I was stubborn, like a prized pugilist, weathered by age and erosion, who believes he still possesses the fixity of purpose and dexterity to defeat younger, undisciplined opponents.

I'd give everything to be able to go back to that place, the waters cool over the skin of my ankles. The world had never looked so beautiful. I wished someone else could have seen the boundless joy we shared, each of us holding her hands, lifting her higher in the air as the waves rolled over. No matter how high we raised her, water tickled the bottom of her toes. That laugh. That sparkling representation of merriment and innocence. I wished I could have taken a jar and imprisoned her laugh, set it upon a shelf. Like a seashell, I could hold it against my ear. Instead of hearing the oceans, I would hear her happiness.

To check the time, I glanced at the display on my phone. Nothing. Again, the coverage was inconsistent and poor. Deeming it useless for the time being, I powered it down. I leaned over and kissed the side of her face, then closed the door to the train car behind me. I moved a few doors down and entered a restroom. They were standard in almost every car, but most of them on this line were non-functional and in dire need of repair. In the winter the pipes froze periodically. I sat down on the closed seat and leaned back. I shut my eyes. In the hallway, I could hear the voices of children running through the car. The train brakes made a creaking sound going around a corner. It sounded like the small tires on that red wagon we bought to ride her around the neighborhood in. My hands shook covering my lips. I remembered that painting. *Page 13*.

Jennifer would have been about two years old. By then she already possessed your beauty, that look of utter brilliance and glamour. Her hair was as dark as the wheels on that wagon. The look in her eyes when she acknowledged you bore right through any assurance or perseverance. The first time we put her in the wagon, she tried to get out immediately. When she kept resisting and fussing on succeeding attempts, she climbed out and ran into your arms. She wrapped hers around your neck and buried her head. You smiled and tugged at the little shoes she wore. They were so small.

You outstretched your arms and set her into the wagon, buckling the small seat belt around her tiny waist. You continued to hold her hands as you climbed into the wagon in front of her. I let go of the handle and stood back, admiring the two of you, the way Jennifer grabbed and pulled at your fingers. I watched you lean closer to her, your hair falling across your right shoulder. It was such a joyous moment, the two of you in passive exploration. I painted her wagon such an intense shade of red. Under the sun, it reflected against your neck and across your lips. You looked so out of place in amongst that child's toy. But you looked out of place anywhere. Your cheeks looked like a frosted strawberry.

Eventually she calmed down enough you were able to step out of the wagon and walk next to me. We buckled her in. We went to such great lengths to keep her safe when she was younger. But as she grew, we failed her in so many ways, too many to recount on canvas or in color. I clutched the handle and began pulling her along. You reached out and grabbed my hand. Jennifer giggled. We barely left our own driveway on some days. But it didn't matter. Walking her down our street a few feet made her happy. I used to paint different pictures and we displayed them on small, wooden easels around our front sidewalk in the grass, so she could pretend she was anywhere she wanted to be. Sometimes she expressed a wish to be a veterinarian, the next the queen of an imaginary, foreign land.

Before long she would climb into the wagon herself and ask us to take her somewhere, to an imaginary landscape where cows changed color when it rained or even once to the enchanting forest of singing trees. Those were the moments I regretted I could not have again the most. Those little episodes of innocence and cleverness the three of us engaged in. Jennifer asking me to paint things for her. Exhausted after traveling, she would come in with sheets of colored construction paper, asking me to draw her a fairy or a group of animals no one had ever seen before. I liked having to enter her imagination, that wonderful world of color and discovery. I'd have given up everything to be there again, inside her mind, lost in a veritable wealth of authenticity and guilelessness. I wondered why we didn't do more things like that with her. We assumed as she got older she would need less and she wouldn't be interested as she once was.

It was the happiest we ever were together, holding hands and pulling her along in that red wagon. I could recall one of the last times she rode in it before outgrowing that sort of childhood adventure. I'm not even sure she ever did, like I said we stopped. It's how I remembered it. It was in the fall. The leaves had changed and broken, leaving many of the trees looking like an artist's model drawing marionette. The colors of our world, our neighborhood were majestic and bold. Jennifer had woken up early and said she wanted us to create a zoo. I stepped out into the morning. Everything smelled like cinnamon. She handed me several, large pine cones and wanted me to make them look like owls. Not long after, I heard her footsteps echo in return. On the floor in a small metal pail, she had placed a bushel of smaller pinecones as well, begging me to make other animals. I sat down at a small art table against the wall in our garage. There was so much history on its surface, old drawings, sketches, her scribbles penned in crayon. I brushed some dust from the table, pushing it onto the floor. I opened a drawer and pulled out some old model paints.

I held one of the geometric shapes within my fingertips and brushed soil from the scales. They were rough and open around the edges. Some pinecones opened up when they were dry and remained closed when they were wet. I held a thin paintbrush and dipped it into white, then at other times silver. The colors were intensely expressive. I dabbed upon the surface of the scales, pushing some color into the center. Not too long after she ran inside to change, I had made her large pinecones look like snow owls, their eyes closed in fatigue. I told her we could make animals with the smaller ones later.

She was so beautiful in her expressions of joy and gratitude. I pulled her wagon into the driveway as we waited for you. Soon, you came through the front door and stood beside me. We didn't need to say anything to each other. You leaned over and wrapped a scarf around her neck and shoulders. Together we pulled her along, past our house and some of the pictures she had placed on easels in the front yard. There were some 'no feeding' signs she had made, several small pools of water and some bold and vivid fish swimming inside of shiny, glass tank filled with flowers. I smiled, appreciative and proud of her wonderment. When we reached the last one, you began crying. I had painted something onto a canvas telling you how much I loved you. I wish I could remember every word, something I often failed at.

When our marriage had broken completely, I packed some of my things temporarily and left. You weren't home. I went into the garage to get some painting supplies. In the back, buried behind her old, rusted bicycle was the wagon. I moved some things out of the way and knelt down beside it. The paint on the handle chipped, the tires riddled by dry rot. The once vibrant, red color had faded into a sad shade of salmon and white. The pictures and the images she and I had painted and displayed in our yard had been replaced by photographs of missing children and police notifications. I don't know what happened to all them. I started sliding back drawers in the desk, hoping to find some remnants of our history. All I could find was empty, blank pages of regret.

There was still a pinecone sitting in the seat where Jennifer had in the wagon. I held it with such a pathetic sense of care. Pieces of it broke off in my hands. I began sobbing. The pinecone covered with silver and white to resemble frost after an ice storm looked ethereal. It had the same sad brilliance and sheen as our daughter's body when it was removed from that pool, the water frozen and taking shape across her extremities. I wiped my palms on my chest, then held my hands up to my face. They still smelled like cinnamon. I closed my eyes, giving access to the aroma to carry me away from the hurt.

I exited the restroom and paused in the small area that connected one car to the next. It wasn't very large. To the right was a window. I could feel a small rush of wind and water escape into the car. I moved closer to the glass and watched the wires and tracks rush by. Everything was in utter perpetual motion, yet it didn't feel like it. The train rolled past another farm in the distance. A lone, gravel road ran along the edge of the property. In the distance, telephone poles remained steadfast guardians, tall, industrial watchtowers of agriculture. Grazing in the plush, emerald grass were several groups of cattle. I remembered our daughter touching ones like them for the first time, reaching through the fence on the McIlheny's farm, in the summer. I could taste the melted ice cream we had to remove from her fingertips. Strawberry with a subtle hint of hope. *Page 23.*

The McIlheny's were so well loved in our community. Schoolchildren oftentimes went to the farm on class field trips to learn about agriculture, farming and animals. They allowed them to help shuck corn, wash blueberries and tend to some of the livestock. In the midst of some humid summers, they served ice cream to local children. They often made their own. We took Jennifer, eager for her to have interaction with others and as always, animals. She couldn't have been more than four. I was walking beside her at the edge of their property, her long, black hair getting caught between my fingers. She leaned up against the wooden fence between the posts and listened to the cows call out. I crouched down beside her and pointed into the distance, where the trees were watching, covered in an incredible blanket of deep green. When she turned her head to smile and laugh in my direction, a small calf had curiously moved closer.

The animal watched her moving fingers, then brushed its moist nose against her hand. Jennifer flinched, pulling away in surprise. Her lips turned down and she began crying. I reached out my hand to touch the cow to show her everything was safe. Our daughter moved closer and reached out her hand. She had such courage, such boldness in someone so young. We should have learned as individuals, gained so much more from her than we did. We never gave enough, to anyone for that matter, only paused briefly to take. The young cow moved closer to the wooden fence and stuck its head between the open rails. I felt utter exhilaration watching the laughter in her voice as the animal reared its pink tongue and licked some of the ice cream off of her fingers. I thought it tickled with the way she reacted. I could feel her happiness in the gentle, repeated tapping of her hand against my chest.

That acreage, that innocent field of soil and industry was different now. Our daughter once waded ankle high in the pond at the rear of the property where that other girl was murdered. There were so little details in the newspaper. It must have been horrible, seeing that. Other children as well felt the cool rush of water expand then collapse around their feet. I wondered what would become of it, their farm and the water. The pumpkins. The gourds. The laughter. I wondered if anything would be able to grow, blossom from the soil that could extinguish the rot and the depravity in what happened. Make people forget.

For a while, from a distance, you watched the two of us walk along the outside of the fence, wandering away from the cows and settling down by a beautiful brown horse. The ice cream had melted all over her hands. You soon came up behind us and began cleaning them off. I stepped back and watched the two of you interact. I've said it before, but you were so much alike. In the distance, beyond a small barn and silo, it looked like rain, the deep, golden fields awaiting nature's baptism. The purple clouds held blackness in their hands, each one ominous.

Yet it all seemed so far away, the silo seemed small and unthreatening. In your bag, you were carrying some colored pencils and a tablet. After asking for them, I traced in against the horizon faint warning signs of impending danger and oppression. It was where I saw you, the clustered buildings, the sense of hope present in the autumn decorations and smells. I never included those details in that painting though. I don't know why. No matter what I painted, it wasn't enough to bring our daughter back, nor any of the other children, nor would it be able to take the violent truth and turn it into a lie.

~

When I stepped back into the car, I could tell she had been glancing through the auction house catalogue. It was opened to a page towards the back. Page 29. That was such a simple painting, placid and serene in its nature. A barn in New England. We were driving north when I pulled over, inspired by the lonely expanse it portrayed. Nothing was more beautiful and transcendent than autumn in New England. In the middle of a deep field was a barn. The agriculture once its companion was long gone, the crops tilled over, their bronze skin shed and piled on the ground. I pulled a small stool and easel out of the trunk and walked a few feet out into the field. You came up behind me, bringing me some colors. Our daughter was with my parents. Some of her things though were still in the back of the car.

There was no place for anything to be concealed. The naked trees higher up on the slope peered down over the out of place building. The surrounding acreage spread out for miles. A light breeze wisped past and carried some fallen leaves. I replicated fragments of them there, in amongst the rest of the summer ruin. What struck me when I studied the barn was the rot lines in the wood structure. The colors from one panel to the next differed in shade and tone. Odd though was the roof was new. I painted it a bone white, a color I hardly used. It lacked any aspects of complication or struggle, something I needed. As I pressed a dark, amber color to the canvas, I waited for the barn to collapse, for its structure to fall into decay and pour out from the canvas and onto the ground in front of me. To begin that delicate balance on the precipice of being forgotten and nevermore. Similar to the ruin you and I immersed ourselves in.

We had been arguing again and our marriage was collapsing. Things were festering, staining the once vivid and bold colors of our union. You had challenged me, even in driving here, about other women, other muses. I held a palette in my left hand and dabbed some color onto the canvas. The corpses of some of the leaves disintegrated underneath your feet. I could feel your lips press against the back of my neck. You asked me what I wasn't given by you in our marriage in a faint whisper. I balanced the brush across my knee and reached back, running my hand through your hair. Together we used to be such beautiful anarchy.

I leaned up and kissed the underside of your chin, your hair falling down across my face. It used to be so soft and welcoming. When I didn't answer, you moved into my perspective and stood in front of the canvas. I watched you walk through the golden field. Not more than a few feet out, it began to rain at the top of the hill beyond the barn. I could see the clouds pushed by the winds, changing shape and distance. The light mist pulled along the declined slope, like a curtain closing. It reminded me of the most beautiful and seductive watercolor I had ever created, one I would never sell. I never showed it to anyone, including you.

We hadn't been seeing one another long. It was the morning after we had made love for the first time. You had moved out from underneath the sheets. I watched you hold them around your body at first. I hoped you hadn't regretted what happened by suddenly covering your nude form, hiding your beautiful vulnerability. The room was dark, but quiet and comforting.

I leaned up against the headboard and studied you. You appeared sad yet content. You looked back at me, your sultry and pouty lips on display. The white sheets you held descended the angles of your body and blanketed around your ankles. I watched you take a step forward and slide the pale green curtains aside, letting the little, natural morning light bless your body, your head tilted to the left. It was raining outside, but everything appeared to pause as nature gazed upon your pale elegance and raven hair. Your unique allurement offset the barren dankness of the morning. I pulled myself out of bed and moved behind you. I pressed my body against your back and wrapped my arms around your chest. Leaning in, I kissed the contours of your shoulders. No matter what happened, I would never regret that moment, even if you ended up doing so. I would understand if you did.

Sitting there in that field, the rains coming closer, you sought refuge in the car. For a least a few minutes, I allowed the rain to bathe the painting, the rich colors I applied sobbing along the white canvas. I put the paints away and allowed the rain to wash over me. On one occasion I looked back over my shoulder and studied you. You didn't see me. It looked like you were crying, but I couldn't be sure, trying to see through the precipitation. Your shoulders rose, then fell. I watched some of the color wash off of the backs of my hands, the construction of the palette and puddle at the spaces beneath my feet. I wished there was a solvent, some chemical that could wash away all the past, the mistakes, the regret that would always remain as a harbinger of what once was and perhaps would always be. You turned, looking back at me, your hand pressed against the window. I wondered if it was possible to be in love with someone, but that somehow, complete happiness still remained out of reach.

~

She was making the slightest of sounds as she slept, her head against the glass. We were nearing the last stop when we would depart to go to the auction. The train rounded a corner and moved past an industrial park, in the foreground along the rails. The colors were dark, cruel and uncompromising. It made me think of where we lived, what had happened. All things there seemed grainy and incomplete. Things would change when someone was arrested for murdering Jennifer and the other children. Regardless, it would be impossible to not remember what had happened.

I was surprised you decided to remain, live there with all that memory, that abject horror and decay. The daily reminders in the newspapers. The tragic anniversaries. The memorials. The vigils. They would forever continue regardless. I wished so deeply you wouldn't. How would you cope with walking past that house? As the cars rolled past the reflections of industry, it opened up upon a large farm, the horizon darkened with disturbing clouds. In the distance was a farmhouse and a silo. Hopefully, the abandoned farm where that other poor girl was discovered, Penelope, would be demolished.

The train slowed to a crawl and I gathered our things. I placed the auction house catalogue in my jacket pocket. I helped her step down from the train, her arms intertwined within mine. I didn't want to let go of her. In doing so, the catalogue fell to the ground on the platform. The winds tossed casually through the pages. The rains quickened some. I watched the water pull the tints from one of the paintings and puddle up on the cement. I couldn't' see which one. In my head, trails of once lush and vivid color dropped over the edge and trickled onto the tracks. I lowered my head. There was no equity in the tragic consequences of our failures.

# THE TEACHER

I told them not to look at the object, but the complete absence of form and perspective, what made it imperfect instead of absolute. Novice students always tried to give definition to an object before they intrinsically understood what composed it, its biology, moreover its architecture. Something considered noble and beautiful could be pestilent and marred underneath.

I tried to make them understand what I meant by moving my hand across the object's lower plain. I continued along the object's composition, admiring its structure and arrangement. Moving towards the front of the room I turned a switch, the impetuous darkness penetrated only by emergency lights housed outside of the building. Faint traces of light compelled through the glass, discovering the object's alabaster nature. I spoke, summarizing where each should have been with their assignments, although there were no grades. An alarm on my cellular phone beeped. I dismissed the class. I moved above a basin and washed the spectrum of charcoals and imbuement from my palms. In the still darkened room, I tried to examine myself in the mirror. I walked over to the window and listened to the rain slip from the branches of trees.

I shut the door to the classroom, stepped outside and watched the rain pool in the sodden grass. While reaching for an umbrella, I minded a foreign color against my skin. I knelt down above the sidewalk and placed the back of my wrist on the surface of a puddle. The color blended into the water, then dissipated. I dried my hand against my slacks then stepped out into the morning. At the edge of the street was a small newspaper machine. I stopped in front of it and closed my eyes when I read the headlines.

The door hadn't closed so I reached inside and took one. Water dropped from the angled umbrella in my hands against each photograph on the front page. I couldn't see who was in them any longer as the images slipped from their margins and came to rest against the edges of my fingertips. The ink bled into my hands, a contagion of pigment and tincture. The longer I stood there the paper wilted, withered and became as lucid as tissue. It broke apart across the plane of my fingertips, yielded,

334

corrupting the asphalt. I restrained sobs when I thought about what had happened to those children. So much loss here, so much irreparability.

Roland and I were never going to be able to recover from what happened in our marriage here. I watched some autumn leaves break free from their seasonal womb and fall into the streets. As I continued, there was no movement, everything subdued and benumbed by the oncoming seasonal change. But it wouldn't last. It repaired itself as human tissue did, membrane and muscles propagating. Yet it took too much time here to rebuild anything, pressed in by the constant economic and emotional hardship. Some of the families here would never be able to reconstruct their lives, regain any semblance of normalcy. I thought of my husband. I wondered who he was going to be again as some traffic in the street passed by me.

Ahead of me there was a man closing the front door to his house. That could have been Roland in disguise, masked under a different identity. Would I have known if it was him? I felt provisional, like a paper doll, a woman trimmed and folded to fit into the life and landscapes of one of his false identities. And if I stood in the rain long enough, I would change as he changed. But it wouldn't be raining. Instead of wearing a wool, cardigan sweater I'd be in a bold sundress which hugged my ample curves. Instead of wearing a bold sundress, I would be wearing a white blouse contrasting against my darkened skin. But at least I would know the truth.

The truth of that false woman though, her experiences, her loss of identity and assurance. Her loss of respect and dignity. I was still so distant and isolated though from what he did, the things he encountered every day I thought would have ruined a lesser man. Or would he have protected that other woman from his criminal identities, that facsimile, sheltered her as well from the oppressive darkness that seeded the clouds with an undeniable sadness.

~

When I crossed the divide into our bedroom I wasn't sure who I would see; a criminal, an arsonist, a forger, an absent husband, an invisible lover. Perhaps there were more. Would I ever know if there were? Deep down inside I needed, was compelled to know everything. I heard noises inside the house. I walked around our room, the sheets still shoved down at the

335

edge of the bed and remembered I had been there only hours ago. I stepped into the bathroom and found nothing. A small lock box was visible at the center of our desk. For only the second time since I married him, it was open. I walked over to it and ran my fingers around the inflammable metal case.

Resting on the top of other documents was a sealed envelope. There was nothing written on the outside. I bypassed it and underneath were several passports and identifications his people had created, dossiers and descriptions of men, inhuman individuals. In each one his eyes were unique, blue, hazel, green, various colors of a schizophrenic rainbow.

"I wasn't sure you were coming back," he said. When he crossed in front of me I wanted to get closer to him, touch his face, to ensure he was real and that I was real.

"I'll be leaving soon. The appointment's in a little less than an hour," I said, avoiding his eyes.

"Are you sure you want to do this?" he asked.

"Yes," I said unconvincingly. He noticed the box on the table. I watched him move over to it, sift through the documents I had removed. I figured he would be upset, but it didn't matter. He paused when he handled the blank envelope and then buried it at the bottom of the pile. I decreased the distance between us. "Who made them?" I asked, gesturing to the still open box.

"Does it matter anymore?" he asked.

"To me it does," I said. I leaned into his body and pressed into his back. "Tell me how all this started," I said.

"Why?"

"I don't know," he said, leaning back into me.

"Who are they, those people?" I asked, glancing at the box, at those facsimiles of individuals whose lives intertwined with and ruined mine.

"They're nothing. Nobody. Weightless, lifeless, soulless things," he said. Through his shoulders I listened to his voice race through my body, corrupting every muscle, every cell. I shivered. "People I used to be because no one else could. Or would," he added.

"Then why is their weight here, crushing me, pressing in on us right now in our bedroom? It's like we're in a crowded subway or a train," I said.

"I don't know," he said. He stepped over to the box, grabbed the lid and then released it. It remained open.

"Did you help to make those men, the ones who silently and without knowledge, made love to me during the night, whispered private things to me that never should have been heard or shared with anyone else?"

"Yes I did," he said. "I helped make them, who they were."

"And still are," I added. "Why?"

"Someone had to help," he said.

"What about me? I needed your help." I paused. "That's never been good enough though, has it? Why? Why this compulsion to be anything else, but my husband?"

"Because it was always easier for me being someone else," he said. His tone and the apparent distance in his words were cold. When his body turned, I stepped back. Surprisingly, I slapped him hard along the plain of his chin and neck. I looked down at my numb hand. I wondered how many other times he had been struck by someone. A small amount of blood gathered at the corner of his mouth. I pulled my sleeve high over my palm and wiped it away. In the pocket of his shirt I noticed, for the first time, a bank envelope and the end stub of a train ticket.

"You're leaving again aren't you?" I said. He moved away from me and grabbed a passport and an identification from the metal box. He closed the lid and instead of locking and replacing it, he let it remain on the top of the desk, as if daring me to look inside again, see all who he was.

"Yes I am," he said. I shouldn't have been taken aback by his tone, but somehow I was.

"I'm asking you not to," I said.

"I'm going under again," he said. I could see him changing already, right in front of me. His hair suddenly changed color, the sensual lilt to his voice replaced by impatience and anger. Usually when I touched him, his skin felt hot, dangerous. Now I felt more apathy than I ever had.

"Is this ever going to stop?" I asked.

"No," he said. No. No. No. No.

"I told you before I won't do this anymore." I leaned in closer. I moved a hand across his abdomen, the beautiful unblemished plain of flesh that was his chest. I touched his throat, discovering the contours of undulation when he sighed. My lips pressed against the corner of his mouth where I slapped him. It must have stung him as he pulled back from me and blenched. I kissed his throat with a violent force I thought myself incapable of only moments before. Soon his mouth opened and I lunged closer, licking the circumference of his lips.

Reaching down I loosened his belt and used my right hand to force his jeans below his hips. He forced his fingertips into my throat then descended them across my breasts. I pressed my palms against his pelvis as he lifted me onto him, and then interlocked my hands behind his neck. I exhaled and closed my eyes. Fragmented words passed from his lips, but I didn't listen. I didn't want to look down and not recognize him.

My legs were still trembling when I slid back the door to the shower. Steam surrounded my body and I used the vapor to conceal myself when the door to the bathroom opened. I covered my mouth so he wouldn't hear me sobbing. Without pause he turned on the faucet, splashed water across his face then moved across the room. I felt nauseous. Soon he dropped some clothes into the laundry hamper then closed the door behind him. When he did, I released my hand from across my mouth and vomited. I bent over and tried to breathe, but I couldn't. Anxiety constricted my lungs.

I stepped out of the shower. I cupped my hands underneath the running water and carried it to my lips. I felt so thirsty. The lucid water washed through my throat. The taste of the sweat from his neck remained though. I cupped my hands again and again, guiding the endless streams of water into my mouth. I shouldn't have had sex with him. The things I said to him. Was there something wrong with me? Why did I feel so guilty? But it scared me, deep into the axis, the pith of my soul. I loved him so much that I became physically ill. With difficulty, I placed my hands on the faucet and turned off the water. The sundress I had chosen slipped onto the floor.

~

It didn't look real, the world outside of the cab I rode in. It all looked like something synthetic, plastic and fleeting. It was all so still, the movement of the water against the trees, the glint from my wedding ring slicing through the gray and the damp that settled in the lap of the wind. I couldn't see him through it all, even when the cab stopped at the light at the end of our street. I pressed my hand against the rear window and watched him dissolve into the framework. Through the glass he looked disrupted, disfigured because of the way the water settled, something frightening, something hideous and misshapen. A gargoyle. A listless stone creature. Statuesque, complicated and dishonest. I leaned in closer. The rains lessened some, but not for long.

Yet in contrast everything collapsed in my mind, the scene behind me. The plush, Japanese maple tree in our front yard descended, splintered against our house. It tore through our lives, the photographs which I now disdained and whose validity I questioned, the memories once sustainable and pure, left barren, doubted and transitory. I turned back around towards the front and whispered to the driver. I wanted to scream. Indeterminable sounds echoed throughout the streets, deafened the innocence and the joy I once embraced here. Tears moved across the flesh beneath my nostrils. The cab idled. There was no going back now.

We were only about a mile out of town when I regained my composure. I pulled my briefcase onto my lap and opened the latch. The papers inside weighed on me. There was no way he would sign them, if he ever came out from under his identities long enough to read them. But I couldn't stay with him anymore. At a stop sign I examined the building on the corner, taken by the craftsmanship, its familiarity. The building was nearly identical to an office I once maintained less than a half an hour from here. It was where I first noticed his allurement, the subtle movements in his hands, the indirectness in speech and his lips parting, the sudden intake of breath giving him pause. I noticed his wrist. There was a silver watch draped over one. I wasn't sure why, but I found his wrist beautiful. It was tender under my touch when I brushed my fingertips across it in his leaving. It would be the first part of his body I kissed.

Not long after memorializing our fragmented and artificial annals, the cab pulled into the parking lot of the law firm I attained to handle our divorce proceedings. I swore the earth shifted under my feet. I stood immobile for a few minutes before I realized I hadn't paid the driver. When he took the money from me I wanted to ask him if it was the right thing to do, going inside. I sat down on a bench in front of the building and stayed there for a while. There was no one I could turn to for guidance.

I used to be able to trust Roland with the emotional things that affected me. But unfortunately that kind of openness and naked integrity was nothing more than a blank train ticket, a passport without a photograph. He would be surreptitious, under for months at a time, leaving me isolated and humbled, stranded in a topographic wasteland of introversion and depression. I thought about his involvement in what had happened here with the murdered children. It was all so horrible, beyond the point of comprehension. I tapped against the lawyer's office door with the back of my hand.

It was as if I only heard every other word he spoke. Reasonable cause. Contested divorce. On what grounds? I hadn't though that far ahead. He kept asking me questions.

*Was he abusive?*

*Was he emotionally cruel?*

The legal terminology was overbearing and exhaustive. Why couldn't anyone understand? There were so many different ways I wanted to answer his inquiries.

*Was there infidelity?*

When he handed me some preliminary information, I slid it across the desk. The paper it was on was tender and amber, like old parchment. I thought about the burn on his back right at the cusp of his shoulder blade.

As I was reading the initial paragraph of the paperwork, the phone buried deep inside of my purse began ringing. Underneath of my wallet I found his watch. I couldn't remember how it had gotten there. I let my fingertips rediscover the stainless steel band. I pressed it against my ear. There was no sound, no consistent, delicate and precise movement. It had stopped. I lifted it higher and watched the light refract off of the deep, black facing. It was like looking into an unending pool of ambiguity. I became disoriented, nauseous.

*Was he an alcoholic?*

*Was there drug use?*

There was love once if that counts for anything.

For me he was transcendent and peerless. I was wearing a shoulder-less evening dress when he came into the art exhibition at the community college, the light from a broken, overhead fixture evaporating against the

340

coldness of his dark overcoat. It had been raining again. I'd never seen a man so poised, but deliberate in his movement, observing an area or object in his perspective then moving on. I admired him discreetly, made note of how his fingertips brushed across a glass, a cheap cotton tablecloth. Oftentimes he would lift up an article, tilt it into the light, examine its weight and structure, each insignificant detail measured and calculated. Nothing was inconsiderable. That's what made him indispensable as an agent.

We passed by several closed classrooms. I felt claustrophobic near him, even side by side in the expansive, vacant hallways. When I broke from him at the end of the evening, he raised his hand to caress the side of my face. I craned into his palm and kissed the inside of his wrist, his beautiful watch pinching the edge of my lower lip.

*Had we seen a therapist together, or separately?*

*Was he neglectful?*

I apologized to the lawyer about the distraction. We started initial discussions about finances and ownership of property.

*What was my yearly income?*

*Did we share a 401K account?*

*Would I be requesting spousal support?*

*Did we have a mortgage?*

*Would I move out of state?*

*Would there be a need for division of debt?*

*Was I stable enough to live on my own?*

*Who is your husband's employer?*

*Did we have any children?*

No. And I don't think we ever would because of what happened. The phone rang again.

Please leave me alone.

Again I didn't recognize the number. I pressed ignore and tried to imagine an ending to all this.

Did I need a restraining order issued against him?

Was he harassing me? I began sobbing.

Did I need a moment?

Yes, a thousand. I need a vast, endless desert of a thousand moments that never cease, never dissolve.

"Can I use your bathroom please?"

I stood from the chair and set my purse onto the floor. I closed the door behind me and walked down the hall. The lights staggered to come on. I stepped inside a stall and sat down. Suddenly I dropped to my knees and vomited into the bowl. When I was barren and used up, I leaned back against the side of the stall and closed my eyes, imprisoning the water fighting to get out. I wasn't sure what to do. The apprehension and unease was encompassing. I closed the door behind me and stood in front of the sink. I swallowed handfuls of cold water. The faux porcelain was stained with a black substance. It looked like ash. It was as if he had been here, burning buildings again and inciting anarchy. I examined the dark marks with my fingertips. The residue was more like black pepper, like gunpowder.

Peter McDonnally.

That was one of the names he had used.

Did eleven years in a maximum security facility for the repeated attempted robbery of a carrier group of armored cars. No secondary education, no current employment was listed on the dossier. Current residence, a motel room on the second floor of the Eisenhower. Paid weekly in cash. No complaints from any of the other tenants about his behavior. No other people were ever seen with him entering or exiting the motel room.

I went there once, to that motel. It happened a little over a month after I found out about his identities. I stepped into the lobby and looked around. The decor was modern, littered with earth tones. In reading the classified index marked 'CASE CLOSED,' I expected something more worn, impoverished. I registered at the desk without baggage and took the stairs to the second floor. I opened the door then closed it behind me.

The room was dim as I drew the thick curtains. I walked over to the window and allowed the afternoon light inside. The bed was fitted with gray sheets and dark brown pillows. It was smaller than I thought it would be. The furniture was sparse, a small table with a television and a chair tucked into the corner. The file said he had lived here for eight weeks. I moved into the bathroom and switched on the light. There was a small tower cabinet above the toilet, pale white towels huddled together. Several of them looked torn. The counter-top on the vanity was an imperfect, distressed black. There were multiple cracks and the caulking

342

was rotted. I dimmed the light and went back towards the window. I pressed my hands against the glass and looked at the row of small businesses across the street. I wondered how many times he had been inside them. This room would have given him a good perspective. Notes said some armored car deliveries were before dawn. There wasn't enough light Roland had said amongst them.

The initial arrest of Peter McDonnally needed to be authentic. Everyone who had gained knowledge of the operation agreed, including his handler. When things were being set up to investigate the series of robberies, he had to drive the area for about 20 miles in each direction to become familiar with the streets, the businesses on each end, the abandoned buildings like the cement factory at the main intersection where the first discussions between criminals took place. It wasn't there now. It was leveled along with several other abandoned buildings in the area. Nothing had taken its place. There were very specific, visual details in the report along with photographs.

The warehouse was covered in soot and ash, crumbled blocks of stone and concrete piled up in front of one of the garage style doors on the inside. The windows were painted over in black. I could see him, walking through the anxious dark, wondering if he sensed comfort in its silence, held in its uncertain embrace. Soon he would huddle around, begin dialogue on how the heist would take place. It was as if I was there, walking behind him, noticing the sweat shine ever so slightly on the back of his neck. Four other men were involved, all with a long history of robbery, assault and grand theft. I couldn't see their faces though, only his. He looked different, edgier, more intense and determined. He was wearing a light blue shirt, several of the buttons missing. When I moved around the dingy table, I could see a series of tattoos on his chest. Another one on his wrist. I wondered if the dark ink would weep down his abdomen if we showered together.

He had schematics on the table in front of him for depositories, traffic routing patterns and alarm panel architecture and construction specifics. Everything on the transit companies that performed the deliveries. Someone on the inside was supplying routing and deposit information to the men he had been sent in to undermine. The discussion was whether the jobs were worth the risk and how many could be planned in succession. It said in the margins he was supposed to comprise the execution of a plan with minimal collateral damage and provide escape routes. The agency had enough to warrant an arrest, but they wanted him in a little deeper.

I would learn they always did, no matter how deep he got. That it was never enough. The room drifted further into silence. I watched him push the chair back from the table. It all seemed so foreign to me, the grime in the factory, the sounds, his mannerisms and the shotgun he held in his hand. I stood in front of him as he loaded it. I watched him run his hands across the barrel, probe the trigger. He took such care with it, as if it were the body of a woman. I stepped back into the darkness of the motel room and closed the folder. I drew the curtains and sat down on the edge of the bed. I pulled down the duvet and cuddled up.

There were many places the human body could take a gunshot wound and not be permanently damaged. In the report were medical diagrams and diagnostics. The scar was still there on his body, starting on the inside of his thigh and continuing straight across the joint above the kneecap. The shot had shattered the bone above the patella. He came out of the alley behind the trust bank wearing a thin Kevlar vest underneath his clothing. The police had stationed a sharpshooter on the roof of the hotel. The alarm triggered in an unsecured room when his group took the entrance-way to the building. It was supposed to be the armored car, nothing else. Oftentimes, some fledgling criminals became anxious or manipulated through greed and excess. Those were his words written in the debriefing. He came out of the building as the armored car pulled up and pistol-whipped the driver on the back of the head.

As soon as an explosive charge blew open the outer steel door, the officer on the roof pulled the trigger. The round tore through the tense flesh and structure above his kneecap like it was tissue paper and exited the other side, though the round shattered some of the bone in his leg. It was an accident. Only two people knew who Peter McDonnally was. Yet due to incurring circumstances, neither was on scene in time. It was the first time he had been undercover and wounded. Hours later all the arrests were made and the men he had associated with were arraigned several days later. According to police and county records at the time of the arrest, Peter McDonnally was treated, released from the hospital and awaited extradition on previous outstanding and superseding warrants in another state.

I exited the bathroom and collected a small cup of water from a cooler at the other end of the hallway. When I stepped back into my lawyer's office he was engaged in conversation with a uniformed police officer. I couldn't hear what words were being spoken. I interrupted their dialogue and caused them both to turn hesitantly. I was nervous during those truncated moments, waiting for him to tell me that Roland was dead. Although I was beginning divorce proceedings, without him, I was as incomplete as his identities.

"Excuse me miss, are you Noemi?" the officer asked after glancing over at my lawyer.

"Yes I am," I said.

"I'm afraid I'm going to need you to come with me," he said. I never told Roland I had gone to that hotel to be near him, to try to understand what he did. I slept uneasily in the rough bed that night, waiting for him to touch the patch of skin at the base of my throat, sometimes wondering if he would injure me in the dark as well.

~

I watched the depressing, drenched landscapes rush by. It was quiet and humid inside the officer's car. The seats in the rear were uninviting and bland, but that would belabor the point. I reached out and touched the metal divider meant to keep criminals isolated and restrained to the back. It was cold and rude, the metal. I imagined him here, Roland, sitting opposite me wearing clothes I had never seen previously. Who was he? His hands were bound behind his back. An officer in the front would be reading his prior record on a small laptop screen. Gambling. Assault. Soliciting a prostitute. Resisting arrest. Would he have cursed, challenged their authority? Mocked them? I could see him leaning into the adjacent door, trying to break the glass. When his attempts at escape failed, he would force saliva onto the barrier in defiance. I closed my eyes and exhaled.

"Could you please tell me where we are going and what is happening?" I asked, growing more concerned.

"When we arrive at our destination, someone will speak to you. Please don't worry," he said.

"When someone says that to you, it cannot be helped," I muttered. I leaned against the window and watched the rain strike the construction of the vehicle. Things here, outside used to have such a different texture and tone to it, regardless of the dilapidation of economy and housing. The winters had been brutal enough. January came quietly wandering in like a stranger. Then the first child was discovered in a backyard pool. Then the second. Then the third. Then Roland became involved and our marriage changed. Or had it always been like that, full of ambivalence and misinformation? To admit though there wasn't love and passion would be untruthful. Now everything was motionless, like a still hourglass after the sand ran down. We proceeded through town and slowed down at times because of the rainwater having nowhere else to go. It puddled in the streets. The tires of the car pressed through and the water careened against the window. I wasn't sure why, but it made me sad.

Soon after we pulled into the parking lot of a closed real estate office. There were several cars parked there already. It wasn't what I had expected. I thought we would be arriving at the hospital where someone would tell me in detail he was gone and he hadn't suffered. Would I recognize him? Would I understand without a doubt it was my husband I was being asked to identify? I was escorted out of the back and stood against the car for several minutes. I raised my head.

The rain was refreshing and felt good colliding with the carbon skin at the base of my throat. I looked towards my left through the front window of the building. Inside I could see people milling around, some occupied by other police. There were shadows on the ceiling in the unit above and lights were on. Soon, I was ushered into the real estate building on the first floor. The officer who drove me here was speaking into the ear of another man. That man began walking towards me, a very heavy look saddled in his eyes. I wondered if any of the men here really knew who my husband was.

"Thank you for coming," he began. "I'm Detective Daniel Mull. I apologize for the vagary in bringing you here," he said.

"Can you please tell me what is happening? Why are all these people here?" I asked.

"Please, follow me," he said. We walked together through the building and out behind the property. It was still raining. A police S.W.A.T vehicle was parked not too far from where we stood. The back doors were open. Mull gestured for me to climb into the back. The sound of the metal was disquieting. He closed the door behind him.

"Why are we speaking in here?" I said.

"Because some of what I am going to tell you cannot be heard by anyone else. A few miles from here there is a situation involving the hijacking of a transit bus. There are several people still on board. We have reason to believe your husband is one of the remaining passengers," Mull acknowledged.

"Is anyone hurt?" I said.

"One shot was fired, but no one, other than the driver, was injured. But he was released by the hijacker because of a medical emergency. I wanted to tell you I am the only one in the department here who knows who your husband is," he added.

"I see," I said. "Then you know the things he's done?" I asked curiously.

"In some regards yes. I know what he has accomplished during the course of our investigation here up until a point. I have had discussions with his handler considering the situation. And I know some of what he has done in the past," he said.

"To be honest, I wished that I did," I said passively.

Mull was quick to respond, so quick that it frightened me. "No you don't," he said.

"So why am I here?"

"We brought you down in case you might somehow be needed. We are hoping we will be allowed to speak to the people on the bus. That's why you're here. I thought it would be prudent to have you around. Do you know if your husband left the house armed this morning?"

I lowered my eyes before answering. "I can only assume so. He said he was going under again," I said.

"Undercover? Are you sure?" he said.

"I left the house before he did, so I can't be certain. How did you know where I would be this morning?"

"I had been in contact with your husband on occasion since he was inserted into our investigation by another agency until I was removed

347

from the case," he said. "I'm sorry, but I was aware of your appointment."

"Why couldn't you people leave him alone?" I said, pressing my hands together.

"He doesn't technically work for me. Noemi, it's what your husband does. It's who he is. You have no idea how many people, how many more children he might have saved by the things he has done," Mull added.

"Detective, I love my husband for who he is. But you couldn't begin to understand what those things have done to me, our marriage," I said. I paused for a moment before I said anything I would have regretted later. "Is he in any danger?"

"I can't answer that with any clarity. We haven't been able to speak to anyone on the bus as of yet," Mull said. "Your husband is an extremely intelligent and capable man. If he sits back and does nothing, there's a chance we can diffuse the situation from here. But he risks his identity and exposure if he tries to do something on that bus," he said. I leaned back against the inside of the vehicle and exhaled.

"What do you think he will do?" I said.

"I honestly don't know," he said.

"I do," I responded. Tears welled up in my eyes as I answered. "He'll try to save everyone," I said.

~

Mull helped me out of the vehicle and back through the rear entrance to the real estate building. I walked past several people on my way through. I hated all them, as if they all had a hand in what Roland had become, what those identities did to him, to us. I didn't even really know them. Mull remained a few feet behind me as I left out into the rain. I was told I could wait in the rental apartment upstairs. The electricity had been turned back on and provisions were being brought over. I guess they expected us to be here for an indeterminate amount of time. I noticed the metal staircase leading up and put my hand on the rail. When I started, Mull stepped in front of me.

"There's other women upstairs in the apartment," he said. "Remember there are other people on that bus besides your husband. Understand this is a difficult situation for everyone involved," he said.

"I know," I said.

"Please try to remain positive. We're doing everything we can to get everyone off of that bus unharmed and back here safely," Mull said.

"Besides my husband, how many people are on board?"

"We're not confirming anything, but considering the circumstances of your husband and what's at stake here, I'll tell you. Four, including the hijacker," he said.

"Do you know the identities of the other poor people on the bus?" I asked.

"Yes we do," he said.

"Who's doing this?" I asked. "Why?"

"That I'm afraid I cannot answer," Mull said. "Even if I could, it's all conjecture at this point."

"Am I ever going to see him again?" I said. As much as I detested the work he did, there was still a nobility in his cause. It would always be there, no matter how hard I tried to pretend it didn't. And it made me love him as much as I didn't want to, or at times wished I ever had. Mull never responded. As I started up the staircase again, a young woman came down and passed beside me. She looked as if she had been crying. The detective went over to her immediately. I finished climbing the staircase.

The apartment was sparsely furnished and was very humid, although there was a window open on the other side. There was a woman sitting on a chair, looking through the rain up the street. I wasn't sure she had heard me come in. I wouldn't have known what to say regardless. I wondered who she was. I set my things down on the counter and headed towards what I believed to be the bathroom. I washed cold, cloudy water across my face, then closed the door behind me.

In the rear of the apartment was a small bedroom, unfurnished. I went into the room and looked out through the back window onto the rear of the property. Several ambulances were parked against the curb on one of the side streets. That street was cordoned off as were several others with wooden barricades. It was raining harder. The temperature had dropped some as well. A small, temporary triage was being set up outside, preparing to handle any possible injuries. There were several E.M.T. workers standing around a steel barrel, shards of flame emanating from the opening. Burning wood glowed in the cylinder. One of them was rubbing his hands together over the barrel. I wondered if I held my hands in the ripe, orange flash, if my skin would burn as Roland's did, bubble up and change.

I remembered holding his hand once in the warm water in a bathtub, stimulated, but saddened by his rough and naked form. There were burn scars on his palm and hand, the back of his wrist. There was a larger pattern on the slope of his shoulder. It was a torn piece of a map of his imperfections, yet I had always tried to think of it as a flawless pattern, an undisturbed and absolute plain of beauty. He told me some things about part of who he was, mostly as an arsonist. But only a partial truth, as it always was and would be. I felt sorry for him at times. When he finally confessed to me, opened up about the things he did, the people he managed to become, I was numbed, frightened and angered by his candor and his righteousness. We were in our living room when it happened, when everything I believed in about us shattered, broken loose from its foundations of steel and stone by lies, truths and false nobility.

"You asked me once if I ever killed anyone," he said.

"Yes I remember," I said. I could still feel the warmth of the bath water and the strength in his body against my skin.

"I shot that woman in a field," he began. I was tempted to interrupt, but instead I watched Roland stare intensely out the window. "Her group was burning a building, a medical clinic. The fire erupted so quickly, was so violent in its movement and voice. It has one, a voice. It whispers at first. As it breathes in, it grows louder, begins to bellow. That's a good word for it. Then before it murders the night and any semblance of hope, it screams. The unpredictable winds pushed the fire to an adjacent building. It was supposed to be empty at that time of the day. Two people burned to death in that tragic mistake brought about by their misplaced anger and false politics. It was my fault it happened. I should have controlled the situation better. Those people, their lives are imbedded in me. I see their burned bodies in the middle of the day, in the ends of the night. I've never seen anything that black before, that dark and absent of anything worthwhile. Yet somehow, I am supposed to forget about all that blackness and come to you," he said.

"Roland," I said. Sensing I was beginning to stand to come over to him, he turned to the left and held out his hand, palm open, signaling for me to stay.

"After I shot that sadistic woman, I watched the rain collide with the heat of her body, warmed my hands and fingertips over the steam coming from the entry wound. I think of that when I watch you step from the shower, can see the warm water evaporating, then rising from your ebony skin. That blackness of your beauty. I used to be able to get lost in that, without reservation, without any sense of fear," he said.

"She and I are not the same. That woman was a murderer," I said in a whisper.

"So am I. I ended up being no more different than those I was meant to destroy." Roland paused and in that stillness I fell in love with his sensitivity and awareness. It was something I hadn't seen. "There's more," he added.

"Tell me," I said, bracing as much as I could. I didn't understand how he could do what he was expected to. Briefly he turned around. I could see his lips moving. It looked they were going to become displaced from his features. The look in his eyes revealed to me in silence, told me everything that hadn't already been said and instructed me and without doubt what to ask. "Did you sleep with her?" I said. I was as scared as I had ever been. I had looked at the truth as an absolute. Yet the truth was never a finality. It only led to more uncertainty.

"Yes," he said. "More than once."

"Oh my God," I whispered aloud, covering my trembling lips.

"It was a way to get closer to her, for her to trust me," he said. "These people were pure corruption. Someone had to stop what they were doing before more innocent people were killed. I never planned it. The situation presented itself and I acted upon it," he said.

I pulled my legs up and huddled closer, almost as if I were alone outside in the cold. "Was she pretty?"

"It's beside the point Noemi. She was a criminal, a tool and nothing more," he said.

"But you still slept with her," I countered.

"It was simply a part of the job, like attaining false passports, changing my appearance. It made the identity all the more realistic. I didn't feel I had a choice," he added.

"Is that what I am? Simply a part of the job?" I asked.

"No," he responded, turning away from me and back towards the window. It had started to rain.

"Did you like sleeping with her?" I asked.

"Yes," he said quickly, a touch of anger in his inflection. "Is that what you want to hear, I liked fucking her? That she was violent, manipulative and cruel? That she was everything I hated, everything I swore an oath to stand against? She was the opposite of who you are. It's what William McCoy wanted at the time, but not your husband."

"I don't believe you. But I'm not sure I can see the difference between them anymore," I said.

"I'm still the same man you married," he said coming over to where I was sitting. He lifted me into a standing position on the floor and grabbed my hand, pressing it against his chest. "I'm still right here, as I've always been."

"But you haven't always been here. I've said that to you before. Remember? You're gone for long periods of time, so long I begin to think you're never coming back," I said.

"I always do come home," he said, reaching up to touch my face. I so wanted to feel the heat from his insistence, his passion. Yet I pulled back enough so that his hand fell quietly through the air.

"Not all does though. There are parts of you scattered throughout all those places I have never been," I said.

"That's not true," he countered.

"It is, you don't see it. But I do more than that, see it. I feel it every time you touch me. Your skin smells like oil, your lips taste like ashes, sad, burnt reminders of what I have lost," I said. He touched my face with both of his hands and leaned in to kiss me. Despite reservations, I let him. I thought of him kissing her, that woman. I wanted to know more about her. Warm tears ran across our lips.

"I love you," he said.

"And I love you, but only you. I can't love any of those others. I don't know who they are. Who else have you been? What else have you done?" I said holding him close.

"It's immaterial what else I've done," he said, caressing my neck with one of his palms.

"No it's not. Nothing you have ever done is immaterial or insignificant in my eyes. You're a wonderful man, but you can't leave me barren on an island alone. I need access," I said.

"We've been through this," he countered.

"Why did you break down when we were in California at the wedding? What happened to you? We've never talked about it," I said.

"I'm pleading with you not to ask me that," he said, increasing the distance between us.

"It's about what has been happening here, isn't it? The murders of those children?" I said.

"Noemi, please. Don't ask questions to get answers you're not prepared for," he pleaded.

"Why? What happened out there? I know you're helping the police here," I said hesitantly. On several occasions I had seen him sorting through documents and photographs.

"Yes I was helping them in their investigation," he admitted.

"Helping them how? What were you doing Roland?" I asked.

"Things no one should ever have to do," he said, his voice genuine and tortured. I moved and pressed my body up against his in front of the window. He kept looking out through the glass. His reflection looked different. "There are some things better left unsaid and undiscovered. After investigating something like this, I don't want you to see what remains," he said.

"What remains?" I said.

"A filth, one which rots from the inside out, especially here," he said, referring to our helpless community. "What I saw, the grainy photographs I examined and the sick films I watched, is something I can never disregard, ever," he whispered. "You want to know what I did. You have to be able to exist, to survive and live, breathe in the deepest recesses of hopelessness and perversion. You have to be able to react with impunity, almost hate sometimes. You're too beautiful of a person to breathe in a place like that," he said. I pressed in closer to his body and wept. I still didn't understand what he had been involved in, regarding the murders here. Then I remembered a name of one of the murdered children. I inhaled and tried to seal in the hesitation. "Please don't push me on this," he said, his voice turning more direct, sterner. Almost combative.

"Who was Penelope?" I asked.

And with genuine intention, I had broken him. With the rain gliding sideways across the glass in the increasing winds, Roland turned around. I had never seen him look that way before, lost and almost pathetic. His body slumped against the wall, unmolested and mute for a period of time. In the quiet shadows, I listened to him tell Penelope's tale, a grotesque and tragic circumstance beset upon the lives of others. Sometimes, lights would peer through the glass and I would see him, a pale wraith maddened by his own inability to remain unseen.

Between the darkness and the light, I watched a man I loved and admired collapse, fall into a realm of anguish and pity, where no one else could go. I could not and would not follow. Penelope was a brave young girl. The poor child. Through his quivering and passive voice, I could hear screams echoing through an abandoned barn silo. Each mirrored the ones I held inside as he described his becoming Jonathan Levin. I sobbed as I should have as he made apparent images he had seen, words he had chosen, only in good cause. Punished by the tools of remembrance, he whispered things I could no longer comprehend or hear about the human condition. I placed my hands over my ears. I wished the world mute. Any words Roland further divulged, broke apart on the surface of the floor, fragments of broken glass, gathered and then forgotten.

~

I stepped out of the bedroom and back into the apartment. The woman whom I had passed on the staircase was sitting on a couch. The silence that lingered in the uncertainty between us was oppressive. Next to the refrigerator was an older model radio. Maybe we would be able to hear some news. Maybe somebody knew what was happening. Anything but the endless expanse of reserve and sullenness. I plugged the radio in and searched for voices, news about anything at all. Most of the channels wouldn't tune in. All I could discover was music on one station. I closed my eyes and allowed the break in the static and the ignorance to wash over me, burn all the remaining traces of doubt and anger I held on to.

The woman sitting on the couch reading something, once calm and poised, stood for a few moments then collapsed upon the floor, clutching pieces of paper against her chest. The material of it resembled burnt skin. I closed my eyes. I thought of the area of flesh on Roland's shoulder. The

354

woman seemed inconsolable as she wailed. I hoped someone downstairs heard her. As I headed towards the metal staircase to find help, a woman came in, the psychologist the police requested to be on scene. Mull said she would listen if I was willing to talk. She knelt down beside the woman and whispered to her in hushed tones. I couldn't help but be moved by her frailty and overwhelming sadness. Tears developed in my eyes and I turned away.

The psychologist helped to raise her to her feet and escorted her downstairs. I moved over towards the entrance to the apartment and watched the rain drip from the crooked and falling gutters, rush down across their shoulders. The gravity of all things pulled away the raindrops, the misery and the corruption and washed it down the metal architecture and across the blacktop. I wished the laws of physics would fall upon me, bend, remove from existence, the love and the hate I possessed for Roland, a love and a hate for which I could no longer take charge. The psychologist, with the help of another officer who arrived on scene, led that poor woman to the rear of the property.

I moved down the staircase, walked through the alley and watched an E.M.T. worker help her into the back of an ambulance. He placed an oxygen mask over her face as she sat down. She was still clutching the papers she had been reading. Whatever it was trembled in the grips of her fingertips. I leaned against the side of the brick façade and looked over at her. At one point she raised her eyes and saw me. I wondered if that would be me sitting there soon. I wondered who Roland would be on that bus.

I stepped over to the steel barrel, the remaining wood giving off a light, peach glow. I rubbed my hands back and forth across the opening. The heat felt soothing and welcoming. The rains continued, but appeared lighter than before. I raised my head higher and let the raindrops fall across my face, crash upon my lips. In that insignificant moment, I wanted to kiss Roland and tell him I was sorry. But I was still leaving regardless.

A man I did not recognize stopped in the space across from me, warming his hands as well. The long sleeves of his shirt were rolled up around his forearms. When he turned his wrist over, I could see a tattoo marking his skin on the underside. With the rain washing over it and the smoke from the barrel, it was clouded, but it looked like it read 'persevere.' When he brushed the water from the ink with his other hand and the smoke faded, it read 'abandon.' I couldn't help but wonder what it meant. I remembered the closed file on Peter McDonnally. The dossier said he had a small tattoo on the inside of his wrist. It read 'antipathy.'

*Peter McDonnally.*

*Did eleven years in a maximum security facility for the repeated attempted robbery of a carrier group of armored cars. Wanted for questioning in the armed robbery of a diamond exchange. Also wanted for questioning in the thefts of precious metals. No known or previous associates. Believed to be last seen trying to cross the border into Canada.*

After Peter McDonnally healed and two years had passed, Roland and his handler put him back into the fold. He tried to get deeper into other armored car heists, but after the failed attempt and his subsequent injury, nothing further along that line materialized. According to notes in the file, as Roland was putting out feelers, he came across a group of men, four in all, that were responsible for a string of the brutal thefts of precious and other metals in surrounding states. The thefts took place at night and in less circulated areas, places one wouldn't consider visible. The only other thing the thefts had in common was they all revolved around areas of freight transit. Trucking depots. Storage facilities. Rail yards. The decision was made to involve Peter McDonnally after the theft of 900 feet of copper from along a rail line outside of New York, which caused the derailment of a freight train comprised of 18 cars. The engineer was hospitalized, one worker killed and hundreds of thousands of dollars of cargo damaged or reported missing.

In the notes written in his handwriting, the idea of getting in with these men was appealing as he was able to improvise and think on his feet when the situation arose. That he would have no trouble adapting. Sad that Roland couldn't seem to adapt to me or being a husband. I wondered what was so difficult about it, nestling in beside me, fitting into the identity of a best friend and lover. Inside the file were photographs of tractor-trailers unloading at a storage depot, vans delivering merchandise and several wide images of a rail yard, which stored train and tanker cars, some containing freight, others empty. In a matter of days, he had absorbed as much information as he could. Attached to a proceeding page was a surveillance photograph of a freight train yard on the outskirts of New York.

The yard, when vacant, appeared as a series of intersecting, steel intestines, a rough display of the autopsy of an industrial art project. Cables were strung from stanchion poles far off into the horizon. There was very little lighting once the sun went down. Surprisingly, considering the stored cargo, the security seemed insufficient, though the depot was isolated in its location. Reading further, a meeting place at an old, abandoned building was established. With his previous history, Peter McDonnally attained schematics of the yard, several weapons and other supplies.

I could see him once again, wearing unfamiliar clothes, the sweat forming on his face and neck. The tattoos I noticed in photographs earlier were duplicated exactly as they had been when Peter McDonnally was first shot and arrested. I wanted him to mark my name on his body, somewhere private, any place so he could remember who he belonged to and who he was. In that little place on the back of his neck. When I kissed him there I could feel his body tense up, his shoulders riddled with gooseflesh.

The building they were planning in was a long warehouse, lined down one side with windows, many of them cracked and distorted. The report was detailed, thorough in its exactness and precision, so much so it scared me. I could feel the hardness of the construction beneath my feet, breathe in the specks of dust and broken cement on the floor. The building used to house a small factory that manufactured welding equipment. Almost standing beside him again, I could see his reflection in a welding mask, noticed the strength in his hands and forearms as he loaded a handgun. I wouldn't have been able to recognize the look in his eyes though, a cold, hard and aggressive stare, one almost reprehensible in its nature. One I had never seen. That man wasn't my husband.

When the rail yard darkened, the group cut through an electric fence at the north end of the property. The phone lines were severed. Most of the time, the cars stored there were empty. But a shipment of aluminum and copper was secured in a train car overnight along the tracks after an accident at the impending destination. There were no suggestions it was more than a coincidence. Notes in the file questioned where some of the information had been retrieved from. There were only three employees scheduled to be on shift. The man in charge of securing the perimeter was rendered unconscious upon their entrance. He was pistol whipped in the back of the head. The poor man. Leaving his body prone and lifeless, one other man and Peter McDonnally entered the office of the facility towards the East, while the remaining men attempted to open the locked train car. The group even knew the number. NR 47290.

The office was more or less a small barn, wooden in its architecture and feel. Touching the photograph, I could sense slivers of pine bore into my skin. Peter McDonnally entered the office and withdrew a handgun, demanding the keys to unlock the train car with the designated number. The worker, a man in his mid-fifties, responded only the companies that stored the train cars and tankers possessed the keys. There was no other way in. Outside on the side of the building were pieces of loose, scrap metal and a small welding torch. The other man brought them inside and locked the door behind him. He turned on the welding torch and pinned the worker against the prefabricated back wall.

At first, the man burned a small section of the wall behind him. Soon, Peter McDonnally watched the man press the torch closer to the worker's flesh and watched it burn. Apparently the smell is something you can never forget. Roland noted that on the back of one of the photographs. The intense and extraordinary stench of death. Peter McDonnally stopped the other man from inflicting further damage and instructed him to go outside with the others. To break into the train car. Roland stepped over to the wall and touched the fingertips on his right hand against the scorched mark. Then watching the torch render inept, the flame falling asleep, Roland noted he stared at the shining, blue stream, listened to the light hissing sound it made when it came into contact with an object. In that truncated moment, William McCoy was born.

I stopped rubbing my hands over the flames as I suddenly felt hot. I wondered if that anarchist he slept with would have taken her hand away or if she would have let it remain, allowed the orange flame to change the surface of her skin. I never got to see a photograph of what she looked like. Many of them were removed or redacted from the file. I wondered if that was intentional. I turned away from the memories and looked at the woman still sitting in the rear of the ambulance. This time, Detective Mull was speaking to her. Over the rain and the noise of my own body, I couldn't hear anything being said. She was still sobbing, holding onto the pieces of paper. Mull turned his head and noticed me. He walked over, umbrella in his hand and ushered me aside, away from everyone else. He looked exhausted.

"What, has something happened?" I asked.

"Again, I preface that I'm only telling you aspects of what's going on because of the circumstances surrounding your husband," he said.

"I understand," I said.

"We've been able to make preliminary contact with the man holding him and the others hostage."

"What did he say? Is Roland hurt?"

"I won't say anything other than no one appears to have been injured. And no other shots have been fired on the bus," Mull said. "We would be able to hear them from here," he surmised.

"Were you able to speak to anyone else?" I asked.

"No. All we were given were assurances everyone is still alive," he said.

"Are you getting any closer to ending this?" I asked. I wanted Roland to step down from the tragic sanctity of that bus and go on with his life. Or lives. Yet I no longer wanted to be stuck with him in this emotional marsh, with no apparent progress, nothing ever moving or changing. This feeling of listlessness was suffocating.

"We're doing everything we can to resolve the situation as quickly as possible," he said. I looked over again at the grieving woman driven away in an ambulance. "Is there anything you need?"

There was no real answer to that question. But then there were so many. "No," I said.

"We've asked that some food be brought to the scene," he added.

"Thank you. I'm not sure I could eat anything right now though," I admitted. The insides of my body felt like an endless chasm of concern and grief.

"Keep yourself strong please," he said. "There is a chance this could go on longer." I walked back through the alley and ascended the stairs back into the apartment. The other woman was still sitting quietly looking out the window. There were the distant corpses of tears in her eyes. I wanted to scream. I wanted to shatter the stillness and the solemnness that permeated the apartment even more so. I grabbed my bag from the counter. I sat down on the edge of the couch closest to the door, frustrated and defeated. Even though I was conscious of the time, I still longed to look. At the bottom of my purse, I rediscovered Roland's watch.

I placed it over my wrist with the knowledge it was too big. The material felt cold against my skin all the way up to my forearm. Again I noticed the small irony in the watch not running. Time was paralyzing, limiting. In regards to time, I would have to reschedule the meeting with my lawyer. Some of the questions he asked resonated with me and others evaporated. I didn't know how to answer some of them. I still had the initial papers he had handed me in his office. I unfolded them and studied the language again. The beginning page listed many of the questions he had already asked me, each listed in the order I remembered him speaking. It made me feel like a character, scripted to fit into one of Roland's identities. The proceeding page was a list of questions he hadn't had a chance to ask.

*Has the love you carried for your husband turned to resentment?*
*Was I worn by all the arguing and too exhausted to even engage with him?*
*Are you having an affair or contemplating having one?*
*When you do talk, does everything eventually lead to an argument?*
*Does the idea of sex with your husband cause you discomfort or anxiety?*
*Would I rather be anywhere than with my husband?*

I would rather be with my husband anywhere else in the world, any rift or island but for here, right now. Yet that place, that utopia doesn't exist. The world we tried to survive in here was cruel and carried with it the weighted baggage of consequence. Because of the crimes and the investigation we fractured in permanence. And there was no one who could change that.

I secured my cellular and stared at the facing. There was nothing notating any recent calls or messages, just the number the police had been trying to contact me from earlier. They said as much. I couldn't hide my disappointment. I was hoping Roland would have tried to call me, convince me, without a doubt, I was making the wrong decision filing for divorce. I scrolled through some of his previous messages from the last couple of days. They were all generic, no moving or inspiring words about his love for me. As contrived and calculated as everything else he did. I wondered what kind of things he said to that woman. I wondered if he told her he loved her. I called the lawyer back and asked if I could reschedule our meeting for another day. Yes, everything was fine. No, I didn't know when. I would have to get back to you.

The rains picked up and I could see water come through the open window and puddle at the other woman's feet. She didn't seem to care much as she stared through the weather and out onto the street. I leaned back in the couch and sighed. I didn't know what to do. I refocused on the rest of the legal paperwork and suggestions. When I raised my hand to run it through my hair, Roland's watch slid down and settled at my wrist. I lowered my arm and unclasped the band, held the watch in my palm. The coldness of the metal made my skin come alive out of reflex.

The last time I remembered putting it on was the morning after he first came home after being William McCoy for the last time. He had been gone for months, down south somewhere burning buildings and inciting uncertainty. In the middle of the night he appeared. I thought again, as I did many times I was imagining, constructing him being here. That he wasn't real. I awoke and saw a light emanating from underneath the bathroom door. When I stepped in and saw his image behind the shower door, I wasn't sure what to expect. For a split second I couldn't remember the sound of his voice. I wanted to hear him say my name. Once. When I saw him he looked exhausted, soiled and scared. After subtle questioning and some arguing, I dropped to my knees and embraced his body, the warm water from the shower washing away everything I didn't know about him.

We made love late into the night. Yet parts of who Roland was must have disappeared within the streams of warm water and sweat. And what remained was unfamiliar and incomplete. When I awoke, he was sitting at the end of the bed, reading something from a file. The burn mark on his back was larger than I remembered. Other scars marked the area along his spine. It looked as if he had been injured several times. There was a large bruise wrapped around the side of his body. I watched him for a little while, wanting to fall back in love with him as he turned through various pages of that file. I didn't need to discover much. I never had. I struggled with the fact he might be leaving again. I wanted to ask him if he was going under again, but would it matter? Roland moved off of the bed, holding a red and beige file in his hands. I closed my eyes, wondering if he would ever be still and satisfied.

Some of his things were on an end table next to me. I picked up his watch and slid it over my wrist. There was nothing unique about it, no inscriptions or engravings on the back of the face. It possessed no value except intrinsically. I tilted the watch from left to right, catching his fleeting reflection in the lustrous, black facing. It was the only constant we had anymore, time. I felt like a prisoner, scrawling marks upon the wall to represent days incarcerated. If I thought about it, I could count the hours I was alone and without him, marked them on the wall. Seeing him close the door behind him, the file gripped within his fingertips felt like finality. I pressed the watch against my chest, its counting rhythm the closest thing I had to feeling his heartbeat sound off against my body.

As I was being reflective, a police officer came into the apartment carrying a box. He set it down on a kitchen counter. Some food, more water and other provisions were brought over. I stood up and grabbed a bottle of water out of the refrigerator. In the box was a newspaper. It was a couple of days old though. I picked it up regardless and carried everything back over to the couch. I welcomed the cold water into my body.

The recent murders in the area dominated the small paper. There were photographs on the second page of all the children murdered so far. It was horrible, seeing their innocent faces. I recognized several of them and not from earlier articles. Several of their faces were pinned to telephone poles on flyers around town. I saw some of the file Roland had when I found him in our living room by the fire, before he had a chance to hide them away. Nothing substantial, quick, sudden images of violence.

But when he relented and finally told me about the case and his involvement is when I came to be familiar with them. And I wished now I hadn't. I folded the paper in half and stared at the photograph of Penelope. The tragic death of that poor 15 year-old girl was enough to break my husband and our marriage in a way. Roland only shared with me sparse details of her crime scene. It must have been horrible for the person who discovered her there and everyone else involved. I thought about her loneliness and my own. I so wanted a child. But Roland would never have children. Not after everything he had seen. Not after everything that had happened.

I wished I could forget some of the photographs and the documents he showed me. Disgusting and horrible images of reckless barbarity and perversion. It sickened me he would immerse himself in that world, allow himself to be corrupted and ruined, even led by such violence. I couldn't understand why he would sacrifice everything, including me, to protect strangers. As much as I had always pressed him about what he did, I recognized the nobility in his reluctance to pull me into that violent pool of violence and perversion. Other than now, I never swam in those waters. I wished I hadn't.

I pressed his watch against my chest, fighting back resentment and regret that accompanied the memories of Roland's admittance to me of his full involvement in the case. Everything had changed when he agreed he would go under again. Whatever chance I felt I had after William McCoy was ruined. Especially when he showed me the last remaining photographs and notes in the file. I couldn't comprehend the things I saw in those images and words, some blurry, some partly redacted, others in focus. I tried not to look directly upon them, turning my head slightly, glancing up at Roland or noticing his watch. The inside of his wrist was the first place where I kissed him. I tried to think of how soft the skin there was, how it once belonged to me. The last photograph remaining was of a young girl, bound with her hands behind her back. She looked frail and scared, her wrists secured by rope, held by what was later determined to be a man. I felt nauseous, trying not to notice the details in the background.

The image shook in the tips of my fingers as Roland took it back from me. The expression strained in his eyes was telling. I took the photograph back from his possession. I didn't want to, but I looked at the girl again. The wedding. Then I remembered the night we made love in the hotel room. I rubbed my wrists where he had grabbed me, felt the heat on the small of my back where he had pinned them in sexual aggression. I cupped a hand over my mouth in sadness, in shock and moved away from him. I felt violated by the one man who should have protected me, honored me with his dedication and sense of decency. That poor girl. I had become a part of it, that barbarity without knowledge, without permission.

I stepped down the steel staircase again and was still greeted by a consistent rain. I peered into the real estate office. People were moving around, a few engaged with the psychologist. Several people were talking on cell phones. Nobody seemed to notice me. I walked out near the front edge of the property and looked around. An E.M.T. worker walked across to the other side of the street carrying a medical bag. There were several men in raincoats as well I didn't recognize. An electrician, with his back towards me, stepped into the building where Mull said other officers were located. Roland could have been any one of them and I would not have been able to recognize him. Perhaps he had found a way off of that bus. If he had though, he would be gone. Underground. Lost in his fiction. And I wouldn't have known. I dropped Roland's watch into the street. I watched the facing break, the deep, black circle shattering against the asphalt, the reflection I once noticed in its beauty, forever lost upon the darkened landscape.

I looked up for a moment, the rain falling across my face. It felt cold against my skin. As I looked out towards where the bus was, everything looked bleak. All the front yards of houses were vacant. A barren birdbath, made from old, rusted watering cans appeared as an admonition, a sign that things of beauty, once innocent and vibrant, wither. Or burn. Like William McCoy. It made me think we all lived right at the edge of destruction. That it was a constant. I closed my eyes when I started crying again, yet didn't try to hide it this time. I took a few steps out into the street when a lone gunshot shattered the temporary stillness of all things.

Made in the USA
Middletown, DE
11 September 2019